At fifty-three, plump, clumsy and kind, bearer of an ancient name and master of Morholm, the big house which had dominated this corner of the fens since Jacobean times, Joseph Hardwick was a man sensitive to familial ties. As he rounded the corner of the kitchen, he was met by a gardener, much out of breath.

'Oh, sir, I've been looking for you. I found a girl in garden 'smorning. Crawled under a bush she had, and laying there like dead.'

'Good Lord! She is not? –'

T R WILSON

Master of Morholm

A Novel of the Fenland

GRAFTON BOOKS

A Division of the Collins Publishing Group

LONDON GLASGOW
TORONTO SYDNEY AUCKLAND

Grafton Books
A Division of the Collins Publishing Group
8 Grafton Street, London W1X 3LA

Published by Grafton Books 1987

First published in Great Britain by
Grafton Books 1986

Copyright © T R Wilson 1986

ISBN 0-586-07038-9

Printed and bound in Great Britain by
Collins, Glasgow

Set in Linotron Baskerville

For Ian Hebb

Mary, or sweet spirit of thee,
   As the bright sun shines tomorrow
Thy dark eyes these flowers shall see,
   Gathered by me in sorrow,
In the still hour when my mind was free
To walk alone – yet wish I walked with thee.

JOHN CLARE, 'Mary'

THE HARDWICKS OF MORHOLM

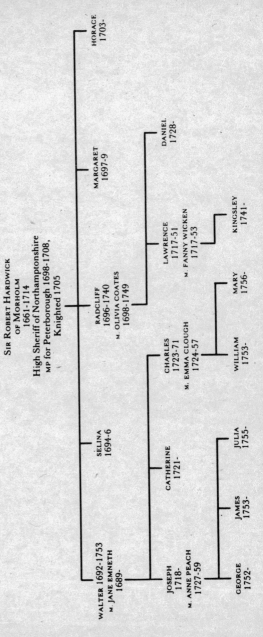

SIR ROBERT HARDWICK
OF MORHOLM
1661-1714
High Sheriff of Northamptonshire
MP for Peterborough 1698-1708,
Knighted 1705

WALTER 1692-1753
M. JANE EMNETH
1689-

SELINA
1694-6

RADCLIFF
1696-1740
M. OLIVIA COATES
1698-1749

MARGARET
1697-9

HORACE
1703-

JOSEPH
1718-
M. ANNE PEACH
1727-59

CATHERINE
1721-

CHARLES
1723-71
M. EMMA CLOUGH
1724-57

LAWRENCE
1717-51
M. FANNY WICKEN
1717-53

DANIEL
1728-

GEORGE
1752-

JAMES
1753-

JULIA
1755-

WILLIAM
1753-

MARY
1756-

KINGSLEY
1741-

PROLOGUE

November, 1771

Sheets of relentless rain were sweeping across the desolate fens.

The narrow road along which the small figure of the girl laboured was almost indistinguishable from the waterlogged fields stretching away in washes of pale colour to the horizon. Mud writhed and sucked beneath her thin, buckled shoes. Her frozen hands held together the ends of a blue shawl around her shoulders, and sodden strands of hair, escaping from her cap, clung to her face. Despite the washing of the rain, the marks of tears were still visible on her cheeks.

A gusty wind blew up, tilting the rain this way and that. In the prostrated landscape the girl seemed to be the only living creature, and the wind bullied her and the rain slapped her with cold fingers. The movement with which she planted one blistered foot in the earth and heaved the other one after it was like that of a machine. Behind the clouds the day waned. The rain increased its onslaught.

Beacons of bright, hard pain flared through the girl's limbs.

Evening announced itself only by the darkening colour of the rain. A man on a packhorse plunged past the girl, and the retreating shape seemed to her blurred eyes to swell and waver like an object seen through curved glass. Her hands holding the shawl were mere clamps; she could no longer feel the soaked wool. Mud had formed a thick crust six inches up her petticoat. Under cover of the deepening gloom the rain and wind grew more malevolent. The girl coughed and coughed again, her face creased and shining like a new-born baby's.

She went on.

Darkness had finally rendered the rain an invisible attacker when the girl saw the lights of a village ahead. There was no one in the flooded street. The first person she saw was an old man standing in the porch of a tavern.

'Lord, child, you're half-drowned,' was all he could say, staring at her from under the dripping brim of his hat.

'Where is Morholm?' she asked.

'Through the village a step. Hard to your left,' he said finally. He continued to stare as she moved on.

Joseph Hardwick was usually the first to rise in his household. Today, nervously excited, he was up and about before dawn. As ever, he postponed the laying of breakfast until the rest of the family should be up, and instead took a turn about the grounds. The torrential rain that had drenched the countryside for the last two days had at last stopped. His boots squelched in the grass and ranks of raindrops filed slowly along the drooping branches of the trees. Picking his way between puddles he explored the bedraggled gardens at the back of the house. He had thought of landscaping them but had never got round to it, and at this time of year they were a stark and depressing sight. A clump of elms at the back led to a gate opening on to the farmland, and here he paused to sniff the washed air. The fields lying west sloped gently, hedged into a neat patchwork; it was a welcome relief from the uniform flatness of the fen country to the east and north. Joseph's eyes were sparkling and appreciative as he gazed, and his face wore that expression of innocence and optimism which Great-Uncle Horace of Stamford, among others, liked to characterize as foolishness. In fact, Joseph was thinking deeply and sadly. Today his eldest son George was to depart for a tour of Europe. Outwardly cheerful about this, Joseph felt the occasion almost as a final parting. George, he knew, did not care for the life of a country squire, and wherever he might make his home when he returned from the Continent in a year or two, Joseph felt sure it would not be back here at Morholm. The days of having his son here at the family home, he sensed, were gone. James too, his younger son, was preparing to go up to London to study law next year. No doubt Julia, his daughter, would remain. Poor, plain, cross Julia.

At fifty-three, plump, clumsy and kind, bearer of an ancient name and master of Morholm, the big house which had dominated this corner of the fens since Jacobean times, Joseph Hardwick was a man sensitive to familial ties. A widower for many years, he had lavished love on his three children, now grown; and also supported in his house his bedridden mother, his mother-in-law, his spinster sister and two shiftless cousins.

Turning to look at the long, low-gabled building, he noted that it was in need of repair. Water trickled in crooked streams from the roofs and stained the ivied walls. He loved Morholm, but he was an impractical man and he knew what the businesslike Great-Uncle Horace said of him; he also knew that his name elicited more respect than his person. Thinking again of the son who was to leave that day, he wondered what would happen when he was dead and George inherited the estate. It pained him to think of Morholm being sold off, as he suspected George would do, but he wanted his children above all to be happy. That was what mattered. As long as they were happy.

The future he found uncomfortable to think about, having spent his life trying to make the present tolerable for those around him. Shaking off some drops of rain-water that fell on him from a branch as if shaking off his troubled mood, he turned back to the house. As he rounded the corner of the kitchen, he was met by a gardener, much out of breath.

'Oh, sir, I've been looking for you. I found a girl in garden 'smorning. Crawled under a bush she had, and laying there like dead.'

'Good Lord! She is not –?'

'No, sir, she's coming to now, but she's blue with cold and wet to the marrow. We laid her in Mrs Reynolds' room.'

In the housekeeper's dim little room above the kitchen, the girl lay swathed in blankets and shawls, a tiny head poking out like that of a queen ant. 'Not dressed for weather neither, sir,' went on the gardener standing at his side. 'Just cap and shawl over her day things. Not even pattens on her feet.'

'I took off her things, sir, to dry them out,' said Mrs Reynolds, her arms folded and her face long and embarrassed. 'She'd have gone straight off with an ague else.'

Joseph was staring at the girl as if he were not listening. 'We couldn't tell what manner of girl she was, sir,' said Mrs Reynolds uncomfortably.

Joseph straightened from stooping over the sleeping form. He had gone pale. 'This is my niece Mary from Wisbech,' he said finally. 'Her father dead but three months since. Bring her to my parlour, Brook. What can have happened? The poor child.' With distracted remarks he attended the carrying of the sleeping girl down to the parlour, where she was buried in a great armchair by the fire. There he chafed her hands, peering anxiously into her white face and listening to her feverish breath. He was going to fetch some brandy when his sister, Aunt Catherine, a sallow, inquisitive woman of fifty, a flowered morning-gown pulled about her plump figure, came down.

'Why, brother, what is this? Found in the garden? Then it must be some drunken slut who – Our niece Mary? Come, you are mistaken. I tell you it is some hussy who has come upon the town, and you must turn her out directly.' As she bent to inspect the girl, Aunt Catherine's peevish face changed. 'And yet it is she! Well, how comes she here? What does it mean?'

'From what I hear of her condition when she was found,' said Joseph, pouring brandy into a glass, 'I surmise that she walked here.'

'Nonsense, she cannot. Almost the other side of Wisbech. And in such rain as we have had! Let us wake the girl; then we may ask her.'

Joseph put the brandy glass down. 'No: we had better leave her be. Catherine, this can have nothing to do with brother Charles's death, surely?'

Charles Hardwick, though younger than Joseph and Catherine, had died three months previously. A widower like Joseph, he had lived in seclusion as a parson twenty miles away and they had seen little of him. At his death his children had gone to live with a relative of their mother's.

'Why, Mary was taken in by that excellent woman Mrs Fleming. Why should she come here? I believe she was hardly ever at Morholm before in her life. Brother Charles, God rest his soul, was always so close in his ways. Unhealthy I always thought it.'

'I shall despatch a message to this Mrs Fleming,' said Joseph, pacing up and down, 'saying that Mary is here, and asking how and why she came. With the roads as they are I do not anticipate a prompt reply. In the meantime let us close the parlour and leave her to sleep.'

As the morning went on, Joseph returned anxiously and often to look at her. The girl's face was losing its chalky colour and beginning to flush, and her breathing was growing calmer and deeper. Dr Milton came and announced no danger of fever. The family, occupied with preparations for George's departure, left her in peace, and at noon the young man and his tutor were ready to leave. At the last moment,

Joseph tried to put him off, his mind doubly torn by these two worries.

'Look at the roads, my son: 'tis like the Slough of Despond. You had much better put off going for another day; you will make no progress today, I feel sure.'

But George, thin and hopeful, was adamant; and so the whole household gathered in the drive to see him off to Stamford and thence to London. His brother James, stocky and quiet, gave him a reserved farewell; his sister Julia, of whom at sixteen the gossips were already beginning to whisper, 'Old maid', put up a pursed, resentful mouth to be kissed; Grandmother Peach twirled her stick; old cousin Daniel croaked, 'Do not pick up any Frenchie ways, George!'; cousin Kingsley, a lumpish oaf of thirty, smirked and waved. Joseph shook his son's hand, and then they were gone. The family returned to the house and the humdrum life which today's brief excitement had interrupted.

Joseph, more moved than he cared to show, softly opened the parlour door and found the girl sitting up in the great armchair. Her vivid green eyes were unnaturally large in her pale face, and wayward strands of brown hair curled from under her cap. She was about fifteen, and small. He was about to speak when she burst into tears and buried her face in the pillows.

Joseph held her hand while she shook with sobs. Her distress made tears prick his own eyes. Then abruptly the girl sat up, swallowed and wiped her face. 'You must want to know . . . why I am here,' she gulped.

'No, no, my child,' said Joseph. 'Time enough for that. Plenty of time.'

'No,' said the girl, collecting herself, 'no, I shall tell you. I walked here to your house, uncle, because the death of my father,' she swallowed, clenched her fists, regained herself, 'because the death of my father meant my removing to the

16

house of Mrs Fleming, whom I detest heartily and with all my soul.'

'Why, my child, you cannot think this, indeed. It is surely a great kindness in Mrs Fleming to take you to her bosom thus. I have never seen her, but she cannot be a bad woman, Mary? Is she?'

'Sir, it is no kindness that moves her to undertake the care of my brother and me. My father wished it because he felt she was the only person he could turn to. He had no money. She is an inconstant woman, sir, her head full of fancies and deceits; and she merely consented to our presence for the appearance it will create to her neighbours of her warmth and compassion – of which I know and have seen she has not any. O! to be in her house, uncle – a foul place: and she goes about it in an old, soiled nightgown, shouting at her husband, who is always drunk, and she flirts beneath his very nose with an evil old rake who visits her. But,' she flushed, 'I could bear this if she did not take my father's name in vain. Always she speaks of him disparagingly, and two nights ago she railed against him, saying that my mother had been a fool to marry him; that it was a mercy they were both gone where all fools go in the end. I spoke up: she struck me. I vowed to leave as soon as I could slip away, packing nothing for fear of arousing her suspicion. I came to you because, though I had but seen you a handful of times, father always spoke so well of you.' She was calm now, not weeping, and there was a vein of defiance in her. 'I know I have no claims on you, uncle. But I shall never go back to Mrs Fleming.'

Joseph looked troubled. 'What are the feelings of your brother on this matter, Mary?'

'He too is leaving, though through no distaste for the house. What little was left to us by father he is making sure to spend, and he intends to take rooms in town with one of his friends. It makes little difference to him. We have grown apart and he laughed at my intention to leave.' She began to cry again and Joseph leant her head on his shoulder, rocking her. 'The world has turned upside down, uncle. I have never known such unhappiness – never known it could exist.'

'I have seen it too, Mary. The world has not been too cruel to me, and I have seen little of it, but I have seen more than people will allow of me. We must simply try to soften our part of it. But your father was wrong when he said he had none to turn to but Mrs Fleming. There is myself.'

'He said he did not wish to burden you further, when you bear so much now.'

'When others need your help, my child, you give it,' said Joseph. 'There are no other considerations. You give it.'

When he left her a few minutes later to sleep again, he found Aunt Catherine lingering about the hall. 'Well, and what does she say?' she demanded. 'Is she out of her senses? I know that must be it. And a message has just arrived from that Mrs Fleming. She says she is distracted with worry for her dear niece, but it happened that she only missed her this morning, being very busy all of yesterday, and sends her regards and asks after Mary's health.'

'Sister, Mary says she is unhappy living with Mrs Fleming. I feel it would be best for us to take her here at Morholm.' Joseph spoke gravely and carefully.

'But surely that cannot be why she walked such a distance, alone, across the Fen, in a storm? No one would ever do such a thing, unless they were out of their senses, as I have held all along.'

'She must have been pitifully wretched to do it,' said Joseph, half to himself.

'Oh, but that was simply grief for her father, as any decent girl must feel,' said Aunt Catherine. 'She will grow to be comfortable there in time. I feel sure Mrs Fleming must be an excellent woman, though of no family. Besides, you must

18

consider, brother, your house is not a haven for every orphan and waif and strumpet to fly to. If they were all to be taken in by gentlemen, what condition would the country be in?'

'Why, everyone would have a home and there would be no more wretches wandering the streets,' said Joseph, smiling. But he was not attending to his sister. The image of his niece's face, sad and mottled with tear-stains but stiffened with resolution, was before his mind's eye, and already he had taken her grieving heart to his own.

BOOK ONE

1

On a cool September evening in 1774, Joseph Hardwick died in his bed at Morholm. With his death an era seemed to close.

He had been ill for several weeks. Dr Milton, the old family physician, had retired from practice, so Dr Villiers had ridden in from Peterborough, bled him, poked him and gone away again. His success rate was never very high, so one more failure would make little difference. Joseph had been nursed tenderly and constantly, but pneumonia had seized him and would not release its hold. On Friday evening his condition seemed to improve a little and Mary was persuaded to leave his bedside and go down for some dinner. Kingsley Hardwick, who of all people cared least about his uncle, went into Joseph's room after dinner, 'to see how the old fellow was', and found him dead. So the old master of Morholm left the house to receive its new one.

It was a chastened company that assembled in the drawing-room that night. Joseph had been like an unsightly pillar that, though abused, keeps a building standing. Aunt Catherine, who had scolded her brother all her life, had taken to her bed on hearing the news. Apart from her, and Joseph's ancient mother, who remained in her room, too old and tired now to comprehend the news, everyone was downstairs. They seemed disinclined to talk, except for Grandmother Peach, Joseph's mother-in-law, a vigorous, vain and ill-favoured old lady, who with the precision of a mathematician was going over every folly and weakness of which Joseph had been guilty since she had known him. Even her harsh tones were a little subdued.

Mary Hardwick, that same girl who had fled to Morholm almost three years ago, was now over eighteen, still slightly elfin in figure and face. Her hair was brown and unruly, her jaw strong, her eyes wide, expressive and sparkling; hers was an intense face, attractive but not easy on the eye. Today she was frozen with grief and a numbing, bewildering sense of having lost a father twice. Joseph had not replaced the memory of her father, but he had joined him in her affections. She recalled her father's death, the brief misery of Mrs Fleming's house, the terrible journey to Morholm. And Joseph's immediate hospitality. She remembered the easy way she had slipped into the fibres of the large household, Joseph's sympathy and kindness, her gradual return to life. The day after she had arrived, drenched and exhausted, in the grounds of Morholm, Joseph had ridden over to Wisbech to see Mrs Fleming. He had stated his intention to care for his niece; she had agreed. Since then her life had been bound up with Joseph and Morholm, her second father and her second home. Aunt Catherine nominally carried her brother's housekeeping keys, but she was wasteful and indolent and showed no objection to having her duties tacitly relieved by Mary. And as Joseph filled a gap in her life, so she filled a gap in his. His sons were in London; James at the Bar, George, as his father had feared, never returning to Morholm after Europe. His daughter Julia showed no hostility to Mary: she was equally distant and unapproachable to everyone. It was natural that her uncle should be the centre of her world.

Now the man responsible for the renewal of her happiness was gone and she felt she could never recover.

Grandmother Peach's harangue gradually petered out like the running down of an old clock and cousin Daniel, dulled by the silence, began to snore in the chimney-corner, his great flat feet splayed out. Mary went up to her chamber but did not attempt to sleep. Instead she sat in her nightgown

24

by the window. Birds nested in the eaves above it and stray twigs and straw, stirred by the wind, tapped at the glass. A bright moon was out, defining the roofs of the stables and outhouses and the long gravel drive. In the distance she could see the warmer light of the tavern in the village. She had cried all she could; now it was effort and very movement that was painful. She realized that her own father's death three years ago had not equipped her to meet trouble. Her happiness at Morholm had rather served to fortify a feeling that she had passed through her share of adversity, that it was a dreadful thing which would not occur again. She sensed with dismay her own innocence, perceiving at the same time that it could not have been otherwise. The first fifteen years of her life spent with her unworldly parson father and her silly careless brother in a comfortable house tucked away in a corner of the Fens; then the new idyllic life at Morholm with Uncle Joseph. Both gone.

Presently she got into bed, but most of the night was spent staring at the familiar maze of cracks in the ceiling above her. By the time she fell asleep, a moist grey dawn was stealing through the window. She dreamt of Joseph, but also in the dream, strangely, were the figures of George and James, Joseph's sons, whom she had seldom seen. When she woke she could tell from the light it was late. No one had come to rouse her. She recalled as she dressed in the autumnal chill how Joseph would sometimes have Mrs Reynolds bring her chocolate in bed. Every time she had felt like a grand lady in a London town-house.

Downstairs she found two sombre-looking men, and a fat woman who kept chewing on something, moving deliberately about. Aunt Catherine, dressed in a dark gown and a mob-cap that covered half her face, came rustling out of the parlour.

'Ah! Mary, at last! I declare your poor uncle has cost you no sleep, my girl – Lord knows, I have not rested a moment

– but there! I was ever a woman of tender heart. Now that you are up, you must occupy yourself as I direct, for there is much to do and I cannot do everything, though it seems the general opinion that I can and shall. The undertakers are here, and a woman to lay out from the village, and I have despatched Kingsley to Stamford to carry the sad news to Great-Uncle Horace. And Parson Medhurst is here in the parlour, and I must needs entertain him on top of all, and Lord knows who else will call as the news gets around. So you must attend your grandmother upstairs, for she is more than ever distracted, though Reynolds is with her; and then I pray you look in my brother's escritoire and find the addresses of George and James, for I must write them directly of their father's passing – poor creatures! I cannot bring myself to open Joseph's desk – 'twould be like disturbing the dead.'

Mary, glad of something to occupy her, went upstairs and along the draughty east passage to the room where Grandmother Hardwick lay. She tried to be cheerful with the ancient lady, who was propped up on a pillow in a giant bed hung with musty draperies, but the room itself was discouraging. One small window looked out over a decaying corner of the grounds where the cesspit was dug, and the room was always semi-dark. But she would not move elsewhere. Mary relieved Mrs Reynolds, who was trying to persuade the old lady to take a bowl of gruel. The air was close and sickly-sweet. Joseph's death had perhaps been better than this decay, she reflected, not comforted by the thought.

When she finally returned downstairs, Mary heard the fruity tones of Parson Medhurst consoling Aunt Catherine in the parlour.

'. . . and your brother was ever a handsome subscriber to the church, ma'am. I remember the autumn of '64 – the year we had those wicked gales. Half the slates were off the church roof, I recall, and when dear Mr Hardwick saw the damage . . .'

Mary opened Joseph's escritoire and found letters from George and James; James's neat, brief, pointed, George's scribbled, rambling, bearing traces of silver-sand, telling of his gambling debts. She felt a stirring of curiosity for her cousins, prompted by her dream. Then, leaving the addresses she found on the table for her aunt, she wandered out into the hall. For a moment she wavered, looking at the portrait of her ancestor, Sir Robert Hardwick, beneath the staircase, idly musing on how sallow and small his face looked beneath the huge full-bottomed wig of his day. Then one of the sombrely-dressed men, carrying a measuring-stick, brushed past her accidentally and with a shudder of irrational loathing she ran out into the garden.

Kingsley Hardwick rode along the rutted lane that led out of the village and on to the Stamford road. His expression was disgruntled. Riding was his passion, and normally at this time he would have been astride a horse anyway, but the very fact that he was forced to make this journey made him resent it. Nevertheless, he had dressed finely, as he always did when going out, in a buff riding coat with a white silk waistcoat embroidered in gold. His wig was tightly curled and heavily powdered, and there was gold edging on his tricorne hat. All this could not disguise the fact that he was a clumsy, lethargic, overweight man of past thirty, with a blank boyish face and colourless eyes. Orphaned at twelve years old, he had gone to live with his kindly Uncle Joseph at Morholm and had quite simply never left. The time had long passed when he would decently be expected to make his own way in the world, but as long as Joseph lived he saw no reason; at Morholm he could eat all he wanted and hunt all he wanted. The big-boned chestnut he was riding had cost Joseph sixty guineas. And here was another reason for his chagrin. He had been able to impose on the susceptible Joseph's generosity for years; but now that he was dead and the estate passed to George ... There had never been much love lost between them. That unfussy heiress with a taste for hunting had better hurry up and come his way.

It was a grey, frowning day that came as a chilly shock after the glories of a hot August. Kingsley cursed at the cool, erratic wind that came sidling across the fields and toying with his coat-tails. Then, as the wind died down, he fell to railing at Joseph for dying in that inconvenient way. It was outside his nature to be fond of his dead protector. Indeed the only person with whom he was on friendly terms was his Uncle Daniel. Daniel Hardwick was another distant relation living at Morholm who owed more to Joseph's great generosity than to any legitimate claims. A sour, flabby, opinionated valetudinarian of forty-five, he had made foolish investments and been left penniless some years ago. Moved by this and a dubious illness, Joseph had taken him in. Lately, feeling on steady ground with Joseph, Daniel had stopped even pretending to be ill. There had better be a renewal of the symptoms now if the old fellow wanted to stay at Morholm, Kingsley reflected spitefully.

He rode past Burghley House, the magnificent mansion built two centuries ago, with envious glances over the stone wall at the beautiful park. Now that was the sort of style he should be accustomed to. Capability Brown had recently been working on the grounds, and large herds of deer were visible in the distance. The Burghleys of Stamford, together with the Fitzwilliams of Milton Hall, whose sphere was Peterborough, were the great aristocracy of the area. Between the two squatted the equally ancient but much overshadowed Hardwicks of Morholm: Lord Burghley, the 9th Marquis, knew Joseph as a fellow magistrate, but that was all. Kingsley rode down into the valley where Stamford, a

flotilla of tall spires, came into view. It was a town on the
Great North Road of some importance and much elegance
and wealth. There were many fine shops in its handsome
streets, built of the local grey limestone. He clattered over
the bridge across the Welland and took his horse to The
George, the great coaching inn with its sign bridging the
street. He was just turning to walk to Great-Uncle Horace's
house in St George's Square, when the clink of tankards
called over his shoulder. He glanced at his watch. Half-past
ten; even in the circumstances, he told himself, it was rather
early for calling. And if he was to be sent on errands like a
servant, after all, he had the right to go about them as he
chose. It must have been at least an hour since he had
breakfasted.

He turned back and went into the inn.

Half-an-hour later, fortified with brandy and veal pie,
Kingsley knocked at the door of Horace Hardwick's narrow
squeezed town-house. He was admitted into a severe,
studious-looking room, where the old man was seated at a
desk beneath a small window that communicated so little
light it might have been a picture on the wall. Old Horace,
bent over a ledger, did not look up but bade Kingsley sit.
He did so, laying his hat on the floor and fiddling with his
riding-crop. Finally, the old man laid down his pen and
turned to look at Kingsley sharply. At seventy-one he was
the oldest of the male Hardwicks and a highly prosperous
merchant. He had entered business while other boys were
still at school and since then had dipped his finger into every
financial pie the county had to offer. He had little to do with
Morholm; as a youngest son he had had to make his own
way and had done so with pleasure. Horace Hardwick rather
despised the rest of his family. The Morholm branch of the
family that had produced Joseph he regarded as fools; the
second branch, of Kingsley and Daniel, were even worse;
the third branch consisted of himself and unfortunately he

had never married. Moreover, with their ancient name, whatever went on at Morholm reflected on him.

'An unexpected pleasure, great-nephew. I seldom receive visitors from Morholm, least of all yourself.' Of all his kin he liked this lazy sponging fop the least. 'What is the nature of your business?'

'My Uncle Joseph died last evening,' said Kingsley, tapping his riding-crop against his boot. As it happened, his blunt, unfeeling manner suited Horace's.

'Indeed? I am sorry to hear it. Joseph gone now, too. I believe I shall outlive every one of you. How did he die?'

'Oh, you know he had been ill for a while: the pneumonia took him last Thursday and he was gone by supper-time yesterday. I found him,' he added morbidly.

'Ah? Well, there it is. I confess I thought Joseph would last a while yet, for all his being a simpleton. When is the funeral to be?'

The George's victuals had fuddled Kingsley's habitually slow mind.

'Mm? The funeral? Oh, I don't believe 'tis arranged yet. Neither George nor James are at home at present. The undertakers are there now, and I believe old Medhurst is preaching in the parlour.'

'I wonder any of you had the sense to call them in. There is regrettably little sense amongst the Hardwicks,' Horace grunted, his narrow unsmiling face set in grim lines. 'Joseph, though, was the greatest fool of you all. If I were master of Morholm there would not be half the leeches sucking my blood as there were his.' He got up with a click of old joints, stood tall and upright, and went to a table where a decanter stood. 'Can I offer you wine? I cannot promise that it will be as good as the ale you got at The George, but I find it palatable.'

Kingsley was too dull to catch the sharp edge of the remark. 'Actually I had brandy,' he said, taking the proffered glass. He noticed the fine lace on Horace's cuffs. The old man had the money to be fashionable, Kingsley reflected, but he went about it in a half-hearted way; his waistcoat was old and stained with snuff.

'I suppose the estate will go to George,' went on Horace. 'I wonder if he will come to live at Morholm permanently, instead of carousing about London as he does. He ought to indeed; it is the responsible thing. It used to be the way of the Hardwicks to have a strong man at their head. Joseph was a disappointment. Now my old brother Walter; there was a man to lead a family. He stood no nonsense. Took after my father – another great man. He saw the Revolution of '88 you know. Saw old Dutch Billy ride through the streets . . .' For a moment the old man's mind wandered amongst uncharacteristic memories. Then he sighed. 'Ah, what a disappointment the family turned out: Joseph a fool, Catherine a scold, Charles with his parson notions. And now only Catherine left.' His manner became abrupt again. 'I fancy George has a little sense in his head, if his blood could be cooled a little. When do you expect him and James here?'

Kingsley shrugged.

'Aunt Catherine said she would write to them today,' he said. Horace made a gesture of contempt. 'Today, tomorrow, never. I say again, 'tis a miracle aught ever gets done in that house. I think,' standing up stiffly, 'I had better ride over to Morholm with you. A little organization would not go amiss. Is it cold outside? I have not ventured out yet this morning.'

Mary took a walk about the village for the rest of the morning, and when she came back to Morholm she found Great-Uncle Horace newly arrived there. An eight-mile ride from Stamford had not diminished his vigour and Mary entered the parlour to find him sitting, upright and acerbic, with his long shanks crossed before him. Aunt Catherine was in full spate, but Horace interrupted her. 'Now, Catherine, I hear the day is not set for the funeral. That is bad management. Can we not arrange tomorrow? What is there against tomorrow? Do you not agree, Mr Medhurst?'

The Reverend Mr Medhurst, Vicar of Aysthorpe and Ufford, a sleepy, agreeable little man, had been comfortably supplied with tea and muffins and had seen no reason to leave while there was still consolation to be offered. Now under Horace's dry, hard gaze, he began to feel a little superfluous. 'Of course, Mr Hardwick, the – er – wishes of the relatives of the deceased must be – er –'

'My dear uncle,' put in Aunt Catherine, 'you must know, George and James are in London, ignorant at this very moment of their father's decease.'

'Surely you do not intend to delay the ceremony until such time as they return? Think how long it will take to reach them, how long for them to arrange their affairs, to return hither! Have some sense, Catherine.'

Aunt Catherine's face slipped into its ill-used expression. 'Very well, uncle, 'tis for you to decide, and not a foolish creature like me. I merely thought it more seemly.' She began to sniff. 'Don't mind me. 'Tis the consequence of a silly, tender heart.' Grandmother Peach, from her corner, snorted with disgust and began to turn her stick round and round between her palms so that the end grumbled and squeaked on the floor.

'Do not distress yourself, ma'am,' said Parson Medhurst, feeling on safe ground again. 'Your brother is this moment one of that happy number on His right hand. He is gone to join the blest above.'

'Praise be!' said Catherine, looking pious. 'I did my best to help him be a good man.'

'A good man, perhaps, but a poor man as head of an ancient and respected family,' put in Horace dryly. 'I think no one will oppose me when I say that as master of Morholm – a weighty title for any man to bear – he was a great disappointment.'

Mary, who was pouring tea for the cleric, froze.

'Yes, indeed, let us not forget that no man is perfect,' said Parson Medhurst sonorously, gaining confidence. 'God forgives them who –'

'He was a natural fool,' said Horace bluntly. 'It is a disease unfortunately rampant amongst the current generation of Hardwicks. I am sure you will not tax me with disrespect when I say that Joseph was, for all his good points, a weak and gullible man.'

Mary gave Parson Medhurst his tea with a trembling hand.

'Ah, 'tis true he was weak,' said Aunt Catherine, 'and often I have had to take him to task for his foolishness.'

'It is the way of the Hardwicks,' went on Horace, shifting his position with a creak of old boots – or old bones – 'it is the way of the Hardwicks to be led by a man who commands respect; the family wheel must be fitted with a stout hub; a true head of the family, in brief. A man such as my father Sir Robert was. We Hardwicks have a tradition of great men, who have made our name what it is. Now, I make no claim to being head of the family,' that was true, Mary thought, for he was too preoccupied with making money, 'no: that title belongs to the inheritor of Morholm. What I am wondering is whether George intends to come back here permanently and take his father's place. Pray, again, do not accuse me of disrespect, but it is time we had someone to provide that order, that masterful quality that was so sadly lacking in Joseph. Joseph, you will all own, was imprudent; he disposed the family fortune in places where it was barely needed, was too liberal with his favours, too susceptible to the appeals of the – er – apparently unfortunate.'

'He took me in when I had no one,' said Mary in a quiet

but level voice which made everyone look at her. She tried to control her trembling. 'And I was not the first to whom he extended his great kindness. I will not stand by and hear him called a fool because of that.'

'Come, Mary,' said Horace, 'I do not deny a certain simple decency in Joseph, very laudable. But we are talking about a great tradition –'

'We are talking about the man who lies upstairs and had a greater heart than all of us!' cried Mary. 'Dear God, I –'

'Ah yes,' put in Mr Medhurst, recognizing his province. ' "And now abideth faith, hope, charity, these three; but the greatest of these is charity." '

'Quite so,' said Horace. 'In the right places.' And calmly contemplating his long reddened hands, went on in his cool urbane tone: 'The time is ripe for a strong and wise gentleman to take his place at Morholm and carry on the family tradition.'

'What he says is right, you know,' grunted Cousin Daniel, speaking for the first time. Clumsily he heaved the newspaper off his fat stomach and waddled to the hearth. There he planted his flat feet and stood, flabby and obtrusive, like a monument of erudition. 'A wastrel such as Joseph had no manner of right to stand at the head of a great family. I mind the time we rode into Peterborough last year, and I had to wait an hour for him, because he would sit and chunter with an old beggar in The Talbot. Gave him all the money he had in his pockets, too. Now I ask you, what is the workhouse for? And suppose that beggar had been a thief – as he probably was – one of those rogues who lure gentlemen to 'em, and then beat 'em about with sticks and steal their gold! The way Joseph behaved – 'twas not conducive to the dignity of a squire. That's what I say.'

Mary got up and faced Daniel. For a long time she did not say anything but merely looked at him searchingly, until he coloured and had to look away. 'You might remember

34

another occasion, uncle. When a bankrupt cousin of Joseph's came penniless to his door and was welcomed with open arms.'

'Ah, well,' said Aunt Catherine uneasily, 'I just pray the Lord may forgive him his simplicities and fooleries, many as they were, and try as I might to cure him of them. For you will allow, Mrs Peach, it was my life's labour to try and put some sense into my brother, and if he died as simple as a child, it was not through my lack of effort to make him what he should be.'

'That boy George'll never settle down,' came the strident voice of Mrs Peach. 'Too many fashionable notions. Could have done with a good leathering when he was younger, if you'd have my opinion. Would have given him it myself, if I'd had the chance,' she added with a rattling laugh.

'Ah! yes,' said Aunt Catherine, 'therein lies another of his father's weaknesses. Irresponsible! Why, Kingsley will tell you of the time I sent him into Stamford to buy lace edging for me, and he ended up paying that villain of a draper over a shilling a yard, because he was too weak to quibble –' But Kingsley, having seen Horace in, had not remained to bandy small-talk, but had slipped away unnoticed and was at that moment on his way to the cockpit of The Angel in Peterborough to gamble a few guineas, or more. After all, Joseph might be dead, but his money remained.

Neither did Mary listen to Aunt Catherine's words for, shocked, repulsed, incredulous and furious, she could not bear to hear any more and fled from the room to the garden where she flung herself down on the damp grass. With a blackbird eyeing her warily from the hedge she lay looking at the sky for a long time.

Julia Hardwick, Joseph's daughter of nineteen, was in the village, visiting a poor family. The man was ill with pleurisy and they were finding it hard to survive. She brought some fresh vegetables from Morholm and a recipe for a draught from Aunt Catherine. She was not sure what prompted her to make these visits: she could not say with conviction that it was pity. She sat a few minutes by the man's bedside in the fetid darkness of the loft in the tiny cottage. Thick eyebrows brooded over the heavy features of her face, the grey eyes and long nose and big lips. Her expression was sour and sullen. Her figure, though full, was sloppy and unrefined, and she dressed drably, as if she were defiantly flinging her plainness in one's face. She was generally declared a 'queer fish' and shunned. The people of this house were too needy to be able to afford to shun her, but they were uneasy with her, and relieved when she finally took her dark, brooding presence out of the door.

As she set out again on the road for Morholm she heard the dull clatter of a horse's hoofs behind her. She turned to see a tall figure reining in his mount beside her. It was a young man of about twenty-three, strikingly handsome, with a keen open face and an intelligent manner. He sat with an easy, big-boned grace; his red riding-coat and white breeches were well-cut.

'Pray pardon the intrusion, Miss Hardwick,' he said in a light musical voice. 'I have just received news of your sad loss. I am at this moment on my way to Morholm to offer my condolences in the absence of my father, who is confined to the house with a fever.' This was Thomas Jarrett, the son of a wealthy wool merchant who lived in a big rambling homestead on the other side of Aysthorpe. 'A most grievous loss to the county. You must be deeply affected; pray accept my sympathy.'

She looked at him with an odd expression in her lustreless eyes.

'Yes, Mr Jarrett, I must allow that I do feel a little sad today. I rather surprise myself. I never thought I would feel

36

anything when he died. You see, Mr Jarrett, no doubt it is a terrible thing to say, but I did not love my father.'

Jarrett was shaken and for a moment his decent diplomatic manner wobbled. 'Oh, Miss Hardwick, I am sure . . . no doubt the shock of your bereavement. I am sure . . .'

'Please do not make excuses for me. It *is* a dreadful thing to own; I am continually amazed by it myself. There really is no justification for it. I suppose it is not in my nature to love. I don't know why. Perhaps it is because no one loves me – do you think that is it? Yes; I do. No, don't say anything; it is true. No one loves me. They make a great show of caring for me, some of them; it makes a good appearance, you know; but they all mistrust me, dislike me, are never easy in my presence; they look askance at me, frown at me, find me odd and unpleasant. Isn't it strange?'

Jarrett, still on unsteady ground, remained deferent and cautious. 'I am sure the lady wrongs herself. The, er, apparently low estimation she holds herself in, others would dispute.'

'No, no. The things you are repudiating you are at this moment feeling. Such an odd, moody girl. Good heavens, it's no matter of wonder that no one loves her. An ungrateful hussy, too, I declare! And *so* plain. Do not deny it.'

Jarrett paused, puzzled. 'I see that you are upset and bewildered, Miss Hardwick, so I will intrude on you no longer. But I still refuse to believe your avowal that you did not love your father as you ought. There, I think you are being –'

'You misunderstand me,' said Julia, suddenly colouring. 'My words are always misunderstood. I – I never said – at least, I did not entirely mean . . . I felt – felt something, indeed, am feeling it now, I think, for my father. People *will* misunderstand one!'

'My dear Miss Hardwick, anyone who does not take the trouble to understand you does not deserve the pleasure of your company – refute that though you may.' An almost tangible pause ensued between them, inviting either of them to speak. Jarrett looked down on Julia with his grey-blue eyes, patting his horse's neck. Her head drooped over her chest, her straggly hair clinging round her face. She broke the silence.

'You are wrong, Mr Jarrett, quite wrong. I want no one to understand me. That would be altogether *too* much.' She seemed about to say something more, but stopped with a little snap of her jaw, as if biting the words back, and turned abruptly away.

2

A great number of people came to Joseph Hardwick's funeral. Aside from the various friends and acquaintances Aunt Catherine, relishing the occasion, had invited, a host of local people from the villages and farms turned up and joined the long shuffling line behind the pall-bearers. By them Joseph had been held in great affection, and it was with instinctive impulse that they pressed forward to speak to Mary, who alone of the family knew them all well. The day was breezy and grey with the shadow of approaching autumn, but occasionally the sun appeared behind the shifting clouds to spill splashes of light on the winding procession. Parson Medhurst, in canonical vestments, bumbled along at the head, followed by the coffin-bearers. Behind them in pairs, with white scarves and gloves, came Aunt Catherine and Julia, Mary and Cousin Daniel, Kingsley and Grandmother Peach. Then there was Great-Uncle Horace, stepping stiffly like an old stork, Thomas Jarrett, sober and handsome, on behalf of his father, the Miltons from Helpston, Mr Sedgmoor the family lawyer from Peterborough, the Wainwrights from Stamford, wealthy and proud and looking rather contemptuous of this country-gentry affair, and among others, to Aunt Catherine's great delight, Sir Samuel Edgington, a genuine old baronet. Then came the servants, and after them, in knots and dribbles, the villagers. They filed into Aysthorpe church, a squat building hardly bigger than the grey stone houses of the village.

Mary did not listen to Parson Medhurst's sermon. She found herself concentrating on peculiar things like the little puffs of steam that his breath made in the chill air of the church, the uneven stone at her feet, the long bag-wig of

Sedgmoor the lawyer. Her own father had been a parson but she was not especially religious. The service, the sober-suited and bewigged mourners disposed uncomfortably about the church, and Joseph Hardwick the living man as he was, seemed at that moment things ludicrously disparate. She just wanted to get the grisly business over. Was she the only one who felt grief, desperate, dry grief, at the occasion? She could not read the faces of her relatives around her. But there was more than grief: there was anger, growing and swelling within her such that she feared its outbreak . . .

Julia sat next to her, her face blank as if she were blind. All these people here, she thought – how ridiculous. As if they really cared about father. They only come to see who else is here and snatch a look at the house and hope he's left them a watch or something. And to look at me. I know they are, this moment. 'What a sour plain girl Joseph's youngest is! How old is she now – nineteen? Looks more thirty. No idea how to dress.' Well, let them look . . .

Aunt Catherine was making free use of her handkerchief. I hope Sir Samuel can come back to the house afterwards, she thought – and the Wainwrights. So long since we had anyone of quality at Morholm. Good of young Mr Jarrett to come for his father – though no doubt he was made to come. I know for a surety the old rogue has scarce been out of the house these two years. They say he has a quantity of money stored up there. Always a tight-fisted old man. Though Joseph was never over-generous, and that's God's truth. No doubt the estate goes to George – but I hope there is a settlement for me for all my trouble . . .

Cousin Daniel's head was nodding. With a jerk he roused himself, flakes of wig-powder floating down on to his shoulders. Wouldn't do to sleep at the old boy's funeral. Not that Joseph would have minded – why, I could roll the old dotard around in my palm. Pox, will this spouting parson never be done . . . ?

Kingsley sat and looked at his shoes. He needed some new ones; these, he thought, are growing scuffed. I hear the fashion now is to have huge buckles that cover the whole foot. In London they say the young men wear their wigs piled high with the hats perched on top. Perhaps George has seen those: I must ask him when he comes back . . .

Old Mrs Peach crouched in her pew like one of the demons in the rough carving on the pulpit, bent over her constantly gyrating stick. She was wondering, at intervals, who would die next, and what was for dinner . . .

When the funeral was over and the body of Joseph buried out of sight in the Hardwick plot, a number of the guests assembled at Morholm to take wine and cake and discuss again the follies and vices of the deceased. To Aunt Catherine's delight the old baronet, who had known Joseph in his youth, came back with the rest. As a personage, however, he was disappointing, for he never spoke a word but merely sat propped up in a corner with a glass of port, occasionally slipping off his wig to scratch the stubbly dome of his head for an elusive louse. Mary's memory of the occasion was fragmented. She remembered Aunt Catherine showing the Wainwrights round the rooms, saying in her most weary and ill-used voice, 'Of course, the furnishings are vastly inferior to what they were – another sad result of my brother's negligence.' And, in the midst of a little group by the fire, Cousin Daniel's voice, loud and arrogant: 'Why, there is a goodly acreage of farmland here – enough to support two houses of this size in a genteel manner, if properly cultivated. But he had no more idea how to farm good land, had Joseph. He was a sad disappointment to this family.'

A sudden smash of glass silenced everyone. Mary had snapped the stem of her untouched glass of port and hurled it to the floor. Powdered heads turned to look at her. Blood ran from her fingers on to her black gown. 'I can scarcely believe my ears!' she cried, her voice breaking with stormy emotion. 'A man like my Uncle Joseph – and *this* is what I hear at his funeral!' Tears were flowing on to her cheeks but she refused to give way to them. Mrs Wainwright gave a cough and held up a quizzing-glass. 'All of you owe him so much. His goodness, his kindness – do they mean nothing now he is dead? You, aunt – and you, Daniel,' he was the nearest to her and she seized his arm, 'do you not owe him something more than – than words like these? I am ashamed – ashamed of you.' She could say no more as great searing sobs filled her throat.

Daniel, sweating rather, patted her hand. 'She's upset,' he said, nodding in explanation to the goggling faces. 'Just upset!' But she shrugged him off violently and ran sickened and desolate up to her room. She seemed to be spending most of her time here of late she thought, as she cast herself down. She had never felt so entirely alone.

It was a dull evening at White's Club in St James's. The big gaming-room, warm with yellow candlelight, was only half-filled. Most of the more notorious and wealthy gamblers had not appeared or were at Brook's across the street, and the scattered groups that remained were playing cautiously; the atmosphere was reserved, almost businesslike. The biggest game was a party of nearly a dozen at loo. One man was dealing to the group around the large green table. Someone whistled a tune and a couple were murmuring to each other gruffly; apart from this there was no sound but the soft patter of cards and the occasional click of a snuffbox. A thin young man with a pleasant, pale face gave an exaggerated yawn and pushed the pile of gold coins in front of him into the well in the middle of the table. He was youthful in appearance, his features keen and mobile with a vulnerable touch to them. His figure, though slender, was well-made; his embroidered coat and fancy stock somewhat showy. At that moment his manner seemed listless and unhappy; he slumped back heavily in his chair and idly watched the reactions of his fellows. There was little emotion marked in the ring of faces around him. One raised an eyebrow and the dealer grunted, 'All or nothing, eh, Hardwick?' A guttering candle brushed wavering shadows across the tops of the gamblers' heads. When the round was over and the young man had lost he stood up, taking a pinch of snuff, trying to appear unconcerned, and play continued without him. He hovered a moment, glancing around. Boredom weighed heavily on his shoulders. Damned wearisome in here today: only the other night he had seen near twelve thousand pounds on a table at one time. Not that he could anything near afford to take part in those spectacular games. Often he found even the lowest stakes one could make here taxing on his limited purse. This gambling, he thought, is a confounded evil business; certainly not the romantic levity he had imagined, unless one was really rich. For some months now the so-called fashionable world had begun to disillusion and tire him; he was coming to the conclusion that it did not live up to its reputation. It had a certain unsteady glamour, but to live in it was to live a life of affectation, and ultimate self-destruction. When he had first come to London in the spring of '73 the glittering novelty of it had captivated him. But after a while its pleasures had become merely hollow to him. For a time he had been able to deceive himself that his life was riotous, gleeful, all he could wish; but now he knew. It was superficial and meaningless – perhaps he had always known that – but what really struck him was that its pleasures were not intense at all. They were disappointing, trifling, and ultimately wearying.

As he went for his hat and started to leave he caught sight of a knot of fops around the fireplace. They were dressed in an extremity of fashion and their posturing and speech were ridiculously affected. Amongst them he recognized Bellatt and Suckling, two fashionable beaux whom he knew and rather wished he did not. He tried to hasten out without being seen.

'Hardwick!' came Bellatt's sharp voice. 'What, departing already, by God? Purse empty already, shite take it? That's not the Hardwick I used to know!' And there was a bray of laughter and a rattle of elegant walking-canes. Reluctantly he joined them, his hat under his arm.

'Not at Mrs Hennessy's yesterday, eh, Hardwick, don't lie, tell me true; were you?' said Suckling.

'No, I fear not,' he said shortly. Good God, look at that fellow, he thought. Things have gone too far. Wig piled up higher than half the women's. And that absurd short coat sticking out at the back – and that tiny hat! And I wondered if I was dressing too extravagantly.

'Should have been there, old fellow – should have been there,' said another whom he did not know, with tassels at the knees of his tight striped breeches. 'The Misses Longman turned out – exquisite angels – dressed like duchesses – worth attention underneath gowns too, though, I'll wager!' There was another whinny of laughter. The young man bowed, made his excuses and left them. As he strode out of the room he heard Bellatt's high-pitched voice rallying after him: 'What, Hardwick, away so early, damn it, the night just beginning! Damned moody fellow of late – crossed in love, I'll wager, eh – by an old bawd? Or thrown out of lodgings for not paying the rent, eh?'

George Hardwick stepped out of White's, welcoming the refreshing coolness of the autumn air. He had considered going to a tavern to drink away the rest of the evening, but instead decided to go back to his lodgings and retire early to bed. Perhaps tomorrow he might go and seek out Mr Alden, his former tutor, who was also in London. They had remained friends for a while after returning from the Grand Tour, but a month ago they had quarrelled and had not seen each other since. He believed Alden was touting some

44

pamphlet he had written. George hoped for a reconciliation; he had no other real friends in the city.

He came out of Piccadilly into Shaftesbury Avenue. The streets were still dotted with people: tradesmen going home, servants hurrying on errands, drunkards who lurched out of back-streets bellowing fragments of songs, dandies with stacked clipping heels, beggars. But the town was noticeably less busy than it had been: it was the end of the season, and a few days before he had seen a group of young bucks mark the official last night by smashing the lamps in Vauxhall Gardens and almost wrecking the place. Such things, he noticed, were growing more and more excessive.

As he passed a narrow alleyway he thought he heard a cry of distress. Thinking it to be a drunk he went on, but as the voice was lifted again he discerned the words: 'Help a blind man, if there be anyone near! Set upon by common thieves, devil take them! I beg you, anybody, aid a blind man to his feet! Purse gone and all! Is anyone near?' The voice seemed cultured and elderly, and he could not help but turn back at its piteous tone. He peered into the alley, a huddled shape gradually materializing as his eyes adapted to the blackness. He stepped forward. 'Are you hurt? Can I help you?' he said loudly, as he detected a movement from the slumped figure at his feet. 'Oh – the Lord be praised – a gentleman at last,' came the voice. 'Thank you, thank you, sir. If you will just take my arm and help me up – the foul thieves.'

As George held out his hand to the man an iron grip suddenly closed about his wrist and held him fast. Almost in the same moment a stunning cudgel blow smashed over the back of his head. The ground loomed up and hit his face and chest. In a fragment of time he was aware simultaneously of lights capering before his eyes and blood crawling over his face and a blinding pain in the back of his head and big coarse hands rifling through the pockets of his coat and the hardness of cobblestones against his cheeks. Then there was a grunt of

'Empty!' and something dropped by his side. A puff of evil breath wafted over his shoulder and he felt the big hands ripping his coat and waistcoat violently from his back. He almost choked as with a savage jerk his laced stock was torn from his neck; then two figures jumped over him and with a clatter of receding footsteps were gone into the darkness of the alley.

He lay still. It did not strike him as odd to find himself cursing aloud for having fallen into a lure. The throb in his head was agonizing and every bone in his body seemed racked with pain. For a long time he could not bring himself to move and remained face down on the grimy cobbles. Then, his whole body wrenched with the effort, he raised himself to his feet. The little blue thing on the ground was his empty purse. He wiped the blood from his face. From the waist up he was clad only in his shirt; his hat also was gone. Swaying a little, he put up his hand to feel the wound on the back of his head, a little burning patch where his wig was matted with blood, but thought better of it and began to stagger out of the alleyway into the street.

The distance to his lodgings off Charing Cross was short, but his journey home that night seemed of infinite length. The pain in his head made him reel and lurch across the road, and once he almost fell beneath the roaring wheels of a carriage. Passers-by clearly thought he was drunk and avoided him. Presently a down-at-heel young prostitute who was doing no business took pity on him and, taking his arm, steadied him the rest of the way.

In his lodgings his landlady bandaged his head and her breathless voice came to him, hollow and indistinct, as if from down a long tunnel. 'I hope and pray they will be hanged tomorrow, though that I say ought never to pass a lady's lips. I declare the streets are no more safe after dark than in my father's time. Taking a coat from a gentleman's back! That *this* should happen to a person living in *my* genteel apartments!' as if it were a personal reflection on her.

Presently, after his frequent assertions that he was perfectly well, she left him. He heard her say something about a letter which had arrived for him, which she had left on his desk, before he sank into sleep.

When he awoke he found he had slithered out of his chair on to the floor. The candle had burnt down and left the room in pitch darkness. The pain in his head was still there, but he felt fresher and brighter than he expected. He fumbled for another candle, lit it, went to the window and drew back the curtains. Then he noticed the letter on his desk. He set the candle by it and peered at the fussy script, recognizing it as Aunt Catherine's.

George read the letter for a long time. Then he threw it down with a sigh and returned to the window where the starry night loomed vast and unchanged above him. Winter would soon be here; they would be burning leaves at Morholm. He fancied he could smell the familiar drifting smoke. 'I must go back,' he said aloud.

James Hardwick was not at all like his brother George. Whereas George was thin and finely-wrought, with something of his father's vulnerability in his face, James was sturdy, of middle height, thick-set and purposeful. His eyes were rather small, giving him a short-sighted look, and he dressed in dark sober clothes and wore his own hair, unpowdered. Though there was only a mile of bustling city between their lodgings the brothers never saw each other, by mutual wish. That evening James was drinking in the chambers of the barrister with whom he was studying, a portly middle-aged Scotsman named Finlayson. A letter like his brother's had arrived earlier and he had been pondering it ever since.

'You're more quiet than usual tonight, Hardwick,' said Finlayson, shoving aside a heap of documents to make room on the table for a second bottle of brandy. 'What's amiss?'

'Father's dead,' said James, and drained his glass. 'Had a letter today.'

Finlayson was a slow man, and liquor did not quicken his intellect.

'What – what – your father?'

'Well, and who else's father? Don't ask details, as people always do,' he pulled the letter from his pocket and tossed it on the table. 'Here, read it.'

Finlayson looked at the wad of paper in surprise and then looked at James. 'What, read your letter? Folk are generally uppish about that, 'specially letters of that kind.'

'Why should that bother me? There's nothing secret in it,' said James, as Finlayson opened the paper and pored over it. There was a pop and a chink and a gurgle as James opened the new bottle and poured out a glass. 'I suppose I must go home for a while. It seems expected of me, though I'm damned if I can see any cause for it. It is not even as if I'm going back for his funeral. Aunt Catherine wants a "family gathering". How ominous that sounds. I suppose we must all sit around and talk about God's will and the Host above and who knows what else. Haven't you finished reading it yet?'

The barrister put the letter down. 'This George – your elder brother, is not he?'

James nodded, brooding. 'And now to claim his inheritance. I certainly do not envy him.'

'Big estate, is it?'

'Moderate. Rich farmland.'

'Wish *I* could just inherit m'living. My father never had nothing but gout, though.' Finlayson sighed and lifted his glass. 'I'd be green with envy if I were you.'

'No, no. I would not wish for a great responsibility like Morholm. One would be tied down by it.'

'So one is by the law.' Finlayson studied James closely. His profession had trained him in reading people and he saw a savagery in the compression of James's thin lips.

48

'Not in the same way. You don't understand my family. They worship a god called tradition. We've been squatting out there at Morholm for I don't know how long, and each new proprietor must bear the burden of that tradition, as well as a wagonload of sponging parasites. No, the life of a squire cooling his heels in the middle of a Fen wasteland holds no appeal for me.'

'Who's this Aunt Catherine?'

'One of the leeches I mentioned. My father's sister.' A bitter laugh escaped his lips. 'I believe my brother's inheritance would be twice the amount were it not for Aunt Catherine's presence.'

'Handsome woman?' said Finlayson with a wet grin.

'She would not still be an old maid if she were.'

'Any other ladies in your family?'

'My sister Julia, who is unmarried and likely to remain so: two grandmothers, one the most ungrateful old harridan you ever met: and my cousin Mary, who I suppose is what you might call pretty, but has no sense in her head.'

'All these living at Morholm?'

'Yes; together with old Daniel, whom father was stupid enough to rescue from the brink of the debtor's prison where he belonged – my father's cousin; and Kingsley, some distant relation, orphaned as a child, and still living off the fat of the land. Inveterate scoundrels, both of them.'

'Tiresome things, families,' said Finlayson.

'And mine is the most tiresome and foolish on this earth,' said James, rising and striding to the window.

'If you won't be offended at my saying it, I conceive that your father – no disrespect – was a small thing soft to let such a brood live off him the way you say.'

'Oh, he was,' said James, his voice muffled by the glass. 'He was the most foolish of all.

'I had better start for home tomorrow morning,' he went on, 'so do not expect me at the office.'

3

The last glow of light was fading across the flat fields when George arrived at Morholm the next day. Of the family only Mary, out in the garden, was there to greet him.

The garden at Morholm was a curious mixture of old and new. Two years ago Joseph had called in a landscaper from Northampton who had done some work before Joseph's interest had melted away and the project had been abandoned. Now an orchard remained as evidence of his efforts, flanked by two pleasant avenues, and there was a flight of stone steps going into a sunken bowl that had been intended for an ornamental pool but was now full of weeds and wild flowers. Though it was so overgrown Mary loved the garden and spent much of her free time there. This evening she had found a last flush of trembling yellow roses in a neglected corner, and she felt a prick of annoyance when she saw the tall slender figure striding from the house towards her, thinking it to be a gardener, whom she regarded as an intrusion in her domain. It took her a moment to recognize George, who she had seldom seen even as a child. As he came up to her with his loose-limbed walk and rakish smile, she thought he looked older than his years.

'Cousin George! I am glad to see you,' she said, extending her hand.

'And I you,' he said, taking her hand awkwardly. 'Though I wish it were in happier circumstances. Is there no one else here?'

'No. Aunt Catherine and Julia are supping with the Townsends over to Thorney: your grandmothers are abed: and Daniel and Kingsley are in Stamford, I believe.'

'H'm. Well, no one knew when to expect me. I received Aunt Catherine's letter yesterday and set out this morning in a post-chaise. It had to put up in Peterborough so I borrowed a horse from old Sedgmoor in town for the rest of the way. This is a grim question . . . but were you with him?'

'I? No. I don't believe I would really wish to be.'

'No. Well, there it is. He's gone, and no amount of lamenting will alter that. For my part I would rather remember him, but not speak of him. Do you agree to that?'

Nothing could have pleased her more than George's proposal. 'Yes, yes indeed. I know what you mean. We have had nothing but talk of him this past week. Let us talk of happier things – or we shall never be content again.'

George breathed the heavy scented air. 'How peaceful the old garden looks! I had forgot what a mellowing effect Morholm has on the soul. There is nothing like this in London. The gardens there are full of vulgar little lanterns and fountains and noisy people.'

Mary smiled. 'I am afraid you will find it no tidier than when you left.'

'Oh, I find a little disorder comfortable.'

'Will you walk round it with me?' said Mary. 'If you are not too tired from your journey, that is. I have had some little trees put in the border there, but I think they are not taking very well.'

He took her arm and she led him round the twisting paths.

'How you have grown, cousin!' he said. 'I declare you're almost a woman.'

'That is nice to hear,' she said, smiling, 'but what of the fine ladies you must have met in London?'

George snorted. 'If by fine lady you mean an overdressed, powdered, affected creature with her hair up to the roof and a bad smell under her nose . . . For my part I would rather see an open face like yours, not daubed with patches. How is it you are here alone? Did you not wish to go to the Townsends' with my aunt and Julia?'

Mary shook her head. 'I am sorry to say it, but I do not in any way relish the company. I could virtually tell you every word that will be spoken by our aunt. I pleaded indisposal and stayed home.'

'I understand perfectly. I once fell asleep when she was talking to me and when I woke she was still talking. And my sister Julia is not the most entertaining companion.'

'No. And yet I think she is not as cold as folk believe. The general opinion seems to be that she is merely dull, but I think if truth were told she is deep down quite the opposite.'

'I never had time for the girl,' said George flatly. 'Ah, well. We Hardwicks are an odd crowd altogether. I take it James is not home yet?'

'No. Do you ever meet in London?'

'No, no. Not James and I – unless by accident. He deplores my dissolution and I deplore his industry. It's a convenient understanding. How was the funeral? I shall just ask this and no more.'

'No better or worse than I expected. People weeping and sighing over him and the next breath counting off his follies on their fingers. There were a good many mourners. The Townsends were there, and the Wainwrights, and a number of other people I never saw before; young Mr Jarrett came on behalf of his father . . .'

'Tom Jarrett! I have not seen him in years. Now that I am here I must renew old acquaintances. Anyone else important there?'

'Oh – there was a very dirty old baronet who came from Deeping. He did not stay long, though I fear the smell of him did.'

They both laughed, a little guiltily. 'Well,' said George, 'I do not envy your being there, I confess.' They were slowly making their way down one of the leafy avenues. As they came to a break in the trees where a gate led out on to the cultivated fields of the farm they stopped. Together they gazed out over the flat and checkered acres. It always seemed strange and charming to Mary to look suddenly out from the shadowy confines of the cool garden on to that broad stretch of green and yellow. Far away they could see two farmhands trudging home after clearing the remains of a late harvest. The cloudless sky was flushing a deeper orange, as if it were being toasted.

'This is all mine now,' said George in a low voice. 'What a daunting prospect. 'Tis like an immense pack being strapped to one's shoulders. You cannot shrug it off and drop it, for it contains all one's provisions and necessaries: if one sells it off, one must sooner or later buy another pack in its place.'

'A wealthy estate like Morholm – and you do not want it?'

'I do not truly know what I want, cousin. I know that I do not want the work and responsibility.' This attitude irritated Mary and she was about to speak out when George, with a curious little half-smile, said: 'I know what you are going to say, and I agree with you. Sometimes it quite disgusts me too.' She thought better of arguing with him. Instead she said: 'If you do not relish life here, why do you not go back to London? You might simply leave it. Let it rot, if you wanted – the choice is yours.'

'Oh,' he leant his back on the gate, stirring the dead leaves with his foot, 'as to that, I am not so very wasteful. And it is expected of me to take my father's place. Family tradition and all you know. Proprietor of the soil, justice of the peace, have the parson to dinner on Sundays, visit the tenants, head of the family, and so on. It's just that I don't feel ready for that yet. Perhaps another instance of my intolerable selfishness. And besides, London is not so very splendid.'

He had awakened an old interest in Mary. 'London! Why, I have heard it is the most –'

'Yes, yes,' he interrupted, 'I daresay much of what you have heard is true. London is a very large city with numerous very important things going on in it. But there is no more happiness to be found there than anywhere else.'

Mary could not believe that London was anything but the most magnificent place on earth. 'Surely – surely it is greatly exciting – diverting?'

'All excitement and diversion palls after a time,' he said, taking her arm as they set out again. 'Having been all through Europe and tasted at length the delights of London, I stand in the curious position of being able to say I have exhausted all the excitement and diversion there is to be had. There is now none left. I have had my life's worth.'

This struck Mary as an absurd thing for a twenty-two year old man to say, and she struggled for words to oppose him.

'What of Bath?' she said triumphantly. 'You have never been to Bath.'

He gave her a droll look. 'A fashionable, watery London; I doubt that Bath holds any undisclosed pleasures, cousin.'

She was about to ask him how he could know without having been there, but stopped as, glancing down, she caught sight of his scarred hands. 'Good Lord! How did your hands come to such hurt?'

'Oh,' he looked at them with an embarrassed face, 'evidence of London's less attractive side. I was set upon by thieves last night when walking home. Luckily my purse was already empty; but I lost a good hat, stock, waistcoat, watch and handkerchief; and obtained a sore head in exchange. I wonder you cannot see the bump through my wig.'

'What evil fiends! Will they be caught?'

He smiled. 'I fear there is small chance of that. They must be apprehended first, and I was stretched on the floor and too dazed to give chase. Yes, cousin, the face of London is as ugly as a demon's underneath the powder. I shall take you there some day, Mary; I believe even your innocence would be shattered by it.'

'If you mean innocence of the world outside this corner of the fens, then yes, I am innocent; but I believe I am not innocent of evils,' said Mary. 'Indeed, I hope not.'

George said nothing, but looked at her askance. Thoughts of London came to her again. 'Tell me more of London. Tell me of the balls and assemblies – I have never been to one,' she said.

'They are exactly similar to those one sees at Peterborough and Stamford, but on a grander scale. The fashion is for great masquerades, though some people think they grow too lewd for this age.'

'Masquerades! Have you ever attended one of those?'

'Scores,' said George, exaggerating somewhat, though he had been to several. 'I went once as a fiend Turk, another time as a jester. Many men go as women – I knew a man went as a fish-wife, though I could never bring myself to don women's clothes. One can often see the finest ladies dressed as dandies and harlequins and ballad-singers. I have seen many dressed as nuns; sometimes one sees popes; and I saw one lady come as a goose-girl, complete with her goose on a gold thread. Often they are somewhat riotous affairs, however – and though they seem delightful at the time, I cannot help but think how ridiculous they are. Similarly with the fashions one sees at St James's. The ladies are bad enough, with their wigs getting higher and more elaborate every day – but some of the young dandies! Macaronis they call themselves – little tight coats and breeches, and jewelled buckles, and idiotic little hats perched on top of piled wigs – some of them powdered bright red! And so many patches on their faces one would think they had the cow-pox: and the whole stinking of perfume and pomade. However, I doubt you see excesses like that out here.'

'Not those, certainly. Kingsley tries to keep pace with the mode.'

'That blood-sucking rogue still here? Though I hardly need ask. And Daniel, I presume. Aunt Catherine antici-pated a mustering of the Hardwick forces at my return – when is this auspicious gathering to take place, do you know?'

'No. Whenever it may be I do not look forward to it with pleasure.'

'Nor I. I expect a prodigious lecture on the duties of a squire, and a great deal of foolishness to be talked. Well, foolishness is an inherent trait amongst the Hardwicks. My father was good and honest, but he was a simple old fellow after all.'

Mary felt her cheeks prickle. 'I have heard nothing but assertions of his stupidity and weakness ever since he died. I begin to wonder at folk's conception of foolishness. Because my uncle had a heart so big and warm that it sometimes impaired his judgement in its generosity, they condemn him for a rustic idiot. His submissive temperament was not the mark of a simpleton but of a man with an infinite deference and respect for others, a love of peace and tolerance. If all this was folly in him then I hope I may lay claim to being equally as foolish.' She realized suddenly how loud her voice had grown. It sounded harsh and incongruous in the soft twilight air. 'I am sorry if I have been rude, but the feelings I give vent to have been building up since my uncle's death at each ungrateful word of my relatives, and I could keep them in check no longer.'

'Why, you cannot conceive how refreshing it is to hear you after a year or more of London affectation. And what you say is quite right, indeed. It is ingratitude to criticize my father. Any weakness of his was amply atoned for by his virtue.'

Mary was a little soothed, though she could not help thinking that he had still missed her point; but she was prevented from pursuing the subject by George's exclaiming: 'Who's that fellow cutting that tree? Is he a new gardener?' He pointed to an elderly man hacking at the trunk of an elm a little way off.

'Oh, yes, he was hired a few weeks ago,' said Mary. They stood and watched the swinging of his axe.

'Why is it being cut down?' murmured George. 'It looks a fine enough tree to me.'

'Why, the garden needs clearing, and winter is approaching. We must have firewood, you know.'

'Ah, yes.' He gave a wistful little laugh. 'I suppose I must begin to think of those things. Why, now what is the fellow doing?'

The old servant, abandoning his axe, was laboriously climbing up into the topmost branches of the tree, which was nearly thirty feet high. Almost at the top he straddled a branch and began to edge along it towards a black tangled shape.

'Only to rescue a crow's nest!' said George incredulously. 'The old dotard. I'm hanged if I'd risk my neck in that fashion!'

At that moment there was a violent crack and the branch supporting the old man began to sag and bend dangerously. With clumsy haste he tried to shift himself backwards, clutching at another limb above him. The broken branch began to fall away, leaving him hanging on to the branch above with both arms, one foot groping at the trunk while the other swung like a pendulum in the air. Mary, horrified, clutched at her cousin's hand and ran to the foot of the tree dragging him after her. 'He'll fall! He'll fall and be killed!' she cried. George, startled and angry, shook off her hand.

57

'It will be the old fool's fault if he is. I've no intention of breaking my neck for –' But she was not listening, for with gasps of panic she was shinning up the bole of the tree. He stood watching stupidly for a moment, dumb with amazement. Fresh rustlings and cracks came from above. Then as she mounted higher he called up to her. 'Mary! Don't be so ridiculous! Come down!' His voice grew sharper with frustration and fear. 'Mary! Stop, you foolish girl! Stop!'

Then the servant himself resolved the affair as he lost his grip with his right hand. He hung suspended by one arm for a second, writhing in the air. Then he dropped. He fell ten feet before crashing into another bough. There was a flurry of dead brown leaves and a creak; then, to the relief of Mary clinging halfway up the trunk, the figure of the old man appeared, hanging from the next bough, having grabbed at it in his fall. He swung his legs down as far as they would go and then carefully jumped, landing on his feet on the grass. Mary wriggled down after him.

'Do you intend to kill yourself?' snapped George, his face flushed.

'Pardon, master – but they say 'tis bad luck to cut down a crow's nest. You shouldn't ha' troubled, mistress: 'tisn't for ladies to go climbing trees.'

'And it isn't for paid servants to go wasting their time trying to save birds' nests,' said George. 'I hope you'll remember that next time you decide to go tree-climbing, man.'

He took Mary's arm and they walked away from the scene. 'And what did you mean by clambering after him like a monkey?' he hissed.

His anger surprised her. 'I'm sorry, cousin,' she said. 'Sometimes I do things without the least forethought. I even startle myself. Shall we go in and have supper now? It is turning a little cold.'

The tension in his face hovered a moment and then

58

relaxed. As they went into the silent house together his manner became easy again and they talked of other things. But at the back of her mind the incident in the garden lingered and she was puzzled by the anger she had seen in him.

Since Aunt Catherine and Julia would not be back till late, or possibly till the morning, and there was as yet no sign of Daniel and Kingsley, they ate supper alone. They sat at opposite ends of the long table, the candles sealing them in a little island of yellow light amongst the curtained shadows of the room. A brisk wind was tumbling about outside and stirring the corner of the Turkey rug on the polished floor, and now and then came the hollow cry of wildfowl flying east across the fen to the river shallows and meres.

'That is a very pretty dress, Mary,' said George. 'All one sees in London is fripperies and frills and extravagant taste.'

'It is my newest one,' said Mary, pleased. 'Your father always said he disliked mourning weeds, so instead I am wearing the dress he himself bought me last Easter.'

'What – the last new gown you had was bought at Easter! I thought he was more generous than that.'

'But you know what he was like. He never thought about things like girls' dresses. I dare say he would have bought me a new gown every day had I said I needed one. I was quite happy: I was never lacking. And, after all, I could not *ask* him.'

'You're the only one in the house who didn't. Did you never go to the shops in Stamford? Aunt Catherine regularly did, as I remember.'

'Oh, she would never ask me to go with her. And if I wanted to go myself, I would have to have an escort, which would mean taking away one of the servants for a day, and I never liked doing that.'

'Well, that is what servants are for!'

59

'Yes – I know. But I never really needed to go. It would have been violating your father's trust to take advantage of his generosity.'

George was silent a moment. 'I suppose you are right; but it all seems a little strong to me. I feel convinced that the old fellow would have wanted you to go and buy yourself a few luxuries once in a while. Indeed, tomorrow you shall. I will ride into Stamford with you. It's not fair if you have been stinting yourself while leeches like Aunt and Kingsley took advantage of the old boy.'

Mary suddenly thought how self-righteous she must have sounded. 'No – indeed I have not stinted myself. I have had quite enough to –'

'All the same, we will ride into Stamford tomorrow morning for your new gown. Now not another word.'

'I fear I do not ride well.'

'No more do I, so we shall stumble along very nicely, I think.'

They sat in silence for a while, listening to the roaring of the east wind off the fen as it threw itself against the walls of the house. Suddenly George gave one of his little half-laughs, a characteristic she had already begun to notice in him. 'It seems strange to sit here alone, in a house usually buzzing with people, at a table usually full. Almost as if we were master and mistress of Morholm.'

'You are the master of the house now,' said Mary.

'Good Lord, don't remind me,' said George.

'But there is no escaping it, George. Now that your father is gone you as his eldest son inherit his estate and responsibilities. No doubt you will become a magistrate like him, and –'

'Must you drum it into me?' said George, the edge coming into his voice again.

'It is a great responsibility, but – well, surely you must have seen impoverished wretches in plenty in London – are

60

you not glad you were not born in their condition? Why, why – even James must earn his living at the Bar; but you need never worry about anything like that again! I know it is not my place to speak like this, George, but I feel sure you will not condemn me – because you know what I say is true.'

'Sound doctrine is the hardest to follow,' he said, and poured himself a glass of wine. 'From the life of a London gentleman of leisure to the life of a country squire in one day is a big step, cousin.'

Between the gusts of wind outside they could hear the sound of horses' hoofs and voices. A few moments later Daniel and Kingsley came in.

'Ah! supper,' croaked Daniel, in the harsh voice that it was impossible to ignore. 'I am half-starved.' He and Kingsley sat and began to help themselves. 'How was London, George?'

'I doubt that it has much changed since your business last took you there,' said George shortly. Daniel liked to pretend that he was still a man of 'business'.

'Now that you are coming to take your father's place, I hope you'll put right all the things he left undone,' said Daniel, settling his stomach against the table. 'I'm sorry to say the family name diminished in stature during Joseph's time.'

George rose, motioning Mary to do likewise. 'Please excuse us. We began supper earlier.'

At half-past ten the stocky, wind-blown figure of James arrived. He had ridden from London in the public coach and looked exhausted. He sat stiffly with them for a while, asking desultory questions about his father. Then, declining any supper, he rose to go to bed. At the door he paused.

'When are we to expect this family gathering for which I have been called home? I can ill spare much time,' he said gruffly.

'Er – I don't doubt that it will be soon,' said George. 'Aunt Catherine seemed to think a little party necessary for my inauguration, so to speak.'

James's small black eyes looked hard at his brother. 'I see.' He went upstairs.

It appeared that Aunt Catherine and Julia were spending the night at the Townsends', so shortly afterwards Mary and George retired. For an hour or two after bidding goodnight to her cousin Mary lay fully clothed on her bed, looking at her old room. Its unchanged aspect seemed at odds with the change in herself: for, with something of guilt and something of pleasure, she felt that old life, of Joseph and quiet security, recede as if it were a hundred years ago.

4

George surprised himself by waking early the next morning. In London he had rounded off each evening with a thorough binge at a tavern and it made him fit for nothing until noon next day. The injuries of two nights ago were now giving him little trouble and he felt bright and eager to do something. He lay a few minutes, letting his eyes roam over the familiar contours of his old bedroom. Perhaps this was where he belonged after all. Then a shadow of doubt and misgiving fell across his thoughts and he scrambled out of bed before it had a chance to overwhelm him.

As he dressed he watched the speckles of rain throwing themselves against the window. He had a mind to look out his old friends – Henry Milton over at Helpston, and Thomas Jarrett.

Mrs Reynolds the housekeeper was crossing the hall as he came downstairs. Even she had a just-risen look about her. 'Oh, you're about, Master George. Shall I have breakfast laid? I mean Mr Hardwick . . .'

'Yes, Reynolds, if you will. Is everyone still abed?'

'All 'cept Master James, sir.'

George found his brother in Joseph's little library. 'You could have had breakfast laid, James,' he said. James did not look up from his book. 'I was waiting for you,' he said.

They ate breakfast in the cold silence of mutual dislike. As children they had never got on and now George found he had not a single thing to say to his brother. He bolted his food and then rose. 'I'm going out, James,' he said, and there was no reply.

Outside he found a carriage in the drive and his sister Julia climbing out from it. As the carriage rumbled away up the drive she glanced briefly at him from the awning of her heavy brows.

'Hullo, George,' she said and shambled towards him.

'Coming home by carriage now and all, Julia? You are rising in the world.'

It was impossible to banter with Julia. 'It is the Townsends'. Aunt Catherine and I stayed the night there. She has remained in Thorney to visit some other acquaintances. The Townsends insisted I use their carriage,' she said in her husky clipped fashion. George dabbed an obligatory kiss of greeting on her brown cheek and she walked past him into the hall. 'I am going out, Julia,' he added after her. There was no reply. What a damned queer set of relations I have, he said to himself as he went out to the stable: Mary is the only agreeable one amongst them.

He rode out on his father's old mount Monmouth, and the symbolism of the act amused him. He could feel the villagers' eyes on him as he clopped through Aysthorpe. Of course, they will stare, he thought: they want to see if the new squire's shocking dissolute life has left any visible scars. Ah, those old fellows outside the Seven Stars are shaking their heads. They don't hold with the likes of me, young popinjay. Well, now they will have to.

The grey limestone cottages of Aysthorpe petered out. The last house, old Nathan Jarrett's big tumbledown manor, lay on his right, the only house in the village comparable in size to Morholm. Old Jarrett's a warm man, I know, thought George, and doesn't spend a penny more than he needs – the place was falling down. George had begun to rein in his horse when it occurred to him it was too early yet for calling. He had better ride on to Helpston.

Back here in the old country, the stark quiet of the broad flat landscape still surprised him. Here the horizon, something you associated with the sea, was a constant presence. Distances were deceptive, for though the country was sparsely populated, wherever you were you could see the next village, even as a smoky blur on the edge of vision. As he rode nothing about him moved but a few birds that dotted the black clay of the fields as though sprinkled from a giant hand.

Though it was still early for calling when he arrived at Helpston, a village on the edge of the brush and woodland of the Heath, Dr and Mrs Milton received him with their customary friendliness. Dr Milton was a kindly man who had practised in the county most of his life. Unlike many of his colleagues he had never made great claims for remedies that he knew were still primitive, and nature had rewarded him with ill-health that forced him to retire from his practice. His only son Henry had had no inclination to follow his father's profession and for the time being managed his father's tiny estate of a few acres; the young man was of literary leanings and did not handle their sparse income well.

Henry Milton was a tall, stooping young man with a hollow sensitive face that seldom smiled. George, his friend from boyhood, sat with him and his amiable, comfortable parents for a while and answered their various enquiries. On being asked where he was on his way to, he answered: 'Actually I came with the express purpose of looking out old friends. Tom Jarrett's is my next call.'

'I must ride into Peterborough today,' said Milton. 'I haven't seen Jarrett in a while. I will come with you before I go into town.'

George set out again with Milton at his side. Both men were more glad to see each other than they cared to show.

'Well, George, are you coming to grace Morholm with your presence permanently?' said Milton, raising his voice to stop the rising wind snatching it away.

'That appears to be the conclusion of everyone but myself,' replied George. 'The flag of family tradition has been placed in my hands, and it appears that I must carry it.'

'Unwillingly?'

'Decidedly.'

'Your father did it for twenty years without coming to physical hurt,' said Milton.

'Ay, and wasted half his fortune keeping the likes of Daniel and Kingsley in luxury. Besides, father was not a guardian of the family tradition. He was a disappointment, so I hear. It appears my coming into the estate represents a Restoration, or should do.'

'And you are a returning King Charles come to grasp the family name with a firm hand and restore it to its place of glory?'

'If you like. It seems my father was not the commanding figure that Squire Hardwick of Morholm traditionally is. Therefore I am looked to for that figure. I fear that is what is to be instilled in me at this family gathering I have the pleasure to expect shortly.'

On arriving at Jarrett's house they themselves led their horses to the makeshift shed that served the old place as a stable, for no servant came to take them. Inside, a tall figure stood up from examining the hoof of one of the two horses. It was Thomas Jarrett himself. His face was red from stooping but the colour disappeared as he straightened, and a broad smile illuminated his good looks as he saw George.

'A wanderer returned,' he said, shaking George's hand. 'Glad to see you, Hardwick! Milton and all. Quite a reunion!' He was dressed very roughly in an old blue coat and boots, and a loose cap covered his unwigged head. 'Only room for one of your horses in here I fear; one of you must needs tie up outside. Excuse the muck. I have just been checking over this beauty. Bought her last week for thirty guineas. When did you get back, George?'

'Last evening. How goes it with you, Jarrett?'

'Ah, much the same. Father now has no teeth instead of two, and suffers from increasing deafness to add to the charm of his company. Aside from that . . . And what of Morholm?

Are we to expect George Hardwick as our squire from now on?'

'If I am asked that question once more I shall go straight-away and live in the South Sea Islands!' said George. 'Will you be satisfied with "I do not know"?'

'I shall say no more, or I fear it will be pistols at dawn,' laughed Jarrett. 'Shall we go inside? Chilly out here. I hope your visit can be stretched to a glass of wine in the drawing-room? Father will be at breakfast for an age yet, trying to chew his toast, poor fellow. The total occupation of his life nowadays is trying to eat and trying to hear and sleeping. He's successful enough at the last, however . . .'

They walked quickly through the increasing rain across the courtyard to the house. Jarrett too is still the same, thought George; same good humour, same clear voice and handsome features. He felt, as he always used to, cheered by his presence.

The untidy, shabby-gilded furnishings of Bromswold belonged to the fashions of Nathan Jarrett's youth, but they were comfortable. Jarrett, after changing, pressing them into chairs and quashing Milton's protests that he could not stay long, produced a bottle of wine. 'Let us drink a toast to the new master of Morholm,' he said with a glint of mischief.

'I fear I cannot join you in that toast,' said George.

'Then you propose.'

'I propose . . .' he brooded over his glass, 'to happiness.'

'What a dull toast!' said Jarrett.

'Why, what else is there?' said George. 'If you consider it, that is all we live for. That is what life is a search for, after all. The least we can do is toast her.'

They drank.

'By the way, Milton,' said Jarrett, 'what is this I hear about you and Miss Wainwright?'

'I do not know,' said Milton with an awkward laugh. 'What is it that you hear?'

'Oh, mere gossip, I presume, but someone was saying they saw you at the Wainwrights' a few weeks since, and that the lovely Miss Elizabeth and yourself were conversing for a long time – the whole evening in fact – and seemed to be more than averagely pleased with each other's company.'

Milton tried to look unconcerned, and said: 'I *was* at the Wainwrights'; and Miss Wainwright *is* lovely; and she did favour me with her conversation, for a while, at any rate; but the rest is pure fiction. I am sorry to disappoint you.'

'All the same, I just cannot help thinking –'

'I wish you could,' said Milton with another dry uncomfortable laugh. He was obviously very embarrassed.

'Oh, good Lord, there were rumours circulating about Miss Wainwright and her beaux even before I went to Europe. Do not bore me with more, I beg you,' said George. 'I shall be thankful when that woman does marry one of her suitors. Talk of some matter else . . .'

They talked, and drank, and midday crept up on them unawares. George passed through the loquacious stage of drink and then began to feel ill. Suddenly he had had enough and wanted to leave. Jarrett was relating a story of something that had happened in Stamford. George ceased to listen and let his mind wander down its own paths. For some reason the word 'Stamford' from Jarrett's tale lingered in his brain, tugging at the strands of memory. There was something connected . . .

Mary. Gowns. Shops. A promise. This morning.

He groaned aloud – so loud that Jarrett broke off and looked at him. How could he have been so forgetful? Visions crowded in on him of embarrassed explanations and his cousin's disappointment and general upset.

'Brandy too much for you, Hardwick?' said Jarrett.

'I just remembered something,' said George. 'I am supposed to be taking my cousin Mary into Stamford this morning.'

'Who said so?'

'*I* said so,' said George, rising suddenly to his feet. 'I promised her last evening. Oh, hang it, how foolish of me!'

'Ho, that's a good way to start, Hardwick,' laughed Jarrett. 'Well, it's too late now. You can go with her after dinner, can you not?'

'Yes, yes, but I said I'd take her this morning, and now I've come wandering out without so much as a by your leave and left her disappointed.' He went to the door.

'Not leaving us, Hardwick?' said Jarrett.

'The longer I stay, the more offence I shall give her.'

'Bide a bit, George, I'll go with you; time I got off for Peterborough,' said Milton.

'Well, and I am not going to be left to drink alone,' said Jarrett, following them.

The wind, peppered with drops of cold rain, cuffed Mary's cheeks as she rode out of Aysthorpe on to the Stamford road. At any other time it would have annoyed her; now she felt almost pleased with it, as a little more fuel for her anger. George had broken his promise and gone out without a word instead of escorting her to Stamford, and she was stupidly, bitterly resentful. When she had risen that morning she had not been unduly disturbed, supposing he had gone on some errand and would be back shortly. But as midday had approached and there was no sign of George she realized he had forgotten (or, she thought, ignored) his engagement altogether. James and Julia had said he had left no word of his business or how long he would be. Her disappointment and dismay grew into a blind anger such that she hardly knew herself. At half-past eleven, telling Julia of her intention, she left the house with as much drama as she could muster and headed for the stables, burning with a desire to make some act of defiance. Well, if the whole point was that it was deemed dangerous and unfit for her to ride to Stamford alone, then that was what she would do. If, she thought with the confused reasoning of anger, I am thrown or set upon by thieves or lost, then it will be George's fault and not mine. Fuming, she had begun to lead the first horse she saw out of the stable. As it happened it was Kingsley's big temperamental hunter. The groom had seen her leading him out and had tried to call her back. 'Pardon, Miss Mary, but you were never thinking of riding out – er – on old Raleigh, now?' Something in his tone had infuriated her further. 'Yes, I am going to Stamford. I am not taking an escort, Clarry. Will you saddle up, please?' He had objected to this so heartily, saying it was impossible for her to go alone, that she had faltered. But then George's words at supper had returned to her: 'That is what servants are for.'

'It is not for you to tell me what I must and must not do,' she had spat, surprised at her own vehemence. The startled Clarry had submitted to her and she had set out with a kind of vicious triumph.

But now, as she trotted along the North road on the broad back of Kingsley's horse, the absurd, petty idiocy of her anger struck her with full force. She bitterly regretted her words to old Clarry. 'I must go back immediately,' she murmured, and without noticing she was approaching a rough depression in the road she jerked on the reins, trying to pull Raleigh to a halt and turn him about in one movement. The bad surface and the girl's inexpert handling upset the big horse and he reared and twisted. With a lurch that seemed to cast her entrails up to her throat Mary was thrown off violently to land with an explosion of pain on her back by the roadside. Luckily the grass broke her fall, but she felt as if her whole backbone were shattered. A dome of grey-blue sky wheeled and spun above her and rain tickled her face. Her mount, after clattering a little way down the road, halted and lingered around nibbling the grass. As she lay groaning and abandoning gentility with fluent curses she heard – or rather felt, through the ground – footsteps approaching. She raised herself up to see a small,

70

bow-legged old man, coming from the direction of a farmstead at the end of Aysthorpe. He was dressed in an old coarse shirt and breeches and his arms and calves were caked with the black clay soil of the area, but he began to help her to her feet with the utmost gentleness. Another man, tall and blond and much younger, was running up behind and took hold of the horse.

'Up we come, my dear. Can you stand? That's good. That was an ugly fall!' He had a florid, bright-eyed face and spoke in the flat, soothing tones of the local accent. 'Are y'all right now. What a lucky chance that me and John was just coming out of house as you fell! That's a sizeable horse for you to be riding.'

Mary was shaken, but the friendly offices of the farmer made her feel better. Before she could stammer her thanks she was being led into the kitchen of the old man's cottage and a dish of tea, 'perked up', as he said, with brandy, placed before her.

'You are very kind. You need not have troubled, I am quite without hurt.'

'Ah, but you sit quiet a minute, mistress – don't be in a hurry to be riding off after a nasty tumble such as you took. Drink that tea, now, and bide a bit. John's tethered your mount outside.'

Sitting in the little kitchen with its roof-beams so low that the young son could not stand upright in it, Mary felt as if that morning's unpleasantness had been a bad dream. The old man was Samuel Newman, a tenant of Morholm land. Her liking for him became admiration when she learned of his wife, who was confined to her bed upstairs and was grievously ill. She offered him money to help but he refused, instead asking only for her advice about a herbal draught for his wife. When finally she left, Newman's son riding with her on a stout farmhorse 'to see her along', she felt happy again and warm with the knowledge that George need never even find out that she had tried to go out alone.

* * *

George, accompanied by Milton and Jarrett, arrived at Morholm a few minutes after Mary had left. He was not clear in his mind what he ought to do, but the first thing must be to apologize to Mary and then, perhaps, to say he would be delighted to accompany her should she still care to go. What he was unprepared for was the news that she had gone. Julia told him. 'She rode out about a quarter of an hour ago,' she said, not looking up from her sewing.

'The devil she did! What – she has gone off to Stamford regardless, then?'

'I presume so.'

'Who went with her? Clarry?'

'I saw her leave alone.'

'Damn her for a little fool! Well, I hardly need have come back, if that's her notion.'

'We would hardly have needed any of this fuss if you had gone with her this morning as you promised,' said Julia, her eyes still on her work.

'I'll thank you to mind your own business, Julia,' he snapped. 'I – I forgot. I am not the first man in the world to forget something, I suppose?'

'What do *I* know of the world?' drawled Julia. Milton stood behind George, uncomfortable. Jarrett sat down and watched with a grave expression. George wavered; his sister always infuriated him, and when he was angry he could not think straight.

'Then you let her go alone, just like that?'

'Pardon me,' said Julia. 'I thought you had just told me to mind my own business. Evidently I misheard you. My apologies.'

'Oh, do not be so damned clever, Julia!' said George savagely. He burst from the house and ran to the stables. 'Clarry!' he yelled. 'Did you let Miss Mary ride to Stamford without an escort?'

The old servant had feared this. 'Well, sir, it was her orders –'

'Damn her orders! What did she take out?'

'Raleigh, sir. Mr Kingsley's hunter.'

'Oh, good God, man, why didn't you follow her? There's a devil of a wind today and it's nigh on eight miles to Stamford and she's but eighteen and no rider! I've a mind to give you your notice, man!' His fury at what Mary had done was all the greater because he knew his own fault of carelessness lay at its heart. Milton had come out to join him and was trying to soothe him when Mary appeared, riding in through the gates, accompanied by a man on a farmhorse. She stopped and thanked the man, who then turned and rode off.

'Well, that was a brief outing,' said George as she dismounted. 'I suppose I have a right to ask what in God's name you think you were doing?'

'As I have a right to ask the same of you,' said Mary. Her anger, which had subsided, was inflamed again by George's tone. 'If you will allow me to speak, I was going to apologize. I realize now that you must have had other business, but this morning I felt you had neglected your promise and I grew angry and tried to go shopping alone. Just out of the village I had a mishap and fell. No, I am all right. A farmer helped me. I saw my foolishness and have come back. That's all.' She took a deep breath, trying to calm herself. 'I'm sorry, George.'

He paused, and they did not look at each other. 'Well, I am sorry too,' he muttered: but they were interrupted then by the arrival of Aunt Catherine in the Townsends' carriage, and in her effusions of welcome at the sight of George the subject was dropped, unfinished.

While this had been going on outside, Jarrett, making himself at home in the drawing-room, attempted to make conversation with Julia. His clothes neat and his face good-natured and handsome he began: 'May I hope that Miss Hardwick is recovering from her grief at Mr Joseph's death?'

73

Julia was silent for a moment, drawing her needle and thread through the material in her lap as if she were killing it. Then she said: 'Mr Jarrett, when you refer to Miss Hardwick, do you mean myself? You might equally refer to my aunt Catherine or my cousin Mary.'

'I shall leave that to your good sense to determine,' said Jarrett.

'I have very little sense, Mr Jarrett, so your question must go unanswered.'

Jarrett smiled, but he was unsettled.

'If you mean my aunt or cousin, Mr Jarrett, I do not presume to speak for them. As for myself, I continue to remark my father's absence, but not to actively regret it.'

'Well, now your brother is here to fill his father's place, so there will be no less company for you.'

There was a long silence. Finally Jarrett went on, discomfited: 'There is shamefully little diversion to be had in this county, do you not think, Miss Hardwick? For a gentleman it is not so bad; there is hunting if he wants it; but I am sure that a young lady, such as yourself, must be frantic for want of amusement. What is there – the occasional assembly at Peterborough or Stamford, a rare ball here and there, a few dinners, calls, outings? You must be very bored.'

'Well, Mr Jarrett, is it not true that that wearying little round of amusements you so accurately describe is all there is to be had anywhere? What else is there in London, in Bath, that is not an elaborated version of what you have named? I fear you cannot convince me we are worse off here.'

'But plenty of really grand assemblies and balls would considerably enliven the place.'

'I am afraid a ball holds no attraction for me.'

'Yet I believe I am right in saying you have never attended one, Miss Hardwick, so are you really equipped to make such a pronouncement?'

'Come, Mr Jarrett, you know as well as I that at a ball *my* companion for the whole of the evening would be the wall.'

'As I believe I said before, Miss Hardwick, you do yourself a great injustice. A lady may not have the most handsome outward favour, yet may be the most interesting woman on earth. A lady may have the finest figure and face, and still be the most foolish creature on earth.'

'Or alternatively she may possess neither beauty of person nor of mind, Mr Jarrett.'

'Or, again alternatively, she may possess much more of both than she will allow, and place herself in a disadvantageous light that others may presume to dispute.'

Suddenly, and for the first time in her life, Julia blushed, not just a touch of pink in the cheeks, but a great flourish of crimson that spread from her neck to the roots of her hair. Jarrett was surprised; but it was then that Aunt Catherine came in with a great flow of talk and Julia slipped away. Catherine had a great deal to tell her nephew of Joseph's death and her grief and numerous other matters, so Jarrett left with Milton.

At last, an hour later, George and Mary set off for Stamford, George to the chagrin of his family deferring dinner to give them more time. 'If you must go, you must,' Aunt Catherine said, 'though why Mary must have a new gown I do not know . . . Go, nephew, do not spare a thought for your poor aunt who has not seen you in an age.'

Mary felt odd and guilty about simply going into a shop with George and spending his money, and intended to be conservative. But the shops of Stamford, which were among the finest in the county, dazzled her and swept away her good intentions, and in the end they had ordered a green satin polonaise gown and a striped underskirt of taffeta. In addition he insisted on her ordering a white ball gown in the pannier style with a train and lace ruffles, though she could not see when she would ever wear it, and a straw hat and some gloves for day wear. George followed her around obligingly but she could tell he was glad when she had finished.

They emerged into St George's Square. 'Is that not Great-Uncle Horace's town-house across the way?' she asked.

'Yes. Did you never go there with my father?'

She shook her head. 'Might we call?' She had a curiosity to see the rich old man's house.

'Well . . . I say, my throat feels parched.' He had a suspicion of the sort of lecture the old man would give him; perhaps a drink would steel him for it. 'I doubt that you wish to come to the Black Bull, so why not go and call on our great-uncle while I just step across for a drop of refreshment? I'll join you in a minute.'

The footman who admitted Mary to Horace's gaunt house was like everything around the old man, dry, thin and austere: but she was surprised to find two ladies in company with her great-uncle in the drawing-room behind the office. One was a big, imposing woman of fifty, richly dressed in a fur-trimmed cloak and a calash, the other a remarkably beautiful girl of about twenty. They and Horace were gathered about a small tea-table. As Mary was announced the older woman gave her a searching glance from eyes that glittered above fat powdered cheeks like over-stuffed pillows. Horace rose stiffly with a polite twitch of a smile. 'Good day, Mary. It is rare to see you in Stamford. How good of you to call. Do you know Mrs Wainwright and Miss Elizabeth?'

'I believe we met briefly at your uncle's funeral, did we not?' said Mrs Wainwright, running her eyes up and down Mary's figure. 'I hope you are bearing up against your grief.' Obviously she remembered Mary's outburst of that day very clearly indeed.

'Thank you, ma'am, you are very kind,' replied Mary,

determined not to give her the satisfaction of appearing embarrassed. She sat and Horace offered her tea. 'Mrs Wainwright and her charming daughter are doing me the honour of calling on me before they leave for Huntingdon, where they are staying for a few days,' he said with desiccated courtesy. Mary saw Miss Wainwright out of the corner of her eye looking at her with an assessing glance. She was dressed finely like her mother, but what looked like ostentation in the older woman only enhanced the beauty of the younger. Her hair was piled high, powdered and topped with a lace head-dress. A fur muff lay in her lap like a little dog. Mary could not help but detect a trace of understandable vanity in Elizabeth Wainwright's finely-drawn delicate face. Taking her tea Mary looked round at Horace's drawing-room. It was spare and inhospitable, with something of the air of a counting-house; she would not have been surprised to see a little row of clerks scribbling away under the window.

'And what brings you to Stamford, Mary?' resumed Horace.

'I have been shopping. George accompanied me.'

'Indeed? Your cousin has returned home, has he?'

'Yes, last evening. James also is home.'

'George is the late Mr Joseph's eldest son, I believe?' said Mrs Wainwright in her emphatic voice. She always spoke more loudly than was necessary. Both she and her husband were of obscure family: Edward Wainwright had risen through hard work and shrewd investing, and now owned paper-mills at Wansford, boat-yards at Lynn and Wisbech, a brewery and maltings in the town, and the largest share in Wiley's Bank, together with a town-house in Stamford and a mansion in the country. Jane Smedley had risen through the equally shrewd investment of marrying him and becoming Mrs Jane Wainwright. Since she had no 'breeding' she tried to make up for it with flamboyantly displayed wealth, which to the malicious and envious eyes of the shabby-gentry of the county only succeeded in exposing her lack of the first.

'Yes, ma'am, that is correct. He is coming to join us shortly,' said Mary.

'And he is returning to claim his inheritance?'

'Indeed, ma'am, Morholm *is* now his estate, but I am not sure whether he intends living there. He has been living in London for over a year.'

'London? Indeed?' said Mrs Wainwright. 'How interesting. It is a while since I was there. I find more diversion at Bath these days. How did he find it?'

'He said he was rather wearied by it,' said Mary, wondering if she was saying the right thing.

'Exactly what I feel. It can try the nerves, do you not agree, Miss Hardwick? Have you ever been in London?'

'No, I fear not, though I should dearly like to.'

'I thought you had not,' said Mrs Wainwright with an indulgent smile that showed large and disconcerting teeth. 'One can usually tell a lady who has. There is a certain air. Now Elizabeth here has been innumerable times, have you not, my dear? She has a large circle of acquaintance. You should go there, Miss Hardwick; 'twould broaden your experience. By the way, how is your excellent aunt – Miss Catherine? We had a pleasant conversation at your uncle's funeral. Such an agreeable woman,' she added condescendingly.

'She is quite well, I thank you, ma'am. She was at the Townsends' for supper last night,' said Mary somewhat coldly.

'Oh, really? The Townsends.' The condescension in her voice became more marked. 'They were with us at our little party recently, were they not, Elizabeth? Amiable people – a pity they have no fashion. Like the Miltons – they were there too. Pleasant company, but – you know – not quite the thing,

78

as they say. Now young Mr Milton, the son – he is a not uncomely young man, if he would but open out a little – but no conversation! I have seen him speak a little to you, Elizabeth, but that is all. Have you met him, Miss Hardwick?'

'He was at our house this morning. He is a friend of George's, I believe.'

'A pity he is so unsociable. I wonder how much he is worth? I am sure his parents do not have half a thousand a year.' Mrs Wainwright had a habit of evaluating people's worth. Miss Wainwright, clearly embarrassed, turned a little red.

'I hope everyone is well at Morholm, Mary?' said Horace, steering the conversation away. They talked idly of this and that, and Mary noticed the way Miss Wainwright had of glancing down at herself in a proud, slightly smug fashion. When finally George arrived and was shown in Mary saw with dismay the glowing flush in his cheeks, and a bold looseness in the way he walked, as if he expected everything to get out of his path.

'Ah, here is my great-nephew George,' said Horace. If he detected what Mary detected he did not show it. 'George, no doubt it is quite a while since you last met Mrs Wainwright and her daughter Elizabeth.'

'It is indeed,' said George. There was a brash edge to his voice. 'I was but a youth when last I had that inestimable honour. Your servant, ma'am. Your servant, ma'am.'

He bowed and in doing so his foot caught the leg of the tea-table and brought it, cups, saucers and all, on to the floor with a crash.

He frowned. 'Dear me, how clumsy of me. You must think me an absolute churl. I am deeply sorry.'

'Do not trouble, great-nephew,' said Horace, his composure intact but brittle, as the footman picked up the crockery. 'I think nothing is broken. Oh, Forrest, have another fresh pot made, will you.'

'These accidents will happen, Mr Hardwick,' said Mrs Wainwright. She was not yet fully aware that he was a little drunk, and was interested in this young man who was now an important local figure.

'How right you are, Mrs Wainwright,' said George sitting down. 'Wainwright – now haven't I heard someone mention that name just this morning? Let me see . . .'

A tiny cleft appeared between Horace's brows.

'Er – Mrs Wainwright was asking how you found London, George,' put in Mary diplomatically. She was unversed in social etiquette, but this was instinctive.

'Yes – I remember,' said George, ignoring her. He laughed. 'Jarrett was teasing Milton about it. He said he had heard a rumour of some understanding developing between Milton and Miss Wainwright, or something –'

'However, people of any pretension to gentility do not countenance rumour,' said Great-Uncle Horace, his lips pursed. Miss Wainwright was scarlet and her mother's nostrils were widening visibly – as if, Mary thought, she were about to snort flames from them at George. There was silence, and Mary quivered with embarrassment. She felt her skin prickle and she fidgeted; she wanted to break that silence but was afraid if she opened her mouth only a squeak would come out. Finally, when the discomfort was such that she wanted to fly from the room, George spoke.

'Oh, good Lord, I hate freezing silences! Look – I am sorry. I will breathe not another word of such attachments – real or otherwise – since they obviously embarrass the lovely lady.' At this Miss Wainwright's colour deepened; she blushed so hard her cheeks seemed about to catch fire. Mary, cringing with shame and pity for Miss Wainwright, felt she wanted to fly at her cousin and scratch at his intractable face. Fortunately more tea was brought in. George passed a hand over his brow. 'God's life, I feel ill,' he murmured.

'Perhaps some tea, cousin?' said Mary.

'I hardly think that thirst is in any way part of the gentleman's affliction, Miss Hardwick,' said Mrs Wainwright with her disquieting smile. George gave his half-laugh. 'Witty, that, Mrs Wainwright. By the by, how are your family? Your excellent father and brother, I mean.' Evidence of Mrs Wainwright's humble beginnings remained in the shape of her father and elder brother, who were unprosperous journeyman tailors in Wisbech. He had touched a sore spot.

'I thank you, sir, they are well,' she replied. 'They are seldom ill. I believe it is due to the healthful, decent, temperate lives they lead.'

'But rather lonely lives, I would say – for I doubt they have their family come to visit them. I am sure you never have the time, shall I say, to see them.'

'Yes, alas, Mr Hardwick, my time is much occupied, often in tolerating bad company. In my position one has to condescend to some people, even though one may despise them.'

George tried to ignore this remark and continue his thread. 'One's family can be such a burden – do you not agree, Mrs Wainwright?'

'Or they can be a saving grace, Mr Hardwick. Why, I have seen the most boorish manners excused in polite society merely because of the good family name of the offender.'

'Oh, quite right – but the worst thing of all, you will acknowledge, Mrs Wainwright, is a boor with no family.'

'Well, Mr Hardwick, as to boorishness, I feel sure there is nothing worthwhile on that subject which I can impart to *you*.'

Part of Mary relished the fact that George was putting down Mrs Wainwright, whom she heartily disliked, but the daughter was plainly uncomfortable and it had gone far enough. 'We must go, George,' she said firmly.

'No,' said Mrs Wainwright. 'Come, my dear,' to Elizabeth. 'I think we have stayed quite long enough.' She rose.

'On the contrary, Mrs Wainwright, you have done no such thing,' said Horace, rising also to show them out.

'Thank you for your kindness, sir,' she said to Horace. 'I am glad to have met you, Miss Mary,' with a gracious nod. And to George, 'Perhaps we shall see you again, Mr Hardwick.'

'But let us not be pessimistic, Mrs Wainwright – fortune may be kinder to us than that,' said George.

'Yes, I think it may, Mr Hardwick – for we seldom patronize taverns,' smiled Mrs Wainwright, and left. As her daughter passed through the door after her, she bent towards Mary and, avoiding her eyes, whispered: 'You said Henry Milton was a friend of your cousin. You heard we are going away for a while. If you see Mr Milton will you deliver him this message – I forgive him.'

Mary nodded dumbly to the young woman, startled. 'I'll do my best,' she said.

'Well, great-nephew,' said Horace testily when they had gone, 'I hope this disgraceful exhibition is not a foretaste of your behaviour as head of the family. It is one thing to come to my house with quite plain signs of drink, but another to indulge in a slanderous exchange with Mrs Wainwright – and worst of all to discomfit Miss Elizabeth as you did.'

'I am sorry for the last,' said George. 'But that Wainwright woman provokes me.'

'Personal dislike should never precipitate a breach of decorum. That is a first principle of civilized life. If I let my personal feelings interfere with my business, I should never get anywhere!'

'I am sorry, uncle, if I have disgraced you,' said George woodenly.

'Not me. It is the good name of the Hardwicks you have besmirched. You must consider that now you are a figure of importance here. As master of Morholm you take on inescapable responsibilities. In your position –'

'Oh, great God, do not begin to tell me of my position,' said George, his face darkening. 'I am hardly likely to have forgot it.'

'You are no longer a swaggering careless youth, George – or should not be. A respectable gentleman squire cannot do just as he likes – at least, he can do what he likes, but only within reason.'

'Do as you like – within reason,' said George, and snorted. 'What an absurd paradox, great-uncle. I shall take my leave before you talk more nonsense.' He swept up his hat and walked out.

Horace shook his head. 'Stupid young peacock,' he said with an air of finality. 'You had better go with him, Mary, else he is likely to have picked a fight with the mayor before he is out of the town. Good-day to you.'

He had turned away but she was not yet ready to go. 'You are hard on him, great-uncle, too hard,' she said. 'It seems none of you are prepared to give him a chance, none of you can – can understand what he feels coming back here.'

Horace was looking at her as if she had gone mad. 'In my opinion he is as bad as his father,' he said curtly.

'If he is only half as good as his father was I shall be proud to own him as my cousin,' she said.

Horace stared at her and then turned away again. 'These outbursts of yours grow more and more alarming,' he said. 'I fear the reckless spirit of Joseph has infected you too.'

'I earnestly hope so,' said Mary.

She followed her cousin and they rode back to Morholm in silence.

5

It was an unusually splendid dinner for Morholm: Mary saw to that, ignoring Aunt Catherine's protests that she should be in charge of such an occasion. There was roast goose, pork, veal cutlets, rabbits smothered in onions, fowl pies, gooseberry tarts, cream and syllabubs, and port, madeira and canary. Only Mary's brother, whom she had long lost touch with, was missing; Aunt Catherine had even had Grandmother Hardwick brought down for the first time in years and deposited like an ancient rag doll by the fire.

But the occasion was memorable, and prophetic, in a way Mary did not like.

'I wouldn't have been here at all if I'd had my way,' said Mrs Peach when Aunt Catherine expressed her joy at seeing them all together. 'My Anne should never have married a great fool-jabey like Joseph. I were against it from the start. If she'd married Fitzjohn Prentice like I said I could have been at the Prentices' mansion at St James's now.'

'What I say is this,' snuffled Daniel. ' 'Tis no use chuntering on over a man's faults when he's gone from this world. Now all well and good: Joseph was a disappointment to this family. I think we're –' He caught Mary's eye and stopped. 'H'm, well, let us look to the future,' he lifted his glass, 'and hope that the new master of Morholm will be a credit to the Hardwick tradition.'

'We have yet to learn whether George intends to reside here permanently,' said Great-Uncle Horace, who was joining the company on sufferance. 'Perhaps, despite all the urging of his family, he would prefer to return to London and its pleasures. It is his free choice, though I think he has

84

sense enough to see the many arguments which weigh in favour of staying here. Are you ready to give your answer, George?'

George swallowed wine and was silent.

'Perhaps the responsibilities of the estate daunt you, brother,' said James darkly. 'Especially after your so strenuous life in London.'

George threw his brother a cold glance. 'I'm grateful for your kind thoughts, James – though I hardly think they were called for. As to your question, great-uncle, I am of course coming to claim my inheritance. I have no real choice. It happens that London is out of favour with me at the moment, but even if it were not I should be compelled to leave it for Morholm. The ties of family and tradition hold me to it.' He threw down his knife with a clatter. 'I am resigned to it. Fortune will do what it will with me whether I kick at its shins or no, so better save my energy.'

There was silence. Mrs Peach muttered: 'Boy still wants a good leathering.'

'Well, George,' said Daniel, 'you know that you are certain to be the local justice as your father was. Now what of all these beggars and vagabonds one sees skulking through the village these days?'

When the men rejoined the ladies in the drawing-room after dinner and George came over to Mary she noticed the hollow look on his face. 'You look wearied, cousin,' he said, sitting down by her. 'I'll wager Julia has been talking the heels off you.'

Mary looked at him dubiously with her bright, candid eyes. She could smell the wine on his breath.

'Oh, do not worry, cousin. I shall not disgrace you as I did the other day. I have learned my lesson,' he said with a wry upward twist of the lips.

'You did not disgrace me, George. I only fear for yourself.'

85

'Oh,' he flapped his arm, 'let us forget about it. When I came home we made an agreement not to speak of my father. Let us extend it to include anything that is disagreeable to either of us. Hm?'

She looked at him. When his eyes were on her his face shed that heavy-lidded expression and became bright, open, more handsome. She smiled. 'Of course, cousin.'

'Well, George, when are you going to look over your land?' said Great-Uncle Horace, stooping over them. 'Your first object will be to ensure the estate is in order.'

Influenced by Mary, George made an effort to be civil. 'Indeed, uncle, I suppose I must cultivate an interest in the land if it is to be my livelihood. I shall make a tour of inspection tomorrow, though I fear I would be little able to tell if it were in a state of ruin. No doubt I shall learn in time.'

'But even supposing you do not, I doubt you would trouble so long as your wine-cellar was well-stocked, brother,' said James, who was seated a little way off with a book.

'Yes indeed,' said George with an uneasy laugh.

James, his head bowed and his tone muted, went on as if he were talking to himself. 'After all, why should you give a hang for your father's estate? As long as you can continue to gamble and drink away your life as you have done so far, then let the farm muddle along as best it can. Nothing matters so long as you are kept fat and idle.'

George was startled. Mary saw with agitation two red spots form on his cheekbones.

'You're uncommonly insulting today, James,' he said. The other groups in the room continued to chatter; only Mary and Horace heard the brothers.

James lifted his hard-grained face. 'I'm surprised you are in a fit condition to appreciate it.'

'Pardon me, James, I appear to be under some misconception. For you to assail me thus with such rudeness, I must have given you offence at some time – but I cannot for the life of me think when. Perhaps you can tell me? What have I done to deserve your scorn? Eh, James? You object to my laziness, my dissipation. Yet surely that is my own concern? It does you no injury, I think! Are you such a coward as to condemn me for defects which hurt only myself?'

'George, I think of all the faint-hearted poltroons in this world *you* have the least right to call anyone a coward.' James's voice was thick. George's face blazed scarlet. Mary, now frantic with distress, saw out of the corner of her eye through the hall door Daniel clambering heavily upstairs to get rid of his wind in decent solitude.

'Pardon me again, brother,' said George. 'I appear to be under another misconception. I thought you had more maturity at twenty-one than to resort to this kind of name-calling. Evidently I underestimated the depths to which you are prepared to descend in your envy.'

'Envy!' James's voice raised suddenly, and there was an instant hush. 'Indeed, you flatter yourself, brother. Envy a drunkard popinjay who –'

'You are remarkably full of words, James – but I cannot help wondering if you have the actions to back them up,' said George. James sprang from his chair and stood over the sitting figure of his brother. 'I am prepared to suit the action to my words, George! But are you?' he roared. Now everyone's eyes were on the two young men. George's face had gone from red to white. A sneer began to form on James's lips. Then, abruptly, George swung out his arm, closed his palm over his brother's chin and gave a heave. At the same moment Mary leapt from her seat and seized his elbow with a cry, trying to stay the force of his push. James, caught by surprise, lurched backwards and fell, his back crashing on to his chair as he went. George leapt up after him, fists clenched. There was a squeal from Aunt Catherine, and Horace began to say something; but it was

Mary, ahead of them all, who made a dash at her cousin and threw herself in front of him. 'No, George, no! What are you trying to do! Stop!' She beat her fists against his chest as he tried to shove past her. 'Stop, I beg you, George! For my sake!'

He halted and looked at her, and she felt the panting heave of his chest beneath her hands. James got to his feet with a groan and stood unsteadily. For a speck of time there was utter silence; then, from the direction of the stairs there was an almighty rumble and a series of crashes. Then came the voice of Daniel, crying amongst a torrent of oaths: 'Well, damn you all, help a man who's tumbled down a flight of stairs, will you? Hoy! Help a man who's broke every bone in his body, by the feel of it! Dying, and not a soul to help him! Devil take the whole stinking crew –'

Daniel was on the bottom stair in a comical, half-sitting position, as if he had just flopped down for a rest. His clothes were dishevelled and his bag-wig lay on the stair beside him like a faithful little dog. The top of his exposed shaven head shone in an outraged manner.

'And about time!' he groaned, as they gathered about him. 'I am one smarting bruise from tip to arse. That top stair is uneven – you must get that seen to, George, or I shall be killed one of these fine mornings. Well, and why are you grinning like a cat, miss?' he added: for Julia – and it was the first time anyone had seen it happen – began to laugh, loudly and hoarsely.

Her laughter was infectious. Even old Horace could not forbear a chuckle at Daniel's expense. George, his anger gone, helped to heave the cursing bulk to his feet. 'I am sorry, Uncle Daniel, indeed, but you did look rather comical at first sight.'

But after Daniel, donning his wig with a look of mortified affront, had waddled off to the housekeeper's room 'to have my mortal injuries dressed', the atmosphere again became prickly. George and James now seemed bent on ignoring each other, but the air felt dangerous, like fire-damp in a coal-mine. Mary noticed that everyone's eyes were on George in a kind of morbid anticipation, and she was about to speak out to break the atmosphere – say something, anything – when George rose and stalked out of the room.

'The new master of Morholm,' snorted Mrs Peach. 'God preserve us!'

Mary, after a moment's hesitation, went out after him. In the musty darkness of the unlit hall the portrait of old Sir Robert under the stairs seemed to loom like another disapproving face. The big front door was standing open and let in a breath of crisp frosty air. She ran out and cast about for George. The moon was bright and there were hundreds of little crystal stars, so that blue-black shadows sprawled around the house. She found him in the garden, leaning against the bole of a tree. He turned his head and glanced at her briefly, then turned away again.

'You are being very foolish,' she said, for want of anything else to say.

'I'm sorry,' he said, in such a stubbornly sarcastic tone that he immediately regretted it.

'Oh, George, I know how it must feel, everyone taking on as they do. I know how desperate you . . . how burdensome it must seem.'

'Do you?' His face was still averted and his head bowed, so that all she could see in the darkness was his back. 'How remarkable your perception is.'

'I can't talk to you when you're like this,' she said, feeling angry with him and sorry for him at the same time.

'That arrangement suits me admirably.'

'George,' she said. Though it was only a week since he had come home she felt she knew him thoroughly. 'James was inexcusably rude, but it might have been better to turn the other cheek.'

'Thank you, cousin, I do not require your advice on what I ought and ought not do.'

'Those things he said –'

'– were entirely true,' said George, moving slowly away. She followed. 'No, George, not true,' she began. He stopped and gave his little half-laugh. The sound of it irritated her. 'You are being foolish!' she said again, exasperated.

'And you, cousin, are repeating yourself,' he said with infuriating archness. He looked up at the dim sky. They had dined late in the afternoon, so now it was well past eight. He gave a little start as she laid her hand on his arm. 'Will you not come inside again?' she said.

'And be stared at as if I were a puppy that had fouled the drawing-room floor? Have those hypocrites drumming "duty" and "position" into me?' He sighed and turned his thin sensitive face to her for the first time. 'It confounds me. What care they for the way of the Hardwicks and all the rest of it, so long as they can live off the fat of the land? A strong hub in the family wheel is the cant – but that's the last thing they would truly want.'

'I know. And why must they condemn your father – does not his goodness stand for more than some futile family tradition?'

'I fear it is the nature of the human creature to condemn where praise receives no reward. Why should they acknowledge father's goodness? Nothing is to be got from it.'

'Well, surely they cannot mean all they say?'

He smiled and took her hand. 'I believe, cousin,' he said, 'you would make allowances for the very devil himself.'

They stood a few moments, and then walked down the avenue to where the wicket-gate looked out on to the farmland. Tonight, but for the stars, the grey expanse of fields might have been a mirror-reflection of the vast sky above. George threw back his head and gazed. 'I often look at the stars,' he said quietly. 'Do you, ever? Folk scratch back and forth with their eyes on this dull earth. If they would but look up, they could see a whole new view, infinitely more interesting.'

She followed his gaze up into the dark sky, and from the expression of intensity in his grey eyes she thought he might have been studying the future that lay ahead of him, written amongst the winking stars.

October was tantalizing, remnants of the beautiful summer alternating with drab days of blowing leaves flying across the marshy levels and yellow metallic skies. James returned to London and his studies and though he was never uncivil to her Mary was relieved to see him go. She took advantage of one of the clearer days to visit old Mr Newman who had been so kind to her. The Lord Lieutenant had wasted no time in nominating the new Hardwick squire as magistrate, and George was attending the sessions that day. She found Newman and his son in the field behind the house breaking up the soil ready for the frosts of winter. They were both delighted to see her and invited her inside, but she preferred to stand out in the middle of the fields with them and feel the wind go scurrying round her lifting her cloak and hair. From here she had a panoramic view of the landscape: a unique landscape, secretive for all its open emptiness. Stamford with its Georgian elegance, Peterborough with its ancient ecclesiastical pride, Wisbech with its bustling docks, were still siege towns, their existence tolerated by the encroaching eternities of rich black earth and water and sky.

Mary turned to Newman. If angels could be old and weatherbeaten, she thought, then he would serve as a model for them. 'How is your wife?' she asked.

He smiled half-heartedly. 'Bearing up, y'know, bearing up.' He paused. 'Well, she's not so good, mistress, nor did I expect her to be. Aye, we've had the apothecary in from

Helpston, and he mixed her potions and what have you; but I don't believe he knows what's amiss. 'Tis her chest that afflicts her.'

'Have you not had a proper doctor in?' said Mary. 'Dr Villiers, from Peterborough?'

Newman shook his head. 'We can't afford the likes of him.'

Mary went into the farmhouse to see Mrs Newman. Up the rude wooden stairs were two rooms, one where John slept among sacks and preserves and the other almost taken up by a big box bed in which lay Mrs Newman. She was a large woman, with a face that looked to have been as bright as her husband's once but was now hollow with pain. Mary was reminded of her Grandmother Hardwick's room in the darkness and the sickly smell; but Mrs Newman smiled and talked in a hoarse whisper, and her husband and son stood smiling back as if it were a party.

It made Mary's heart heavier than if they had wailed in despair; and after taking a dish of tea with them she left in low spirits. There was the sound of horsemen behind her as she returned through the village, and she looked up to see Thomas Jarrett and Henry Milton. She had seen Jarrett about the village and knew him for a friend of George's, but had seen little of him at close quarters. Now as he reined in his horse and smiled down at her she thought how handsome he was.

'How d'you do, Miss Mary,' he said, removing his hat. 'You stand there as a living contradiction to me. I have been saying there is no beauty in the county, and I find a jewel in Aysthorpe of all places.'

As he was tall and mounted it was difficult to talk, so he got down and Milton, after a moment, followed suit. She brushed her hair from her face and returned Jarrett's dazzling smile. It was an unknown luxury to be complimented by a handsome gentleman – and Thomas Jarrett was extremely handsome. She felt gratified. 'You flatter me, sir, and are most unfair to your county. Have you not met Miss Wainwright of Stamford? I did recently – she is the loveliest creature I ever saw.' Almost before she had finished speaking she realized her mistake. The rumour that George had talked of at Great-Uncle Horace's was something to do with Milton and Miss Wainwright. At the same time she remembered the message she had been given. She cursed her tactlessness.

Jarrett laughed. 'Why, as to that, Miss Hardwick, I hardly feel qualified to speak on the subject of that lady's charms – am I, Milton?'

Milton raised his eyebrows. 'I don't know, Jarrett, are you? I am not, certainly, if that is what you infer.'

Jarrett smiled and changed the subject. 'We were just on our way to see George, Miss Hardwick. Is your cousin free to see two useless dogs of friends?'

Mary explained George's engagement that morning. 'But we may find him at Morholm by this time. And if not, I shall try to entertain you, should you still like to come. Er – I believe,' she added, 'my aunt is out calling, and Kingsley and Daniel also.' She had noticed the look of misgiving on Jarrett's face; she was growing used to people's feelings about her family – and growing to share them. Jarrett smiled again. 'I think we understand each other, Miss Hardwick. Perhaps we shall see more of Morholm now that George is home.'

'I hope so, Mr Jarrett,' said Mary.

Milton watched them, a little aloof. To bring up the subject of Miss Wainwright! Obviously she had heard the rumour. He would go along to Morholm, but only to see if George were there.

They led their horses the rest of the way to the house. Outside the stables Mary said aside to Jarrett, feeling she could trust him, 'Will you go in, Mr Jarrett? There is something I am charged to say to Mr Milton.'

'Eh?' he said, and then after a moment, 'Of course, Miss Hardwick,' and slipped discreetly away while Milton was still dismounting. Mary watched him walk in with his easy stride, and then turned to Milton, who was standing uncomfortably waiting for her to go.

'Er – Mr Milton – a few weeks ago when I was in Stamford, I had the honour of meeting Miss Elizabeth Wainwright who asked me to deliver to you this message.' She paused, wondering how best to say it. Milton shifted his weight and glanced down at her hands, evidently expecting a written message.

'She – er – went away to Huntingdon for a while, I believe,' she went on.

'Yes, I know.'

'Ah. Well. She said for me to say she forgives you.'

His eyes remained fixed on the floor.

'That is all she said.'

'Thank you,' he muttered. 'Very gracious of her, I am sure.'

'If – perhaps I heard wrong – if that was not the message you anticipated –'

'No, Miss Hardwick, I had anticipated no message, but now that I hear it I see that it is quite typical of her. Well, you may tell her –'

'Indeed, Mr Milton, I cannot say when I shall meet with her again, if ever.'

'No.' He frowned. 'No, of course not. The message, Miss Hardwick, is in reference to some remarks I made to her, which it was her whim to take offence at. I hope that has satisfied your curiosity.'

'Indeed, I had no wish to pry –'

'No, of course not.' His face had gone stony. She thought him rather rude; she wondered, as they walked to the house, what Mr Jarrett saw in him.

* * *

94

When Jarrett went into the house ahead of them he found George there to greet him. With him was a girl of about seventeen, dressed in an old dimity frock and a ragged shawl, with lank hair and the vacant look of the destitute. Her name was Amelia Seddon, and she had been wandering about the local villages sleeping on doorsteps for a week. A constable had brought her to the magistrates and George, moved either by compassion or attraction, or at a loss as to what should be done with her – he was not sure which – had proposed to take her on as a maid at Morholm. He explained all this to Jarrett while the girl stood in the middle of the room like a market calf in the ring, gazing about her with heavy colourless eyes.

'But, Hardwick,' said Jarrett, leaning against a chair and regarding the girl doubtfully, 'do you need – and can you afford – another servant at Morholm?'

'I don't know.' George shrugged. 'What does it matter? We can make room for another. I had to do something with the girl, rather than throw her out of the parish.'

'Perhaps she is unversed in the manners and graces required of a servant,' said Jarrett.

'Oh, you do pick at things, Tom. She will learn. Can you curtsey, girl, and say "yes, sir"?'

The girl looked at him blankly. Jarrett grunted. 'Perhaps you have picked up a half-wit, George.'

'Come along, Amelia, surely you can do that? That's what you're engaged for,' said George. The girl looked from one man to the other, dumbly; then bobbed and said in a husky voice: 'Yes, sir.'

'There you are, Jarrett,' said George, turning to his friend triumphantly. 'What else is required of a maid?'

'Nothing, except ability to do every kind of housework.'

'Oh, she can learn easily enough,' said George. 'Are you not going to congratulate me on my charity, Jarrett?'

'If you like,' said Jarrett, 'but hardly on your taste, old

fellow. Though I suppose if she washed her face, and put on some proper garments, she might not look uncomely.'

'You doubt the honour of my intentions?' said George, laughing, but a slight frown on his brow at the same time.

'My dear fellow,' said Jarrett, 'I do not doubt your intentions for a moment.'

As George sent the girl to the housekeeper Mary and Milton appeared. 'What has detained you two?' he said.

'I had a message to deliver to Mr Milton,' said Mary, wishing he had not asked.

'You did? To Milton? How so?'

Jarrett interrupted him. 'He was just as inquisitive as a boy, Miss Mary,' he said. 'Ignore him.'

Mary glanced gratefully at Jarrett. 'Who was that strange girl we saw in the hall, George?' she went on.

'An unfortunate whom he has saved from the gutter with promises of an apron, a roof and three or four pounds a year,' said Jarrett. 'Along with the estate he has acquired a taste for philanthropy, have you not? By the way, now that you rule the roost here, are you not going to bring out your cousin more? Beauty will wither buried here all the time.'

'Do you really think she has beauty?' said George, looking at Mary.

'Don't mind him, Miss Mary,' laughed Jarrett. 'It's merely his way.'

'Well, I don't want you getting any braggarty ideas of yourself, cousin.' He tried to banter, but seemed faintly annoyed. 'However, it's true she sees little of life here. Did you know she has never been to a ball? At almost nineteen.'

'Shameful,' said Jarrett. 'But I believe I heard your sister say the same thing recently. This is an aberration you could right, George.'

'Oh, Julia,' said George dismissively. 'Well, Tom, what you say is all very well, but we are hardly in a position to give a ball in this place. Besides, in London they irritated me with their endless posturing.'

That night as Mary was snuffing the candles in the panelled hall and George was climbing the stairs to bed he suddenly turned and spoke down to her.

'Mary, what Jarrett was saying about a ball today, do you think it worthwhile, if it could be arranged? What do you feel?'

'It would be wonderful,' she said. 'I should love it – and so would everyone else, I am sure.'

He smiled wryly. 'Well, I fear I am out of favour with the Hardwick brood again today.' There had been mutterings of 'unseemly' all day at his acquisition of Amelia the maid, and Daniel, who had been in an ill-temper ever since his tumble down the stairs, had grunted, 'Extravagant young puppy!' many times over. George had eventually agreed to call in Dr Villiers to look at the 'wounds' he had sustained to soothe him.

'Do not heed them, cousin. You acted kindly and for the best.' As he seemed to hesitate she went on: 'Your friends Mr Jarrett and Mr Milton are very agreeable. But Mr Milton is very reserved.'

'That's his way,' said George, who rarely thought about his friends. 'What to hold a ball in honour of I don't know. In honour of my arrival sounds a thought conceited. Of course it is only a notion.'

'But I am sure it could be arranged. The whole neighbourhood would be glad, I am sure.'

'Yes, yes. Perhaps I shall think of it on the morrow. Now I'm going to bed.' He turned as abruptly as before and went upstairs.

6

After leaving Morholm that morning Henry Milton parted
from Jarrett and rode home to Helpston, a small village,
surrounded by the woodland of Helpston Heath, at the end
of which his father's unimposing house of grey stone stood,
enclosed by ragged trees which were the haunt of crows and
rooks. He spent the rest of the day inside trying to put the
accounts in order. His friend George had probably already
forgotten there was even a rumour about him and Miss
Wainwright; but Milton was in no such state of happy
oblivion. The thought of her prevented him from working,
from resting, from thinking of anything else.

He had fallen in love with her at a party at her home at the
end of the summer. Only his father's name and, probably, he
bitterly reflected, a need to make up the numbers, had
caused him to be invited. The Wainwrights were very
wealthy and rising fast; they had a house in the country as
well as in Stamford; Mr Wainwright was a burgess of the
town and likely to become mayor. Even now as he thought
of their beautiful daughter he suspected it was almost wholly
a physical attraction she held for him. She was vain, selfish
and rather trivial, he told himself as he irritably scribbled
down figures; she was obsessed with her own appearance,
yet any allusion to it seemed to embarrass her. But, he
realized as he threw down his pen and paced around the
little library, he could not rule and reckon up his feeling for
her as he could those accounts. Even an unprejudiced eye
might have pronounced her to be the finest woman in the
county, and to Henry Milton who, apart from his mother
and sisters, had known scarcely half-a-dozen women in his
life, she was the personification of beauty.

It was a miracle or, if there were such a thing, he thought, a mixed miracle – that they had ever spoken that night. She was as reserved as he was. But he could adapt to company if he had the motivation, and a glimmering he had discerned of an impish sense of humour among the beauty had drawn him to her. They had talked together all night: since then he had not seen her. If that night was all, all there could ever be, then in fact he ought to be grateful for it. Hold on to it. Few men could boast of the same.

But his tongue had been loosened too much that night. He despised her parents, seeing through their pomp, and had said almost as much to her. He had been surprised when she took offence. Judging people by his own cultured standards, he tended to hold them in contempt if they fell below them; he recognized, deplored and could not help his peculiar form of snobbery. He meant to try his fortune in London with his pen one day, though at the moment his father could not spare him. He admired Richardson and the poems of Collins and Thomson, and had been entranced by Mackenzie's sentimental novel *The Man of Feeling* that had appeared a few years ago. Applying the feelings these inspired in him to everyday life in Northamptonshire left him in a curious position. He had offended Elizabeth that night: but the message Mary Hardwick had given him today had only served to reinforce his torment of mind. He saw an arrogance in it which irritated him; and to convey it by Miss Hardwick, a girl he hardly knew, and give her such an advantage over him . . . And yet she 'forgave him'.

After an uneasy night's sleep he woke next morning desperate to see Elizabeth Wainwright's face again. He wondered if they were returned from their stay in Huntingdon yet, and with some embarrassment asked his mother at breakfast.

'The Wainwrights, Henry? They returned last week, I believe.'

After another hour's deliberation he set off for Stamford to call at their town-house. He prayed that they might be home, but if they were he did not know how he would face her. He left his horse at The George and walked up to Barn Hill to the Wainwrights' roomy, expensive town-house.

A liveried footman answered the door. 'I am sorry, sir, the family are at their country residence,' he said, and gave Milton's plain coat a contemptuous glance before he closed the door.

Milton, thwarted in his first attempt, chose to ignore an inward voice which told him this must be a hint from fate. He wanted to see her more earnestly than ever, and collecting his horse he set out for the Wainwrights' country place. He had never seen it, but he knew it was somewhere between Fotheringhay and Elton, close to Elton Hall, home of the Probys. No doubt they were on visiting terms, he thought gloomily. It was a distance of about ten miles, and he hoped his old horse, which was the only one they had, would not protest too much.

The monotonous country to the north suddenly dipped as he approached Elton and gave way to the beautiful bowl-like valley of the Nene, the fertile fields in the distance a misty blue lattice-work with a winking glimpse of the river. Despite his agitation he stopped to admire the view at the top of the plunging slope and took off his hat and wiped the sweat from his eyes. A villager carrying a pail came labouring up the hill and he stopped him to ask directions.

Then he put on his hat and set off, his heart pounding harder than ever.

The trouble was one simply did not go calling at someone's country house. If you were part of their set, yes, certainly, but he . . . On the strength of his acquaintance it was a presumption. Mrs Wainwright had been courteous to him at the party, he had to give her that; a call at their town-house might not have been taken amiss. 'Business in Stamford this morning emboldened me to take this opportunity of seeking to renew the honour of the acquaintance of Mrs Wainwright and her charming daughter.' 'Ah, Mr Milton, of course.' But here – impossible.

He was roused from these thoughts by the appearance of chimneys and roofs in the trees above him, and he came upon the Wainwrights' country house almost by accident. It was a plain and bulky Palladian building with a short drive through turreted gates, and not as impressive as he had imagined. But already his nerve had gone. What could he hope to say? It might even be taking several steps backward to do such a clumsy thing.

He rode home again, with rain beginning to fall heavily, cursing under his breath his bad luck, his folly, his excuses.

Thomas Jarrett also did some travelling that day, but not with his friend's impulsiveness. His father was too infirm to make his monthly business call at the house of old Horace Hardwick and so his son had to go instead. Stamford was busy today with carts and sedan chairs crowding the market square and there was a constant ill-tempered jostling on the narrow pavements to avoid being elbowed into the stinking refuse of the gutter.

Old Horace, receiving him in the office at the back of the house, was cordial but soon came to the point. 'With age a man's faculties may become impaired, Mr Jarrett. I fear your father does not share the relatively undiminished vigour with which I am blessed. Of late I am afraid he seems to have lost his old adroitness where business is concerned.'

'He is not a well man,' said Jarrett.

'He has my sympathy,' said Horace. 'But this does not alter the fact that he is my debtor to the sum of eight hundred and fifty pounds.' He rolled his pen between skeletal fingers. 'Naturally, Mr Jarrett, your father being an old associate of mine, I'm prepared to extend the term until, say, the new year. But I shall need some security. You say your father cannot now leave the house. Are you prepared to act for him, sir? Or shall I foreclose now?'

'Of course I will act for him,' said Jarrett. 'I shall do everything in my power.'

But it was a bad shock. His father had always jealously guarded the running of the business and Jarrett was unprepared for this. He left Horace's and proceeded to the house of Mr Thornton Wiley, the banker, in Broad Street. The front room of the house opening on to the street was the bank office; behind it, in the private parlour, he found Mr Wiley, a rotund greasy man, sitting over a late breakfast in slippers and dressing-gown and a cap in place of a wig. When he stated his business Wiley eyed him narrowly.

'Your father's account here is confidential, you know,' he said, wiping his lips with the edge of the tablecloth.

'He is ill and cannot leave the house,' said Jarrett. 'From now on I have agreed to act for him.'

Wiley grunted and poked his head into the bank office. 'Pass me that ledger, Lewis,' he said, and returned bearing a large dusty book. He shoved aside the breakfast things and opened the ledger out on the table.

'Spare me the details,' said Jarrett. 'Just tell me how much he is in debt.'

A few minutes later Jarrett left Wiley's and went to fetch his horse. It was beginning to rain heavily, and that, he thought ironically, was appropriate. His father owed the bank, with interest, nearly two thousand pounds. Then there was old Hardwick's debt; and for all he knew a hundred other smaller obligations. He had known his father's business was weaker than it had been, but he had never imagined . . . Old Jarrett retained his thrifty ways in trivial things, but he was now too senile to revive a failing mill. Jarrett calculated rapidly in his head as he rode out into the pattering rain. If prices continued to fall, unless the firm's fortunes looked up drastically, and soon, he estimated his father would be in the debtor's prison before next spring. He spurred his horse home.

Bromswold, the big haphazard house of old Nathan Jarrett, presented a gloomy aspect that day under the grey sky. The neglected grounds in which it stood were poorly drained and had been mashed by the drizzle until now the house looked as if it were floating in a swamp. The sound of rain trickling off the uneven roof in hundreds of little crooked waterfalls gurgled all about Jarrett as he opened the door and went in. He found his father at the dining-room table amongst a litter of half-eaten food and dirty crockery. The old man took so long over his meals that he seldom bothered to get up from the table except to hobble to a close-stool or to bed. He was a wizened, withered old creature in a bob-wig and thick spectacles; he seldom washed himself or changed his clothes, so he had an unmistakable smell about him. His son threw off his hat and stretched out on a sofa wearily. 'Well, father,' he said. 'You have left me quite a task.'

'What's that you say? Oh, 'tis you, Thomas. Pass me that dish of butter, will ye?' said the old man, his words attended by a little spray of saliva and crumbs.

'Father, when was your steward last here?'

'Eh? Old Trent? Let's see. When would it be. Tuesday? No, I tell a lie, 'twould be Wednesday, for on Tuesday –'

'How did he say things were in Wisbech? With the mill, I mean?'

'Oh, I don't hearken to half what the man says, my son. Now I come to think of it, I mind he said things weren't going so well as we could wish, mebbe. But he's often said that afore.'

'Father, do you know how much money you owe?' said Jarrett, exasperation and anger in his voice.

'Mmm? To whom, my son?' The old man dropped a spoon in his lap and it smeared his waistcoat.

'To Wiley's, for one.'

'Old Thorny Wiley! Haven't seen him in donkey's years.' He left the spoon where it was and picked up another. 'I wonder how he is. I mind his wife Joan was your mother's great friend, God rest her.'

Jarrett stood up irritably and went to the window. Through the grimy leaded panes he could see a dismal view of the stripped fields towards Helpston, the day dying across the misty levels with bloody orange stains. A hedger in leather coat and leggings was trudging home to the village, and a few huddled sheep were visible in the distance beneath the bare ash-trees.

'What d'ye see there so interesting, boy?' said the old man tetchily.

'Nothing, father,' said Jarrett. 'Absolutely nothing.'

'Then stop mooling about and lift me to the stool. My old joints won't move. Come, d'ye want me to shite in my breeches?'

Jarrett sighed and helped his father from the table.

George Hardwick also made an important journey that day. He rode out at eleven, after thinking hard for the whole of the night. He was going to arrange a lavish ball. The cost he did not contemplate: the plan was enough.

The place he chose at last was Stilton, a village about eight miles from Aysthorpe. Stilton gained any importance it had from being on the Great North Road and in consequence boasted a large and thriving coaching inn, The Bell, which had an assembly room which had accommodated balls in its time but was now mainly used for business committee meetings and gentlemen's clubs. Morholm had not been designed for such entertaining, and the usual venues for balls, the Stamford Assembly Rooms and the Peterborough Guildhall, which doubled as a magistrates court, were fully booked.

In The Bell he took a brandy while he inspected the

rooms. It was a spacious and handsome building. As he stood and looked at the assembly room with its high ceiling and heavily draped windows he fancied he could see the flicker of many candles, the glitter of glass and jewels, hear the swishing of silk and lace, the tapping of leather heels and silver buckles, the hum of voices and the wheedle and squeak of an orchestra. He pictured elegant ladies parading about the room. The thought pleased him in spite of himself. That reminded him: he must go into Stamford and see if Mary's ball gown were ready yet.

After making arrangements with the landlord he left the inn and rode to Stamford. Now that his idea was being put into action he felt lively and the listless dissatisfaction that had been afflicting him dropped away. He found himself loudly upbraiding the unctuous seamstress in the shop because the promised gown was not finished yet, and demanded that it be ready by the end of the week – though the ball was fixed for the fifteenth of November, a month away. But he also gave the underfed needlewomen who worked in the gloomy back room of the shop an extra crown each. Then he headed for home. He wanted Mary to be the first to know.

He found Mrs Peach and Daniel crouching on either side of the fire in the parlour, but no Mary.

'Oh, you're back,' grunted Daniel in a sour tone when he came in. For some reason he had chosen to blame George for his falling downstairs. He shifted his legs with a grimace of imagined pain. 'Villiers has been in to me this morning. Ouch! He says there are no bones broke, but I did not like the look on his face when he said it. I wonder whether he is not holding the truth back from me. He bled me and bound my ankle and left some potion or other. Damme if I think I'll ever be right again with his treatments. I never knew a doctor yet could cure my afflictions.'

No, thought George, it's unlikely you ever will. But his mind was elsewhere. 'Where is Mary?' he said.

'Gone gallivanting somewheres about,' said his grandmother. 'Everyone's forever gallivanting hither and thither in this house.'

'Excepting those too mortally injured to stir,' muttered Daniel.

'Where did she go?' said George, suddenly angry. He had wanted her to be here.

'Don't know. Didn't say. No one ever does,' snapped Mrs Peach. 'Just phht! Out they go.'

George turned away. Damn Mary! Why wasn't she here? What business had she to go wandering out? His mood changed, became abruptly resentful. He barged out and went to the library where he remained till dinner.

Mary was at Newman's farm. The sight of Dr Villiers calling on Daniel that morning had stirred the memory of Mrs Newman suffering in the big box bed. Joseph had settled a large sum on her for her marriage; but also in a bureau in her room she had about forty pounds for her immediate use. As Dr Villiers was leaving at noon she had cornered him and asked him to come and see the old lady. The physician would do anything as long as he got his fee, and after he had gone to the cottage and peered down Mrs Newman's throat and bled her and left instructions with the farmer, it was Mary who paid him. She would only accept Mr Newman's thanks and not his offer to pay back the money; she knew he did not have it. Two hours slipped by chatting with the family at the cottage before she returned to Morholm.

George curtly made his announcement to the whole family at dinner. He watched their reactions but Mary he did not look at.

'But what is your reason, pray?' fluttered his aunt.

'Something must be done to enliven this infernal place,' said George. 'And must there be a reason?'

'But so soon after your father's death, nephew? Surely disrespectful! I ha' never heard the likes of it!'

'Oh, nonsense – father would have approved entirely.'

'A costly extravagance,' said Daniel. 'Frittering away the estate on such falalleries. And I suppose I must go without my doctoring to help you meet the cost.'

'No, Daniel, you will not.'

'Well, if George has set his mind to this, there is nothing we can do,' said Aunt Catherine. 'It seems to be the fashion for the young to ignore the counsels of their elders – but then, no doubt, nephew, you will find plenty of others of your fanciful turn of mind who care naught for keeping up a seemly appearance.'

'Of course,' said George, his eyes cast down, 'those who do not approve need not attend.'

'Why, as to that,' said Aunt Catherine, ' 'twould look even more unseemly if *I* were not there. But of course I must have a new outfit.'

Mary looked at George, who had clenched his fists and closed his eyes to contain his anger. She felt, turbulently mingled, pleasure and pity and reproach and exasperation when she looked at him. He opened his eyes, and her gaze seemed to disquiet him. With studied carelessness he said, as the others talked among themselves, 'Well, Mary, and what have you been about today?'

She decided it was best not to tell him. 'Oh – just walking in the village,' she said. The prospect of the ball excited her and she wanted to ask him all about it: but she feared that in this mood she would get nothing from him.

'I don't know what you think of this ball notion,' he went on. 'I begin to wonder whether it is such a good idea. It will hardly be the most fashionable of gatherings, with the sweepings of gentility that can be gleaned from this forsaken county.'

'I shall look forward to it with the greatest pleasure. You know I will.'

'I fear you may be much disappointed. By the by, I stopped into Stamford this morning to see about your dress. I fear the ball-gown we ordered will not be ready in time.' He knew it was not true, but he took a perverse delight in lowering her hopes.

She sensed his queer mood and with the sense came a fiery response. 'Well, you said it would not be a fashionable gathering,' she said. 'I would only have felt uncomfortable in it, and I doubt it is of any consequence to you whether I wear it or no.'

At that she saw the colour come into his face and he left the table without a word. She tried to continue eating, but anger and sorrow choked her. She tried to think of the coming ball, but it all seemed to have been spoiled.

George retreated to the library: he could feel his father's placid homely influence in here, though he scarcely ever touched the books that lined the walls. He was idly looking along the shelves, seeing nothing, when the door opened and Amelia Seddon, now decked out in the cleaner garments of a maid, came in with a shovel and coal-scuttle. Evidently Mrs Reynolds, who called the girl a trollop but all the same was a motherly woman, had given her a thorough scrubbing. Her face had lost its grimy sallow aspect and her dark lank hair, also new washed, was tucked inside a mob-cap. She did not see George, who was inside an alcove made by the bookshelves. She went over to the cold fireplace and began to rake out the ashes. Silently he took out one book from the shelf level with his head and watched her through the gap. Her movements were heavy and noisy; she was a sloppy, big-breasted, big-rumped girl.

'Hello, Amelia,' he said. She started and dropped the shovel and turned. Even when she jumped her motion was cumbrous, as if she were acting. She looked at him with her emotionless cow eyes. 'Sorry, sir, didn't know you was in here,' she mumbled.

'How are you settling into your new position? How are the other servants treating you?' He could hear the angry blood still thumping in his head, and his words seemed to come out stilted.

'Well enough, thank you, sir.'

'Good. Good.' They stood a moment or two, he frowning at her, she returning his look dumbly. Finally she said: 'Shall I go out, seeing as how you're here, sir?'

'No, finish what you started, by all means, don't mind me,' he said. She stooped and resumed her work.

He took up a book and made a pretence of reading it; but still he watched her, glancing up and then down and then up again, the blood pounding harder in his ears and the deep, knotted anger channelling itself into an unreal lust.

Amelia finished her work and rose and almost in the same moment he stood up. The girl, carrying the shovel and coal-scuttle, turned. Shot through with frustrated impulse he seized her round the waist and pulled her to him. The coal-scuttle and shovel crashed to the floor. For a moment she did not resist, and she felt like a dead weight in his arms as he clutched at her. Then with the same cumbrous slowness of movement she broke free of him and bent to pick up the scuttle and shovel. He slapped her lightly across the rump, trying to laugh it carelessly away. With an expressionless face the girl opened the door. He began to say, 'Just a joke, Amelia,' a needle of lacerating self-loathing already shooting through him, but she was gone.

A great number of people were to attend the ball held at the Bell Inn, Stilton, by George Hardwick, Esquire, of Morholm. George himself had, in a burst of industry when the idea first took hold of him, made out a list of guests, but he had reckoned without Aunt Catherine's seeing it.

'Why, nephew, you cannot invite *them* – did you not hear the scandal? – and if you are to invite *him* you cannot have *him* – they fight every time they meet: and if you are to have the Townsends you must have Lydia – did you not know she was out?'

George knew better than to argue, but he felt riled when she noticed he had missed off the Wainwrights. His intense dislike of Mrs Wainwright remained fresh within him, but Aunt Catherine, unaware of his encounter with her in Stamford, was adamant. It was impossible not to invite the Wainwrights – they were the most fashionable people. Finally it was Mary who persuaded him to ride into Stamford and offer an apology with the invitation. She wanted the Wainwrights to be there because she had a burning curiosity about Elizabeth and Henry Milton, who was also invited. Milton often came to Morholm to see George and she noticed how preoccupied he seemed.

When he learned that the beautiful Miss Wainwright was to be at the ball – for George's reluctant apology and invitation had been accepted – Milton viewed the coming event with mixed feelings. He was not sure he wanted the wound re-opened and had been keeping busy in the hope it would heal itself. But still she floated into his thoughts unbidden every hour of the day, even overshadowing his concern for George. Milton was glad of his return from London, for he had few close friends, but he doubted George's capacity to take to this life. On one rare occasion he had met George on the estate with the steward, and the incongruity had struck him: George in shirt sleeves helping to mend a fence. 'Our dear sovereign's namesake,' he had said wryly, 'Farmer George.' But he had looked as if he wished he were somewhere else.

Mary's ball-gown was ready in time, but in addition George had to provide new clothes for the rest of the family. He baulked especially at a new suit for Kingsley, but drew an ironic satisfaction from realizing how absurd he would look in the affected coat he had insisted on. Daniel's doctoring he continued to pay for; but unknown to him Mary again took the opportunity of engaging Dr Villiers to attend old Mrs Newman.

Dr St John Villiers was a hard-faced, tight-fisted man of forty with a fashionable practice in Peterborough for whom his fee was everything and sick labourers nothing. But even he had qualms about continuing to receive Miss Hardwick's payment, for he knew that Mrs Newman was dying and there was nothing he could do. He hoped he would not be called in again.

7

Mary stood before the mirror in her room surveying herself in the gown George had bought for her. It was the evening of the fifteenth of November. The weather – for it was not really the season for travelling to a ball – had co-operated; it was cold but clear. Her stomach felt tight and she ran over her worries like an inventory: how did one greet people, what were the steps for the minuet, the cotillion, how did she carry her fan. Then she looked at herself again and marvelled.

Mrs Reynolds, who produced new resources on every occasion, had piled Mary's long brown unruly hair off her forehead and powdered it, with a few curls dangling round the ears. Aunt Catherine had offered a little box of anti-quated face-patches but Mary drew the line there; though she did not say so she thought that fashion made you look as if you had the pox. The dress was a revelation. The snow-white tiers of lace rustled whenever she moved, and she had to be careful with the swinging of the wide panniers. And the low square-cut bodice showed a lot of her, more, she realized with amusement, than she thought she had. An exquisite emerald necklace, lent by Grand-mother Peach, set off the dress and her sparkling eyes to perfection.

Her life at Morholm had been lived through the senses: dressed in an old smock helping the housekeeper brew ale or dip rushes for candles, trudging lashed by wind and rain in pattens across the wet fields by the Long Ditch, going barefoot in the summer when Morholm was marooned in an aching yellow ocean of wheat and mustard, her awareness of her body had been simply as the vehicle through which she experienced the pleasures of being alive, the rhythm of the seasons and the world of sensations in the spacious fertile country where she lived. Now it was as if she were awakening to a different awareness of her self, a world of experience that had always been there but which she had somehow never noticed.

Dear George for arranging the ball. Her cousin had grown into her life almost imperceptibly in the last couple of months. Changeable, truculent, exasperating, he was yet at Morholm an element of humour, of charm, of unpredictability that she warmed to. Even his moods she had managed to understand or at least cope with so far. She would dance the first with George. In an impulsive, red-faced moment he had already asked for that. And she knew his friends, Mr Milton and Mr Jarrett, so she need not fear going without partners. Two months ago she would not have believed she could have been this happy. She must remember to thank George.

George too had taken pains with himself; a buff coat cut away to show the embroidered waistcoat. His lean face was half-raffish, half-boyish as he turned to greet Mary descending the staircase in her splendid gown. He took her hand, which was as damp as if she had been clenching her fist. 'Well,' he said, and smiled nervously.

'Both dressed up to the nines, eh?' Kingsley broke the tension by appearing in his new outfit, for they had to smother their laughs. His short coat stuck out at the back in Macaroni fashion and his fat thighs in tight striped breeches with tassels rippled like sides of meat on meat-hooks.

Thomas Jarrett was to ride with them in the post-chaises George had hired for the occasion and arrived at Morholm punctually, dressed in a plum-coloured coat and silk breeches. His courtesy even softened Mrs Peach who, wearing her new wig and carrying a polished stick, asked after his father in a cracked parody of a girlish voice.

Mary never forgot the ride in the chaise to Stilton. The fields too seemed to have put on their finery, silver white with frost, and the night was netted with stars and a brooch of pinkish moon. Sometimes she glanced out of the window to make sure the other carriage with the gentlemen was following, until Aunt Catherine made her put her head in for fear her hair would come down. Kingsley, who could not dissociate any pleasure from being on horseback, rode behind on Raleigh.

The Bell was glowing with light as they drew up outside, and hired footmen in livery greeted them as they descended. A waft of warm air laced with smells of food and drink came out of the open door like a hot breath. A smattering of villagers had turned out to watch the guests arrive, and Aunt Catherine sailed in ahead of George with her head held high and surveyed the assembly room with critical eyes. It had been scrupulously cleaned and lit and two small committee rooms at the side had undergone a hasty conversion for cards and refreshments. A band from Stamford was noisily tuning up. While George congratulated the inn-keeper Mary watched the other guests filtering in. She recognized the Townsends and Mr Sedgmoor the attorney with his wife and sons. She saw too the gangly figure of Henry Milton enter with uneasy nonchalance.

The next twenty minutes was the most intimidating time for Mary, for it meant endless introductions to people of apparent consequence. Aunt Catherine took it upon herself to steer her about the room, displaying her to the arriving guests, as she had not before been out. There were many second, and approving, glances for the striking girl with the strong line to her jaw and the wide candid eyes who was hitherto known only as old Joseph's niece. 'Mr and Mrs Townsend – young Mr John Townsend, and the Misses

Sophia and Bridget: Dr and Mrs Milton,' (a plump and kindly couple), 'ah! Mr Van Druyten and Miss Emma.'

George, after circulating a little, stood by and talked to Jarrett while the other guests arrived. 'I've seen little of you lately, Jarrett. Where have you been hiding?'

'Sorry, George. Not choice but compulsion. Father's no longer fit to run the business alone, so it falls to me.'

'Well, when you get time, come over and look around the estate. We're having trouble draining the long field towards Nunton and you might offer some advice.'

'Thank you, I will. Milton's on his toes tonight,' said Jarrett, nodding in the direction of Henry Milton, who was standing a little way off watching the door askance as if he were afraid it might sneak up on him.

'So he is,' said George. 'What is the matter with him?'

'Perhaps he awaits the arrival of Miss Wainwright.'

'Eh? Oh, her. Is it true, then, concerning those two?'

'So far as I know they have only met once, but made their feelings pretty clear on that occasion.'

'Ah, there come the Wainwrights now.'

Like a conjurer displaying his last trick with a flourish, the doors at the end of the room yielded up the figure of Mrs Wainwright, looking not merely large but immense in a pink silk gown with huge panniers. Beside her stalked Mr Wainwright, a preposterous absurdity next to his imposing wife. He was a stooping, dried-out, clerkly man in a scratch wig who looked out at the world testily through narrow spectacles. Behind them came Elizabeth, beautiful but dressed with somewhat unnecessary splendour. It was odd, thought Mary watching them, that two such individually grotesque people as Mr and Mrs Wainwright could have produced such a beauty as their eldest daughter; but whatever strange chemistry had gone to make the lovely Elizabeth had failed with the Wainwrights' second daughter Wilhelmina, a sallow-faced nonentity who tripped like a shadow behind her sister. Mrs Wainwright greeted Mary briefly, totting up the cost of her gown with one glance, and then advanced on George, conscious of the rank that wealth gave her and doubly conscious of the deference it failed to elicit from this arrogant squireen. The condescension in her voice was faint but perceptible as she returned his grudging salutation. Her little eyes darted from side to side as she assessed the company, looking out for anyone richer than herself. A little way off Henry Milton watched. His contempt for the woman was as hearty as his friend's, but it took second place to his overpowering attraction to Elizabeth, the sight of whom had made his heart pound and his chest tighten until the excitement and apprehension inside him became almost a pain. All he had to do, he told himself, was pick up where they had left off; she had forgiven him; that was all he had to do.

By now the main body of guests had arrived, scraped together from the scattered numbers of gentry who inhabited that bare countryside. Old Horace Hardwick had reluctantly made an appearance. Sir Samuel Edgington, the vile old baronet from Deeping, had arrived, a solitary title, and with him an equally vile and even older woman who had one tooth that dangled from a stringy gum and who turned out to be his mother. There were a couple of large parties from Peterborough, and in a corner Parson Medhurst sat with his spinster sisters, lending a little gravity to the proceedings. By the time Aunt Catherine had finished steering her round Mary was overwhelmed, and she was glad when her aunt at last let go of her arm. She stood still a moment, fanning herself awkwardly. She had already forgotten half their names. Never mind. She knew the ones that mattered. To her left she could see Thomas Jarrett, taller by a head than the whole company, good-naturedly receiving Mrs Wainwright's condescending greeting. His handsomeness struck her with redoubled force beside the fat corsetted woman. When she had first met him at Morholm she thought him the most attractive man she had ever seen and now with the lights and music and her own costume she began to feel a queasy light-headed excitement, as fine-drawn as the lingering note the violinist was coaxing from his instrument. Then at a signal the band struck up 'God Save The King' and stirred her from her reflections.

Henry Milton swallowed wine and watched Elizabeth Wainwright. They are right when they say 'heartache', he thought, because that is precisely what it is . . . an infernal tightening in the throat, a pain in the chest, a hollowness in the stomach. How ridiculous, he thought, that the sight of a certain combination of features arranged in a certain way should do this to a man. His father was a doctor – perhaps he should ask him about it. He smiled at the homely sound of the band as it struck up the anthem, and felt better. He noticed George had drunk nothing and was glad, for he took an almost fatherly interest in George, whom he liked and felt he understood above all people. Then his eyes fell on Miss Wainwright again, this time on her brilliant smile, which did the impossible by doubling her beauty.

He took another glass of wine.

The dancing began, and leading it were George and Mary. George, because he was not concentrating too hard, danced well tonight.

Mary's curiosity about Henry Milton and Elizabeth Wainwright was still at the back of her mind as she danced. She had grown to like Milton better over the weeks, and with a vein of romanticism was pleased with the notion of uniting the reserved Milton and the statuesque Elizabeth. She glanced aside at the other dancers. Thomas Jarrett was dancing with one of the Townsend girls. She noticed a gaggle of suitors pressing Miss Wainwright for a dance, but Milton was not among them. She could not see him anywhere. Finally Miss Wainwright accepted someone. As they formed up again Mary thought she saw Milton's pale face staring like a full moon in the furthest corner of the room.

Aunt Catherine, foreseeing that no one would ask for Julia's hand, had forced Kingsley to dance the first with her, and the ungainly pair were now drifting back and forth, not even looking at each other. Satisfied that all her charges were on the floor, she sat and babbled to Great-Uncle Horace.

'Not at all a fashionable gathering, you will acknowledge, uncle – but then it never met with my approval. A ball so soon after brother Joseph's death – I declare people must be talking. But then the young have no respect in these times of ours, as you have heard me observe before now. Cousin Daniel, have you not? Mrs Peach, have you not heard me observe that? I thank you ma'am. Hmph! Mrs Wainwright obviously thinks herself very fine. Of course it shows, you know, for all their finery. No family. No more family than that footman.'

Daniel, seeing Dr Villiers nearby, seized his chance to pursue his favourite subject. 'Ah, Villiers,' he said, rising with a groan and hobbling over to the physician. 'You're here, I see.'

Villiers inclined his head, a tall spare man with a face as cold and grey as a scrubbed stone floor. Tonight his taste for fashion had overcome his avarice and he had chosen to come instead of visiting a man at Whittlesey who had had his face bitten by a dog.

'Now, man, what about this ankle of mine? You said . . .'

Aunt Catherine, noticing finally that Horace too had slipped away as she chattered, moved over and assailed Sir Samuel and the Dowager Lady Edgington.

'My lady, Sir Samuel. How good of you to honour our little assembly.'

The eyes of the ancient lady studied Aunt Catherine for a moment from cavernous sockets. Then she spat expertly on the floor.

'Don't know you, ma'am, I believe.'

Aunt Catherine glanced uneasily at the spittle. 'Er – I am Miss Catherine Hardwick, my lady, the present mistress of Morholm.'

'Ah? Oh, now, didn't your brother die or some such?'

'Indeed, ma'am, I have recently lost my dear brother Joseph.'

'Thought so. Sammle, you 'tended the funeral, ain't it so? What did your brother die of, ma'am?'

'Alas! The pneumonia.'

This seemed to disappoint the old lady. She stuck a skeletal finger up her nose for a while and then said: 'I had an uncle once who died when a madman threw a close-stool at his head. He took a deal of time going . . .'

The first dance came to an end and George conducted Mary to a seat.

'Who has been teaching you the minuet?' he said finally, a little breathless.

'Mrs Reynolds, of course.'

'When did the housekeeper ever dance the minuet?'

'I don't know. Perhaps she is really a fine lady who has fallen on hard times.' She remembered what she had told herself to do earlier. 'Thank you, George.'

He smiled, the boyish smile that made him look younger. 'For dancing with you?' he said. 'Or do you think I arranged this whole affair just for you?'

'Even if you did not,' she said, 'I shall always think of it so. Thank you, George.'

There was a pause.

'But did I make any mistakes, or do anything amiss?' she asked.

'I believe we were the best couple on the floor,' said George. 'Tom, were we not?'

Jarrett, who had come up to them, laughed. 'Indeed you were. But since if I danced with you, George, it might create an odd impression, I beg the favour of the next dance from Miss Mary.'

Mary, surprised, hardly knew what she said as she accepted. George refused a glass of wine and after watching his friend lead Mary out on to the floor went over to Henry Milton, who had sunk into a shaded corner and was visibly quivering. Milton looked up with pale eyes as George patted his shoulder.

'Come, Milton, not dancing?'

'I have managed to resist that temptation, George, yes.'

'Miss Wainwright seems in no light mood,' said George. 'She has refused everyone this dance.'

'Indeed.'

'Are you not going to try your fortune?'

'Why? I dance poorly, I do not like to dance, and since she has refused so many prospective partners it seems highly unlikely that I shall be favoured.'

'I thought you were fond of Miss Wainwright,' said George.

'I spent one evening with her at a party,' said Milton irritably. 'I had a long and reasonably pleasant conversation with her. That is the sum total of our attachment.'

'Yes, Henry. I'm sorry.'

There was a long silence. Milton drew a deep breath.

'Perhaps I shall ask her for the next.'

Mary danced the second minuet with Jarrett and suddenly the excitement of the evening began to take on a magnified and overpowering quality.

He danced in a graceful amateur way and if his step went out of time he did not try to cover it up but laughed and shrugged at her engagingly. Whenever they parted in the steps of the dance she found herself waiting with an excited apprehension she did not understand for the moment when they met again and touched. She wondered if she had drunk too much wine and if others were noticing her exhilaration and realized she did not care.

'I see the price of corn's on the down again, ma'am,' said the charming dowager.

'Indeed, my lady?' said Aunt Catherine, 'I didn't know it.'

'You don't know much then, ma'am,' said Lady Edgington, hawking and swallowing, 'and that's a fact.'

'In our opinion, Mr Hardwick,' said Dr Villiers, 'a course of regular bleedings will be essential, or further swelling may develop above the ankle.'

'Why, Villiers,' said Daniel, ''tis swelled like a pumpkin now. I'm of the opinion there's more in this than meets the eye. I took a sore tumble, Villiers. I've known men half my age never rise up again from less. Why, I knew a gentleman once had a footman who but tripped on the kitchen step . . .'

George was circulating and trying to be courteous and pleasant, and was to a fair measure succeeding. But he was eager for the next dance to begin so that he could rejoin Mary. Immediately the second ended he glanced towards the dancers. He saw Mary smile brilliantly as Jarrett bowed and conducted her to her seat. He had taken a step towards her when suddenly, like an apparition, Mrs Wainwright appeared before him.

'Mr Hardwick, a most pleasant assembly. Have you met Mr John Redburn?' Mrs Wainwright seemed to have forgiven George and decided to be cordial. She was unaware of what an inopportune moment she had chosen. He smiled and replied, cursing her between his teeth. His sight of Mary was blocked by the immense form of Mrs Wainwright and the nonentity she was introducing. As she chattered on the fragile thread of his temper stretched and threatened to snap. As she finally moved on he heard the music begin again. Then he saw that Aunt Catherine was pressing Kingsley to dance with Mary and she, hardly able to refuse, was taking the floor with him.

George gave way to his vexation and turned and went into the card-room.

Henry Milton's legs were so unsteady as he walked from his corner across to Miss Wainwright that had anyone been watching him they might have thought he was drunk: but it was a ferocious nervousness that was making every fibre of him quiver so uncontrollably. As Elizabeth turned to face him the delicious scent of her washed over him. Her white gown was cut low to show her shoulders and her skirt was looped up with crimson velvet bows above a mauve-striped underskirt. She was like a vision. Ignoring the other suitors around her – powdered, pretentious youths and a couple of elderly squires with lewd twinkles in their faded eyes – he spoke. 'Miss Wainwright. A pleasure too long postponed. Might I hope to have that pleasure doubled by the honour of this dance?'

He felt himself reel as without hesitation she turned away from the others and took his moist hand.

As she danced with a silent and wooden Kingsley Mary watched Milton and Miss Wainwright take the floor with an inward smile. She also saw that Jarrett was dancing with Julia, and her heart warmed to him again. She did not see George go into the card-room.

To Aunt Catherine's relief Mrs Townsend had joined her and helped shoulder the burden of entertaining the baronet and dowager, who were proving highly unsociable and were at that moment sharing the dross in the bottom of a dirty snuffbox.

'This wine has a very taking flavour, ma'am,' said Mrs Townsend. 'Do you not find it so, Lady Edgington?'

The old woman took a glass and swallowed the contents. Then, after sucking her gums for a moment, she said: 'Thank'ee, ma'am, I b'lieve if I was to get on my knees and lap up the puddles our horses leave in the yard my palate might be equally as tickled.'

'. . . a wart the size of a sovereign, with enough hair to cover a baby's head!' concluded Daniel, jabbing at Dr Villiers' chest with his forefinger. 'What do you think of that, sir?'

'A truly remarkable case, sir,' said Dr Villiers, wondering how he could escape. Details of human physiology did not interest him, and he loathed Daniel Hardwick. 'Ah! Dr and Mrs Milton! I am sure what you were saying, Mr Hardwick, will be of great interest . . . how are you sir, ma'am? Will you excuse me a moment?'

Leaving the good-natured Miltons to suffer Daniel he slipped away.

The evening was unusual in that Kingsley Hardwick, who had been to three balls in his lifetime and on each occasion had drunk wine all the time and not said a word, had finally found some company who pleased him. Mr Van Druyten was an elderly corn factor from Peterborough, a man who lived for hunting and shooting, and father of a daughter who nursed similar affections for the chase. Emma Van Druyten freely let her fingers do the office of a handkerchief and had a face that was mainly chin, but she was the first woman to storm the battlements of Kingsley's heart. Her knowledge of horses won his rapturous admiration; and she had an authentic smell of horse about her. Her knowledge of dogs was equally extensive. 'D'you keep dogs, Mr Hardwick?' she asked him.

'Some,' he answered evasively. There were four or five wall-eyed brutes who prowled around the stables at Morholm that he called his.

'One of my best bitches has just whelped, y'know, sir. A fine litter. Perhaps you would care for one of the pups when they are growed? There was half a dozen, and one born dead. I put it in the pocket of my cloak, as I recall – I'd show it you, but I left my cloak in the powder-room.'

Great-Uncle Horace rarely talked about anything but business unless more trivial conversation might be to his advantage, so tonight he went into a tête-à-tête with Sedgmoor, the family lawyer, for the rest of the evening.

'What d'you say to this fuss in America, Hardwick?' said Sedgmoor. 'Continental Congress indeed. A parcel of rebellious rogues setting themselves up as if they were of some account.'

'It need never have got this far,' said Horace, who was an ardent Whig. 'North has mismanaged the whole thing. If the king had for a moment even listened to their grievances – '

'Grievances?' Sedgmoor wagged his big powdered head. 'Mere braggart posturing. A little force and they will back down.'

'If you imagine that three million colonists across a wide ocean may be kept as slaves without disastrous consequences,' said Horace, 'you and your party are more blindly stubborn than I believed.'

The card-room was a tiny place, accommodating a very few tables at which elderly or bored people were playing. George did not intend to stay long. He was playing with two Townsends and a fiery young woman whose independent air astonished him until he found out her name was Alicia Knaggs-Landgreebe and realized that with such a name she would have to be independent. He heard the music in the ballroom end just as another round began. Fruitlessly he tried to hurry the play and drank his wine with furious

124

haste. He won the round and started from his seat as the next dance struck up. He pushed through the little knot of people in the doorway and glanced around the crowded room where couples were already forming up in the middle of the floor. Above them all he recognized Jarrett's head, moving beside Mary's.

He felt his new-found patience draining away as he snatched another glass of wine.

When Kingsley finally relinquished her, Mary had sat and tried to compose herself. People wove endlessly around her and the room was becoming crowded. She watched them and tried not to look for Thomas Jarrett and looked for him, frantically.

His voice spoke in her ear.

'Miss Mary, I – '

She turned with a start and they both laughed. 'Miss Mary, I – I hardly dare . . .' He seemed at a loss, and his face was flushed, as if with embarrassment.

'Mr Jarrett, if you are asking me to dance, you are doing it very badly,' she said, smiling. 'I have half a mind to go and dance with my cousin Kingsley again and listen to his charming conversation.'

He laughed gaily as they went out on to the floor. 'I hardly dared ask,' he said. 'I fear I monopolize you. We shall start a gossip that will be right round the county before tomorrow noon.'

'Then we shall be doing folk a service,' said Mary, and at his enquiring glance went on, 'We shall give them something much better to talk about than the price of corn.'

He laughed again and then said, low and haltingly, 'You favour me greatly, Miss Mary. I can scarcely express . . .'

A searing, choking emotion seemed to fill her throat, and her words came out scarcely audible. 'You need not fear monopolizing me, Mr Jarrett, indeed you need not.'

'How did you find Huntingdon?' Milton asked, as he and Miss Wainwright sat together, uncomfortably.

'I liked it well enough, though it is not half so fashionable as Stamford,' she replied, her eyes cast down on her elegant hands. They were long-fingered, which he liked.

'I wondered whether to call at your place near Elton, but I thought I might not be welcome.'

'Oh, but you should have – I'm sure Mama would have been agreeable,' she said, forgetting herself. She lifted her eyes to his, and they were blue and bright; then, as if ashamed of her show of feeling, she dropped them again. 'At least, I fancy she would.'

'I apologize for my dancing. I was never adept at the art, and I fear I have been out of practice,' said Milton. She did not make the customary contradiction that etiquette suggested; one thing about her that he was beginning to notice was that her character was entirely frank, no soft edges – almost hostile.

'Where is your friend Mr Hardwick?' she said. 'Can it be he has left his own ball?'

'I thought he was with Miss Mary – no, she's with Jarrett. Well, she seems more than happy with him.'

'More than can be said for poor Mrs Townsend,' she said. Mrs Townsend had been prevailed upon to dance by old Sir Samuel, who was now stumping back and forth with her, raising dust like a horse. They laughed, and it was as if their laughter burst through and broke the surface tension between them. Suddenly two bold and fashionable young women, with faces rouged and patched, hair piled up in turbans, and gowns parted in front to reveal tiers of lace, appeared before them.

'Well, Elizabeth, not dancing? Never tell me you're fagged already! Or is this gentleman detaining you from the floor? Don't believe I've had the pleasure, sir,' said one in a loud voice. He looked at them with distaste as they were introduced, recognizing them as two of a party from Stamford. He noticed too that when Elizabeth spoke with them she made what seemed to him a silly attempt to imitate their affected manner. When they had sardonically criticized the quality of the ball and moved away he felt a worm of annoyance and dismay as he sensed aspirations that she could never meet in him.

'Just moozes about, usually with a glass in his hand, ma'am,' said Mrs Peach, who was expounding the evils of George's character for the benefit of Mrs Milton. 'He's no man to bear the Hardwick arms – not that we've got any arms, mind you, ma'am. Nor a carriage to put 'em on come to that. Ha! I wish you could have witnessed the scene when the younger boy James came down after Joseph passed on. They quarrelled and near came to blows. No love lost there. No love lost. Family's going to ruin.'

When he saw Jarrett and Mary dancing together again George went back to the card-room but did not resume play. The tables had filled up in his absence, and he felt, besides, indisposed to play again. Instead he stood in the entrance and watched another game, unseeing. He was unaware that Daniel had puffed to his side until he spoke. 'Well, George,' he said, 'not dancing?'

'No, uncle,' said George, without looking round, 'I don't believe I am – normally my legs move in a rhythmic fashion when I dance, so I believe yes, you're right, uncle, I am *not* dancing.'

Daniel glanced at George blankly. Sarcasm was lost on him so he resumed. 'Hardly the most brilliant of occasions though, is it? They've no notion how to fit out a ball these days. Why, I remember the balls we had in London when I was your age. I mind the skirts of the men's coats were as wide as the women's. And you always wore a sword then, you know. Had to. No telling when you might have to fight for your honour – '

But George had walked away.

'Where d'you buy your saddles, Mr Hardwick?' inquired Miss Van Druyten.

'Er – Blackmore's,' replied Kingsley, who was captivated by this woman who knew each dog by its pugmarks and who had once re-shod her own horse when, on a hunting trip, she had called at the smithy's to find the blacksmith ill in bed and his tools lying idle.

'Blackmore's, eh? Used to formerly m'self. Generally go to Nesbit's nowadays; workmanship's better, I conceit; I always find Blackmore's a mite hard on the arse.'

Kingsley replied, with the gallantry of adoration, 'Er – perhaps our housekeeper could make up an ointment for you . . .'

The dance came to an end and Jarrett bowed to Mary. As he did so his face came closer to hers and for a moment she looked straight into his dark frank eyes. She felt an odd thrill go through her; it was like a wave of concentrated excitement that transmitted itself into a tingling physical sensation.

'Will you take a little refreshment?' he said, his voice colouring the formal request into a warm and confidential question. He took her hand and led her to the refreshment room.

'Now, was this evening not worth waiting for?' he said, presenting her with wine.

'I would not exchange it for the grandest assembly in London,' she said.

'And let us not forget the man who arranged it all for us,' he went on. 'I think we owe George a vote of thanks.'

'Oh – yes,' she murmured, realizing guiltily that she had indeed forgotten her cousin. She wondered where he was. As if in answer to her thoughts George appeared before her and bowed shortly. She noticed how hot he looked.

'Why, George, you've been neglecting us. Tell Mrs Wainwright to go hang, and join us,' said Jarrett.

'Thank you, Jarrett,' said George, not looking at him. 'I believe the next dance is mine.'

'Oh – ' Mary hesitated, suddenly confused. George's thin intense face stared down at her, and she was disconcerted. She recognized that look in his eyes, and recoiled from a darkness there that seemed at odds with the gaiety of the evening.

'I plead guilty,' said Jarrett, coming to her rescue. 'I'm afraid I've been monopolizing her and preventing Miss Mary from expressing her gratitude to you for arranging her first ball for her.'

'Upon my word, Jarrett, don't flatter her into thinking the whole business is for her benefit,' said George. Her cousin's perversity made Mary flush with anger. Jarrett looked uncomfortable. 'I see Milton and Miss Wainwright. I'll ask him to introduce me. Will you excuse me?' He bowed, and Mary watched him walk away with his tall big-boned gait.

'Far be it from me to lecture, cousin,' said George, 'but a lady should not be seen dancing with the same gentleman all evening.'

If he had meant it half-jokingly, it came out stiff and pompous. She frowned. 'I had a higher opinion of you than to think you cared for proprieties and wagging tongues,' she said. 'And why have you suddenly decided to teach me how to behave?'

'Somebody has to,' he snapped. They stared at one another for a moment. He passed a hand across his face. 'I'm sorry,' he said. 'I'm sorry, Mary.'

'Don't let's quarrel, George,' she said, her anger cooling. 'Not tonight. It's such a lovely evening. How does it compare with the balls in London?' she went on, babbling a little with nerves. 'Mr Milton is still with Miss Wainwright, look.

She certainly is beautiful. I believe that's the first time I have seen him smile.'

'I believe it's the first time *I've* seen him smile,' said George. 'He must be drunk.'

She laughed, the tension easing. 'George, I think you have been taking lessons from Daniel on how to be uncharitable. They are an odd match, aren't they? And I fear Mrs Wainwright may not approve. Yet in a way they are not unsuited.'

'Yes, they both blush a lot and say little,' said George. 'When we mentioned Miss Wainwright to him a while ago he strenuously denied any attachment. But then old Milton's like that. He's one of those folk who are so on their dignity they think it's a compromise of it to acknowledge love – or – any of that carry-on.'

'And last season we went to Bath. One is introduced to all sorts of people. Mama tried the waters but found they did not agree with her.' Miss Wainwright was coming out and talking at length about her family and their wealthy life, but he was content to listen. Her voice was cultured and precise; he envied her it because his own was gruff and tinged with the flat vowels of the fen accent. He admired her beauty while she talked, the long clean lines of her legs under the rich skirts, the slender white forearms below the elbow-length lace sleeves. Her hair was powdered now, but he had seen it without, and it was of mesmerizing fairness. The reason her beauty was not more universally remarked upon was that she seemed actually embarrassed by it.

Even as the strains of the music grew louder, he was unaware that the next dance was beginning until he noticed that shadows were falling around them and looked up to see a ring of men pressing for her hand. He felt a spasm of pain as he realized he was not the only man on whom her beauty made an impression. He waited tensely while the men bobbed around them like drinking birds, trying to outdo each other with extravagant bows. Then he heard her cool shaded voice say: 'I am afraid I have already promised this dance to this gentleman, have I not, Mr Milton?' and a moment later he was leading her out on to the floor with his heart pounding in his ears.

Across the other side of the room George was leading Mary out. Suddenly a very young man – a boy almost – appeared before them, with a bold frown on his pimpled face. 'I believe, sir, the lady promised me this dance,' he said, and seemed about to snatch her hand away.

'You must be mistaken,' said George, 'I – '

'Let us ask the lady,' said the young man. 'She cannot fail to recollect, I feel sure. Do you not remember your promising this to me directly after the last?'

Mary, confused, tried to remember. She had danced the last with Mr Jarrett, and consequently had eyes for no one else, but as they made for the refreshment room – had not someone approached and said something to her? She had not really listened, but whatever was said seemed to require some acknowledgement, so she had nodded and said 'yes'. That must have been this young man. She noticed that both he and George had hold of her arm, and though her cousin's grip was the tighter it was a trembling one. She heard him hiss 'Young puppy,' and was beginning to feel apprehensive when Thomas Jarrett's voice broke in on them. 'Ah, Mr Sherborne, I was just looking for you. Have you met Mrs Sedgmoor? She has been asking to meet you all evening.' Jarrett had appeared behind the young man with the lawyer's wife, and with a discreetly firm hand was pulling him away. Reluctantly the young man gave up and bowed to Mrs Sedgmoor.

'How good of Mr Jarrett,' said Mary, watching his tall figure move away again. 'I'm sorry, George. I must have answered that young man, but indeed I never meant to. Come.' She tried to speak lightly, but the hardness was in his eyes now and he muttered 'Young puppy' again as they went on to the floor.

'That was a most strategic intervention, Mr Jarrett,' said Julia, going up to him. He turned, surprised to find her beginning a conversation. 'But does it not occur to you that the other young man may have been in the right?' She watched him from the corners of her heavy-lidded eyes.

'Oh, I daresay George would have sent him off had I not detained him, anyway,' said Jarrett.

She gave a snort. 'Do you really think my brother would have done that? It strikes me as highly unlikely, Mr Jarrett.'

'Perhaps. But an act of kindness never goes amiss.'

'An act of kindness? You're on dangerous ground, Mr Jarrett. A cynic would tell you that no man that ever lived ever lifted a finger but out of self-interest. Even the most selfless acts of heroism may be seen as mere manifestation of egotism.'

'Would you call yourself a cynic, Miss Hardwick?'

'I?' There was the snort again. It was bitter and scornful. 'I call myself nothing, Mr Jarrett, but an ignorant girl who will live out her days in the decaying country house of a decaying family. Those are my limits, Mr Jarrett, and I do not presume to go beyond them.'

'Why do you not attempt to, Miss Hardwick? I feel sure you are more than capable of doing so. But to return to the original question. Is it not possible then that I may be simply desirous of helping George and Miss Mary? They are both, I hope, my friends.'

'I think I *must* be a cynic, Mr Jarrett. Please pardon me, but I simply cannot envisage how anyone can take pleasure in witnessing the pleasure of others. It always vexes me until I could be sick.' Her thick lips pursed. 'That is why I find this ball so wholly disgusting.' She turned and stalked away.

8

'George, you've given us a marvellous evening,' said Jarrett.

The air in the refreshment-room was hot and oppressive, as if the smells of perfume and pomade and plain greasy food were weighing it down. George had made a mistake in the last dance which had discomfited him so much he had gone wrong again. He was in a bad temper.

'This little unfashionable gathering? Come, Jarrett, there are limits to compliment,' said George.

'Why, who needs fashion? I have not enjoyed myself so well in an age. Perhaps your coming back to be master of Morholm marks the beginning of a new age here. I know that I'm very glad of it.'

'I could always detect the sarcasm in your voice, Jarrett,' said George. 'I can't see why you must flatter me thus, however.'

'Good heavens, George, what's the matter? I'm not being sarcastic. I'm sure everyone will reinforce my opinion and join in my thanks.'

George was becoming more and more hot-tempered, Mary noticed. She flashed him a reproachful glance, but he was not looking at her.

'Why, here's Milton to back me up,' said Jarrett. 'Miss Wainwright, how do you do? Come and help us convince George we are enjoying ourselves.'

'No one is ever happy in truth,' said George. 'A person may pretend to be, but deep down he knows he is miserable.' He looked at Milton; the two of them, in past long confidential evenings of drinking and philosophising, had concocted this and many other epigrams which they thought witty and profound. But now Milton shrugged his shoulders and said, 'Well, if we are not really happy, this is a most delightful delusion.'

'Well said, Mr Milton,' said Mary. 'Now, George, you are outnumbered.'

'Really, Milton, I had credited you with more intelligence – ' George began: but there was a glow about Milton's face, as he held Miss Wainwright's arm, that he did not associate with his friend. He turned around. 'Good heavens,' he laughed, 'look at old Villiers and Mrs Townsend behaving as if they were twenty again. Is there any sight more absurd than two elderly people trying to recapture their youth?'

'I don't ever want to be old,' said Mary. 'I can't blame them. I want to live my youth to the full and not regret it.'

'When I look at my father,' said Jarrett, 'I can scarce believe he was ever young: he seems to have been old all his life. I'm determined not to be like that. These are our golden days, you know; let us make them days to remember. I feel these waning months of '74 will remain in our minds for a long time . . . a time of awakening . . . our all coming together, this ball, George's becoming master of Mor-holm . . .'

'Why must you harp on that so persistently?' interrupted George. 'And why this fulsome praise of youth? Ay, one has vigour and all the rest of it, but one is so infernally confused in one's mind and heart that one cannot appreciate the compensations. I think age must be preferable; it has more security; when one is fifty one's back aches too much for one to get involved in all the idiotic troubles that plague us now.'

Mary looked at her cousin dubiously. Another time Milton might have agreed with George, but with Miss Wainwright he was bright with gratification and hope, and Jarrett's idea of their 'golden days' seemed both charming and possible.

As the room was quickly filling up Jarrett suggested they

find seats for the ladies before all the food was gone. In the resulting crush there was only a small square of standing room left, and George was about to step into it when the young man Sherborne appeared – from nowhere, it seemed – and blocked him. The youth held a plate of something which he lowered to Mary's shoulder and offered to her. She thanked him and refused: but he remained where he was, stubbornly, stupidly, still holding the plate, and merely listening to their conversation.

'I wonder how many people throughout the land are sharing just such an evening now,' said Mary. 'There must be scores in London alone.'

'Perhaps one day you may go to one of those,' said Jarrett.

'Oh! I hope so indeed. But I would not exchange this evening for the grandest of them. Have you ever been in London, Mr Jarrett?'

'Yes, but not of late. I think Miss Wainwright is better qualified to speak on London than I.'

As Miss Wainwright began to tell them of London somebody brushing past George dug an elbow into his ribs and like the last turn of a key in a clockwork toy it prompted him into movement. He took a step forward and tapped Sherborne on the shoulder and said, trying to sound brisk, 'I say, move aside, will you, these people are with me.' The young man looked round with an uncompromising frown, then turned his head. 'I may stand where I choose, I think,' he said. Mary saw, with a dreadful lurching feeling in her stomach, George's face pale and a vein, ticking, stand out on his forehead. He seized the young man's collar with one hand and pressed the other against his waistcoat and pushed. Sherborne, caught off balance, stumbled backwards and fell with a little grunting exhalation of breath. His elbow caught a small table which wobbled and fell over, scattering plates. Mary and Miss Wainwright jumped to their feet, and amongst the hubbub came Great-Uncle Horace's authoritative voice saying, 'Come, what is this? Are you hurt, sir?' There was the scrape and whine of the band tuning up in the main hall as Dr Villiers helped Sherborne to his feet and the young man dusted down his coat. Then Horace, mindful of the preservation of family dignity and observing the potential violence in Sherborne's mutinous eyes, was leading the young man away, saying in dry soothing tones: 'Most hot and oppressive in here, sir, I think a little air might be beneficial. One may easily lose one's temper on these occasions.'

George was staring, as if in a trance, at the stooping footmen picking up the broken plates. Mary was used to feeling disappointment and incomprehension at his actions, but now as he turned and spoke shortly to her she was overcome with bitter resentment. 'The dancing is beginning, cousin. Shall we go?'

For a moment she made no reply. Then, looking away, trembling, she said, 'I cannot believe you wish to dance, George, when you seem determined to spoil every pleasure you can. I have already promised this dance to Mr Jarrett. Miss Wainwright, you were saying –?' With linked arms the two couples moved away. Jarrett was trying to hang back to say something to him, but George did not want it. Suddenly Aunt Catherine was at his elbow.

'Why, such conduct in public, nephew, indeed! I vow I shall die of shame. Are you trying to make the Hardwick name a laughing-stock? Lord knows your father brought it low enough.'

'Boy's drunk, I'll be bound. Can't hold his liquor no more than a parson.' That was Mrs Peach.

'Fortunately the young man has left, George,' said Horace. 'He has more decency than you, it turns out. It is high time you stopped this sort of thing. You are the head of the family now. This kind of disgraceful episode may be allowable in a London gambling-den, but not here, and not for the master of Morholm. Have you no esteem for the tradition of the Hardwicks.'

George made a move for the door. He caught a glimpse of Milton and Miss Wainwright and Mary and Jarrett dancing as he went: then he was out in the cold darkness.

He walked unsteadily to the stables behind the inn. The air was crisp and sharp with the smell of fallen autumn leaves under a light frost. An owl swooped low with a hush of white wings. In the stables there was a pungent odour of horse sweat and dung and old leather. He saw the fat outlines of the horses' rumps as they twitched nervously at his coming in. Peering into the gloom he said 'Hallo! Groom!' The horses jumped at the sound and one gave a little throaty grunt as if in annoyance. 'Hoy, groom, here!' he called, putting one hand to his spinning head and the other against the wall to steady himself. His anger was swelling and surging within him and he himself feared its outbreak. A man in shirt and breeches appeared in the back of the stable; he held a guttering candle whose flickering light fell in brief moving patches all over the walls.

'Sir?'

'I hired two post-chaises. These are the horses, are they not?'

'Aye, sir.'

'Saddle one up.'

'Sir? But – I can't –'

'It is not your place to argue with me and I order you to saddle one up!' His words echoed metallically round the stable. I'm just a bit drunk and overheated, he told himself; I'll feel better once I get home; after all, I am missing nothing by leaving.

The groom had finished and George led the horse out, swung into the saddle and set off at a canter on the north road to Morholm.

A few minutes later another man left the inn and walked

round to the stables. It was Kingsley, whom Great-Uncle Horace, anxious for the preservation of Hardwick dignity as much as for George's personal safety, had despatched to follow him to make sure he did nothing foolish and came to no harm. Kingsley's normally sluggish intellect had been deadened by liquor to almost total inertia, so he did not object to being sent on an errand. Besides, he no longer felt the pull of any amorous obligations because the Miss Van Druyten who had briefly captured his heart, sharing his taste for hunting but not for fashion, had made fun of his townish wig. He had the groom saddle Raleigh and trotted out on to the road.

Mary and Jarrett, Milton and Miss Wainwright danced a couple more dances after George had left; then, feeling very hot, and observing that several other people had drifted out of the main doors without general remark, they agreed to take a breath of air before continuing the dancing. Skirting round the inn, they came upon a path, hugging the edge of a kitchen garden and leading to a wicket gate. Others had gone through to admire the fineness of the night and they followed, emerging through the gate into a paddock with the first straggling trees of a copse ahead of them.

'Shall we go on?' said Milton.

'Yes, let's go a little further,' said Mary, her arm in Jarrett's. 'The air is so fresh, and the moon will light us on our way.'

The ground was not muddy so they went on, finding a smooth worn track through the copse. Jarrett and Mary led, through the quietness and the coolness and the darkness that seemed as one, so that she fancied that a loud noise might change the temperature and flood the place with light. Above her was a spiky network of branches with jigsaw glimpses of inky sky between them and occasional stars which flashed among the black threads as if in rapid motion.

'Are you quite warm enough?' asked Jarrett in a low, almost whispered voice. 'I should have brought your cloak.'

'No, no, I am not cold,' said Mary. But as if by instinct she moved closer to Jarrett and held his arm more tightly.

'Miss Mary, I cannot begin to tell you what a particular joy this evening has given me,' he said, and stopped. Hot, unruly emotion churned within her, constricting her throat until she felt it would be a lancing pain to speak: but confusion relieved her of the necessity, for she could not think of a single word to say.

Henry Milton was usually embarrassed at such close physical proximity, and he knew that Miss Wainwright was doubly so; but tonight the darkness and solitude seemed to make things easier. His feelings at being with her, formerly so consuming, so desperate, almost dark, were transmuted into something much more tender, warm and quiet. He lifted an overhanging branch and held it for her to pass under. She did not smile or thank him or even look at him, but he felt the pressure on his arm grow fractionally tighter.

Soon the trees thinned out and they came to a grassy bank which looked out on to the endless plashy plain of Farcet Fen. A breeze, slightly chilled as if it had just blown across a patch of ice, came skipping across the level fields and danced around Mary's shoulders, and she shrank nearer to Jarrett. Then, as they all began to shiver a little, Milton suggested that they return. With unhurried steps they made their way back towards the yellow light of The Bell.

There was not a single light to illumine the dark shapeless mass of Morholm when George arrived. Grandmother Hardwick was asleep, Matthews the steward had already trudged over to the gatehouse, Clarry was snoring in his closet expecting no one for a couple of hours, Mrs Reynolds, having entertained the farmhands with dishes of tea and finally sent them off to their homes, had fallen asleep in the kitchen where she sat, and Amelia was in bed. George did not take his horse to the stables but let it wander where it would. With steps made haphazard by anger and drink he lurched into the hall. A trace of light came from the fire in the kitchen at the end of the passage leading back from the stairs, but there was not a sound in the house. The door unlocked and all, thought George, and no one come to attend him. Neglect. Damned neglectful swine. What did he pay them for? He spent his wretched days supporting a crowd of worthless people. He would put his foot down. He went down the passage and was about to shout something indignant and masterful when he checked himself. No – he would creep silently into the kitchen. The effect would be better if he could catch these skiving servants sitting idle. Moving stealthily was difficult in his state, but when he pushed the kitchen door open Mrs Reynolds was still soundly asleep by the fire. Her mouth was slightly open, a faint comfortable rattling noise coming from the back of it, and her big motherly breast was slowly rising and sinking. She reminded him of a sentimental engraving he had once seen, and for a moment he was softened, a moment long enough for his attention to shift from reprimanding her to noticing a tiny crack of light from another door next to the cellar. Where did that lead? He seldom came round the back here. Must be the closet where the new maid sleeps. Moving through a dream-like fog of fermenting fury he opened the door and stepped into the tiny room, half-closing the door behind him. Amelia Seddon was sitting up in the bed that almost filled the closet, dressed in an old cotton shift that revealed the deep shadows of her heavy breasts, mending some garment by the light of a stub of candle. She started and lifted up her eyes, surprise rendering them less lifeless.

'Mr Hardwick,' she said, and then she put the sewing

down and her voice changed, became a clumsy husky cooing. 'I was wondering when you'd come to see me . . .'

Kingsley arrived at Morholm a few minutes after George. George's horse, left on its own, wandered into the orchard, so Kingsley did not see it. Following George for a little way, he had realized he was heading for Morholm and so had slowed down his pursuit and carried on home himself. If his cousin met with an accident, he would come across him on the way. Now, as he took his horse to the stables, he could see that the front door was still open. Satisfied that he had completed his mission in seeing George safely home, he quietly unsaddled Raleigh and went into the house. Seeing the glow of a fire in the kitchen, he went down the passage with his slow silent tread, intending to get Mrs Reynolds to find him something to eat. He found her still asleep by the fire, but muffled sounds were issuing from a little room to his right, of which the door was slightly ajar. He peered in.

What he saw, had it been part of some disreputable play on the stage, or a cheap bawdy plate in a smoking-room, would have raised a smile to Kingsley's lips. But when the figure being greedily embraced by a now naked Amelia was his cousin George, and his observing them placed him in danger, quite different feelings were excited in his slothful heart. He slipped away quietly and went to the bedroom which he and old Daniel shared. There he lay and pondered for a long time on what he had seen.

Presently George, his anger and desire spent, emerged from the tiny room, pulling the door shut. A sickening tiredness was stealing over him and with the realization of what he had done came a growing sobriety. He glanced at Mrs Reynolds, still sleeping peacefully in her chair. Then he staggered upstairs and toppled on to his bed and lay staring at the blackened room made obscurer by his own darkness.

* * *

At The Bell the evening drew to its close and Mary found herself being handed into the post-chaise by Mr Jarrett. Aunt Catherine followed and Mary said 'Aunt, I have not seen George. Is he not here?'

'Don't speak of him, Mary. He took off – that stupid groom tells me on one of the chaise horses – and now we must borrow one from the inn – and I must needs stand by and see the good name of the Hardwicks dragged through the mud for a second time.'

'I must be busy most of tomorrow,' said Jarrett to Mary softly, 'but may I call on you early in the morning?'

'I shall be sadly disappointed if you do not,' she whispered. He smiled and then turned to hand Julia in. 'I hope you have enjoyed your evening, Miss Hardwick,' he said.

'A most enlightening evening, indeed, Mr Jarrett,' she said.

'Might I inquire as to the nature of the enlightenment?' he said, but she settled back beside Mary in silence. He handed old Mrs Peach into the carriage and closed the door. As the carriage jolted out of the inn yard Mary craned her head out of the window, shrugging off a clucking Aunt Catherine's restraining hand, and waved to Jarrett's diminishing figure. She hung perilously out, straining her eyes, the wind tugging her hair into its old disobedient tangle, until he was out of sight.

Book Two

1

The morning after a lavish party, no matter how enjoyable, never goes unattended by feelings of disappointment, regret, and a degree of nausea. Henry Milton counted himself very lucky when he woke on the morning of the sixteenth that the expected feelings, though present, were slight indeed.

All the time as he dressed and shaved he marvelled at his good fortune. Now he understood why Shakespeare's sonnets, which he had read with an appreciation of the poetry but a mistrust of the sentiment, were so passionate. This was what had prompted the poets to write those verses which he had thought must be insincere, this sign that the woman he worshipped might feel some tender emotion towards him.

All through breakfast he went over in his mind every moment of last night, trying to extract and savour some extra delight from the memories. And when he could think of it no more he turned to looking forward to seeing her again very soon, for at parting last night he had begged leave to call on the Wainwrights this morning and had been granted permission. And when his mother began to talk about how pleasant the evening had been he had to get up and excuse himself for fear of letting his feelings show.

He went out into the yard, into a windy morning, and a few autumn leaves came chasing each other round his feet. It was early yet but he had to get out, out in the open, for these overflowing emotions could not be contained indoors. He took out his horse and set out on the Stamford road. Wind lifted his coat-tail and stock and the ribbon in his hair, cuffed his new-shaven face. The clatter of his horse's hoofs and its snorting breath were cheerful in the clean morning.

Of course there were doubts, worries: when were there not? Last night's display of feeling from Elizabeth had been little enough. Perhaps it was merely politeness, condescension even? But she would not behave that way out of courtesy; she was not a courteous type, and he knew it, and loved her still. Did she love him? Impossible to say. Possible to hope – too possible, for did he not hope that every moment of the day since he had first seen her? Did she like him? It appeared so. If she did not, it was a most unpleasant and laborious game she was playing with him. Would she do that – bring him on for fun, when really she felt nothing? That too was possible. But the signs, the hints of something deeper, cried out that it was highly implausible.

Of course, if something definite were to grow up between them, he must make his addresses formally to her parents. There was another difficulty – he had no money. No doubt her settlement would be sizeable – very sizeable. Would Mr and Mrs Wainwright look favourably on their eldest daughter marrying a fortuneless young man who, in all honesty, was nothing? They probably already had her marked down for some baronet or Member of Parliament who would connect them with some great name. But his family were respectable, if genteelly impoverished: his grandfather had probably had Mrs Wainwright's father make his breeches for him. Yet supposing the Wainwrights would not give their blessing to the marriage, and Elizabeth had to choose between keeping her settlement and so marrying some candidate of her parents', or taking her chance on Milton and becoming accustomed to a much less wealthy life than she had hitherto led? It all came down to whether she loved him. And of course, though he might try his best to be worthy, that was up to her.

Just a moment: whither was he galloping so eagerly? It

was too early yet to ride into Stamford and call on her. He suddenly remembered George. What had made him so odd last night? If he had not been so absorbed he might have had more time for him. He would repair that wrong now. He would like to see Mary Hardwick too; his opinion of her was going up. And she had been part of last night.

He rode on towards Morholm.

When Mary got up she found in the dining-room Julia and Kingsley. Julia was often an early riser: occasionally she aided Mary in the housekeeping, which she otherwise supervised alone. But it was surprising to see Kingsley, who only rose early when he was hunting. As she ate breakfast she even thought he looked slightly restless, as if he had something on his mind. It was rare for Kingsley to have anything on his mind.

Mary could eat hardly a thing and soon hurried out to let her spirits be carried higher by the buffeting wind. What mattered Julia's sour gaze following her out – sourer than ever it seemed this morning, and tinged with mockery – on such a day. She ran with long strides out of Morholm gate, along the village path that was still muddy with dew and over the stone bridge that spanned the stream. On the sedgy bank a lanky girl followed a string of geese, looking like an immense forlorn goose herself. She gazed after Mary, and so did several village women, crossing the green in pattens to go stick-gathering. She could not have cared less. She ran past the little church with its square of turf a bright emerald green with dew, past the blacksmith's where smoke was already curling up to the sky, and through the dark cut in the trees at the side on to the open field. The wind, coming from the north across the fens which were an enigma of level distances wrapped in a smoky blue mist, was damply, bitingly cold. A boy was driving a mixed herd of sheep and pigs around the stubble field to glean the last remains. In the distance she could see the haze of a willow grove marking where old Mr Newman's farm stood; to the left, a line of trees marking where the road ran straight before twisting into Aysthorpe; to the right, obscured by more trees and other dwellings but just a few minutes away, Mr Nathan Jarrett's house Bromswold. Lucky, undeserving stone to house such a treasure, she thought!

She ran towards the highway, hoping to see a coach or something she could wave to, and as she approached it a figure on a horse appeared. She recognized the bony unaccomplished horseman as Mr Milton and ran towards him waving and calling. Seeing her, he pulled his horse up and swung to the ground with a confidence she did not expect in him. They were both a little out of breath and they stood gasping and laughing at each other for a moment.

'We are two early risers, I see, despite our late hours last evening,' he said. 'I was coming to see George, but I doubt he is astir yet?'

'George? Oh – no.' For a moment a shadow fell across her as she remembered George and his behaviour last night. 'No, I fear not. But how fast you were riding! Were you going to burst in on him and drag him from his bed?'

'I am afraid I have been riding about like a madman,' he laughed. 'I could not even face my books today; I felt compelled to ride out.'

'I too,' she said. They were walking along together, he leading his horse. 'But is Morholm to be your only call today?'

He looked at her for a second, then laughed. 'No – I believe the Wainwrights are expecting me this morning.'

'Really?'

'Yes indeed – though with what feelings I am expected I daren't say.'

'I feel sure it is with delight and anticipation on one lady's part,' she said. He smiled. Small courtesies became warm and confidential in Mary; she said them because she meant them.

They had gone on a little way, talking easily and pleasantly, when a horse, fully saddled and bridled, came clopping, half-nervous, half-friendly, towards them from behind the hedge.

'Why, whose can this be? The animal is wet and shivering,' said Milton, trying to make the animal approach so he could grab its reins.

'Oh – I seem to remember that George came home on one of the carriage horses last night, yet Clarry found no extra one in the stables this morning. This must be it.'

Together they caught the bewildered, chilled horse which George had left to wander last night and gradually induced it to be led along with Milton's. At Morholm they took the horses to the stable and were turning for the house when the tall striding figure of Jarrett appeared from the direction of the village. He waved and hurried towards them.

'So, I've interrupted your secret meeting,' he smiled. 'Good morning to you, Miss Mary. I hope I am not calling too early?'

'No, indeed,' said Mary. As if he could be too early!

'Milton too! Glad to see you again. This is a happy meeting.'

As they walked to the house she and Milton explained about the stray horse. 'The poor beast must be fearfully bewildered,' said Jarrett. 'Have you seen George this morning?'

'No, he is still abed. I think he had better remain there for the present.'

'One must sympathize with him,' said Jarrett. 'It is all too easy, after having been heady with anticipation of some coming event, to throw oneself into it too rashly, and to consequently spoil one's enjoyment of it. And one must remember, George has been thrown into some confusion these last months, with the changes in his life. This must help account for his behaviour. One drinks a little too much, one becomes heated – it is so easy to do. I think it would be best if it were all forgotten. George was ever the most impetuous of us all. I feel sure a gentle word from those he holds dear, now and then, would allay his recklessness.'

Mary felt a pang at his words. 'Indeed, I do try, but he takes no heed of me. Come, talk of something else.'

Mary almost gasped aloud at the sight of George when he came downstairs: he was ghostly pale and dishevelled. It was a constrained and disapproving family that greeted him and Milton, prickly with discomfort and anxious to see Miss Wainwright, rose and said he must leave, and Jarrett did likewise.

George, not moving from the chair where he lolled, spoke for the first time. 'Did you not say you wished to see round the estate, Jarrett?'

'Er – yes, certainly.'

George rose suddenly and walked to the door. 'Then come. You have the time, I hope?' Without waiting for an answer he turned to Mary, who had risen also, reluctant even to lose sight of Jarrett. 'I think *you* have seen over the estate enough times, cousin. Do not trouble yourself to accompany us.' He was out of the room without another word. Jarrett, after paying his respects to all, with a special bow and a smile for Mary, followed, and Milton with him.

'Will you not come too, Milton?' said Jarrett, as they walked down the windy drive.

'Alas, no: I am engaged to call upon the Wainwrights this forenoon,' said Milton, moving towards the stables.

'Ah,' smiled Jarrett. 'Well, that is not an engagement I would prevail upon you to break. Goodbye, then.'

George and Jarrett walked out over the fields in silence, George a little way ahead, eyes bent to the ground. They came across Matthews the steward and George told him to join them. 'Mr Jarrett here wishes to look over the estate, and I am little appraised even of where our land lies, so you had better come with us, Matthews.'

Matthews was a brisk man in his fifties, with a florid face the purple-red colour of a washed-out beetroot and a way of walking on the outside of his feet which gave him an odd gait, as if at each step he took he changed his mind about which way he was going. They trudged across the gently dipping country south towards the woods at Upton, a last outer vestige of Rockingham Forest, and then east towards the edge of the wild marshy country of Helpston Heath and the flat moist fields near Peterborough. Here the drainage had failed with the recent heavy rain and the fields where they grew turnips were awash. Men were at work digging out the long geometric ditches which were clogged with rank silt. Presently George said he wanted to go no further and sat down on the grass in the lee of the hedgerow. There he covered his face with his hands and apparently fell into abstraction. Jarrett continued to speak with Matthews.

'And northward before you, sir, lies Fitzwilliam land. To your right is Sam Newman's tenancy. He's farmed there for years but he's failing, and can scarcely work the land. His wife's like to die and he seems to have lost his old spirit.'

'Surely it would be best to let the land go for fox-cover,' said Jarrett. ''Twould be more convenient for game.'

'I don't believe Mr Hardwick's a hunting man, sir,' put in Matthews mildly.

'No . . . no, of course,' said Jarrett. 'I think you may as well go back to your work, thank you, Mr Matthews. I expect we shall return to the house shortly.'

The old steward waddled off, and Jarrett turned to his friend. 'Well, George, shall we start back?'

George, after a moment, got up and without looking at him began walking towards Morholm. Jarrett followed.

Starlings, borne haphazardly on the wind, wheeled over them.

'Matthews tells me Newman is a poor tenant. Have you not thought of getting rid of him and letting the land go?' George glanced to where Jarrett indicated, then lowered his eyes again. 'No,' he said without expression. The figure of Mary came into view at the gate leading into the garden of Morholm.

'There is your charming cousin,' said Jarrett, waving his hat to her. 'You are lucky indeed to have her company every day.'

'Jarrett.'

They stopped.

George had spat the word out as if it were something nasty in his mouth. Without raising his eyes he went on: 'I wish to say something. I hope you'll listen.'

Jarrett stood still and looked at him, his handsome face slightly surprised. The wind tugged impatiently at the ribbon in his hair.

'I – I just hope – I damned well hope you mean it – because if you don't, if you're not sincere and – honourable in intent – I – I –'

George's face was crimson and covered in little beads of sweat. He could say no more and turned away, trembling.

'Your cousin awaits us,' said Jarrett quietly. 'Come, George, shall we keep her waiting all day?'

George did not move.

'I shall go then. She will be very disappointed that you will not rejoin her,' said Jarrett, and went on towards the house.

George remained where he was, motionless in the middle of the paddock that backed on to the garden. He lifted his head when Jarrett reached Mary, and saw her eager clutch at his hand, the smile lifted to his face, heard the warm throb of her voice, even from here. He watched them walk together to the gate, saw him set off through the village, saw her waving and waving to him, until he was out of sight, and long after. Eventually George began to make his way to the house.

He had reached the courtyard behind the stables when Kingsley appeared. 'I say, George,' he said, and hesitated.

'What is it?' said George, impatient and inattentive.

'I've just seen Amelia with frightfully red eyes. I thought I heard her crying earlier. I don't suppose you know if anything is amiss with her?'

George felt his heart dive into his entrails and lurch back again. He looked at Kingsley, but his cousin's face wore its usual sleepy expression.

'Why should I?'

Kingsley gave a slow, barely perceptible shrug, as a tortoise might make. 'I merely wondered. I wasn't aware there was anything at Morholm to make her unhappy, that is all. But perhaps someone else may find out.' He paused, briefly. 'Perhaps Mary may find out, don't you think? She is usually adept at winning people's confidence. If there were any cause for the girl's distress, I feel sure Mary would be most interested.'

George said nothing, but stared intensely at a point on the breast of Kingsley's scarlet riding-coat.

'Dull affair of yours last evening, don't you think?' went on Kingsley. 'I came back early too. There's more diversion to be had at home than at a ball, don't you find?'

George still did not answer, and presently Kingsley turned towards the stables. Then he checked and turned back again. 'Oh, I say, George, I was considering going into Stamford to order a new suit. Really, 'tis not fitting I should look like a scarecrow.'

'I'll give you my draft on Wiley's bank,' said George after a long time.

* * *

The Wainwrights' town-house in Stamford was full of glass and gilded mirrors so that it seemed wherever you looked you saw yourself reflected. Milton sat in a fiercely elegant drawing-room and took tea out of preposterously small and fragile tea-cups without handles, while silent footmen glided in and out with trays and cutlery so stealthily they might have been stealing them. Mrs Wainwright, resplendent in a rich brocade gown, her hair thick with powder and decorated with all sorts of combs and beads, her fat face made fatter by cosmetics, ruled over the morning from amongst cushions that matched her dress so cleverly that Milton thought she must change the furnishings with her outfit. Mr Wainwright, in an old coat with wide skirts and a cap covering his bald head, sat by the window with becoming insignificance and read a London newspaper. Elizabeth, in a pink silk of typically unnecessary fineness, sat next to Milton and looked beautiful and spoke to him now and then. Wilhelmina, as plain as her sister was lovely, did most of the talking, ignoring her mother's silencing looks. 'I hear you are a poet, Mr Milton, is it true? I have heard that poets are the most exquisite lovers, and I only wish someone would write me some verses – but all the gentlemen I know are perfect ogres who can scarce write their own names, I believe. But what am I talking of. I do run on so –' thereby convincing Milton that her fluent inanity was infinitely worse than Elizabeth's silence. But Mrs Wainwright was friendly enough, and her snobbishness, though always in evidence, was never directed at him, and if it had been he thought he would have tolerated it with Elizabeth at his side. They talked of the ball.

'A pretty evening in its modest fashion,' said Mrs Wainwright, 'but a pity Squire Hardwick behaved in such a boorish manner, though in confidence it was no more than I expected of him; and I was rather surprised at the ball's being held at all, so soon after old Mr Joseph's decease, and the family only just out of mourning; but then it is well known the family is declining, as most of these old families are, you will acknowledge, Mr Milton; they have only their pride left, though more than enough of that; and I don't doubt Mr Hardwick is an excellent gentleman, only he cannot control his liquor or his passions; and no matter what may be said to a gentleman's credit, to say that to his detriment is the worst thing one can. Of course, I am aware that Mr Milton is a friend of Mr Hardwick's, and mean no disrespect – but even Mr Hardwick's friends must allow . . .'

This he bore well too; but presently other callers arrived and quickly separated him from Elizabeth. The realization broke over him again – and he felt sad and sick with it – that other men were attracted by her and came to feast their eyes on her beauty as he did. Perhaps she had a string of hopeful lovers tied to her finger. But it seemed unlikely judging by her behaviour to the two young men who arrived, together with two young ladies whom he recognized from the ball last night. They were all fashionably dressed, elegantly bored with everything, and talked with an odd mixture of sentiment and callousness; they laughed much, wearily and inanely. From the snatches he observed of their conversation, when they drew off and left him with Mrs Wainwright, Elizabeth seemed somewhat out of her depth.

'Elizabeth, as you may imagine, Mr Milton, has many admirers,' said Mrs Wainwright. 'I think I can say with all modesty that my daughter attracts some of the most eligible men in the county to her side. But as to the matter of possible union with any of them – for matrimony, you will allow, is something a young lady such as she must look to at some time – as to that, I feel I should not press her. She is young; she has a wide choice; I think I should trust her to make her own decision wisely. Young ladies of fashion, I believe, should know their own minds; and I am not about to press upon her any match which is foreign to her tastes and preferences. Love is a thing much talked of in these times of ours, but in matters nuptial it too often, I fear, takes second place to material considerations. Marriages of convenience do work, in plenty, as you may observe anywhere,' perhaps Milton thought, there was some personal significance in her words, 'but I think, perhaps, they should be avoided when there is some reasonable alternative.'

And she gave him a smile much warmer than he had thought her capable of. They were prevented from pursuing the subject, however, by the arrival of an elderly couple who seemed to be particular friends of Mrs Wainwright, and who claimed all her attention, so Milton found himself talking to her husband. Mr Wainwright was of such a spare, shrivelled constitution that he seemed to have been systematically pinched all over as a baby and had been in a peevish humour ever since. He tapped a page of his newspaper. 'This business in the American colonies. What a deal of fuss over nothing. Put them in their place. What do we maintain troops there for, if not to put a bridle on their whining? One sharp blow is all it needs.'

He murmured something in reply but it was drowned by a loud burst of laughter from the group around Elizabeth; he heard her voice in it too, fractionally late. Mr Wainwright scowled in their direction. 'That Hugh Woodhouse again. Always some fop or other sniffing round my Elizabeth. Wish a few of 'em would draw off and look at Wilhelmina instead – I doubt we're ever going to get anyone to take her. You wouldn't know Woodhouse, would you, Milton? The fat fellow, there. I've no love for the man, but he is the son of a baronet, and it would be a worthwhile match for her. But I'm damned if I can tell who she's a mind for, if anybody: she might as well be made of stone. I just wish she'd nod her head one way or t'other. Let her marry Woodhouse and I'll be content: there'll be more peace at any rate. I suppose that would make her Lady Woodhouse some day. Hullo!

They're pointing at you, Milton. Seems they require an introduction.'

The two young women he had met last night were calling him over with suppressed giggles in their voices. He could tell they thought him a perfect yokel, and that, together with his grave face, had led them to seize on him to make fun. The women he knew as Miss Maria Graham and Miss Harriet Thackray: they were handsome, in a bold uncompromising way. Hugh Woodhouse was a big portly man, with a peculiarly heavy mouth and jaw – almost a muzzle – as if he had two whole sets of teeth in there, and he had all the confidence of a man with money, power and strength. Milton noticed that instead of a wig he wore his own hair, ribboned and powdered; men of fashion were beginning to abandon wigs in this way and Milton was glad he had never started wearing one. The other, a little rabbity man, who was appropriately called Mr Warren, had the reputation of a wit, though Milton would never have guessed it.

'Mr Milton, you're a scribbler, I hear?' said Miss Graham. 'D'you write love verses? I would dearly like to receive one. Come, do you, eh?'

'Maria, you fright, as if he would send one to you!' said Miss Thackray. 'I'm sure the gentleman has better taste. Or perhaps Elizabeth has received some such verses, eh, Elizabeth?'

Miss Wainwright, struggling between her natural embarrassment and an attempt at an affected laugh, looked uncomfortable and nearly choked.

'Ho, I see, Elizabeth, then they are not of the kind to be repeated, eh?' said Miss Thackray.

'Those are the best kind!' said Miss Graham, and there was a roar of laughter.

'Bigod, Maria, if that's the kind of thing you want, I can scribble a few suggestions that might interest you!' bellowed Woodhouse, and the laughter rang round again. This time

Milton saw Elizabeth laugh, copying their affected manner. He did not join in.

Talk went on in this way, but he recoiled further and further from it. It sickened him to see the refined, reserved Elizabeth trying to join in. They talked of the ball, and how agreeable it was to have George Hardwick in the country, because there was simply no one who could make a laughing-stock of himself so well as he: and Woodhouse said, in a supercilious way, he wished he had been there – it sounded a most amusing little affair: and Mr Warren said had they heard that old Rowland of Matherby's mistress had had a stillborn child, and they gave it to the housekeeper to dispose of, only her lunatic son, who was twice as mad as everyone in Bedlam put together, had got hold of it, and was carrying it around like a doll, and wouldn't let anyone take it from him, and Rowland had been heard to make a joke about 'The family name literally being dragged through the mud' – which anecdote they found extremely amusing, though it made Milton feel sick – until finally he took his leave. Their presence prevented him from speaking individually to Elizabeth, though he ached to, so he bowed and thanked Mrs Wainwright and left. Their patronizing remarks followed him, indiscreetly loud.

2

Thomas Jarrett was soon invited to dinner at Morholm: at Mary's suggestion, though Aunt Catherine needed little prompting. He arrived, a little late, in a white coat and sober cravat, handsome but, Mary thought, looking tired. 'Is your father's health still not secure, Mr Jarrett?' she asked him at dinner, her eyes searching his face. He smiled at her, briefly but warmly. 'He is pretty much an invalid, Miss Mary. He needs much tending,' and she wondered at the effort that his good spirits must cost him.

Old Daniel had not had such a polite listener for years: and when he began to recount his most whopping stories, particularly his meeting the Duke of Marlborough – who was dead before he was born – Jarrett flashed Mary a wry glance so that she almost choked suppressing her laughter. After dinner Daniel, in his sweetest mood, called on Mary to play the spinet and sing.

'Very well, uncle,' she said, getting up, 'but you must promise me you will not weep when I play "The Soldier's Lament".'

'That I can't promise!' said Daniel, getting out his handkerchief, and there was a general laugh.

Her father had been musical and had taught her to play: it was her sole legacy from that old life. She played Daniel's favourite and then a short canzonetta and then called on Jarrett to sing with her. 'Come, Mr Jarrett, this is an easy part – see, you come in here.'

He accepted with good grace – 'It seems an ill reward for your hospitality to hear my singing, but on your heads be it' – and when they had sung a Scottish air and been applauded Mary looked around for George.

He had retreated to a corner with the Stamford Mercury and did not look up when she touched his shoulder. 'George, will you not join us? This song has three parts, and –'

'I don't sing,' he said, his face a little flushed. She was determined not to be upset. 'But it is a small part – you and I and Mr Jarrett can –'

'Sing both parts yourself, cousin,' he snapped, suddenly getting up and going to the door. 'You ought to be able to do that.'

She looked at him, and hurt was quickly succeeded by wrath. She turned without a word and went back to Jarrett at the spinet.

George was gone, slamming the door behind him.

Henry Milton was also at that moment walking out of a dinner party. He had gone to the Wainwrights' fresh and expectant; he had seen what he inwardly feared, Elizabeth giving all her attention to her fashionable friends, hanging on their every word and trying, pitifully as he saw it, to imitate them; he had been all but ignored by her; and so, disgusted and miserable, he had taken his leave as soon as was possible. Going into the Black Bull in St Mary's Street to get his horse, the smell of ale and smoke – not an odour that usually attracted him – touched some nerve newly exposed by his mood and shot him through with an impulse to get roaring drunk. He entered the crowded tap-room, with its walls lined with pewter and beer barrels piled up to the ceiling. The air here was so thick and rank with tobacco smoke, with the stench of sweat and grimy bodies and clothes, of beery breath and cheap spirits, that he moved through it almost like a swimmer. He finally reached an empty bench and ordered brandy; he disliked the stuff but some perverse instinct within him told him to feed the fire of hate. He had been drinking long enough for a haze like a veil to appear a few inches before his eyes when he saw

George enter the room. His face wore a pale, drained look and there was a hard, bitter glint in his eyes that Milton recognized. When he caught sight of Milton his features registered only a mild flicker of surprise, as if he were in the grip of some more overwhelming emotion. He too ordered brandy and joined Milton.

'Becoming a tavern-crawler like me, Milton?' he grunted. 'I thought you were dining with the Wainwrights.'

'I was,' said Milton, wondering whether to tell George why he had left; but his friend said nothing more, and seemed occupied with his own thoughts, so he remained silent.

Presently George lifted his head and said, as if it had just occurred to him: 'Is not life the most – the most damned, bewildering, frustrated –'

Milton was ready to agree with him in his present mood, and nodded before George had finished.

'Why do we trouble ourselves with it?' went on George. 'Why – why can we not merely shut our souls away from all the – ridiculous business? But we cannot. The closest we may get is to be drunk – enclose ourselves in the fr-friendly screens of liquor.' He motioned the inn-keeper over. 'So let us do so, while I still have a little money in my pocket that my family has not appropriated.'

Milton only remembered the rest of the evening as a kind of tableau of fragmented, disparate elements: he remembered drinking, and drinking, until the bitter stuff flowed down his throat almost unnoticed; he remembered the smoke in the room growing thicker and thicker like a fog, but it no longer irritated his eyes, for the brandy numbed him; he remembered talking to George almost ceaselessly, saying the first thing that came into his head, and he remembered George talking too, in the desultory, rapid, often witty way he had when drunk; he remembered their leaning together closely in order to hear each other's words above the general noise, and several times bumping heads and laughing absurdly because it did not seem to hurt. Things after that he began to remember with less precision; George suddenly stood up and lifted his arm, like a puppet being taken up by a puppeteer, and said: 'Why, look, there's William – William, Mary's brother,' and went over to a little knot of men and women by the hearth. 'How are you, cousin?' said George, with the uncomfortable heartiness of intoxication, slapping William on the shoulder. Mary's brother was a grinning, simian young man of twenty, shabbily dressed. He seemed a little surprised at his cousin's friendliness and smiled uncertainly. 'Have a drink with us, my dear fellow,' George went on, pouring brandy shakily into William's mug.

'Thank you, indeed, George, I will,' said William, not about to question such an invitation. 'I hope my sister is well?'

'Blooming . . . blooming,' said George, 'but how goes it with you? We have seen nothing of you in any age.'

'Well, to speak truth to you, cousin,' said William, 'I fear I am in somewhat pressing straits.'

'Indeed? T-tell me.'

'Well,' went on William, encouraged, 'this gentlewoman at whose house I lodge – an excellent woman, but a severe – has taken it into her head that she must have her rent by tomorrow, just – would you believe it – when my finances are at their lowest. You know how it is with these matters. I cannot pay – and I fear as a result I may be homeless tomorrow.'

An idea, small and shabby enough in itself but polished up by his drunkenness into brilliance, sprang up in George's mind.

'What is this sum you owe?'

'Oh,' William shrugged, 'a paltry sum – a mere three guineas.'

'Three guineas indeed?' George began to fumble in his pocket. 'Hardly worth the mentioning. Here we are. 'Tis a pretty pass for the world to come to when a man suffers for want of three guineas.' He pressed the money on William, who was not slow in accepting. Milton, who did not believe William for a moment, remembered seeing the young man shake the coins from his sweaty fingers into his pocket; they reminded him of the feet of a queer lizard he had seen on display at a travelling fair – they seemed to have the same stickiness.

'A damned unreasonable woman she sounds, William,' went on George. 'But then all d-damned women are unreasonable, don't you think?'

'Indeed, George, she's not the most agreeable creature – and as a matter of fact I have been looking about me for new accommodation.'

'Oh? Then I tell you what.' George laid a hand on William's shoulder, swaying – 'you shall come and stay at Morholm until you find a suitable situation.'

'Oh, really, cousin, I –'

'No, no, no,' said George, 'you shall come. You have seldom visited the old pile, even as a child. We'll make room. Everybody else you care to name is there.' A shadow of unhappiness crossed his face. 'So come! When may I expect you?'

'Well, George, as you insist. I fear I shall not be able to arrive tomorrow, but the day after, I hope.'

'Excellent! And –'

He stopped abruptly, his eyes fixed on a figure behind William.

'Good Lord! Amelia?'

A girl, dressed in a plain cotton frock and with a mug in her hand, turned and looked at him with the face of Amelia Seddon. And yet it was not Amelia's face, for this girl had a clear rosy complexion, whereas Amelia was spotty and sallow. Beyond that there was no difference.

'Beg pardon, sir? Oh, my, of course – you're thinking of

me sister, Amelia. People are always mistaking us, one f'
the other. You wouldn't be Squire Hardwick, now?'

George nodded, still amazed at the resemblance.

'Of course. I heard tell she was serving at your house, sir.
I'm Beth Seddon, see; we're twins. Our own father used to
have trouble telling us apart, you know, specially when he
was well in his cups, and saw four of us!'

The group she was drinking with laughed at this, and
George and Milton, initial surprise over, laughed too. And
the next period of time – it might have been an hour, it
might have been two – was the one Milton had most trouble
in remembering. Somehow, he recalled, he and George
joined the party which included William and Beth Seddon
and various unremarkable Stamford characters, and though
they were the sort of people he had never imagined himself
consorting with, he remembered laughing and drinking with
them as if they were his lifelong friends. Then he remembered
George looking at the girl Beth in an odd way, with a kind
of feverish half-smile he did not at all like; then somehow –
for a kind of soporific heaviness was settling on him, like
some loathsome dust, obscuring everything to a dreamy
haze – somehow George and Beth had their arms around
each other and she was, innocently enough, kissing him and
giggling, not appearing to take it very seriously; but George's
face was rather more intense. Milton could not guess the
thought that was racing round George's head at that moment, and physically manifesting itself in a throbbing at his
temples: yes, he had done it with one twin, why not the
other? She too was every bit as willing. The irony of it was
too amusing. For the moment all he could see was the
absurd, hilarious side. The group were beginning to empty
their mugs and button their coats. 'I'd better be going, too,
Squire,' the girl was saying. 'Then let us escort you out,'
said George, and he and Milton went with them out into
air so cold after the heat of the tap-room it was like a slap

in the face. William and most of the others, after many slurred farewells and brash parting jokes, departed one way down the street and into the darkness; Beth and another girl turned to go a different way. George retained his hold on Beth's arm. 'Come, Beth, no last kiss?' he said.

'That one was supposed to be the last, Squire,' she laughed.

'Are y'coming, Beth?' said the other girl, already a little way off. 'I've to be up early on the morrow.'

'Oh, you go on, Susan, I'll come after you in a minute.' The girl went on and her footsteps died away.

Milton, feeling dazed and increasingly sick, leant against the wall and heard the two kissing for a few minutes, Beth occasionally making half-hearted attempts to pull away but showing no real desire to do so. Then, abruptly, he saw George pull himself away from the girl's embrace with a wrench. Through the fog of his intoxication Milton's sight was unsteady, but George seemed to be shuddering with real loathing. The girl put out her hand to touch him and said, 'Come on, Squire, what's to do?' but he shrugged her off violently. 'Get away from me,' he muttered. 'Get *away*!'

The girl looked startled for a moment: then her expression changed to one of pure contempt. 'Poor bastard,' she said. 'You pitiful bastard. You should know, Squire, not to start a job you can't finish.' She turned with a laugh to Milton. 'You'd best take your friend home, sir. 'Tis past his bedtime.'

They listened to her footsteps receding in the distance. Silence fell, and the stars watched the two men standing in the streets of Stamford below. Milton put his hand on George's arm. He had had enough of this. 'Come on, George, let us go.'

'You must despise me, Milton,' said George. 'For before God I despise myself.' Suddenly – it made Milton start – George screamed, 'DAMN ALL THE HARDWICKS TO HELL!' long and at the top of his voice. Then he began to run. Milton stood transfixed a moment, the shout ringing in his ears and echoing round the streets as if the whole town were repeating George's words in an obedient chorus. Eventually he stirred and began to run after his friend. He seemed now to have lost all voluntary power of action: he did not know why he was running, it was an impulse born of instinct. But in that absurd gallop down the darkened street, with the rush of cold wind on his face and the hard smack of the cobblestones on his feet he grew sober again; and at the top of Barn Hill he came across the Wainwrights' house, one chimney standing up against the sky. There were several lights about the house, yellow and warm with a glow of peace and domesticity. It seemed the guests were still there. He too might have been amongst them still, if he had not left straight after dinner in rage and jealousy. Surely it would have been better to stay with those fashionable creatures than to spend the evening in this manner.

The harsh frightening noise of much glass breaking stirred him from his thoughts. Some distance further on in the square George was hurling stones into the darkened windows of his great-uncle Horace Hardwick's town-house. He was cursing. Already two whole windows were destroyed, and George was stooping for another stone. Lights were appearing in Horace's house.

Milton ran to George's side and caught his arm, but already the stone had crashed through a pane, sending splinters tinkling all over the street. There was the sound of voices and footsteps inside. Milton began to drag George away. 'Come along, George, let's get our horses and be off quickly,' he hissed.

The door opened, framing the figures of Horace and a servant in yellow light. Milton tried to hurry the reluctant footsteps of his friend. George's curses were coming in occasional gasps, in an ebbing fury. Milton glanced back over his shoulder at Horace's house, but the old man was calling his servant back in, and Milton heard him say: 'Do not trouble, Forrest. It is that disgrace of a great-nephew of mine — our new head of the family,' (this with a snort). 'I will attend to it in the morning.'

It was a long and laborious business for Milton, dragging the half-defiant, half-contrite George back to the inn for their horses and persuading him to mount up and go home. By the time he reached his own home at Helpston a baleful grey dawn was breaking over the Heath.

When the slow, misty autumn dawn finally lightened Mary's room she was already up and dressed and looking at herself in the small mirror on her dresser. It had never occurred to her to examine her face for beauty before, and now she studied her reflection with something of the curiosity of a new acquaintance. Her mouth was over-generous, her cheek and jaw too strong . . . it was hopeless really. But the bright sparkle in the green depths of her eyes was unmistakable and even startled her. She hoped, her stomach fluttering, that Mr Jarrett had understood her last night when she had mentioned her habit of going for a walk by the stream every morning. To be disappointed now would be unbearable.

At last she left the house, earlier than usual but unable to rest a moment longer: but when she emerged from the trees that screened the parsonage into the low open field that ran east to Borough Fen he was there. He was standing on the narrow wooden footbridge that spanned the stream, his back to her, rather bowed as if deep in thought. He did not hear her approach and when she touched his arm he jumped.

'I did not mean to startle you — ' she began as he spun round, and then stopped, stirred and troubled by the intensity in his eyes as he looked at her.

'You've come,' he said. 'When you said that each morning you . . . I hoped . . .'

She turned her head, unable to trust herself to look at him any longer. 'The old women in the village say you can tell your fortune by watching the sticks in the stream. Was that what you were doing?'

'I was watching the moorhens,' he said, 'until one decided I was not respectable and they bolted with a great fuss. I must say my pride is a little wounded,' he added.

She laughed, and then tinglingly aware that he still gazed at her returned his look. His face was as handsome as ever but there were dark smudges of tiredness under his eyes. Moved by anxiety she said, 'Mr Jarrett, are you not well? Tell me.'

'I am well, indeed,' he said. 'But my father is not, Miss Mary. He is failing. And with him, his business. Large debts he has built up, I would never have believed. He is not sound enough in mind or body to deal with it himself, and so I must do it. It means a deal of work, a deal of travelling. Sometimes I am wearied to despair. But all the time, listening to old Thornton Wiley's complaining, or Trent's accounts, which I fear are Greek to me, always I think of you.' He smiled nervously. 'You intrude on my business affairs most impudently, Miss Mary.' Her face was averted again, staring down at the bubbling stream. 'And now I fear *I* have been impudent.'

'No, Mr Jarrett,' she said, and her hands tightened on the wooden rail of the bridge. 'No, you have not been impudent.'

He followed her gaze down into the water. 'Well?' he said.

She looked up at him, not understanding.

'You said you can tell fortunes by the sticks in the stream,' he said. 'Will you not tell me mine?'

The flat landscape seemed to be spinning around her and she tried to stop herself colouring and blushed even harder.

'I think,' she said, staring without seeing at the water scurrying over the rocks, 'I believe . . . it will be a good one, Tom.' She was aware that he had taken her hand and that she was returning the pressure. 'I hope so. And I believe mine will be too.'

Presently they turned and crossed the bridge and made their way across the fields, arm-in-arm, towards the village. She breathed as if for the first time the sweet smoky air and gazed at the autumnal country around them, her country, the one she loved for all its uncompromising starkness: the heavy clay earth stripped of crops, the bare elms looking gaunt and shivering against the endless sky hung with ragged banners of purple cloud, Aysthorpe church tower itself like some thick, stunted tree-trunk. She did not see the figure of George in the distance, leaning on the fence at the back of Morholm garden.

It had been a humiliating session for George that morning. Horace Hardwick, realizing the cost of replacing his broken windows, had chosen for once to concern himself with Morholm and had ridden over early to 'attend to' George. 'It is not the cost that concerns me, great-nephew, it is the principle,' Horace had said when George had told him he would pay for the damage. 'I object strongly to having the good name of the Hardwicks thrown, flouted in my face by – by –'

'A young puppy?' George had put in. 'Who is now master of Morholm . . .' That had angered them. Soon they were all saying their piece – Aunt Catherine, Mrs Peach, Daniel – '. . . hoped you were the man the family has been waiting for . . .'

George put the cant from his mind. Now that he was out, he thought, he ought to attend to the estate; go and see Matthews, visit his tenants, inspect the livestock, superintend the new drainage. He felt little inclined for it, but it might occupy his mind. He watched the figures of Jarrett and Mary walk slowly down to the village. At least he had been spared the humiliation of being scolded in front of her.

He walked over to Matthews' gatehouse with a heavy tread.

As he came on to the path that skirted the gatehouse and led to the north road he saw Kingsley approaching on horseback. 'Ah, I say, George,' he said, dismounting and leading Raleigh up to him.

'What is it?' George looked down into the plump bland face. There was a trace of an expression on it that disturbed him.

Since the night of the ball and his observation of George in Amelia's room Kingsley had done a good deal of thinking, and his confidence had grown. With the rogue's eye for the roots of unhappiness he had descried the influence Mary had on George's feelings, and realized that he knew something that would throw George entirely out of Mary's favour. And he foresaw, too, the barrage of scorn and abuse George would get from the others if it were known. This could be put to excellent use. It was time to be more explicit.

'Er – George, I wish you might speak to Amelia. She is becoming most neglectful. I cannot remember the last time my bed linen was changed. She is acting most oddly, weeping half the time.'

'Why cannot you deal with her, if you have a complaint?'

'Oh – I would not presume to interfere – it is you who has the most influence over her, I think.'

'What do you mean?'

There was a long pause. Kingsley's horse stamped and tossed his head, as if it found the conversation unpleasant and did not want to hear any more.

'Must we keep up this pretence any longer, George?'

Kingsley's voice was as cold and hard as his heart.

George swallowed. 'I – I will have a word with her,' he said mechanically.

'Oh – and another thing,' Kingsley went on, 'old Sir Samuel at Deeping has offered me the chance of a fine hack for forty guineas. I really cannot miss such an opportunity.'

Suddenly George wanted to hit Kingsley, to mark that deceptively sleepy, boyish face, and make the blood flow from it. But that would be the shortest step to his opening his mouth –

'Then – then you had better call on my banker.'

'Thank you, George.'

Kingsley went on his way.

That afternoon Julia made her weekly visit to the house of Thornton Wiley, the Stamford banker. Mr Wiley had three daughters, Jane, Kate and Constance, who were the nearest things to friends Julia had; she did not really care for them, but her mother had been a great friend of Mrs Wiley, and so, obedient to typically Hardwickian tradition, and for want of anything else to do, she was a regular caller there.

They were joined at dinner that day by Francis Sedgmoor, the eldest son of the Hardwick lawyer. Young Mr Francis, as he was called, was an intelligent, well-looking young man who suffered from a slight stammer and had a cleft between his brows which gave him a quizzical expression. He was known as a local 'catch', for his father had done well for himself, and the Wiley girls were quick to make up to him; but there was an added piquancy to their pleasure in his company today, for it was a long-standing subject of gossip with them – and it certainly seemed to be true – that young Mr Francis had a taking for Julia. Whether it made any impression on Julia it was hard to tell from her brown expressionless face, but throughout dinner Sedgmoor, placed next to her, pressed food on her, asked after her family, complimented her on her looks (to the smothered giggles of the Misses Wiley) and put his earnestness as a suitor beyond dispute.

'I declare, Julia,' said Kate when they had retired to the drawing-room and Mrs Wiley, a peaceable woman, had taken up her needlework, 'you have quite made a conquest of poor Mr Francis.'

'Why do you say "poor"?' said Julia. 'He will be a rich man, I hear.'

'You are provoking, Julia. I did not mean poor in that way.'

'Of course you must not take it too much to heart, you know, Julia,' said Jane, who as the eldest liked to patronize, 'for he has the politest manners of any gentleman in town, and a girl who has not had admirers before may find her head turned by them.'

Julia was inured to this sort of thing, and she allowed herself a small secret smile of pleasure that underneath it all they were jealous of her.

'Well, for my part I dearly wish that something would come of it,' said Constance, the youngest, who was sixteen and good-natured and resignedly afraid that she was over-shadowed by her sisters. 'There has not been a wedding in town for so long. I thought Elizabeth Wainwright would have settled on someone by now. What a marriage that will be!'

'She has set her cap at Hugh Woodhouse, Sir Geoffrey's son,' said Jane. 'She is insufferably proud and thinks she belongs in his country mansion, and appears not to mind taking second place to his dogs and horses.'

'The wedding would be no pleasure anyhow, for we would have her dreadful mother quizzing us as if we were cottagers,' said Kate. 'Julia, why does not your brother the Squire marry? Though I hear he is sowing his wild oats plentifully enough!'

There was a general laugh and a look of reproof from Mrs Wiley.

'Oh, yes, make him marry, Julia,' said Constance, 'I would dearly love to see inside Morholm.'

'You may not be disappointed in that,' said Julia casually. 'Since the ball there have been obvious signs of an attachment between my cousin Mary and Mr Thomas Jarrett.' As she said it she trembled a little and she had to lay down her teacup carefully.

For a moment this news silenced even the sisters, and there were only gasps. Then Kate snapped, 'Thomas Jarrett . . . the lucky creature! How I hate her!'

'Tell us more, Julia,' said Constance. 'When is the wedding to be? Is it all fixed?'

'There is no more to tell,' said Julia, and her eyes were stony beneath her dark brows. 'Is there nothing in your silly heads but weddings?'

'Don't be cross, Julia,' said Jane, 'tell us. Has Mr Jarrett —'

'Sshh!' hissed Constance, for the door had opened and there with Mr Wiley was Thomas Jarrett himself.

'Well, and what are you little fools staring at?' growled Mr Wiley. 'While you sit chattering I have business to attend to. To keep you in your wretched finery. Come through to the front office, Mr Jarrett, where we shall be away from these hyenas and can hear ourselves think.'

He stumped past them and Jarrett followed, saying good-day to each of them in turn. Julia did not acknowledge his greeting.

In fact she said nothing more for the rest of her visit: but when it was time for her to go, and a servant showed her out through the now empty front office, she noticed that on Mr Wiley's desk Jarrett had accidentally left behind his snuffbox. It was a neat enamelled box with the initials T.S.J. on it, and it was the work of a moment for her to scoop it up and slip it inside her muff.

Clarry, as usual, accompanied her on the way home, riding a few paces behind her. He did not see her feverishly pressing the little box against her cheek: but he could hardly fail to notice, with astonishment, when she suddenly leant back in the saddle and hurled the object with savage violence into the bushes.

3

Mary thought every visitor who arrived at Morholm now was Thomas Jarrett, and it was a not entirely pleasant surprise when she ran downstairs one morning at the sound of the door to find her brother William standing with his baggage in the hall.

She had spent the weeks since the ball in a dream-like, almost oblivious state, a state where a rarefied joy was constantly with her, to be marvelled at and turned over in the hands like an infinitely beautiful and precious gem. Time spent without Tom was strange, a kind of no-time, a void, such that when she looked back she could scarcely even remember it: she could only sit in her room or walk about the country, trying to hurry the empty minutes by. Even the housekeeping she went about in a distracted manner, hardly knowing what she was doing.

One thing was for sure: it was not as she had read in the novels, the sentimental novels for which Mrs Peach had a weakness. She had read *Sir Charles Grandison* and thought it very foolish: *The Man of Feeling* had made her laugh out loud. Love was not that tinkling elegant business, she knew now: it was richer, darker, and strange. Her only wish was that she could share her happiness with her cousin George: but life at Morholm seemed barely tolerable to him. They saw little of him, and he spoke less.

She could not feel glad at the sight of her brother: he was much changed. 'Cess take me, sister,' he cried as she came down to greet him, 'you ha' got a woman's figure on you at last.' He wore a wide-brimmed hat and his hair loose in what he thought was a very sporting fashion.

'What brings you here, William?'

'Why, didn't you know? Cousin George invited me. What a dear fellow he is, and what a hothead!'

'How – how have you been living, brother?'

'Inquisitive miss! Why, as a gentleman of leisure. A smart fellow like me does not want for means. And what of you – I hear you are being courted. I did not think you had it in you, sister. What snares have you laid to trap some poor fellow, eh?' He laughed hoarsely. 'But where are the Hardwick brood? Let me greet 'em.'

They were in the winter parlour, and having an argument with George.

'I tell you, nephew, I want a carriage today,' Aunt Catherine was saying. 'Why we cannot set up a carriage of our own I don't know. I am tired of riding, and besides, we cannot have the Townsends thinking we cannot afford to travel otherwise than on horseback.'

'We can't,' snapped George.

'Oh, by the by, George,' said Kingsley, 'it turned out that Sir Samuel had another fellow after that horse, so he pushed me up to fifty. I trust you did not mind?'

George's lips tightened as if in sudden pain. 'No, of course,' he said in a low voice.

It was then that William came in.

'Why, William,' said Aunt Catherine, 'how come you here? And with baggage too.'

Oh, God, thought George, I forgot about him coming. 'Oh, yes – I met him in Stamford – he is looking for new accommodation – I invited him to stay at Morholm in the meantime.' God, how drunk I must have been! One more leech on my back. Why on earth did I do it? To please Mary, I suppose. What a mess.

'Why were we not told, George?' said his aunt. 'Of course, I shall have to do all the arranging, as ever.'

'Turning Morholm into a lodging-house, George?' said Daniel.

William stood grinning and trying to look very rakish through this. Mary watched him dubiously. He had never been very trustworthy and all in all she could not understand why George had invited him. Unless he had done it to spite her.

'Of course,' said William, 'if I am not welcome, I can easily . . .'

'No, indeed, 'tis not your fault, William,' said Aunt Catherine, with a significant glance at George, who was slumped in a chair with a frowning, weary face. 'You are welcome, I'm sure, if the master of the house sees fit to invite you, even if he tells no one of it. Nothing is prepared – and I must have Reynolds set another place for dinner – and there! I asked dear Mr Jarrett to dine, when I met him yesterday, and so he will be coming too –'

'Oh, but he will not mind being put off,' said Mary eagerly. 'I can walk over to Bromswold now and tell him. Mr Jarrett would not mind.'

George leapt from his seat and turned on her. 'Oh, naturally your precious, agreeable Jarrett will not mind! Oh, *do* let me go and call on him and make my simpering calf-eyes at him and fawn at his feet! You are so pathetically obvious, cousin!'

Mary felt tears spring to her eyes, but they seemed to bring anger with them. 'Is mockery all you are fit for, George? I sometimes think it is a pity *you* cannot show a little of that decency of Mr Jarrett's! And is that not why you mock it, because you so wholly lack it?' Passion had seized her now and she could not stop. 'God, I have been so mistaken in you, George. I had hoped . . . But at least now I see what you are really like. Thank you for showing me.'

'Why, damn you, Mary –' he began, but she had already run from the room.

* * *

It was not until that day that Milton plucked up enough courage to call on the Wainwrights. The previous day he had spent in agonies; old Mr Horace had undoubtedly seen him with George two nights ago, that wretched disgraceful drunken night, and though he himself had smashed no windows he thought Horace must have condemned him merely for being involved in such a business; and the old man was on good terms with the Wainwrights, he knew. If he had told them . . . what would Elizabeth think of him? He could hardly bear the pain of such a speculation, but neither could he face the next call at their house.

Yet soon the discomfort of delay, and ignorance of his fate, became heavier than the terror of the prospective call, and so that morning found him seeking and winning an audience alone with Mr and Mrs Wainwright. Mr Wainwright, seated in a chimney-corner (Milton could not help reflecting on the absurdity of making a chimney-corner grandiose, as this was with rococo wood-carvings), wore his habitual expression, that of an animal caged because of its sullen temper, but on the overfed face of his wife, where there was usually an expression of aloof politeness, was a look cold and uncompromising. Milton's small reserve of hope began to drain away.

He decided that he had better make a clean breast of the whole thing; and so, speaking in a grave, submissive tone, he said that he guessed from her demeanour that the lady had heard report of his recent conduct in Stamford that placed him in a bad light, and in view of the petition he had come to make to her (it seemed natural to address himself to Mrs Wainwright alone, so dominant was her presence) he saw fit to present his own account with no evasions or euphemisms. It was true that after leaving this house he had met his friend Mr Hardwick of Morholm at the Black Bull Inn, and there had allowed the temptations of liquor around him, which he was not in the habit of indulging, and a certain selfish and needless melancholy of spirit, to lead him into a disgraceful state of intoxication, under which he was sure inside the inn he had acted in a slovenly and boorish manner; but once outside again, he had striven to regain a modicum of sobriety and decency, and had so far succeeded as to have done his best to prevent the acts of vandalism committed by Mr Hardwick on his great-uncle's house. If this was not enough, he went on, to lift him from the shadow of Mrs Wainwright's disapproval, then in view of the intimate nature of the suit he wished to press, he would take his leave.

Milton stopped, a little breathless, and realized how stiff and pompous he must have sounded. The humour of his abasing himself thus to a woman he despised was not lost on him: so this was what love had brought him to. But to his relief the large ugly smile spread across her face.

'I am sure, Mr Milton, we may forget completely an affair in which yours was a relatively blameless part.'

'Ay, he sputters it out well enough,' grunted Mr Wainwright, and went back to his newspaper.

'And now,' said Mrs Wainwright, 'I think I may guess at your suit: you have taken a fancy to Elizabeth, and wish to try for her hand.'

Milton, rather surprised at her mode of expression, stammered his assent.

'Well, indeed, Mr Milton – and Mr Wainwright joins his voice to mine in this – you have my full permission to woo her, and win her, if you can do it. No doubt, Mr Milton, you think me a worldly woman; and I know that you have nothing to offer my daughter in the way of fortune. I own it would give me great pleasure to see Elizabeth united with a knight, a baronet, whatever. But it would give me greater pleasure to see her united with one in whose company she was happiest. Whether you are to be that one, Mr Milton, I cannot say; neither can I say whether worldly considerations or the simple power of love will finally sway Elizabeth – she is not a demonstrative child, as you may know, Mr Milton. I dare say you are surprised at what I have said: but it is a great deal of thought and experience that has led me to the conclusion that no amount of money and fashion can take the place of matrimonial felicity. And now, shall we go into the drawing-room, and see Elizabeth?'

For the remainder of his call there Milton's feelings were a mixture of delight and guilt. Delight, because he was free to court his goddess, and today, looking more beautiful than ever, she seemed pleased to see him, and talkative, and friendly, and confiding: and guilt, because he realized the ugly prejudice of his early impressions of Mrs Wainwright. He had blinded himself to the genuine warmth that still survived in her. Eventually – it seemed but a few minutes – it was time for him to go. Could it be that he saw a similar reluctance to part in Miss Wainwright's perfect face, as he took his leave? Or was it his own love deluding him?

He could not tell – but he hoped.

It was an iron-hard December, and horses' hoofs rattled on the frozen earth as if on cobbles. In the mornings the fields were covered in a chill wet mist that sometimes came only as high as the waist; often at a drenching, violet dawn Mary would see the threshers going off to their work as strange legless, truncated creatures. As the day went on, darkening instead of brightening, flurries of stinging sleet came horizontally off the fens, penetrating hoods and cloaks. The pump in the yard froze, and in the stables Kingsley's dogs huddled together in a mangy heap. When Morholm had been built in the year of the accession of James I by Geoffrey St John Hardwick for his new bride Anne-Margaret Warboys its heavy Barnack stone and timbers had been laid with an eye to the cruelty of the Fenland winters: but the passing of a hundred and seventy years had taken its toll. The shutters leaked and chill draughts whistled constantly down the two dark upstairs passages with their fumed oak panelling. The heavy drapes at the windows of the winter parlour at the back of the house billowed and flapped, and often when Mary rose in the morning she had to crack the ice in her water-jug. The skies were sprinkled with wheeling black shapes, rooks and crows and starlings on their way to the reedy banks of the icy streams and meres. The flood plains of the Welland and the Nene valleys froze and one afternoon Mary went with a party of villagers to skate on the frozen meadows north of the river near Peterborough. Only the dykes were unsafe and she stayed there with them until a molten coppery sun dipped over the horizon dragging rust-coloured stains across the ice and firing the distant towers of the cathedral.

In Stamford the usual fair was held, and George gave the servants at Morholm the day off to go to it. The family had all been invited to dinner by Thomas Jarrett that day, including William, who was staying at Morholm for Christmas; though George had declined, saying, 'I hate dining out.'

Milton, in alliance with Mary, tried to persuade him to go, concerned about his way of life; but he knew he was out of favour with George at the moment. When Milton mentioned George's health and low spirits, his friend dismissed the notion that he should care about anything enough for it to make him unhappy. 'It is the natural state of mortal man to be wretched, Milton, as you will find out when your foolish infatuation fizzles out as all "love" does.' In compensation for the indifferent reception Milton's calls got from George, Mary always greeted him kindly and they found a pleasant friendship growing between them. They were both eager young lovers, and had an immediate sympathy.

* * *

The Morholm party came the quarter of a mile to Bromswold in a hired carriage, at Aunt Catherine's insistence – 'for such a smart wide drive, 'tis a pity to waste it'; and Jarrett, standing in the doorway, obligingly affected admiration for their grand entrance so as not to disappoint them; with an open smile of welcome and a kind word for everyone, and a special warm smile for Mary; and apologies for the absence of his father, who was rather too poorly to bear company, but who sent them his regards; and many expressions of disappointment at George's still not being persuaded to come. And as he led them into his comfortable parlour there was not one of them there but thought Thomas Jarrett the most delightful gentleman they had ever met.

But only Mary guessed his exhaustion. After a morning of the usual work of salvaging his father's once-prosperous wool business – meetings with Trent the steward, interviews with irate creditors and bankers, and audiences with the scarcely less irate employees at the mill – he had come home in midafternoon to find his father unconscious in his chair, a bowl of gruel upset all over the floor. These fits were growing more frequent and Dr Villiers' purges and doses of Peruvian bark seemed to do little good. The old man was incontinent now and he made a noisome burden as Jarrett carried the hunched figure in his frogged velvet coat gone shiny with wear upstairs to his bed. The strain was apparent on the young man's face as he welcomed them. While Aunt Catherine was making a great to-do of removing her cloak Mary squeezed his hand secretly. 'God bless you,' he breathed.

There was no light visible in Morholm. George was sitting in darkness in the library. One candle burnt by the side of the bed in Grandmother Hardwick's room, and the heavy curtains were drawn. Mrs Reynolds, who had stayed to tend her, sat and sewed by the sickly light. It was in this peaceful atmosphere that the ancient lady in the bed had a seizure that convulsed her small body and made her gasp and cry out, clutching at her breast. Mrs Reynolds started up and grasped the trembling, knobbly hand. Grandmother Hardwick's sallow old face went pale and bluish. Mrs Reynolds, with little puffs of distress, hesitated, then hurried to the door. 'Hang on, hang on, my dear!' she cried. 'Must send for Dr Villiers.' She ran to the top of the stairs. 'Master Geor— Mr Hardwick! Oh, sir, come quick, your grandmother's been took bad!' She peered down into the gloomy hall, half-listening to the moans of the old lady, half-listening for an answer from George. There was none. 'Oh lord, oh dear,' muttered the housekeeper, beginning to bustle down the stairs. 'Mr Hard—' She was cut short as her hurrying feet trod on the hem of her gown and she was pitched forward. She tumbled noisily down the first eight steps and came to rest on the landing-step, her head bumping against the wall. She did not move. Grandmother Hardwick continued to groan from the bedroom above, her cries forming now and then into pleas for help.

George, sitting in the library, thought of the grim scene he had had with Amelia earlier that day. She had not wanted to go to the Stamford fair: she said she wanted to stay here with him. Since he had gone into her room in half-oblivious rage the night of the ball he had never touched her, never gone near her. But her invitations were constant. He had seen the voracity of her appetite that night – God, he had seen it. Yet now, her invitations were subtly changing into veiled threats. It had been a battle of wits this morning before he had finally packed her off with the other servants. He poured another brandy and, hearing a commotion upstairs, wondered vaguely what was going on. Perhaps he ought to go and look. No, it couldn't concern him . . .

It was a contented party that moved to the table at Bromswold: in the empty landscape society was little to be had and they were enjoying the change in their drab routine. But Mary was keenly aware of George's absence in the big family group and Jarrett, in tune with her thoughts, remarked it too. As they sat he said: 'I still regret that a place is empty at my table.'

'George?' said Aunt Catherine. 'I pray you don't speak of him, Mr Jarrett. The boy is incorrigible.'

'Perhaps, but he is my oldest friend. I – wish he were here.'

'Oh, there is no understanding him, Jarrett,' said Daniel. 'Lord knows I've tried to knock some sense into his head.'

'No – I am resolved,' said Jarrett, getting up again. 'I will have one last try to persuade him to come. 'Twill take but a few minutes to run over to Morholm and see him: I hate the thought of his being alone in that silent house while we make merry. Pray excuse me just for a little.' And quashing their protests, Jarrett left the house.

Mary watched him go and only when she turned back to the table did she see that Julia was watching her with a vivid, alarming intensity in her eyes.

No one came to answer the door when Jarrett arrived at Morholm, and it was not bolted, so he went in. The utter darkness of the echoing hall startled him. 'Hallo!' he called. His ears caught the sound of faint groans upstairs. He fumbled for the banister and began to sprint up. He almost trod on the motionless figure of the housekeeper on the landing-step and, bending down, could only just discern who it was. 'What on earth has been going on here?' he said aloud. 'Need a light . . . George!' he called. 'Are you here – George?' The groans from above grew louder. He sprinted up the rest of the steps and hurried down the passage in the direction of the cries. Here he could see a light. He found old Mrs Hardwick gasping in her bed, almost doubled up. Speaking gently to her he seized the candle and the jug of water by the bed and hastened to revive Mrs Reynolds. When she finally came round she showered him with apologies for 'tunnying down' but he turned them aside. 'Attend to the old lady,' he said, 'while I get Dr Villiers.'

Jarrett ran outside to the stables to get a horse, but found the doors locked. He would have to run back to Bromswold to get his own. He made his way back in a matter of minutes and quickly explained to the family in the dining-room before departing for the doctor.

They all returned to Morholm, some of them annoyed at this misfortune occurring just when they were ready for dinner. Mary rushed into the hall ahead of the rest and started up the stairs. A solitary candle burnt on the table where Jarrett had left it, and illumined the figure of George below, emerging pale and haggard from the library, looking around him with fogged eyes. For a moment all her affection for him swelled up strangely within her as she looked at him, her dear cousin George; then she remembered her grandmother upstairs and disdain and disappointment returned.

She turned away from him.

With Grandmother Hardwick's death the next day Horace was left the oldest of the Hardwicks and the last relic of a Carolean world in which Morholm had been a great place was gone. After the hard frosted earth in the Hardwick corner of the churchyard had been broken by the sexton and two helpers and the old lady laid to her rest there was some argument between Aunt Catherine and Daniel as to just how old she was, until Parson Medhurst consulted the parish register and confirmed Aunt Catherine's belief of eighty-five, much to her triumph.

On Christmas Eve Henry Milton called on George. He found him in the stables checking over Monmouth, who had gone lame. Milton was struck by how haggard his friend looked. He was concerned about the way George was living – solitary, unsocial, drinking too much. That his health was suffering was obvious already.

'How are you, George?' he said, his breath steaming in the cold. 'I am sorry I have not called of late.'

George said nothing.

'George – forgive me if I pry – but I am concerned for your welfare.'

'There is nothing wrong with me beyond my disgust at being lodged in this infernal human skin, and the after-effects of the medicine I take to relieve the mortal wretchedness.' He patted Monmouth's neck.

'But – forgive me again – you seem so unhappy –'

George gave his habitual snort at the mention of emotion.

'If the life of a squire is intolerable, why not go back to London?'

'What is to be so relished in London?'

Milton sighed. He wished George would not get into these moods. 'Well – if not London – anywhere, to get away.'

'From my responsibilities?' He made a gesture of contempt. 'If only I could. But besides, is this perambulation to cost nothing? God knows there will be little enough of the estate left soon with all these leeches devouring it.'

Suddenly Milton put the question he had never ventured on before.

'Must you tolerate the leeches then? Can't you be firm with them, for God's sake?'

Immediately he was sorry. He seldom spoke cruelly to people and he had certainly never touched George on a nerve like that. But before he could stammer an apology George had turned away saying: 'I wish to God you'd leave me alone. Go on, get out!'

On his way out Mary saw him and invited him to stay awhile and take tea. It was impossible to refuse Mary's gentle hospitality, and he felt besides that he wanted to talk.

Only Daniel was there, snoring by the fire, so he was left alone with Mary at the little tea-table. He offered his condolences on their recent bereavement.

'Yes, it is sad. But, bless her, she was terribly old and tired. And how are things with you, Mr Milton? I hope your parents are well?' She gave him a cup of tea.

'Thank you. Yes, father is rather better, and they enjoy their customary good spirits.'

'And Miss Wainwright? I have not seen her of late.' She wondered if she were being rude, but he smiled warmly.

'Yes, indeed. I have called on the family frequently in the last few weeks. I –' he hesitated. He had come hoping to broach this subject with George but knew now it was pointless. Mary was a cordial and sympathetic girl; he liked her more and more; perhaps he could talk to her.

'Er, M-Miss Mary,' (for some reason he always had difficulty in addressing her), 'I wonder if I might confide in you.'

Mary was surprised and rather pleased. 'Indeed, Mr Milton, if you think it will be of any use to you, I shall be only too glad to be your confidant.'

'I – think I hardly need tell you that I am very much enamoured of Miss Wainwright.'

'Yes.'

'From Miss Wainwright's parents – at least, from Mrs Wainwright, if you understand me –'

She smiled.

'From them I have received full assurance that should I engage her favour so far as to think it reasonable to make her a proposal of marriage, I am free to do so. I am glad to say that Elizabeth's – Miss Wainwright's mother, about whom I see I have been unfair in the past, puts her daughter's marital happiness before her marital status. She is under no illusions about my financial situation, and I hope Elizabeth is under none too. I have no money, and my

186

inheritance will be little. Indeed any kind of fortune I shall ever aspire to must be made by my pen, and I am not so vain as to make claims for that.' He shifted in his seat. 'It is on this subject that I had hoped to ask George's advice. But you know how he is – he laughs such matters to scorn. This worldly manner, this cynicism of his, is something I myself used to affect, when I was much in his company, but it is something I find myself more and more mistrusting. It is a destructive, blighting outlook; I see its effect growing in George, and wish I could find more time to be with him. But something else occupies . . . my very being . . . and I must see it to its resolution.'

'You are very much in love with Miss Wainwright, are you not, Mr Milton?'

'If I could only convey how much –'

'Don't try, for I understand. I believe I have the same feelings for dear Mr Jarrett. We are in a similar position.'

'Then you must know – for Elizabeth to be my wife is the greatest felicity I could hope for. Yet I hesitate to ask her.'

'Do you feel she would not accept?'

He made a helpless gesture. 'Sometimes I feel that my company is as delightful to her as hers is to me. Then I am on the brink of proposing. Yet – am I deluding myself? I beg you to tell me your opinion.'

'It is so difficult to tell what lies beneath Miss Wainwright's – if you will forgive me – haughty exterior.'

'You speak only the truth.'

'You see, I am afraid of raising false hopes. Yet if you really do put some faith in my view –'

'I do, indeed.'

'Then I would advise you to propose to her. That you are ardently in love with her is clear, that you would be a devoted and affectionate husband I feel sure, that you are a sincere and good-natured man I – think I know.' (This with the faintest tinge of a blush on both sides.) 'That she is fond of you and glad of your company I assure you I have seen with my own eyes. That she should have received, accepted and encouraged the devoted attention you have given her, and now refuse to continue it to its conclusion would, I think, be thoroughly reprehensible on her part: but I also think it unlikely. But, Mr Milton, whether she will accept you, I cannot say. If she loves you, as I hope she does, then I think it would be vile in her to sacrifice that love because of material considerations, and in such circumstances I think you would be well rid of her, if you will pardon my saying so. That I speak with such conviction on this subject, Mr Milton, is because of my own love for your friend Mr Jarrett. I – I am not afraid of saying that I think he may be making an offer of marriage quite shortly . . . in which eventuality I hope you will give us your blessing.'

'A union between two people whom I hold in the highest esteem and affection would be immensely gratifying to me. Jarrett is an excellent fellow, and I am sure will be an excellent husband.'

'Thank you, Mr Milton. I – I am afraid my advice has not been very conclusive.'

'On the contrary, you have eased my mind greatly. Much more, in fact, than George would have done, I fear.'

'Dear George! I have tried so hard to understand him. He hardly seems to notice me, anyhow,' she added with a wistful laugh. 'More tea?'

When finally Milton left and rode off towards Helpston he reflected that, however his love fared, at least he had found a friend who, he felt, would never let one down. The strange tension there had once been between them was now gone, as if it had never existed. With Mary as friend, Elizabeth seemed almost a figure from fable or myth; but, thinking of the suit he had to press, that was not an encouraging reflection.

4

There was a clash at Morholm over the Christmas festivities.

Aunt Catherine and Mrs Peach planned for a Christmas dinner of great expense, but Mary was adamant that they should keep open house for the villagers as Joseph used to.

'Whatever it be, it appears I must pay for it: but I had much rather feed empty bellies than overfull ones,' was George's only comment: so in the end they compromised, with the open house on Christmas Eve and the dinner on Christmas Day.

Apart from the family there was to be Jarrett, the Sedgmoors and the Townsends. It was to be a dinner such as had not been seen at Morholm since Mary's grandfather was a young man with a large fortune in the days of the Old Pretender, and now that Grandmother Hardwick was gone only Great-Uncle Horace could remember times like that. As well as numerous pigeon and fowl pies, mutton and veal, and fish, there was to be a fine roast goose and roast swan, and to follow there would be endless tarts and sweetmeats with the plum pudding.

There was morris dancing on the village green and a party of mummers came to give 'Jack the Giant-Killer'. Morholm was hung with evergreens, holly and box berries, and two gardeners heaved in a great yule log to put behind the fire. On Christmas morning clouds of the dense grey texture associated with snow hung on the horizon, but the snow held off and the guests had no trouble getting to Morholm. Dinner was late and continued for three hours. Something of the festive spirit seemed even to have got into George, who played the cordial host well and flattered Mrs Townsend till she bridled like a girl. Julia, for the first time Mary could remember, had a new gown: its rich scarlet played down her brown colouring, and the bodice set off her full figure. Young Mr Francis Sedgmoor, placed next to her, was captivated. If her appearance was for his benefit she did not match it in her behaviour to him: but once towards the end of the evening Mary saw her laugh at a joke he made. A little snow began to fall soon after dinner ended and seemed to promise more, so the guests left earlier than intended to avoid being caught in a blizzard. Only Jarrett remained – to most of them he almost seemed one of the family – to take coffee and talk in the warm parlour.

It was then that he told them of a friend he had in London who had offered him a set of excellent lodgings, free for a month, in return for a favour he had done him. Jarrett said he was sensible of a wish amongst the family to see London, and as he himself knew the city quite well he would be glad to take them all there for a short stay. Should the expenses worry them, he said, then for the company of a family who had shown him so much hospitality, he was more than willing to help defray these. Unfortunately the time he could have the lodgings was only during the first quarter of the year, which meant they would not see Vauxhall Gardens, for instance but fortune permitting, a March visit would not be entirely dull.

His suggestion was received with delight, but, as Aunt Catherine said, 'We had better appeal to the master of the house before replying, Mr Jarrett.'

Mary turned to George, who was half-asleep in an armchair, almost with desperation: her eyes sought his but he would not look her way. 'George,' she said softly.

'If you want to go jaunting off to London in the tail-end of winter you are welcome to do so,' he said. 'It's not as if you ever pay any heed to me anyway. But don't ask me to go too; for my part I am sick of London, and can think of no more appalling prospect than wandering about the city with the March winds under my coattails. I think I would prefer to be alone in this dreary place.' And he would say no more. It was clear, however, that the others had already accepted. A minute later a group of villagers arrived singing carols, and as was customary they went out to the hall to let them in and give them slices of yule cake and spiced ale.

The singers, led by the choir from Aysthorpe church, were a ragged collection of farm workers from the villages round about: they had already called at Lord Fitzwilliam's and were well-oiled, more spirited than tuneful. One old man accompanied them on an antique fiddle.

Aunt Catherine, thinking Mary could not hear, was whispering to Mrs Peach. 'Dear Mr Jarrett! I can see what's behind this. It will be a London marriage for him and our Mary, I know. Such a delightful gesture! And it will be so much more fashionable to have a wedding in town.'

'Indeed, aunt, you run ahead of yourself,' said Mary. 'There was no suggestion of such a thing.' But she smiled as she said it, for with a sweet, sickish glow inside she knew better.

The villagers began to sing 'Remember O Thou Man', and the melancholy charm of the carol hushed them all. Even George was visibly moved, and at the end of it Mrs Peach croaked, 'You are a poor looby of a grandson, George, but it is Christmas and you may kiss me.'

'How can I refuse such an invitation?' said George, bending to kiss the whiskered cheek, and there was a general laugh. Only Mary noticed Julia, in the shadows at the back of the chilly hall. She had never known Julia to shed a single tear but now she saw she was weeping, silently and desolately, tears streaming down the heavy curves of her neck and breast, and tearing the handkerchief clutched in her hands to tiny shreds.

* * *

It was a fortnight later that George ordered Mary to stop seeing Jarrett.

The whole family was there, for 1775 had come in bitterer than ever and no one had stirred out in the cold that threw itself in gusts of stinging wind at the marooned house. They had begun to talk of the trip to London when George said in a loud voice: 'No.'

Such was their surprise that they all fell silent.

'I think you had better abandon this notion. I am not happy with this attachment I see growing between – between Jarrett and you, Mary.'

Mary, who was kneeling at the fire, glanced up, startled.

'Why, what are you talking about, nephew? Do you –' began Aunt Catherine, but Mary cut her off.

'George, what can you mean?' she cried, rising to her feet. 'Mr Jarrett, your old friend – how can you –'

'I am master here, damn it, am I not?' shouted George, his blood rising. 'The stout hub, and all the rest of it? I disapprove of your consorting with Jarrett and I tell you that as long as you are under my roof you shall have nothing to do with him! Do you understand me, cousin?' He stared into Mary's face as he had never ventured to look before.

For a moment she thought she was going to strike him: strike him as hard as she knew how.

Just then Mrs Reynolds came in. 'Beg your pardon, sir,' she said, 'but 'tis Amelia, and – someone else. She says she wants to see you and – the whole family . . .'

Amelia Seddon stepped into the room, looking sulky as ever but flushed with a new determination. Behind her, in a shawl and dangling a rusty bonnet, like a distorted mirror-image, came her twin sister Beth.

'What the devil –' said George.

'Ay, you might well speak so profane,' said Amelia. ''Tis no more'n I expect.' She looked round at the others. 'I come here to – to accuse my seducer and ravisher.' The melodrama with which she said the words was almost risible.

'I believe you have been reading too many foolish romances,' said Mary. 'Now what are you –'

''Tis true!' said Beth. She pointed a finger at George, shakily. 'He tried to ravish me too. In Stamford 'twere. One night when we met at th'inn. But I fought him off.'

'You lying little minx,' hissed George. Aunt Catherine gave a little muffled shriek: but Mary had stepped forward. She glared at the girls. 'I do not believe a word of this,' she said calmly. 'What jot of proof do you have?'

'What proof?' said Amelia. 'I'm with child. By squire . . .' She began to sob, dryly, as if trying to make herself cry. George had gone very pale. Mary, in loyalty to him putting aside what he had said just before, gripped his arm.

Kingsley, who as usual had appropriated the settle closest the fire, rose to his feet and sighed deeply, like a man burdened by conscience. 'I fear I can keep silent no longer,' he said. 'Alas, George . . . the night of the ball, when we came home early, I – I observed George . . .' He turned to the others and spread his hands with an expression of outraged decency. 'It's true, I'm afraid.'

Mary let go of George's arm.

George looked for a moment as if he would hit Beth, and under his stare the girl flushed and hung her head. But he did not strike her. Instead he flung the brandy-glass he still held into the hearth so that it smashed into hundreds of pattering fragments. 'So now I am to be a moral outcast . . . a leper,' he said in a low voice. 'Very well. Very well. What are morals, for God's sake? What is anything in this world but part of a great – sickening – joke?' And he was gone from the room.

He lurched out to the stables, quickly saddled a horse and rode away with a thunderous clatter of hoofs on the frozen yard.

At Morholm, amongst the animated discussion and exclamation, only Mary was now very quiet. She stared into the fire with misted eyes, feeling sick to her heart, and suddenly all hesitation was removed. Her path was clear.

George rode at breakneck speed, with no thought of his direction. The freezing wind cut his face like a blade but he was hardly aware of it. He did not slow down his furious pace, but a destination formed in his mind with the desire for a drink. He made for Wansford, where there was a great coaching inn where they knew him well, The Haycock. The village was sometimes called Wansford-in-England and the legend went that during a flood a farmhand who had gone to sleep on a haybale had woken to find himself floating downstream; inquiring where on earth he was, the reply came, 'Wansford, in England'. This scene was comically painted on the inn-sign and George saw it with grateful recognition as he clattered over the stone water-bridge and into the inn yard.

Inside a glorious fire roared in the huge grate and cast comfortable red flickers about the room. From elsewhere came the smell of a roast, and there was a cosy clink of glasses. It was like stepping into another world from the naked cold outside into this uterine warmth. George slumped on to a polished settle. The landlord came oozing towards him, servility tempered by mild surprise at the wind-blown figure, hatless, with a face like thunder.

'Mr Hardwick, sir, a pleasure to see you. I hope –'

'Bring me a brandy,' snapped George, and the landlord, with a backward glance, shuffled away. George stretched out his boots towards the fire. The sound of conversation in the room, which had died down at his entrance, now rose again, and he caught snatches of it. Old Joseph's young profligate – so it was true about the Hardwicks – family going to the dogs – not like the old days. . . The landlord returned with his brandy. As George brought the glass to his lips he lifted his eyes and saw, as if he had risen genie-like out of the fumes of the liquor, Thomas Jarrett. He was emerging from the dining-room. When he noticed George he smiled and moved towards him. George set down his brandy untouched and suddenly his head swam with boiling, irrational animosity.

Jarrett came up to him, his handsome face friendly and smiling. George felt that surge in his veins, that crawling all over his skin, that urgent drum-like pounding in his chest. Hate and frustration, violent, irresistible, without reason, bubbled and mounted and boiled over.

'George, my dear fellow, an unexpected pleasure –' was all Jarrett had time for before George leapt from his seat, overturning the table, brandy and all, and launched himself at Jarrett with full force. He grasped Jarrett's coat lapels and went down on top of him; George was the smaller and weaker man but his adversary was startled and taken off guard. Almost before Jarrett knew what was happening George was hitting him, with strength he never knew he had, square in the mouth. His third blow fell short for Jarrett had got his knee under his stomach and one hand on his throat and shoved him backwards. He landed heavily against the wall. Jarrett was climbing to his feet, blood running from his mouth, clearly not about to return hostilities, but in a moment George was up and, his fury unabated, threw a swinging punch at Jarrett that caught him on the side of the head and made him stagger back and then fall. Immediately George was on him. By now the landlord was buzzing round and round them, entreating them to stop and consider, and begging for someone to help him separate them; but no one seemed disposed to come between the two young men. George saw the split lip that came from his fist and he raised it again in a kind of ferocious exultation. That's it – mark those good looks – split your knuckles and spoil that supercilious handsome face. He aimed a blow at Jarrett's face but Jarrett half-parried it by catching his wrist with a strong grip. With his other hand he gripped George's chin and pushed and succeeded in rolling George off him. Jarrett began to stagger to his feet but George lashed out from where he lay and caught hold of his ankles and heaved. Like a felled tree Jarrett toppled and crashed against a table, scattering plates. George lunged forward and hit him again, but Jarrett was already in no state to retaliate. With that last blow all the fury seemed to drain out of George and he stopped, just as the landlord reappeared with two grooms whom he had been to fetch. George left a handful of money on the table and went out.

The landlord, puffing, helped Jarrett to his feet. 'Dear me, Mr Jarrett, I hope you are not badly hurt. Sarah, some water here, quickly – pardon, sir? Oh, dear me, there is no need for you to apologize, sir, an unprovoked attack by Mr Hardwick. I observed it all – a most dishonourable action – I thought he seemed inebriated when he came in. Let us bathe that wound, sir. Sarah hasten, girl! Now sit here. Odds my life, your head is most wickedly cut, sir. Booth, bring a little brandy here – pardon, Mr Jarrett? The damage? Oh, think not of it, sir – see, it appears Mr Hardwick has had the decency to leave money for it, at least – no, I won't hear of it, Mr Jarrett . . .'

Only after about half-an-hour, patched and totted up by the kindly landlord, did Jarrett feel well enough to leave. He refused with thanks the landlord's offer of a man to ride with him and see him home, and set off alone and aching, keeping his horse to a gentle pace. The cold air revived him somewhat and gradually he began to straighten up and stir his horse to a trot towards Aysthorpe. But waves of nausea broke over him as he came into the village. Every step his horse took shuddered through his body with a jarring pain, a pain that, after a period of numbness, was growing, taking a stronger and stronger grip on him. He rode slowly down the drive to Morholm, drooping in the saddle. In the parlour window he caught sight of Daniel, who lifted a hand in greeting and smiled. Jarrett smiled back but it produced a vicious sting in his torn lip. The pain made him reel and, to the evident consternation of old Daniel in the window, he slid off his horse and on to the ground in a faint.

Great-Uncle Horace was at Morholm. Scarcely had the sensation caused by the twins died down – Amelia had been dismissed by Aunt Catherine, and told she would be 'provided for' – when Horace arrived to tell them that old Nathan Jarrett had been declared bankrupt. Creditors had moved into Bromswold this morning and were claiming the furniture and the house.

They were discussing the matter, and Horace was remarking what a pity it was that such an excellent young man should be involved in such a misfortune – although he was one of the creditors and had foreclosed on old Jarrett last week – when Daniel exclaimed at the sight of Jarrett toppling to the ground outside, and Mary, with a scream, rushed out to him. Servants were summoned and they bore the long drooping figure into the house and laid him on a couch.

'Why, poor Mr Jarrett! What can have happened?' fluttered Aunt Catherine. 'What a day! Julia, my smelling-salts.'

Mary chafed his hands, Daniel poured a little brandy between his bleeding lips, and Aunt Catherine waved her smelling-bottle. 'He is most horribly bruised,' said Mary, trembling – trembling both with distress and with the electric thrill his presence always gave her. 'And see here on his head – a most fearful knock he has had. Oh, Tom, what has happened?'

'It appears he has been in a fight,' said Great-Uncle Horace. 'Some ruffian attacked him, probably. Ah! he is reviving.'

Jarrett stirred and opened his eyes. Mary gripped his

hands. 'It's all right. You are safe now. Are you badly hurt?'

Jarrett smiled weakly and rose painfully to a sitting position. 'I am afraid I have been a nuisance to you. I fear I stirred out too soon after my mishap . . . should have rested longer.'

'Take another sip, sir,' said Daniel. 'Who was it? Some vagabond after your purse, I'll be bound: the country is full of 'em.'

'It was a mere brawl . . . not of my choosing. It does not matter.'

'But who was it?' said Mary. 'Who could do such a thing?'

'I am bound to tell you, if you insist, that it was George.' Mary's eyes widened. 'It was in The Haycock at Wansford. He saw me and made what I hope was an unprovoked assault on me. I cannot think what I have done to precipitate this. We have always been good friends.'

'That stupid young puppy,' grunted Daniel. 'Where is he now?'

'I do not know. It was nothing serious. I dare say he will apologize and make some explanation when next I see him.'

'And on a day so distressing for you, too, Mr Jarrett,' said Mary with love and pity, looking into his face. 'Yes, we have heard. Great-uncle brought us the news. Never fear. I am here with you.' She spoke the last words in a whisper and he smiled feebly at her. No amount of cuts and bruises, she thought, could mar that beauty.

'You must stay at Morholm tonight, Mr Jarrett,' said Aunt Catherine. 'You must. I will have Reynolds make up a room directly.'

Jarrett protested a little more, but he was clearly too exhausted to be moved. A servant was sent over to The Haycock where old Nathan Jarrett was staying to explain this. Jarrett had dinner with the family and old Horace, who rode home in the evening, showed a special cordiality to him:

198

Mary suspected a trace of remorse even in her parsimonious great-uncle.

Before Jarrett retired Mary managed a few words alone with him. 'I fear I am rather a poor figure for you now, in more ways than one,' he said, a blush barely discernible beneath the bruises.

'You know me better than that,' she said gravely. 'It is my cousin who appears a poor figure to me now. This afternoon,' she went on with an effort, 'he forbade me to see you any more.'

'Good God! George? Perhaps it is better if I leave, if my presence will mean trouble for you –'

She put a gentle finger to his cut lips. 'I am not afraid of George,' she said. 'Go now and sleep, my love. Everything will be all right.'

At least, Jarrett noted, there had been no cooling towards him on the part of the family because of his sudden and drastic change in fortune. As he undressed painfully in the semi-gloom of the candle-lit chamber he noticed, on the inner wall, a small bright yellow spot, like a glow-worm. Going closer he saw it was a crack in the wall through which light was coming from the adjacent room. In idle curiosity he bent down and put one eye to the crack to see whose room it was.

It was Julia's room; and it was the biggest shock of Jarrett's life to find, as the girl undressed, that Julia had the most magnificent body any man ever hoped to see. Beneath her sun-coarsened face and masses of heavy black hair her body was white and unblemished, with shapely limbs and large rounded breasts. And then he saw that a framed picture was lying on the floor of her room. There were several fingertips showing clearly in a thick layer of dust on the top, as if the picture had just been moved after hanging in one place for a long time. Julia's room was brightly lit with several candles, which seemed odd.

He went to bed and thought hard for a long time. When he woke in the morning he looked through the hole again; Julia was already up and gone. He dressed, and as he went down the passage he glanced in at Julia's room. His surmise was right. The picture still lay on the floor, and on the wall was a rectangle of bright white among the yellowing whitewash, showing where it had hung. The picture must have been hung there, long ago, to cover that crack; and it was clear that Julia had taken it down deliberately and lit up her room so brightly, so that he would see her.

George had not come home all night.

'He is probably asleep in a gutter somewhere,' said Aunt Catherine at breakfast, 'and let him stay there is what I say. Will you not stay at Morholm, Mr Jarrett?'

'I fear I will get but an indifferent reception from the master of the house,' said Jarrett. 'I must go and see my father. My aunt and uncle from Spalding are coming down to take charge of him: he is to live with them. Then I must find lodgings.'

After taking a fond farewell of Mary, Jarrett left. She watched him go from the window of the parlour, and a fierce love for him seemed to well up and thicken her throat like threatening tears. It was the fiercer because of the anger that was fuelled in her by the thought of George.

Later in the morning George arrived home, having spent a wretched night in a tavern. He shut himself in the library and would see no one.

The garden of the Wainwrights' town-house in Stamford was not large but beautifully laid out, with a fountain and an obelisk and a timber-framed summer-house built into the town wall; and it was round this garden that Milton found himself walking with Elizabeth in the cool of the January morning.

She was wearing a fur wrap and her arm was warm and firm in his. Frost still sparkled on the grass and the shrubs and on countless spider webs that festooned the hedges, as if there had been a miniature party the night before and the decorations had been left up. The fresh beauty of the scene was echoed in Elizabeth, whose cheeks were touched with red by the chill breeze and who was unusually talkative. Milton himself had dressed finely, putting on a new cravat and even powdering his hair. As she talked excitedly to him of their house near Elton which was being refurbished and the grand ball they would have when it was finished and smiled and laughed and squeezed his arm he felt he loved her so dearly he could hold back no longer. He stopped and took her hand and looked into her lovely face.

'Miss Wainwright,' he began, 'Elizabeth . . .' He could not tell whether that was a blush forming or merely a growing bloom from the cold. 'I am sensible of a deep affection for you, as I am sure you must be aware. Can I – can I dare to hope that that affection is in some way reciprocated?'

She seemed desperately embarrassed, as he had foreseen. She looked down at the ground: it was definitely a blush.

'Indeed, Mr Milton, I – I am always glad of your company,' she finally said after what seemed an age. Milton relaxed a little. Well, it was something to have got thus far. He was very uncomfortable himself, and the humour of the two painfully shy people engaged in such a conversation was not entirely lost on him.

'You see, I'm –' he was going to come straight to the point but lost his nerve and skirted round it, 'as you must be aware, I am not wealthy. Any fortune I ever make must come from my pen if it is to come at all, and that is a doubtful thing to rely on. I am very much in love with you, Elizabeth, and –'

(She was so very red now, and seemed almost on the point

of running away, that he lost his thread for a moment.)

' – What I am trying to ask is if – it is too much to hope – if it is possible you could ever consent to be my wife . . .' There, it was out now, he thought, and a proper mess he had made of it too; it would not surprise him if she did turn him down after that.

She seemed to be half-choking, and now he saw what the authors meant by the phrase 'covered with confusion'. Finally she said, as if in a desperate attempt to put off her answer, 'You must first consider . . . my parents . . . you must first –'

'I have already spoken to them, and they have given their consent to my speaking to you about this.' He hated to break down her last defence, but he must have an answer.

'I – I really cannot reply now, Mr Milton – it is something I have not given thought to . . .'

'But you will, I beg of you, give some thought to it now?'

'Of course – I shall consider all you have said, but . . . oh, please do not press me, Mr Milton!' she said, looking into his face with a lovely appeal that would have made him consent to anything she said. 'I cannot say – let us go on as before for a while – do not urge me . . .'

He patted her arm. 'I understand. Forgive me if I have distressed you. We will talk of other things.'

'Dear Mr Milton – please promise me you will not be angry or impatient with me.'

He nodded, surprised. She leant forward and, clumsily enough, kissed him on the cheek and then hurried inside.

Never, never would he be angry with her, he said to himself as he galloped out of Stamford and on to Morholm. Never, never. He must see George, or Mary – anyone. As he rode past Bromswold he noticed that the windows, which were usually heavily curtained, were bare. He thought it odd and so he dismounted and went up to the house. A gruff man in shirt sleeves flung open the door at his knock and said 'What now?' Milton was so taken aback that he could say nothing. 'If it's the Jarretts you're after they're not here. The old fellow's gone bankrupt and it's all to be auctioned off.' And he slammed the door again.

Milton went on to Morholm where Mary received him. She told him – with some agitation, he noticed – of old Jarrett's ruin. She told him of the brawl between George and Jarrett. She told him of the accusations of the twins yesterday – here he looked very grave. Finally she told him – with tears fighting her words – of George's forbidding her to see Jarrett any more.

'Why? What is his reason for this?'

'Oh, I cannot say. This was before his father's misfortune was made known to us. He merely said he disapproved and – and that as long as I was under his roof I must abandon the attachment. He behaves so hatefully to me now. We were such good friends, not long ago.' She gave way to silent tears. Milton was moved; her face was becoming almost like that of a sister to him now, and he hated seeing it so distressed; but he never knew what to do in the presence of tears. He was glad there was only Julia in the room, and she was in a chimney-corner and could not see them.

'You say he is in the library now?'

She nodded, wiping her eyes. 'But he will have no one to see him. Matthews wanted to speak to him but he would not let him in.'

He patted her hand in brotherly fashion. 'Perhaps he will give me an audience,' he said, though he himself was not so sure. 'I will try and reason with him.'

On his way out of the room Julia rose from her corner. 'Mr Milton,' she said, 'if you are going to the library, perhaps you will return this book: my brother will not let me in.'

'Of course.' He took the book, which was the third volume of Smollett's *Humphry Clinker*. On an impulse he said, 'Did you enjoy the book, Miss Hardwick?'

'Very much,' she said in her abrupt way. 'Apart from –' She stopped.

'Go on.'

'I was going to say I found the character of Lydia is drawn with too much sentiment, something of which Dr Smollett's works have always been happily free.'

He was surprised, and interested. 'You have read all Dr Smollett's books, Miss Hardwick?'

'Yes indeed. Do not look so amazed, Mr Milton. There is really very little else for me to do.'

'Indeed, I did not mean to. How do you feel Dr Smollett compares with Sterne as a humorist?'

'He is less inclined to archness and whimsy, but lacks breadth of imagination. I think –' She seemed for the first time to notice his interested expression and stopped abruptly. 'But my ill-informed prattling can be of no consequence to you, Mr Milton, so good-day.'

She had shut up like a clam, to his regret. He had often suspected there was more to Julia than met the eye and she seemed to have given him a glimpse before as suddenly withdrawing it again.

George consented with no very good grace to see him. He was going over the accounts: Milton thought he looked more sick and saturnine than ever, but he did not mention it this time. But when he broached the subject of Mary and Jarrett he got an angry reaction.

'I suppose *you* are going to tell me what to do now, Milton? If that is the case I think you had better leave.'

'Indeed, I – Have you heard that the Jarretts have gone bankrupt?'

George looked at him keenly and his dark brooding expression sharpened for a moment. 'Is that so?' Then he turned away again. 'All the more reason. I won't have her marry the son of a mendicant.'

'Are you sure you can stop her?' said Milton.

He did not mean to offend but once again he found himself being ordered out. He tried to console Mary before leaving.

When George finally emerged at dinner he re-emphasized that there was to be no more Jarrett at Morholm. 'I want none of a man who cannot handle his own affairs, and neither should you.'

'You speak as if it were his fault!' cried Mary. 'It was he who had to struggle, he who had to bear the burden of trying to save the situation!' Her tears were over now and she was newly defiant. 'You sicken me, George! If you had been in his shoes the collapse would have come a lot sooner!'

The glance he shot her then was so intense that she stopped.

'Ay, you talk out of your arse, grandson,' said Mrs Peach. 'The young man's no pauper. Any number of respectable positions are open to him.'

'And a better notion of respectability he has than some young puppies,' said Daniel.

'I will not have him in this house,' hissed George.

'Fie, nephew,' said Aunt Catherine, ''twere a better action on your part to lodge him here. I hate to think of our poor Mr Jarrett living in wretched inn rooms.'

'I harbour enough parasites,' said George. He spoke coolly. 'I shall instruct the servants to tell me if he comes here, or if when escorting Mary out she ever meets him. They shall be dismissed if they do not co-operate.'

Mary turned to the window so that he should not see her tears of anger. George had gone too far. If he wished to waste his life that was no longer any concern of hers. He would never stop her seeing Tom. Never.

* * *

To Mary's surprise she was taken aside by Julia that evening and beckoned to come into the front parlour. Once there Julia closed the door and took her hand.

'You know I have to do a lot of calling and visiting in Peterborough, without Aunt Catherine,' she said. 'I get about a good deal with only Clarry escorting me.'

Mary, puzzled, opened her mouth to speak but her cousin silenced her.

'Don't say anything. Mr Jarrett went to take a room at The Angel in Peterborough, did he not?'

Mary nodded. She had never known Julia to speak to her like this before.

'Well. If you like I will act as a go-between for you and Mr Jarrett. I can take your letters or whatever and perhaps arrange times and places for you to meet – tell him when George will be out of the house – things like that. Shall I do it for you? Nod if you want me to, now: don't say a word.'

Mystified by her manner, but overjoyed at the thought of being able to keep in touch with Jarrett, Mary nodded. 'But –'

'No, not a word! If you want to write a letter to him, go and do it now. I am going out early tomorrow morning. Go now.'

The next morning Julia set out, accompanied by the old groom Clarry, to visit the Sedgmoors in Peterborough. Clarry rather preferred escorting Miss Mary, who always talked pleasantly to him on the way; Miss Julia never said a word and today, he noticed, she seemed more preoccupied than ever. Yesterday the young master had told him to see that Miss Mary never met Mr Jarrett when he escorted her out. He could not understand why, for Mr Jarrett had always seemed a nice young gentleman, but the master had given him no reasons. No, it was not like the old days when Mr Joseph was the squire . . .

Peterborough was a town on the edge of the fen of three thousand inhabitants and no great extent but with a fine market square dominated by the imposing front of the twelfth century cathedral. There were two members of Parliament and one in recent years had been Edward Wortley, husband of the authoress and friend of Pope, Lady Mary Wortley Montagu. Three splendid inns, The Angel, The Talbot and The Cross Keys looked over the square and competed for the coaching trade. In the middle stood the Butter Cross, where the magistrates' court was held; the lower storey was completely open and was used for public meetings and marketing. It was Saturday and as usual the Marketstede was crammed with people, and carts and sedan chairs could hardly move for the press. With difficulty Julia and Clarry threaded their way past Butcher's Row behind St John's Church, with a fetid stink of offal in the air, and guided their horses to The Angel. Clarry was given leave to go and visit his sister who was in service at a house in Priestgate, and told to meet Julia with the horses in two hours' time. Julia, however, after a brief visit to the draper's, returned to The Angel. She asked a pot-boy which was Mr Jarrett's room, explaining that she had a letter to deliver to him. The boy directed her to a door in a narrow passage and left her. With an air of unusual agitation she knocked and waited. There were noises within and a moment later Jarrett appeared in his shirt sleeves.

'Miss Hardwick,' he said, looking startled. She did not say anything but he stood aside to let her in. As she entered she glanced around at his few possessions, his coats and boots, a few books on a desk by the window where he seemed to have been writing. He offered her a chair but she remained standing.

'I have a letter here from Mary,' she began. 'In the light of my brother's behaviour I have volunteered to act as a go-between for you.'

He took the letter. 'That will be a great pleasure. But I hope it will not be necessary to put you to the trouble for long. I hope to effect a reconciliation with George if it is at all possible.'

She was looking straight at him. It was a very bold gaze for her. He returned her look and said:

'Why did you want me to see you in your room the other night? Pray, do not for a moment think me offended – but why?'

She was silent. She seemed to quiver like the distorted air above a fire. Jarrett took a step towards her and put his hand quite gently to her neck. 'Why?' he said again and the next moment she was kissing him and her fingers scratched feverishly at his shirt. Then she pulled away again and looked at him with the same fierce direct gaze. 'Now do you understand?' she said in a voice so low it scarcely carried. He seized her roughly and kissed her while with fumbling fingers she undid the lacing of her gown. His fingers touched the heavy swell of her breasts above her bodice. With their mouths still locked together he reached back with one hand to yank the curtains to and then began to pull off his shirt.

It was an hour later when Julia furtively emerged from the Angel Inn into the cold January sunshine. As she went past the tap-room door she did not notice Kingsley Hardwick, sitting there drinking, just as she had not noticed him an hour earlier when she had come in. But he had noticed her, both times.

Julia brought Mary a letter from Jarrett saying he could meet her early next morning in the copse behind the parsonage. She was easily able to do this without detection and the next morning found her running across the frosted grass into his arms. After the first effusions of greetings and love, however, she grew melancholy in spite of herself. 'It is so sad, so *wrong* that we have to meet like this,' she said. 'George has blighted everything.'

'I still hope for a reconciliation with him, my darling,' said Jarrett as they walked together. 'Somehow, I must be able to. I know his odd moods of old.'

She shook her head sadly. 'I fear there is little hope of that. But he must be out all morning on Thursday, so you could come to Morholm then: the others will be glad to see you.'

'This reminds me – our proposed visit to London is still most definitely to take place.'

'But –'

'You see, this friend, of whom I told you, in London, can still supply us with lodgings, and what is more he is fairly certain that he has found me an excellent position in a mercantile house in the city, which I may take up in April.'

'Tom! How wonderful.' She kissed him. 'I hope to meet this friend.'

'And you shall. I can scarcely express my gratitude. Of course this is not fixed as yet. You see, the head of this firm puts great trust in the integrity of my friend – Charles Macmillan – and asked him recently if he knew of anyone to fill a position of promise that had been vacated. Charles gave a good report of me – God knows I hope I can live up to it – and believes he has secured it for me.'

Suddenly her face fell and she cast her eyes down. Would this not mean he would be living in London? But when she looked up again he was smiling.

'I know what you are thinking. But would it not be a good notion to combine the visit to London, my acquisition of a new living – and a wedding?'

She was in his arms with a cry of joy. 'Oh, my lover, you know my answer . . .' He lifted her off the ground and spun her, and she buried her face in his shoulder and breathed in the sweet smell of him.

'A London marriage will be pleasing to your aunt and the others, I'm sure,' he said, lowering her gently down. 'Of course I have to be sure you do not dislike the idea of our living in London, if my hopes are realized?'

'I will go anywhere with you,' she said quietly.

'And you know I am not wealthy, though if Macmillan is right I shall be tolerably secure. We shall not live in grand style.'

'It matters not a bit,' she said. 'And besides, there is my settlement from my uncle.'

His face darkened. 'That must be for your discretion only. The fact that his wife brings him an income must not turn a man from making his own.'

'Everything I have is yours, Tom.'

'But let us keep this quiet for a while,' he said. 'Nothing is sure yet.'

'One thing is sure,' said Mary, and she kissed him with a fierce and possessive passion. 'I love you dearly.'

5

In February the ice on the marshes began to melt and the iron-grey stare of the sky softened with an occasional ray of sunshine. Mary continued to meet Jarrett through the mediation of Julia. Sometimes he managed to come to Morholm when George was out and was welcomed by the family. He told them that the London trip was still on and that he hoped for employment there. Aside from these meetings, Julia arranged occasional trysts for Mary with him in Peterborough and Stamford; Mary had won Clarry over to her side and persuaded him not to tell the master when she met Jarrett. Their meetings were brief and consisted of short arm-in-arm walks and tender conversation on what they would do when they were married and when to announce it. Julia would never accept Mary's thanks for helping her, and seemed to grow actually restive and angry when she tried.

But it was a frustrating time for Henry Milton. For a couple of meetings after he had broached the subject of marriage with Elizabeth Wainwright he did not mention it again, for he could tell she wished he would not and he did not want to jeopardize what ground he had gained by putting too much pressure on her. But people of fashion began to call more and more often, and he saw to his distress the attraction their absurd posturing had for her. Was she so desperate to be one of a crowd? Did she care so little for her own self-respect – a thing that mattered greatly to him? What was it about these people, who to him were so false, so affected, that made her court their society? But his only reply to these questions was puzzlement and incomprehension.

It was Hugh Woodhouse who troubled him most. Milton had taken an instinctive dislike to the man the first time he had seen him: he personified everything he hated. He was rich and did not appear to appreciate it; he was a snob; he was powerful and used his power indiscriminately; he was thoughtless and dull and seemed to honour nothing of beauty or constancy or grace; rather he seemed out to destroy all such things with his crass blunt brutality, just as he often destroyed the Wainwrights' china tea-cups with clumsy swingings of his bear-like arms and embroidered coat-tails. When Milton dined at the Wainwrights' in February it was Woodhouse who got the honour of escorting Elizabeth in to dinner, and Milton had noticed how carelessly and brutishly he grasped her arm, that fair slender arm that he himself would hold with trembling gentleness as a priceless gift. 'Dear Hughie,' the little toady Warren had said to Milton on that occasion, smirking. 'Isn't he a *bear*? Isn't he a perfect *bear*?' And when Woodhouse talked to her, it was all things of interest to him only – his hunting and gambling – things Milton thought could not interest her.

And yet she liked him. As March came in Milton saw that he had a genuine rival. That was partly why, when he and Elizabeth were alone together one March morning, he finally revived the subject of marriage. This time she stopped him before he had even finished speaking and refused to discuss the subject.

He was worried, too, about George. His hope that his friend might adapt to the life of a squire seemed vain now; the estate, even he could see, was neglected. George, though he denied there was anything wrong with him, seemed in one long wretched depression that Milton could not account for. He was drinking heavily and rarely stirred from Morholm; his face was hollow and pale and his hands shook. Once Milton ventured to suggest he call Dr Villiers in to be on the safe side, but George would have none of it: he only wanted to be left alone, and Milton found his old friend hardly had time for him now. His only comfort was the friendship of Mary, who was uniformly kind and hospitable. But he also found, to his disappointment, that when he attempted to speak to Julia about books again – interested by her unguessed-at knowledge – she actively seemed to avoid him, almost as if she was ashamed of herself.

March brought the surprising news of Julia's engagement to young Mr Francis Sedgmoor, the lawyer's son. Surprising it was initially, but once the first exclamations were over, it had been, as Aunt Catherine said, 'clear all along'. After all, young Mr Sedgmoor had made tentative advances a good while ago, and Julia had been out calling at the Sedgmoors' in Peterborough frequently of late. Aunt Catherine was greatly pleased with the match. She had never dared hope for anything nearly as good for the girl, and moreover it seemed to have sweetened her niece's character; Julia seemed much more pliant and sociable these days. She was taking pains with her appearance also; and it was striking to see how much more presentable she had contrived to make herself.

It was one evening, when George was about the estate, that Jarrett came to Morholm as he had arranged with Mary to speak of their marriage. He had not yet been told of Julia's engagement and he offered his congratulations.

'In fact this is most auspicious news,' he said, smiling round at them. The whole family, as well as young Mr Sedgmoor, was there. 'For I have come today to ask whether I have permission to marry – to marry my dearest Mary,' he took her hand, 'permission which I already have from the lady herself.'

'Why! my good Mr Jarrett,' exclaimed Aunt Catherine, 'as if you need ask! There is no one here but gives you their blessing – never mind what George says. What a happy week this is!' And she shed a few graceful tears among the inquiries and congratulations. Retaining Mary's hand Jarrett went on: 'I have not ventured on this before because of my doubts about my financial position. I could not bear to think that I should be in the nature of an encumbrance upon my wife because of it. But now, I am happy to say, a short visit to London this week has confirmed that I have secured a position of great promise in the mercantile there. Which brings me to our trip to the capital: why do we not hold our nuptials there? Make this a wedding trip? Then Mary and I can look about us for a home, just before I begin in my new office in April. Moreover – would it not be even better if we had a double marriage occasion? Would that be agreeable to Mr Sedgmoor and Miss Julia?'

Francis Sedgmoor, who ever since Julia had accepted him had been in a permanent blush of pride, was delighted. 'That would be marvellous. What a memorable occasion it will be! Er – do you agree, Julia?'

'Of course,' said Julia, taking his hand. She always seemed to agree with him: which Mary thought strange in such an uncompromising girl as her cousin.

'My good friend Macmillan has lodgings ready for us in Moorgate – he is leaving London soon, you see, and he is very kindly offering to us, free, for a short period, the rooms of which he is landlord, before he sells up. He is an estimable man, and I am sure you will be glad –'

He broke off. George, a riding-coat about his shoulders, his hair dishevelled by the wind, stood in the doorway.

He did not storm or curse, perhaps because he had had no drink that day, perhaps because of the constant weariness that was on him now. He merely threw down his hat and took off his gloves and said: 'I thought I told you I did not want you in my house. You had better get out.'

'Mr Jarrett has been here many times in your absence,

214

George,' said Aunt Catherine. 'We won the servants over to our side: that is why they did not tell you.'

'George, I wish –' began Jarrett.

'I said get out.'

'George, you had better know that Mr Jarrett and I are going to be married in spite of your opposition,' said Mary.

There was a silence, a bitter, tangible silence, like an evil smell in the room. Mary never forgot the expression of contempt on George's face as he looked at her. She felt sick and hot and had to turn away her head from the hollow gaze of those heavy-lidded eyes.

'I continue to oppose it,' he said finally, in a husky voice, 'but I suppose I cannot prevent it.'

'George, the wedding is to be a London one, later this month, together with that of Julia and Mr Sedgmoor,' said Mary. 'All the family will be going. I hope you will come too?'

Mary wanted George to say yes, to smile, to get up and shake Jarrett's hand and kiss her just as her cousin should: she wanted it so badly she clenched her fists and prayed.

'Have you said all you want to say, Jarrett?' said George. 'Then get out.'

The wife of the kindly old farmer Mr Newman had lingered on through that hard winter. Many times when Mary had called the woman had seemed on the brink of death and the old man and his son had been hushed and subdued; yet miraculously the invalid would rally again and sit up in bed and disperse the pain-graven wrinkles of her face in a smile and ask for a dish of tea. Whenever the occasion arose Mary got Dr Villiers to come and see her and she paid his fees, but eventually even the hard-nosed physician had been overcome by scruples and told her that it was pointless her paying for his attendance any more, as it was only a matter of time. That was in February. The day after the announcement of her engagement she remembered that she had not been to the farm for several weeks. Oppressed by guilt and a fear she hardly dared acknowledge she hurried over there that morning.

She did not ask Mr Newman and his son anything because they merely burst into tears where they stood in the yard and continued to weep and brush their hands across their eyes, leaving streaks of dirt like smeared face paint.

''Twas three days ago, mistress,' said Mr Newman when he could at last speak. 'Straight off like that. I warn't even with her. But she warn't in no pain at the end – do you think –?'

'No, no, I am sure of that,' said Mary. 'She's at peace now.'

'Thank you, mistress, it heals me to hear you say it. But oh God! what are we going to do?'

As his father could not go on, John Newman, muscular and blond, continued, crumpling the handkerchief that Mary had lent him between his fingers: 'It's been such a hard winter for us, you see – for everyone, I suppose – there's many on the fen didn't see it out – but somehow . . . When me old ma was here, it didn't seem to matter that we were as poor as churchmice. The lease on the farm's long run out, y'see – though Mr Hardwick's left us be so far – but we can't pay the rent again, that's for sure.'

'The only thing,' said Mr Newman, 'is to sell up what's ours, our bit of stock – the calves and the horse and a few poultry. But it's precious little we'd get in these times.'

A few moments later Mary was running full pelt across the slushy fields, ochreous water spurting up over her shoes and staining the hem of her frock, back to Morholm. She must speak to George.

Whilst Mary was at the farm, Milton, accompanied by Dr Villiers, had arrived at Morholm. Milton had grown so concerned about his friend George's health that he had presumed to ask the physician to come and see him. He was still doubtful about George's reaction and was not sure whether he would submit to a medical examination, but it was worth a try. They found George, as usual, alone in the library.

'Hullo, Villiers,' he grunted. 'What brings you here?'

Dr Villiers tapped his gold-headed physician's cane and bent his heavy brows towards Milton. He was not going to take responsibility for the explanation.

Milton cleared his throat. 'Er, George, concerned as I am for my friend's health, I took the liberty of asking Dr Villiers to come and see you to, er, put my mind at rest on that score.'

George's reaction was as he had feared.

'I consider that damned presumptuous of you, Milton. What has that to do with you? Besides,' he rose and poured himself a glass of wine, 'you have wasted Dr Villiers' time: there is nothing wrong with me, unless wretched boredom is in the medical textbooks.'

Dr Villiers refused the glass proffered him. 'But Mr Hardwick, will you not allow me to give an opinion? It is sensible in a man to have an occasional consultation with his physician, even if he thinks himself in perfect health. It is no trouble, I assure you. I am often over this way to attend your uncle Mr Daniel, and your charming cousin has often found occupation for me –'

George froze, his glass half-way to his lips. 'My cousin?'

'Indeed, Miss Mary; the lady –'

'Is she ill?'

'No, indeed: she has called me in to attend on one Mrs Newman, a farmer's wife living quite near here – a tenant of Morholm, I believe, sir. Apparently your cousin owes some gratitude to this family and, as the old woman was in need of experienced medical attendance, repaid it by enlisting my services. A most generous gesture, I think. Of course,

I only asked reduced fees of your cousin, but,' he spread his large professional hands, 'a mortal man must earn his bread, you know, Mr Hardwick. You seem quite surprised, sir: I thought you would have known of it.'

'No,' muttered George in a voice Milton did not like. 'I did not.'

'Unfortunately – though I did what I could – I was unable to check the course of the woman's illness, and I have ceased to make calls there. Now, as to yourself, sir –'

'I have told you I require none of your prodding,' said George, 'so you had better leave. Good day to you.'

He would have no more of them, and Milton well knew that flushed look of suppressed anger on his friend's face, so he and Dr Villiers left. In the hall Milton said to the physician: 'I am sorry to have taken up your valuable time. My friend's obstinacy is something I had underestimated. If you will send me your bill –'

Dr Villiers held up his hand. 'Pray, Mr Milton, do not speak of it – I could hardly charge for such an attendance. And your friend's disease is quite plain: it is his way of life. He is quite clearly drinking too much, and as to work or exercise – he does not hunt or shoot, I believe? No – just so. You will allow that his manner of living is – not to mince words – dissolute?'

Milton could not deny it. They went out to the stables.

'It is a malady suffered by many young men of his temperament, Mr Milton, and I think we need not trouble ourselves. Of course it has been the death of some, there's no escaping the fact. It merely depends on Mr Hardwick's own fibre, what becomes of him. Good day to you, sir.'

Dr Villiers mounted and rode away. Milton was just about to set off too when he saw Mary hurrying through the gateway. She smiled a greeting to him but seemed agitated.

'Mr Milton, George is in, isn't he?'

'Yes, I have just been with him. Is anything wrong –'

'I'm sorry, Mr Milton, I've no time to lose,' she said, running past him into the house. When an idea like this took hold of her she could not delay. She was about to knock on the library door when it was abruptly opened and George appeared before her.

'George, I was just coming to speak –'

'Good, and I sought you too. What did you mean by that business of getting Villiers in to the old farmer's wife?'

Mary was so startled she could say nothing for a moment.

'Why was I never told? Why must you do this behind my back? Good God, the – the presumption of it! With your own money you paid that old windbag just for a farmer's wife?'

'Indeed, George, I am sorry that I –'

'If you must needs do such a thing,' he went on fiercely, ignoring her, 'why could you not come to me? God knows I pay for enough extravagance – why not join in? Why did you have to go skulking – sneaking – behind my back in this fashion?'

She had never seen him so angry. She took a step backward.

'It was because I expected just such a reaction that I did not come to you,' she said. 'Why must you censure me for something done in good faith?'

'Oh, you make me sick with your eternal good faith,' hissed George. 'I believe half of it is to gratify your own self-importance.'

'Good faith is not something you are conspicuously well versed in, George,' said Mary, furious and near tears. 'Besides, you need trouble no longer: Mrs Newman is dead, and Mr Newman all but ruined.'

'Well, the country is too thickly populated anyhow,' said George. In his rage he did not mean what he said – half the things he said he did not mean – and he did not see how deeply his words offended her. His passion led him on: 'You seem to have contracted a deplorable habit of intimacy with bankrupts, cousin.'

He saw the colour come into her face.

'I hate and detest you, George! Hate you, do you hear?'

He brushed past her and went out.

When he had gone she sat alone in her room and the tears – of pity for the Newmans, of distress from the row with George – fell at last, silently, on her shaking hands. She had meant to ask him to help the Newmans. It had all turned out very differently. Suddenly, for no apparent reason, she remembered a September evening last year – how long ago it seemed! – when George had come home from London and they had walked so pleasantly together in the garden. He had changed towards her so much since then. She was stirred from her reflections by Julia, who came up to tell her she would be going into Peterborough tomorrow, and would take a letter to Jarrett for her.

The vengeful urge to hurt someone, to get your own back, once it seizes hold, is inexorable. It must run on to its climax, though behind it there may be a perfect realization of its folly and prospective tragedy. That someone else may be much more hurt in the process is immaterial, as it was to George when, leaning on a gate that morning and looking out over the fields poorly farmed by old Newman, he had an idea.

Jarrett descended the stairs of the Angel Inn after an enjoyable hour with Julia.

Her passion astonished him and left him a little dazed. He had visited brothels in London in his time and had known what was called a Posture Woman do amazing things. But with dowdy, sullen Julia ... Perhaps if he had known he would have pursued her instead of

Mary originally. But now things were working out doubly well.

Above all, the torrid sessions with Julia were infinitely better than the dismal couplings available at the brothel in Stamford he used to visit. It was a dingy house behind Water Street where the river ran out of the town; the back gave out on to the river bank and was slowly crumbling into the water, and poisonous damp crept up the walls of the apartments. Jarrett did a good job of curbing his appetites in daily life – acting was his supreme skill – but that did not destroy them, and though the business of leaving his horse at The Black Bull and skulking through dark streets to the tawdry house had been embarrassing – and dangerous in a gossip-ridden town like Stamford – it was very necessary. But that particular freezing night in January had proved unexpectedly useful. His partner in the brothel was a new girl: Beth Seddon.

He had been immediately struck by the resemblance to the maid Amelia at Morholm and his questions had soon revealed more. 'Ay, sister's there. She's a one. She told me she led squire on till he topped her. She can't never get enough . . . Shite knows how she managed, though. I had a bit of a knap wi' him one night at th'inn but he wouldn't go no further.' A few guineas had persuaded both sluts to make those accusations to the family. George, he perceived, had been an obstacle to his complete power over Mary, and though he had charmed that idiotic family of hers – even over the hurdle of his father's ruin – he thought George suspected him. If George still had any influence over her, that would kill it finally. Out of near disaster luck was being thrown at him and he had only to put out his hands and catch it . . .

In the tap-room an old man was seated on a pile of luggage, sobbing into his coarse red hands, while a much younger man stood, blond and uncomfortable, next to him.

He thought he recognized them and went up to speak to the younger.

'Pardon me – aren't you from that farmstead near Morholm?'

The young man nodded, and finally stammered: 'Newman's the name.'

'Ah, yes, of course. You – er – seem to be in some kind of trouble.'

'Ay, sir, it's been one thing after another. First the old girl died. She was sickening a long time, see. Then Squire Hardwick come and turned us out.'

'Squire Hardwick?'

'Ay, from Morholm, y'know. What wi' mother's illness, we know we couldn't manage the land proper. 'Twas all going downhill. Our lease was long run out, but Mr Joseph was always good to us, and left us be. Squire Hardwick give us a price for our own stock, fair enough. We buried the old girl only last week,' he added, glancing down at his father who continued to weep heedless of them. 'He's no younker any more – too old for all this upset,' he went on in a lower voice. 'I don't know what we're going to do. We've bare forty pounds in the world between us. We'll stay here tonight, but,' he sighed, 'I don't know what's to become of us.'

When Mary learned of this from Jarrett she felt she could never bring herself to look on George with fondness again.

Late that evening Jarrett was in his room at The Angel when a potboy showed in, to his great surprise, Kingsley Hardwick. Jarrett, barely refraining from a smile at Kingsley's curled and powdered head and gold waistcoat stretched grotesquely across his paunch, offered him wine and a chair. To his renewed surprise, they were refused. 'Well, my good sir, and what can I do for you?' There was not the slightest suspicion in Jarrett's mind of what Kingsley, blank-faced and lethargic, was about to say.

'I know about you and my cousin Julia,' said Kingsley, never one to beat about the bush.

Jarrett's heart gave a lurch and his bowels slackened sickeningly for a moment before he regained his composure and realized that to outwit this dullard would not be too difficult. His mind worked furiously as he walked to the window and casually looked out at the spires of the cathedral brushing the smoky evening sky. 'Indeed? And no doubt this knowledge is something you cannot but hope to use to your advantage.'

Kingsley sat down with an air of satisfaction, his boots creaking. In the midst of his mental calculations Jarrett thought it typified Kingsley that when he wore boots they creaked and when he wore shoes they squeaked.

'Mr Hardwick,' Jarrett began, 'I know that you are not a man lacking in intelligence. You are a man of the world. I think I may speak freely and with expectation of understanding and sympathy.' He paused, but Kingsley made no reply.

'I am planning to elope with Julia,' went on Jarrett. 'When we all go to London for this marriage trip, a great deal of money will necessarily go with Julia and with Mary. Julia and I will take that money and then head for the continent. My prospective position in the mercantile is a myth. That is our plan. I am quite confident of its success; I have the whole of your family in the palm of my hand; but if you will give us your help, I can feel more confident. In return for this, you see, you will get a share. I will tell you how you can help when the time comes. It will, I assure you, be well worth your while.'

Jarrett's handsome face smiled down at Kingsley's ugly one. He could see the buffoon was attracted by the proposition. 'Of course,' he went on, 'this will be a much more profitable arrangement for you, for should you care to – er – put the screws on now, as it were, there is not a lot I could give you – compared with what you will get in a couple of weeks' time.'

At last Kingsley nodded. It had not turned out quite as he expected, but he could see no difficulties in this new situation. 'Very well,' he said, 'but you will not tell Julia I am party to your scheme?'

Jarrett agreed to that, and they shook hands in a business-like fashion as if they had arranged the sale of a horse.

While at Morholm preparations began for the trip to London, an invitation arrived to an informal party at the Wainwrights' town-house in Stamford. Though it was to Mr George Hardwick and family that it was addressed, George was the only one who declined the prospect of an evening 'being sniffed at by that puffed-up old harridan'.

The Miltons also received an invitation, and it awakened in Henry conflicting feelings of elation and foreboding. He knew well who else would be there: Hugh Woodhouse and his circle of hangers-on. They had been with Elizabeth the other morning when he called: Woodhouse, Warren and the Misses Graham and Thackray. The two women, very grand in feathers and turban head-dresses and silk polonaises, had monopolized him, deliberately, it seemed to Milton, while Woodhouse paid Elizabeth his desultory, charmless addresses. 'I damn near broke my neck taking a fence the other day, Miss Elizabeth,' Milton heard him saying, copiously taking snuff. 'Damn near broke my neck,' and he wished he had. The man treated her like a pretty toy which engaged the attention for short whiles and could easily be laid aside. When finally Milton escaped from the two women and the wretched little creature Warren – who made a joke about him directly his back was turned – he joined Elizabeth and Woodhouse. He could see the confusion she was thrown into by being caught between the men to whom she was Elizabeth the human being and Miss Wainwright, glittering lady of fashion; and in the end she treated him distantly and in a brittle, careless manner. And Woodhouse seemed to think him almost beneath notice. As he thought of the coming party he felt almost as if he were going into battle.

The whole Hardwick family was to go to London to see the girls married, except for George, who remained as surly as ever on the subject, Great-Uncle Horace, who dared not risk losing a penny by an absence from the office, and so declined the journey on the grounds of his age, and Mary's brother William, who had departed after Christmas as abruptly as he had come, telling Mary slyly that he had found employment in Stamford. From his manner she guessed it was of doubtful nature, and did not enquire into it. Meanwhile Mary also wrote to the younger son James in London and secured his promise that he would join them for their nuptials. Jarrett wrote to tell them that their departure was now set for the beginning of April, and as March petered out Mary felt as if she were floating in her excitement. Under Aunt Catherine's supervision a good deal of her nieces' money was to go with them for the purchase of trousseaus and all the 'necessaries', as she put it, as well as all the family jewels and a substantial sum extracted from George in order that the celebrations should be worthwhile. Young Mr Sedgmoor expressed a little apprehension of robbery on the way, but he was soon quashed by Daniel. 'Why, my boy, these are not the days of highwaymen, y'know; the roads are as safe as you could wish now. The North road's too busy, if you ask me.'

There was only one shadow on Mary's happiness. She wished she could bring George round to going with them, but he would have none of it and refused to talk to her. If he would only be friends with her again, and come to London and wish her well, her joy would be complete. But even enlisting Mr Milton's help did not move him.

Aunt Catherine found the Wainwrights' party wonderfully opportune, for as well as Mrs Wainwright herself there were several distinguished members of local society present to whom she could boast of her going into town ahead of the season, and of the excellent matches that her nieces had made. Jarrett too was there (Mrs Wainwright had hesitated as to whether to invite him after the Jarrett mill had closed, but he still seemed to be on a respectable footing, and such was the young man's overriding charm that her doubts disappeared as they occurred to her), and Mary sensed with pleasure the envy in the room as the news of her coming marriage, now officially announced, buzzed around the guests. During the evening she found herself talking to two young women who were introduced as Miss Graham and Miss Thackray. They had extravagantly dressed and powdered hair and patched faces and they cast critical eyes over her clothes and figure. Yet Mary detected the envy in their superiority, and glowed with pride; it was she, not they, who had captured the heart of the handsome Thomas Jarrett.

'Faith, Miss Hardwick,' said Miss Graham, 'I'll wager poor Elizabeth – you know her, of course – is jealous of your trip to London. She adores town, you know, or tries to. Poor girl, she tries so hard to keep up with the mode – and who wouldn't struggle, with that hag of a mother,' she added. 'All her money bags can't hide her vulgarity. That's why Elizabeth is flirting – poor dear, she's not very good at it – with old Hugh over there.'

Mary followed Miss Graham's gaze to where Miss Wainwright was talking with a big unhandsome man in silk breeches and stockings embroidered with clocks. Mr Milton, she noticed, was some distance away with the Townsends.

'He's the eldest son of Sir Geoffrey Woodhouse, over at Peterborough,' said Miss Thackray. 'I believe he's taken a passing fancy to Elizabeth – if he can take a fancy to anything beyond a horse and a bottle of wine. Elizabeth's overwhelmed at such attention, you know. To marry a baronet's son would be just the thing. Of course, there's still her other suitor, young Mr Milton,' here both women laughed, 'Milton the poet, the ardent wooer. I believe she has some affection for him. But if it came to a choice between affection and a title I know which she'd choose.'

'Perhaps our gallant Mr Milton had better steal in one night and sweep her off her feet and carry her off from the clutches of the evil baronet,' said Miss Graham.

'There's Mr Milton, see,' said Miss Thackray. 'Oh! if looks could kill!'

'Perhaps our poet will challenge Hugh to a duel,' said Miss Graham.

'I wonder what weapon he would choose – slingshot?'

'Oh, I say – Mr Milton's joining them. Looks as if Milton's not prepared to lose his paradise!' And in their screams of laughter at this pun she left them.

But Milton was to have no success with Miss Wainwright that night; and it was Woodhouse who led her into supper. Milton was forced to resort to escorting Aunt Catherine (an act which delighted her – she later confided to Mary that 'she was always being told how gracefully her years sat on her, and what further proof could one need, than the fact that she had been distinguished by a good young gentleman such as Mr Milton'). For her part Mary wished her friend had been able to distinguish a certain other lady. Although Mr Milton could not compare with her Mr Jarrett, Mary was fond of him and could only think him vastly superior to that pompous buffoon who was his rival. When at last, late that night, the Morholm party left Stamford for home, she felt almost guilty in her happiness, so dejected had Mr Milton looked.

* * *

On the great day Mary was roused very early, for the coach left for London at six; she would be on it with Julia, Aunt Catherine and Mrs Peach, together with Clarry and a new maid they had hired from the village to replace the ill-fated Amelia. Jarrett, Mr Sedgmoor, Daniel and Kingsley would follow next day. She had hoped that George might rise early to say goodbye; but he did not appear, and after a bite of breakfast Aunt Catherine was urging her to hurry and put on her cloak, the horses were ready; then she was climbing on to the back of a stamping horse; then they were clopping down the drive, away from Morholm, in a little procession, their horses' breath steaming in the moist spring air; then winding through the village, where a shepherd's dog ran with them for a few moments, yapping excitedly. When they got on to the Stamford road, Mary gave the old country a last fond look. The dew was like silver on the flat fallows, catching the tender rays from a sky of blue eggshell transparency. There were a few nestling primroses and cowslips beneath the hedgerows, and somewhere a thrush was singing with sweet and piercing clarity. From the rushbeds of the river meandering to Southorpe Mill a ghostly grey heron rose up and with slow flaps flew over them in the direction of the distant brown smear of Helpston Heath. Past Burghley House, they dipped into the grey stone elegance of Stamford, the church spires soaring around them as if presenting arms. Beneath the gallows-sign of The George they dismounted, and Mary found herself doing what she had often dreamed of, sitting in the coffee-room with 'London' over the door, where travellers waited for the north coach to take them to the capital, where she was to see the sights and visit the theatres and the gardens and perhaps live for the rest of her life. Aunt Catherine was paying for the horses to be taken back to Morholm, and giving orders that it was to be no one irresponsible, now; and Julia, who seemed just as excited, was squeezing her hand in an affectionate manner

Mary had never seen her use before. Grandmother Peach, in her best frizzed wig, was telling them she remembered the Duke of Cumberland coming to this very inn after Culloden back in '46 – ay, she remembered looking out of the window in St Martin's Street where she lived and seeing him there on his horse – 'twas the year her Anne married old Joseph, she remembered – and then there was a noise of stamping and jingling and shouting commingled, and Mary glimpsed a very buttoned-up coachman going into the tap-room for a tot; and then they were hurrying out to the coach, and as their luggage went up Aunt Catherine was telling Clarry, who had been furnished with an old duelling pistol that hung on the wall at Morholm, to keep a close eye on the strongbox that was concealed among it – ''tis not the money I fear for, but my dear mother's locket' she added. Mary heard a voice by her side, and she turned to see Mr Milton.

'I have come to see you off, as I won't be able to see you married,' he said. 'I wish you all the happiness in the world. Jarrett tells me you may settle in London.'

'Yes, we think so,' she replied. 'Oh dear! That means –' She had not thought, in her elation, that she would no longer see Mr Milton – or George. 'But we will write you,' she assured him, 'regularly. And you must be the first to come and visit us. Oh, Mr Milton,' her excitement bubbled up with renewed vigour, 'I am so happy, and expectant, and – oh, there is so much ahead of me!'

He smiled, trying to show a happiness for her that he did not feel because of the wretchedness in his own heart. Sensing this from the hollow look on his face, she said: 'And – and I earnestly hope, dear Mr Milton, that you may attain such a joy as I have.'

He could not manage another smile, still less speak, but he was grateful for her kindness. The coachman was climbing into his place.

'I must go now. Mr Milton – I – my cousin George will be virtually alone at Morholm while the family is away. I hate the thought of him in that silent house while we – I mean, despite all the things that have happened, it seems so sad.'

'I understand. I shall go and see him as often as I can.'

'Thank you! I shall feel so much more easy. Goodbye! I promise we'll write!' She squeezed his hand and climbed into the coach. Milton gave his good wishes to Julia, paid his respects to Aunt Catherine and Mrs Peach, and then stood back and watched the coach rumble off towards the Great North Road.

Milton fetched his horse and made his way slowly home. He was sorry at this parting, and angry with himself because he could only give it a distracted, absent-minded attention. For he had called at the Wainwrights' again since the party, and had had an increasingly careless – no, damn it, it was hostile, she was actually hostile – reception from Elizabeth. And her sister Wilhelmina had spitefully made some oblique comment about Woodhouse that left him in no doubt as to whom Miss Wainwright was now directing her attention. Milton was a man given to abandoning hope rather quickly: he had done so a hundred times in the course of his love for her. There was a certain curious perverse pleasure in it, when at the back of his mind he knew he was exaggerating. Yet now he wanted to cling on to hope and found it slipping away; and the voice at the back of his mind seemed this time to be saying he had lost her.

The coach rattled and jolted out of Stamford and the Great North Road stretched away before it, a narrow raised causeway flanked by unmade road, but pregnant with romantic associations. They juddered slowly and unsteadily down the steep descent to Wansford that had brought many a coach to grief, and crossed the narrow arched bridge over the Nene at a careful pace. Then it was on briskly past the Wansford paper-mills to their first change at Alwalton, after which they were out on to the long and lovely stretch towards Alconbury Hill. It was along here that Aunt Catherine, despite the bruising motion of the coach, contrived to fall asleep, until they began the climb up to Alconbury, when Mrs Peach woke her. 'We're coming up Stangate Hill, Catherine.'

'Oh! Lord! Prepare yourself, Mary, Julia: this is a notorious resort of highwaymen. God protect us!'

But they met with no trouble, and even the gibbet on the hill was bare. They changed at the Wheatsheaf and went on. By the early afternoon they had passed through Eaton and arrived at the Sun at Biggleswade, where they ate a welcome meal. Then, after a break that seemed all too short, it was on towards Baldock. The novelty of travelling began to wear off for Mary now and she was impatient to see London. The jolting, rattling miles continued to Stevenage, where they changed at the famous Swan Inn; then came an easier stretch, for the sun which had been lurking behind the clouds at last appeared and illumined the pretty Hertfordshire parkland with its woods and orchards and pastures and lodge-gates. She drifted into sleep for a while, and her thoughts of London were just melting into the more colourful form of dreams, when she was roused by Julia as they halted to change at Hatfield. When they set off again Aunt Catherine told her their next stop would be Barnet, and then they would be almost there. At this news the excitement began to well up inside her again and, refreshed by her nap, she watched the fields and villages, already turning grey with twilight, moving past the window and realized how far she was from Morholm, further than she had ever been in her life.

At Barnet they changed at the Green Man and traversed the dreaded Finchley Common without incident. The coach

toiled up Highgate Hill and passed through the charming
little village, descended slowly, and then began the arduous
struggle along the rutted watery track of the Holloway Road.
Then they picked up speed through Islington, passed the
Islington Gate and urban London swallowed them up.

The size of London, as they rattled towards their final
destination, astonished Mary, who had never seen a town
bigger than Stamford. First there was what seemed like a
long chain of blackened villages set amongst scrubby fields
with drifting smoke from brickyards. Then a maze of cobbled
streets, steep and sharply turning and crowded so that the
coach could hardly get along, and almost brushed the smutty
walls of the houses, so that sometimes leering faces, of frowsy
pox-ridden women and deformed beggars and emaciated
children, were briefly pressed against the coach windows.
The children were everywhere, scuttling in gangs like rats
behind the coach wheels; and there were many half-wild
dogs and cats and even pigs in the smoky alleys. The stench
was overpowering, and as they drew nearer the heart of the
city the noise of traffic and the cries of pedlars and hawkers
still out in the twilight was like bedlam. They began to
glimpse grander buildings, squares and crescents of tall
white houses that looked like palaces as the street-lamps
were lit. As the coach fought its way down Gray's Lane to
its stopping place at Holborn Mary caught sight of glittering
creatures in the mass of sedan chairs edging along like a
tide; men with their hair loose and powdered and narrow
cutaway coats, and women in daringly plunging gowns.
When the coach stopped it seemed strange to be suddenly
motionless in the midst of this whirling, eddying activity.

Jarrett's friend Mr Macmillan, to whose kindness they
owed their lodgings, was to meet them, and they had only
just climbed out of the coach when a voice close by them
rose above the general noise: 'The Hardwick party, I believe?
I am Charles Macmillan.'

Mary was surprised when she turned to look at the gentleman who waited on them. She had automatically envisaged Jarrett's friends as tall, good-looking young men with broad smiles; this Mr Macmillan was about thirty, little taller than herself, and plump and inelegant with a mottled complexion; and although his manner was as deferential and obliging as Jarrett's, he had about him a kind of latent ugliness that she found disconcerting. But he led them most courteously to the carriage he had waiting, supervised the loading of their luggage and chatted amiably to them on the way to their lodgings.

'I hope you will find your rooms satisfactory. They are not large, I fear, but then to country people like yourselves I expect everything in town will seem horribly cramped. I myself am leaving London shortly, as Tom has perhaps told you; that is why I have sold up this house. My purchaser does not take possession until two weeks' time, and as my tenants have left already, I was glad to offer you the use of the place, such as it is, for this happy period. May I be so bold as to inquire which of the ladies is to make my friend's wife? Ah, I see: you must be Miss Mary Hardwick, of whom Tom has written me so much. Miss Julia – I am honoured – Mistress Catherine – charmed, ma'am: and Mrs Peach: a pleasure to meet you.'

The rooms, though they did not look spacious compared with Morholm, seemed grand with their high ceilings and carved fireplaces, and they looked out on to a street near the Moorgate that Mary felt could alone afford her months of fascination with its parade of beggars and rakes, carriages and drays, squalor and finery. After changing they sat down in a snug dining-room to a meal with Mr Macmillan, who throughout was politeness itself; Aunt Catherine and Mrs Peach were clearly impressed with him. When dinner was over their host announced that he had a hired carriage ready to take them for a drive about the evening streets, and it was on that excursion through the lamplit April dark that the spell of the city fell on Mary. She saw such fabled structures as the Tower and St Paul's as if in a dream. The Thames astonished her, for the Nene and the Welland at home were green, rushy places of moorhens and swans, whilst this, though scarcely bigger, seemed one solid mass of shipping, so that she fancied she might walk across to the other bank without getting her feet wet. Mr Macmillan obligingly pointed out and described everything they should see, but it was another source of surprise to Mary that he seemed so indifferent to it all — surely custom could not dim the fascination of this? But he was a friend of Jarrett's, so she could not think he could be really insensitive.

When she lay down to sleep that night, memories of all she had seen that day still flashing in her mind like the coloured blobs that dance before the eyes after looking at a strong light, she thought of that great multitude of people surrounding her. How vast this city was, how important its business: how insignificant this young provincial girl. Yet how bustling too was her own world of the self, how giant the importance of her love and hope and excitement. Thus trying to reconcile the macrocosm and the microcosm she fell asleep.

6

The next evening Jarrett, Daniel, Kingsley and Mr Sedgmoor arrived in high spirits. With the attentiveness of both
Jarrett and Mr Macmillan they settled in wonderfully well,
and the weather was clear and fine. That day, and the day
following it, were the happiest Mary had ever known. The
exciting scenes round her and the love of Jarrett, bound in
with the wonderful knowledge – it was still heart-stopping
every time she thought of it – that shortly she was to become
Jarrett's wife, and begin a lifetime of further happiness.

They explored London fully, travelling along the river by
ferry-boats. Jarrett was always with them, guiding them
pleasantly, never patronizingly, explaining and recommend-
ing what he knew, sharing their interest in what he did not.
Aunt Catherine investigated many expensive dressmakers
and outfitters, assuming an air of great discernment. 'You
must be on your toes with these people,' she said, 'for they
may spot a provincial a mile away, and assume they can
pull the wool over her eyes. It does not do to appear rustic
– really they are such snobs! And I am sure half of them are
mere upstarts of no family – that pompous madam this
morning, Mrs Peach, did you mark her? – a more mealy
complexion I never saw. Yet a tall wig and a gilded fitting
room makes her turn up her nose at me. The daughter of a
footman no doubt.' Mr Macmillan, who seemed to be a very
busy man, could not accompany them; but he was often
with them at their rooms, and was pleased to show them
the newspapers and journals he had bought in the city.

It was their third evening in London when they all stayed
up rather late, diverting themselves with talk, with parlour

games and conundrums, and with drink, and only when Aunt Catherine caught sight of the clock and made a great bustle in retiring did they make their way to bed. Young Mr Sedgmoor, a man normally given to temperance but waylaid by high spirits, was a little tipsy, and Jarrett and Macmillan stayed up to see him safely to his room and undress. When everyone was gone they sat in the parlour with their pipes and talked in low voices. The fire had dwindled to a red wink and the darkened room was taking on that chill forsaken emptiness that rooms have in the small hours. There was a smell, rather stale, of smoke and wine, and a brisk wind could be heard muttering down the chimney. From the bit of fire and their pipes they could see only faint lineaments of each other, like touches of white chalk on a charcoal drawing.

'Thank God they've gone at last,' said Jarrett. 'What a strain entertaining people of such intellect!'

Macmillan grunted. 'I've never observed you to feel the strain of being polite before, Jarrett.'

'No.' Jarrett laughed. 'No, it's true. But I don't want to do it all my life. One does tire of crawling to worthless people.'

'Surely you would not count yourself particularly worthy, Jarrett?'

Jarrett laughed carelessly, the musical laugh that bewitched everyone. 'True again. But tell me, how goes it with you? Are things still as according to plan?'

'Yes, I'm pretty confident. I've withdrawn everything I've made from Firman's and it's a tidy sum altogether. Then there's the money from this place, as well as from other less desirable properties I've sold up.'

Jarrett chuckled and knocked out his pipe. 'If only old starchy Firman knew the source of the money that's been lying in his vaults.'

The sources of Mr Macmillan's money were manifold, but

236

they ranged from the doubtful to the downright swindling. Much came from a profitable line in the peddling of potions and nostrums to get rid of unwanted pregnancies, sold to the gullible and desperate, which often had no effect, sometimes induced ill-health, and occasionally killed, together with other drugs and cures – aphrodisiacs, vomits, purges, youth-elixirs – all the most unscrupulous quackery. Then there were forgeries and swindles, the occasional robbery of jewels from ladies, and the hiring out of vile lodgings at ruthless prices. He had also been a pimp.

'And no one is on to you, you're sure?' went on Jarrett.

'Well, naturally, I cannot be sure. I am modestly confident. But it can only be a matter of time. That is why I am getting out now, while my fortunes are at their peak. I have got us a little carriage to facilitate our flight, and I have arranged for Will and his cronies to be ready for us about midnight. They often make the Channel crossing to smuggle brandy and they'll ask no questions. Then I have acquaintances of our sort in Dieppe with whom we can arrange the disposal of our profits.'

'Very good. We must pack them off tomorrow evening to the theatre. Julia will plead a headache to stay behind, and then make her way to a rendezvous we have arranged – a rendezvous she doesn't know will never be fulfilled on my part, the little fool. That oaf Kingsley is to remain behind too, to secure us access to the old bitch's room where sit the blessed strong-box and jewel-box. They've a deal of valuable jewellery, you know, Macmillan, that's been mouldering away in that Fenland pile for years: I was quite surprised. I dare say it will make my gains level with yours.'

'I suppose you feel no regret at the way you're treating these women?'

'My dear Macmillan, I have had great enjoyment out of Julia – indeed you would not believe the capabilities of that girl by looking at her. And my undertaking could not have gone on without her. The indolence of dear drunken George, and Mary's somewhat – abstracted state of mind, meant the housekeeping began to be left to her, and many a draft George gave her on Wiley's bank has come my way. For our – elopement – of course. And poor young Sedgmoor – when I noticed him sniffing round her I told her to form an engagement with him. It was an excellent cover for our activities . . . and of course it meant dear George laying out the money for her marriage too. And Mary has been a most charming companion. Indeed, at the beginning, when I first realized father was sure to go bankrupt, I fully intended to marry her if I had to. It was a way out of the poverty I saw coming when the firm collapsed. The settlement her uncle left her is most handsome. But a lifetime of marriage . . . I did not relish it. Luckily, the intervention of Julia helped me to see this profitable alternative. But to return to your question, it is no use my saying I care for their feelings when I do not. I care for their money and my comfort and advancement. It would be the attitude of every person would he but admit it. Moreover, my dear fellow, "love" is far more transient than folk believe. Mary was half-way to loving George when I stepped in. And he loves her still, I can tell. You see, I'm quite a little Richardson in my way, aren't I, Macmillan? They would have one believe that the affairs of the heart are inextricably complex, but when one is possessed of an analytical and disinterested mind as I am, one perceives they are really monstrously simple.'

'And what of the future? What are your plans?' said Macmillan.

'Oh, with as much money as we shall have, who needs plans? For the moment,' he stood up and stretched, 'I shall go to bed. Goodnight, Macmillan.'

'Pleasant dreams, Jarrett.'

* * *

In the countryside around Morholm spring had finally come and left daubs of green painted all over the landscape. Most of all the grim silence of the winter months was gone; cuckoos called from the Heath and the sky was speckled with swallows, the pasture was full of lambs with tremulous new voices, the stream that fed Aysthorpe gurgled in lively spate, and the voices of the shepherd and the herdboy were loud and healthy.

Yet in Morholm, as if in another world, the silence was so complete and so depressing that George was repeatedly forced to get outside and merely wander about the farm and the village to escape it. With no one there but Mrs Reynolds to look after him, no distraction of a scavenging, scolding family, his mind was horribly free. If ever he had wanted to concentrate his mind – not that he ever had – now was the time. But he did not want to reflect now, now of all times, for there was nothing to reflect upon but a kind of empty vastness, a nagging, sterile despair, an endless aching futility. He felt he would go mad with thinking and thinking, and seeing nothing before him still but a terrible vacancy. Drink was the only answer, drink and more drink, though he knew it was no answer at all. And he felt so ill all the time – his head ached and buzzed, he sweated and shivered, his hands shook. Alcohol and inactivity had brought this on him, he said to himself. In fact he was responsible for everything, his own wretched uselessness lay at the bottom of it all.

No, no, he told himself, it was merely the world, the world was like that and he had always known it. It was a laughable sham – hadn't he and Milton always said it? Though Milton seemed to have changed. But he himself still had his eyes open; life was a sick joke, it wasn't to be taken seriously, man was an absurd creature and there was no use in expecting much from being one. That was what he had established in his mind, his ideas since a youth. There were a few scummy, ridiculous pleasures, to be taken as you liked, to make the thing worthwhile, and the rest was cant.

His erring footsteps took him to the churchyard, and he went and looked at the graves of his parents. That of his mother was old and moss-grown. She had died when he was nine years old, but the memory was not a catastrophic one. So long as his father Joseph had been there, nothing seemed to have real significance; his father had been so unobtrusively strong, so full of love that he well supplied what was missing. For the first time, as he stood in the flowering churchyard, George realized the immense loss Joseph must have felt at the death of his dear Anne, a crushing loss that George had never observed to get the better of his father. His parents had not been similar characters; she was a more forceful person than Joseph, always kind, but strong-willed and often abstracted. She had been subject to fits of depression and illness, and it was an exceptionally long one of these that had carried her off. Ah, how wrong one could be about people! He had always thought of his father as the most agreeable and well-meaning of men, but not a man of any fibre, any singular virtue. Yet Joseph had suffered, and smiled while he suffered. More than I can do, thought George: I don't smile in comfort. Yet have I really suffered?

No, no, it was man's lot to be in a kind of wretched limbo, and it was not worth worrying about. Yes, it was true, not long ago he had allowed himself to get like the rest of them. He had pretended to himself that the world contained something really worth having. He had let hope take hold of him, that feeling of blithe childish anticipation, that bright-eyed waking in the early morning as if the world was just beginning. Hope, he told himself, was really a destructive, malignant thing. There was no good in it, it was treacherous, it was cruel. He was glad, he thought, that the illusion had been shattered for him. Man and man's life was stupid, nasty, vulgar, grubbing and worthless, and it was dangerous folly to persist in the belief that it was not. Who was that author his tutor Mr Alden always used to be pressing him to read – Swift, was it? Anyway that author seemed to think similarly, though George had never been a scholar. Well, what did it matter? What did anything matter?

But that was the cruel paradox. It did matter.

It was the day of the Stamford bull-run, and Milton emerged from The George where he had left his horse to find St Mary's Hill jammed with yelling apprentice-boys and sportsmen, blocking his way up the street.

It was a barbaric practice, and both it and its counterpart in Peterborough were coming under criticism from citizens who wanted it banned; apart from its cruelty it caused much damage to shops and vehicles. A heifer was released from the market and chased and tormented through the streets to its death by a bellowing, bloodthirsty crowd. Milton thought it a brutal and degrading business and especially hypocritical in a town with pretensions to elegance like Stamford. He saw the crowd, with the bull somewhere in its midst, moving his way, and hurried back down the hill towards the river. Once they were set going they were likely to trample you underfoot. He stopped on the bridge opposite Lord Burghley's hospital and looked back. He could see the bull now, not very large, snorting with fear and rage and wheeling this way and that to face its tormentors. A savage and mangy dog ran suddenly from its master's side, black lips curled back over foul teeth, and attacked the bull. The maddened beast, finding at last an individual to wreak its frantic revenge on, lowered its head and tossed the dog like a rag and trampled on it with dancing, sideways steps. There was a great howl, part anguish, part hilarity, from the crowd, and in that moment the bull broke away and ran clattering down the sloping street. Suddenly bull and pursuers were roaring towards Milton. There was no time to run; he could only flatten himself into one of the bridge bays while the bull with a flash of panicked eye-whites and the sweating, screaming mob streamed past him. As the last stragglers went hooting by he heard a splash behind him. The bull had plunged into the river and with frustrated jeers they were hurling stones at it.

Trembling and rather sick he walked up to the Wainwrights' house. He was bitterly sure he must present a pathetic figure, turning up at the place more frequently than was polite and hanging round a woman who had suitors at her beck and call. And besides, Elizabeth turned out to be not at home. Mrs Wainwright was, and was happy to see him, 'but my daughter and some friends are calling at Mr Woodhouse's.' Where else? thought Milton. Without Elizabeth there he had no inclination to stay, but it was impossible to leave immediately, so he took tea, in no very good humour, with Mrs Wainwright and Wilhelmina. It was an aggravation to have to endure Mrs Wainwright's snobbish talk – he hated the woman again now – and, even worse, the detestable Wilhelmina's hints – 'Why, mama, I declare Lizzie is for ever at Hugh's nowadays – I think she must be taking measurements for carpets and curtains, eh, Mr Milton?' He set off finally for home in a savage mood, but it had changed to a sluggish desolation by the time he reached Helpston.

Milton's father had recently had a heavy fever and, though he was recovering, the air was still redolent of excessive heat and hot draughts and broths and rasping coughs. Also they were having the first floor decorated so upstairs there was a smell of whitewash and the sudden glare of repainted walls, and the equipment of decorating lay everywhere. Milton always recalled that distinctive offbeat air at home when he looked back at the events of the next few days.

Mrs Townsend was with his mother in the parlour and as he went through to the library he heard her talking. '. . .

and it seems that Miss Elizabeth Wainwright and Mr Hugh Woodhouse are rapidly coming to an understanding, and people say they are sure to become engaged soon. Such a perfect match!'

Yes, a perfect match, thought Milton sourly, perfect in a way a match with him would not have been. Elizabeth was rich, Woodhouse was rich: she had a fast-rising name, he would soon have a title. Love did not come into it – what need love with such dazzling credentials? He wanted to hate her but could not; instead he loved her so intensely he could not sit or stand still for a few minutes at a time. He felt always that he must get on and do something to resolve this dreadful anguished uncertainty. The thought of Elizabeth and how desperately he loved her lodged itself like a dull, rough-edged stone in his soul.

In this mood a visit to Morholm to see George was an irksome duty, but he had promised Mary, and beneath his emotional turmoil there was still concern for his friend. He rode over to Morholm in a gentle scented dusk. George was very low, and he was drunk, but Milton thought he seemed pleased to see him under the indifferent mask. They exchanged the usual restrained greetings and when George said 'How goes it with you, Milton?' it was rather a relief to pour out his feelings.

'Oh, George, I hardly need tell you how very much in love with Miss Wainwright I am. No, don't scoff, George, let us be earnest –'

'Good Lord, Milton, let us be anything but earnest! You know that is the last thing within my power. But go on.'

'It is just that it is the most crushing, overwhelming feeling, to love and oh, to need someone so much. You feel your heart will burst. Are you listening, George?'

George was slumped with his head on his hand and his eyes closed. After a moment he said: 'Yes. Yes, I'm listening.'

'Well, but – oh, how can I explain – when you feel that

– that your hopes are no more, when you perceive that you are not favoured as . . . Oh, I doubt if you can understand me, can you, George?'

George raised his head and for a moment his face was frank and young and open as Milton had not seen it in a long time. His lips trembled and he seemed to be on the verge of saying something that had been very burdensome to him. 'Milton – I –'

Milton looked at his friend and suddenly felt an immense pity and affection for him; he was glad George was going to be frank and serious with him at last. Then George faltered, his face clouded over and became wry and cynical once more, and he turned away. 'Oh, I forget what I was going to say, anyway. Let's have a drink and talk of something else.'

'Mary, my dear, are you quite ready? Come, let me look at you. Hm, yes, a pretty figure you shall make, I think: of course at the theatre there will be ladies of the highest fashion, but I think we shall not be entirely put to shame. Hm, I am not sure about the dressing of your hair: it is a pity you want a little height: but there, 'tis done now, and better less than more, as my mother used to say: no one favours a gawky girl.'

It was Aunt Catherine speaking, standing in the vestibule of their lodgings, on the fourth night of their stay in London.

'Where is Julia?' said Mary, escaping from her aunt's primping fingers and addressing young Mr Sedgmoor. 'She will be late.'

'I th-think she may not be well,' said Sedgmoor, his pleasant face a little puckered. 'Will you go and see her?'

'Of course,' said Mary. Slightly uncomfortable in her finery she went down the passage to Julia's room, resisting the urge to run as she often did at Morholm. There in summer, to the outrage of Aunt Catherine, she often went barefoot in her oldest and most comfortable print frock: and she felt a strange flash of regret for the freedom of that old life as she knocked at Julia's door.

The room was in darkness: but a tireless, pellucid light seemed to come unreflected from the eyes of Julia, lying on her bed. 'Julia? Are you not well?' said Mary: she could hear her cousin's breathing, intensely sharp and fast.

'It's nothing, Mary,' said Julia from the bed. 'I have a bad headache, and I fear I had better not come to the play tonight.' Mary found her hand in the darkness. The palm was feverishly hot. 'Can I get you something?' said Mary. 'Some sal volatile?'

Julia shook her head. 'Nothing. It is merely the excitement. I will be better for the rest. Tell Francis to go to the play with you and the others.'

'Shall I send him to you?'

'No. No.' Julia's grip tightened. 'No, he will only fuss.' The grip on Mary's hand grew tighter: then Julia abruptly let go, almost as if pushing her away. 'Go now, and enjoy the play.'

Jarrett and Mr Macmillan had arranged the outing to see the famous Garrick at Drury Lane, but were not coming themselves: Jarrett was helping Macmillan to wind up his accounts before his friend left the capital. They were waiting in the vestibule to see them off and when Mary came back from Julia's room Jarrett took her hands and looked at her admiringly. 'God's life, I have half a mind to come to the play after all,' he said.

'Now, Tom, you promised to help me,' said Macmillan. 'I must rob you of your escort this evening, Miss Mary.'

'I never dreamed I would find a rival in a cost-ledger,' laughed Mary. 'Mr Sedgmoor, Julia has a bad headache and prefers to stay in and rest. No, she insists that you go.'

'Such a pity!' cried Aunt Catherine. 'Daniel, you say Kingsley is not coming either? Well, he probably wishes to spend the evening at a gambling-club or some such. The carriage is waiting for us – well, Mr Sedgmoor, we shall have you with us at least. Pray take Mary's arm, Mr Sedgmoor; and cousin Daniel will escort Mrs Peach. I must go without escort, alas – the penalty of my position.'

Young Mr Sedgmoor still seemed a little troubled about Julia, and Mary had to keep reassuring him as they got into the carriage. At the last moment, as with a jerk they began to rattle off over the cobbles, she turned to wave to Jarrett. But he had already closed the door.

When they had gone Jarrett hurried to Julia's room and went in without knocking. She was standing in green velvet travelling habit, with a three-cornered hat trimmed with lace, her eyes luminous and her face glowing. A bag containing clothes was on the bed. He smiled and took her in his arms.

'All is ready, darling?' he said. Julia nodded and kissed him. 'But I wish we could leave together. Can't we –'

'Now, Julia, you know we cannot be seen leaving together. It's only a short walk to the corner I've described to you. Wait there and I shall be with you in a carriage in less than half-an-hour. In that time I must collect my own things together, secure our little fortune and then we shall be on our way. Kingsley will be no problem, and Macmillan is in his room with reams of papers. Go now: hurry.'

'In a moment. Oh, dear Tom, I do love you!'

'I am convinced of it, my love.'

'Tell me you love me.'

'Do you really need to hear it again?'

'I need to hear it always, always. Tell me.'

'Very well . . . I love you, Julia.' Her eyes roved over his face, glowing feverishly and possessively. He turned. 'But go now, darling, there will be time for all this later, lots of time, when we are together.'

'For ever . . .'

'For ever. Go now, my love.'

Julia picked up her bag and with a last hungry embrace of Jarrett, hurried out of the house and away into the night.

Jarrett left Julia's room and entered Macmillan's. Macmillan tied the last string round his baggage and turned to his friend. 'She's gone, then?' he said.

'Yes, thank God. I wonder how long she'll wait? Looks like rain too.'

'We won't have to pass the spot where she's waiting, will we?'

'My dear Macmillan, I do believe you are experiencing scruples! No, we'll go another way. You've sent all the servants out of the house, I presume?'

'Yes, all.'

'Well,' said Jarrett, 'we'll carry our baggage down to the hall now. Our carriage came a while ago: the money for it is paid and the fellow who brought it sent away. All is ready. I've told our friend Kingsley to stay in his room till we come for him.'

They carried down their bags and the box containing Mr Macmillan's ill-gotten fortune. Then they remounted the stairs and entered Kingsley's room.

'You have the key to the old woman's room?' said Jarrett shortly to Kingsley, who stood grinning sheepishly by the window.

'Certainly I have. Damned difficult it was to get too. You'll find the money, jewels and all in there. What would you have done without me, eh?'

'What indeed,' said Jarrett.

'Now about my share –' Kingsley began, when he found his arms pinioned by Macmillan, who had crept behind him. He just uttered a little cry before Jarrett raised the heavy cudgel and brought it down on his head. Kingsley sank to the floor and Jarrett and Macmillan left him there, a scarlet stain slowly spreading over his powdered wig.

Quickly they unlocked Aunt Catherine's room and emerged with the Hardwick jewels and the money that had gone with Mary and Julia. In a few moments they were in a carriage, Jarrett driving, with thousands of stolen pounds between them, speeding through the streets of London; and then they were speeding out to the coast; and in the small hours they were on a little smuggling-boat, crossing the Straits of Dover on a calm sea beneath a bright star-pricked sky.

Earlier that day Milton found on calling at the Wainwrights' that he was not the only visitor; there was quite a gathering there in the gilded morning-room. Warren and the Misses Graham and Thackray, the Wileys, the Van Druytens, he saw without really seeing them. For he had seen Elizabeth, in the middle of them all, smiling and blushing, her arm through Hugh Woodhouse's arm, and Mrs Wainwright came up to him with the falsest smile ever seen and his head swam as he realized that his worst fears had come true and he heard Mrs Wainwright say, distantly as if in a dream: 'We are glad to have you here, Mr Milton – just a little impromptu gathering to celebrate my daughter and Mr Woodhouse's becoming engaged to be married: an unofficial declaration you understand, but it is all fixed. They are to be married next month.'

They gave him a seat and wine – 'Not really the time of day for wine, of course, Mr Milton, but I think the occasion demands it' – but he hardly knew what was going on, stunned as he was. And perhaps the worst thing of all, when he was sufficiently roused to face the ordeal of offering Elizabeth and her fiancé his congratulations, was her cold and indifferent manner, as if they had never met before. That was too much to bear, and he took a very hasty leave of the party, almost running out of the room. He made his way – he scarcely knew how – to the George Inn, and there sat in an almost empty tap-room, brandy before him and despair within him, blinking and frozen and seeing the room through a pearly mist.

He spent the rest of the day in there, drinking in a corner, and he was left alone and not disturbed, so pathetic a figure did he make. It was late afternoon before he got up, paid his bill, and set off for Helpston with the light dying slowly across the Heath.

George ate and drank nothing that day. He could not sleep either. Mrs Reynolds was solicitous but he said she could do nothing for him. He spent the time wandering around the village and the house and the garden, and everywhere he saw memories and despair.

It was in the garden that he lingered. He remembered a pleasant September evening, a head bobbing amongst tall flowers. He remembered a tree being cut down. He remembered a night when he had stormed out of the house into this garden, and a comforting voice, and a pair of gentle hands. He remembered much more, and each memory was a dagger.

He rode north, leaving the last fields of Morholm farm and crossing Helpston Heath, where spring was speckling the woods with primroses and the banks of the narrow dykes were thickly crowned with celandines amongst rank furze. He came to the ancient viaduct of Lolham Bridges spanning the Welland, and leaned on a stone bridge bay to watch with a perverse fascination the white ropes of water threading the stony bed. This place had held a horrid fear for him ever since, as a small boy, one of his father's gardeners had fallen in and drowned during the fierce winter floods that swelled the river at this spot. Now it was quite docile and musical and there were only glimpses of its restless irresistible currents like muscles beneath a smooth skin. The gurgle of the sinuous water below mesmerized him and his thoughts

seemed to flow on to it, sharing its rhythm and drifting with
it in calm motion out to the waiting sea.

Julia stood alone on a street corner, clutching her bag, that
night. She wished she had a watch because she was sure it
was long past the time Jarrett said he would come and pick
her up in the carriage. Then they were going to fly, north
he had said, though she didn't care where. She would begin
a new life. It would be wonderful. They would never be
traced, no, she was sure of that. But where was Jarrett?
Perhaps he had been delayed. Perhaps the others had come
back from the theatre unexpectedly. Perhaps she had better
go and see. No, she had better wait. Time was bound to go
slowly under such circumstances. It was starting to rain.
She didn't care about that. But if only Jarrett would hurry
up . . .

Very late that night Aunt Catherine, Mrs Peach, Daniel,
Mr Sedgmoor and Mary came back from the theatre. The
evening had been a great success. The diversion of being in
a box in a London theatre had been enough for the two
older women; Mary and Mr Sedgmoor were still laughing from the one-act farce, 'The Deuce is in Him', that
had followed the main drama; and Daniel, claiming to be
discerning in such matters, said Garrick was a superior
performer; he had seen better, but not for a long time,
no, not for a long time had he seen anything better. It
was a well contented party that alighted from the carriage and went up the steps, chattering and laughing, to
their lodgings.

    They found not a light burning inside, which surprised
Mary a little, for she had expected Jarrett and Macmillan
to appear, bright and hospitable, and ask them how the play
was. There was not a sound in the house, and the fires had
gone out and left it chill and musty.

'Well! I must say I did not expect the gentlemen to have retired before our return,' said Aunt Catherine. 'But there, doubtless they had been working very hard, and were quite fazed.'

'I wonder how Julia is?' said Mary. She went up and walked into Julia's room. It was darkened and empty. 'Strange,' she said, and went out into the passage. 'Julia!' she called, 'Julia, where are you?'

Mr Sedgmoor, his thin young face anxious, joined her. 'There is no one in the parlour,' he said, 'and no servants in the kitchen.'

'Why, the girl is nowhere to be found!' said Aunt Catherine.

'Not here? How can this be?' stammered Mr Sedgmoor, looking more and more distressed. Then they heard Daniel's voice raised in undisguised horror. 'Good God! Here, help here, quickly! Oh, good God!' He had gone into Kingsley's room and found his nephew lying unconscious on the floor, a livid gash on his head and a heavy bloodstained cudgel nearby. The others crowded in, panic growing. Daniel knelt and lifted Kingsley's head gently. 'Sedgmoor, some brandy here – stand back, give him air – I thank you, sir – I hope it will revive him – Lord, what can have happened here – see! he stirs.'

'It must be housebreakers – housebreakers must have got in,' murmured Mary. It was several moments before the full horror of her own words sank in. Then Mr Macmillan – and Mr Jarrett – were lying somewhere like this.

Before she could turn and fly to Jarrett's room Kingsley painfully opened his eyes and spoke. Luckily for him he had a few of his wits about him. 'Jarrett and Macmillan – the rogues . . . they have taken off with everything . . . I tried to stop them . . .' There were cries of disbelief.

'But what of Julia? Where is she?' said Mr Sedgmoor, trembling.

Kingsley thought it best to pretend innocence. 'I don't know,' he breathed.

They soon discovered the truth. They found Jarrett and Macmillan's rooms stripped bare. Then they discovered their own loss. And amidst the cries of distraction and fury and vengeance and Mr Sedgmoor's plaintive: 'Where is Julia? Where is Julia?' Mary, her world slipping away beneath her feet, ran wailing and hysterical down the stairs and out into the rainy street.

She did not know how long she ran, the rain and wind pelting and battering her, how many circles she ran in, how many times she stopped, panting for breath and weeping and stupidly calling Jarrett's name. Her cloak and evening gown were soon soaked but she was aware of nothing but her despair. Suddenly, as she turned another corner, a hand seized her arm and there, her hair lank and dripping, her eyes glaring, was Julia.

'Julia, Julia, Mr Jarrett's gone,' sobbed Mary, not thinking to ask why her cousin was here. 'He's taken all our money and gone, him and Mr Macmillan, they've run off.'

For a moment Julia was silent and the rain splashed noisily. Then she hit Mary across the face. 'I know. I know, you foolish girl! I know he never meant to marry you! He was going to run away with me! It was me he loved, not you, Mary! Me!' She slapped Mary's face again and again, her voice rising to a shriek. 'You! You don't know what love is! It's me that Thomas Jarrett loves. He's been tricking you all along, don't you see? We have been lovers all this time, real lovers, do you know what that means? He was going to take your money and run away with me!' And suddenly Julia, from being towering and furious, shrank and wept. 'But he hasn't come,' she whimpered. 'We were going to start our life together – but he hasn't come . . .' Then she turned and ran down the street as

Mary sank to the ground in a swoon and the rain danced on her.

The next thing Mary remembered was waking up in bed next day, emotionally collapsed and shivering with fever. No one knew how long she had lain in the rainy street, but they had searched a good while to find her, in the carriage and on foot, and she had a bad chill. She lay in the bed and stared and sombre figures, indistinctly seen, moved like phantoms about her: Mr Sedgmoor, Aunt Catherine, Daniel, Mrs Peach, Kingsley, a doctor. Through the same strange haze words spoken to her came disjointed and indistinct and hardly comprehended: 'How are you, Mary?' 'How are you?' 'How is she?' and 'No trace of them,' 'No luck.' Gradually as the day went on and she lay there things grew a little clearer and slowly she gathered that 'they had been unable to trace Jarrett and Macmillan: it was unlikely now that the villains would be found', and that neither was there any sign of Julia, though it was reported that she had spent the night at a tavern. And then she slept again, and soon it was the next day, and she began to feel a little better bodily, and evening came down and they lit a candle by her bed; and then came news. A messenger had ridden thither from Stamford with a letter from Great-Uncle Horace, telling them that George was missing. He had left the house, telling no one of his destination, and had not returned home the night before. There was still no trace of him.

BOOK THREE

1

As the light of a soft, scented day at the end of April faded the London coach drew nearer to Stamford. It was none too soon for the people inside the coach, tired in body and tired of each other's company. On one side of the coach was a very fat old man who had been drinking all the way and divulging himself of the most extravagantly misanthropic views. On the other side was a man of fifty, a shambling, lumpish creature whose coat and waistcoat and breeches were all in shabby snuff-brown and whose very cravat was nearer brown than white; and a young man of twenty-two, dressed severely and with the utmost neatness in a blue coat with a spotless white waistcoat buttoned up very high. He wore his own hair uncurled and tied with a small ribbon. His face was a hard and immovable one, as if it were carved from wood; his eyes were small and shortsighted but his nose and mouth and jaw had something very strong and handsome about them, giving him a grim, limited attractiveness. He had said little on the journey, exchanging the odd remark with his brown-clad companion, and most recently snapping at the old misanthrope opposite: 'I wish to God, sir, you would give us some peace. If you are so ill-satisfied with the world, I suggest you leave it – I feel sure it will not miss you.' After this there had been silence for some time; now the young man, leaning forward to look out of the window, spoke again.

'Still the same,' he said, glancing at his companion. 'Not a missing tile replaced, not a face that has changed its expression, not a blade of grass stirred in the whole county since last I came.'

'I was rather expecting everywhere to be two feet under water,' said the man in brown.

'Oh, we are only on the edge of the fens here, and the country is well-drained, though I have seen Stamford flooded once. Here is the town, Finlayson; prepare yourself to be stared at. Everyone knows everything that is going on here.'

Mr Finlayson smiled, a peculiar action that looked as if his ruddy face were falling in on itself. Actually the barrister's face showed traces of his having once been a 'good-looking dog', but those looks had crumpled and collapsed and blurred like a picture being devoured by flames. 'This is nothing to the Highlands, you know, Hardwick,' he said. 'Why, people are in such an infernal rut there they scarcely know which king is on the throne. Mysterious disappearances are pretty well unheard of.'

His companion frowned. 'Well, it is something I could well have done without. I hope my family understand the sacrifice I am making in coming to take the late lamented's place.'

'Never known a man regret leaving the law,' grunted Finlayson.

'It is not the fact of its being the law. It would be the same if I were taking orders, or in a mercantile house, or anything. I am giving up a career I have worked hard at. You know I have worked at it, Finlayson—you know I would have made a success of it, far more than you ever did.'

'Can't deny it.'

'For years I always wanted to break free of that mouldering Morholm life. I was glad I was the younger son; I was glad George would inherit the estate and I would be left to make my own way. George could sit and stew with the flock of cousins and half-cousins about him and I could get away from all that, that which I detested. It seems however I had underestimated my brother's weakness of character.'

'Well, perhaps he may turn up,' said Finlayson.

'Two weeks and no news of him? I'll believe it when I see it. Likewise with this Jarrett fellow. What a mess from one girlish infatuation.'

The older man eyed him narrowly. 'Ah, Hardwick, you don't understand the affairs of the heart. You've a great deal of sense, but you fall down there.'

'What a sentimental old fool you are, Finlayson! Affairs of the heart – are we to include there the liaison between my cousin Mary and Jarrett – as well as my sister Julia? A charming business, I am sure, that ends in two creatures jilted, one broken in spirit and body, the other refusing to return to her family and supporting herself in London God knows how! I hope *I* may always miss out on such affairs!'

'Ay, well, 'twas a bad business. But perhaps Jarrett and that other rogue will be caught soon.'

'You think so? I would not wager a penny on it. Ay, I have taken out a warrant for their arrest, but we shall be most diabolically lucky if we ever hear of them again. It is over two weeks since they made off. No, what galls me is that everyone was taken in by Jarrett in the first place.'

'The fellow was a charmer, it seems.'

'All the more reason to be on one's guard. No one ever makes an action but in pursuit of his own welfare. It is not easy to be universally agreeable; it must be worked at; and no one goes to all that trouble without a motive. If my family were not such a pack of worthless, shallow creatures ... However, things are going to be different now that I am master of Morholm. I tell you, Finlayson, I have been in two minds as to whether to abandon the place to its fate as it appears my brother has done. The mouldering old pile does not belong in this age, at least not in its present state. But I have decided otherwise. I am disgusted at a large estate going to waste as it has; at so much money being squandered through greedy, sponging good-for-nothings; at having my name sneered at as a sign of decadence and folly. Oh, it is not that I am anxious to restore the Hardwick tradition and our great name to its old glory, any of that nonsense. But what I am going to restore is economy, firmness, stability. All that is superfluous shall be shorn away.'

'You sound very determined.'

'Have you ever known me not determined in something I do? Oh, I dare say initially I shall be made quite a figure of – I shall be just the head of the family they have been waiting for, the wheel being fitted with a stout hub at last. But I think they will find they do not truly want their own wishes. However, we are here at last. I hope someone at Morholm has remembered to send horses over for us.'

The coach rumbled under the arch of The George and into the inn yard. The dwindling light was now rosy, staining the beams and limestone and the latticed windows of the inn so that it took on the appearance of a varnished oil-painting. James Hardwick and Mr Finlayson alighted from the coach and went into the inn, the older man's rolling gait affording a bizarre contrast with the younger's purposeful stride.

James inquired and found that Clarry had brought horses for them from Morholm. He was told to wait awhile and they took some refreshment in the tap-room.

'Now, I say, Hardwick,' said Mr Finlayson, 'you're sure your family won't take exception to my coming down here with you for a while?'

'I shall see to it they do not. I am in charge now and if I choose to have a friend stay with me then my dependants must accede to my wishes. Beggars can't be choosers, though these beggars have been enjoying that freedom during both my father's time and my brother's. I know you cannot stay for ever, but at least I shall have conversation that is halfway intelligent for a time.' He snorted. 'I can just picture it –

there will be old Daniel or Aunt Catherine, hypocrites that they are, sniffing something about "bringing intruders into a house of sadness, I declare".'

'Oh, I say, Hardwick,' said Finlayson rather anxiously, 'I hope I won't be a little *de trop*?'

'No, no – I shall see to it. I shall not have a house of lamentation. It is all over. So George *has* disappeared: so Mary *has* been jilted, hoodwinked and robbed; very sad; but she will get over it, and the sooner conditions are made more favourable for her doing so the better. So Julia *is* staying in London somewhere and refuses to return to the bosom of her family; very well, worrying will not bring her back; she will come if she wants to.'

'You're a very firm man, Hardwick: I only wish I were like you. But this cousin Mary of yours – I do feel sorry for her.'

'Yes,' said James, 'she is the only one I feel disposed to pity in all this. She was a little fool in allowing Jarrett to gain such a hold over her – but she can't help being a fool. She, at least, never took advantage of father, or George, I surmise. She is someone with a right to a place at Morholm, at any rate. But there are others upon whom I am not inclined to look so favourably. How do you feel about riding to Morholm, Finlayson? Are you a good horseman?'

'Why, the last time I bestrode a horse was up at my father's place in the Highlands when I was a lad. But, if I fall off, I am not of a build to come to any harm.'

'I need to stretch my legs a little first. Let us walk a while around the town. You may see what kind of a place you are come to.'

They stood aside at the entrance to the inn yard to let in an open wagon loaded entirely with ducks. 'Those will be from the decoy at Borough Fen,' said James. 'Introduced by the Dutch drainers, I believe: a long tunnel affair leading to a pond where the decoys are placed. A most prodigious amount are caught; but I believe our local curiosity is in decline now that so much of the fen is farmed.'

There were few people about in the streets as dusk settled over the high rooftops. In St George's Square the shutters were going up on the market stalls. Finlayson shambled obediently behind James, who walked with his hands clasped beneath his coat-tails, looking about him with a critical eye.

'This is where my Great-Uncle Horace lives,' said James, stopping suddenly. Finlayson looked up at the narrow, frugal town-house. 'Thought you said he was rich?'

'He is, through not wasting money on external show. Come.' James walked on.

'Aren't you going to call?' said Finlayson, hurrying after him.

'Call? No! I hate calling, and the old fellow does too. Besides, he will probably be at Morholm to receive me.'

They walked on up the High Street and across Red Lion Square where from the massive church of All Saints came the peal of bells.

'Hm, I wonder what is going on at the Wainwrights',' said James. The grand Wainwright house in Barn Hill was brightly lit in every window and two carriages were drawing up outside. 'Mr Wainwright was once an errand-boy for a counting-house, and his wife's origins are even murkier. They are now probably the richest people in town,' went on James. 'Hullo, there's Henry Milton.'

Milton emerged from the Wainwright house and hurried down the steps, his eyes cast down, his hands fumbling with a pair of gloves. He did not see James and would have walked straight past had not the other called: 'Mr Milton, good evening to you!' He turned to see his friend's brother and a man he did not know; he wanted to merely return the salutation and go, but he knew that would hardly be polite.

'I am glad to see you, James,' he said, without the other's

formality. Milton had mainly been George's friend but he and James had known each other as boys. He had never really liked James, however, and he wanted to talk now least of all. 'Are you home permanently?' he asked.

'Yes, I am. Just arrived. This is my friend Mr Finlayson. Yes, I am abandoning the law to take charge at Morholm. A bad business about George, Mr Milton; there is no more news, I presume?'

Milton shook his head.

'One should not despair, but I regret to say it's my belief that my brother is at the bottom of a river somewhere. His drinking, his unstable state of mind, I fear –'

'I believe otherwise,' Milton said shortly. The two men exchanged a cold glance.

'Well, time will show,' said James. 'And this business about that rogue Jarrett – you have heard the details, I presume?'

'Immediately I heard that the Morholm party had returned last week I went to call on them, and learned everything. I suppose they have not been traced – Jarrett and his accomplice?'

'No, they were efficient rascals, and it is unlikely now they will be caught. Enquiries have discovered Macmillan, the accomplice, to be quite a consummate villain. Jarrett must have been in contact with him and his nefarious activities for some time. Tell me, what is the great occasion at the Wainwrights'?'

'Didn't you know? Well, no, of course, you wouldn't. Today saw the marriage of Miss Elizabeth Wainwright to Hugh Woodhouse. I have just been to the reception. A very grand affair, needless to say.'

'Miss Wainwright and Woodhouse?' James was musing aloud and did not mean to be rude. 'But didn't I hear, the last time I was here, something about you and –' He stopped.

'About me and Miss Wainwright?' said Milton. His face was wry and sallow, like that of a man trying not to be sick. 'No, no. That was nothing. Nothing at all,' he said with an ugly little twist of a smile, and put on his hat. 'Good evening to you.' He went away, quickly.

'A friend of yours, Hardwick?' said Finlayson, when Milton had gone.

'Not really. A friend of my brother's. He used to write poetry and such stuff. Seems to have grown very sour suddenly. Well, shall we start for Morholm now?'

Mary was having a walk around the garden – her first since the terrible night in London two weeks ago – when James came to Morholm. Aunt Catherine had pressed Kingsley to walk with her but she preferred to go alone. So she wandered among the sweet-smelling tangle, shawls packed about her shoulders, Mrs Reynolds watching her from the kitchen.

She was still slightly frail from her fever caught in the rainy street that night. For a week she had had to remain in bed in their lodgings in London, with chaos around her. The news of George's disappearance; the fruitless wait for news of Jarrett and Macmillan; the search for Julia; lamenting, cursing, groaning all about her; and within herself, joining forces with the ravaging effects of her illness, her own private chaos, as she struggled with ideas that would have been the blackest of nightmares before, ideas that seemed the enemies of hope, sanity, happiness, of very life itself, yet were now facts that must be accommodated in her mind. Jarrett did not love her, Jarrett had been making a fool of her, Jarrett had been having an affair with Julia, Jarrett had run away with their money, Jarrett her idol, her god, her life-blood was not only gone but had never really existed. These ideas pounded through her all the time of her illness, ideas somehow turned by the demons of her fever into a physical awareness, a rhythm, a boom, a pulse, a sound, a texture, a smell. Jarrett was gone, Jarrett was gone . . . And then a new demon had come and flapped something else before her face, something she had not let sink in yet: George was gone, George who had seemed so worthless and yet was so worthy, George, the basis on which almost unknowingly she had built her life after Joseph's death, George had disappeared without trace.

And at the back of her mind, like a gnawing, battening worm, the embryonic realization of why . . .

In a way she was glad of that fever, for had she been well in body at that time she thought she would have gone mad with grief. As it was, much of it had been worked out in that week of sickness – yet no, the grief had not been reduced, it was as if the lump of it had been pounded out flat like gold leaf. Now she was just evenly, resignedly wretched. She did not weep at all; tears seemed much too fulsome and graceful for this barren emptiness.

Yesterday she had heard from Mrs Townsend about Miss Wainwright getting married to Hugh Woodhouse, but she hardly registered any surprise or regret: the world had all gone wrong, and so it merely fitted into place.

When James arrived she felt something like relief, for at Morholm all was disorder and vacillating aimlessness, and she was already aware of the dominant presence James could take on. In London, the day after the catastrophe, Daniel had had the sense to send for him from Gray's Inn, and he had immediately taken charge of the situation. During the week they had remained in the city until she should be well enough to travel home, it was James's sturdy figure she remembered most clearly amongst the shades flickering about her room, it was James's grim penetrating gaze from the ring of faces around her that seemed to have the most to do with reality. It was he who questioned her about her encounter with Julia on the rainy street corner, and later showed the letter they had received from her:

I suppose Mary has told you about Jarrett and me. We were lovers for months. After what has happened I can never come back to the Family, so you had better not waste time looking for me. I am living in London, I won't say where. Do not try to find me. I won't come back. I am perfectly able to support myself so forget about me: that ought to be no matter of Difficulty to you.

JULIA.

James had made enquiries after her, but to no avail. When he arrived at Morholm that evening with Mr Finlayson, however, he had more news of her; he had received another letter from her, reiterating what she had said in the first, in more hostile and emphatic terms. Aunt Catherine was quite overcome: 'Why, James, I declare my poor heart will break. All this is too much for me to support – I was never strong, you'll acknowledge, Mrs Peach – I declare 'tis too much . . .' Mr Finlayson gallantly offered her his handkerchief.

'Well, if my sister is intent upon this course, then I intend to let her pursue it. It will be better than having her moping around here,' said James. 'And as we are all gathered here, let me say a few more things now. This family has been hit suddenly by a good deal of misfortune. I am not going to begin an argument, but I believe it was not a conspiracy of various phantoms of ill-luck that brought all this about. This family has had a lot to answer for, not only in this latest business, but consistently in the past. Never mind that outraged face, aunt, you know it as well as I. I am not going to harp on it; but now that I am in charge here I want you to know it. There are going to be changes. There has been a great deal of cant for a long time about someone to uphold the Hardwick tradition; it seems my father and my brother were both disappointments in the capacity they were meant to fulfil. Well, I shall be this upright man of strength and decision and all the rest of it; that is why I am beginning now. Let me say to Mary that I am laying no undue blame to her in this; you, cousin, have suffered much.' He paused. He was standing before the fire with his hands under his coat-tails, looking steadily at the circle of people around him, their faces lit orange by the flames.

Aunt Catherine stirred uneasily. 'Why, I must say, nephew, I am sure I do not know what you can mean about this – our behaviour – I think I must have misheard you. But what you state as your intentions are most commendable, indeed.'

'Let the young man go on, Catherine,' said Great-Uncle Horace, who had come over to Morholm to greet his great-nephew. His narrow old face was puckered with interest.

'I shall go on, sir. I noticed on my introducing my friend Mr Finlayson here that there were looks of disapproval. I gather it is thought offensive that I should bring a stranger here at a time like this. There must be no more of that attitude. George is gone; very well, if he lives, which I doubt, there is nothing to lament, and if not, tears and gloom will not bring him back even supposing you should want to. Jarrett is gone; very well, we are better off without the villain –'

He was interrupted by a dry, groaning sob from Mary. 'No, no, no, don't speak of him . . .'

'He was a villain, Mary,' said James, with no change of tone or posture, 'a completely worthless, vicious scoundrel. We must not cover the fact. We must be glad that what he got away with was not more, and concentrate on making the management of the estate more efficient so as to recoup those losses. The estate and its finances must be administered: and as George is missing presumed dead that responsibility passes to me, as Mr Finlayson will confirm.

'For a start, Morholm has too many occupants. I wrote to Mr Sedgmoor last week and was appalled at the state of our finances, the result of parasitical extravagance. There shall be no more taking advantage of one man's weakness to support another's idleness. Cousin Kingsley, you must find yourself a situation and accommodation before the end of next month. The same applies to you, Uncle Daniel; your health is perfect now, and has been for longer than you pretend. The end of next month: I shall have neither of you in this house after then.'

Kingsley's big bland face registered no greater emotion than if he had detected a faint unrecognized smell on his clothes, but he was more startled than he had ever been in his life. Daniel, meanwhile, was swelling and puffing and fidgeting like a pot on the boil. 'Damme, nephew, this is an unfunny jest,' he spluttered.

'Come, I am being quite reasonable. As for you, aunt, and grandmother, your taste for finery at the expense of the estate must be curbed. And another thing – I may replace some of the servants; they are fat and lazy, and there are lords in London who would be glad of the perquisites they get. I am saying this now so that no one will be under the wrong impression in the future. Now, I am going to see Matthews.'

James was gone in a moment, leaving his family stunned and silent. Daniel shifted uneasily and spoke to Kingsley. 'The lad is not in earnest, you know,' he said.

'Well, I must say,' said Aunt Catherine, 'I do not think James need have spoken quite so severely. I am sure he is shaping into a fine young man, but to be so severe . . . I am in no fit state for such things, what with poor George gone, and Julia and all, and our hopes for Mary all disappointed.'

'Pray do not distress yourself, ma'am,' said Mr Finlayson, producing another handkerchief from somewhere. Aunt Catherine's figure was plump and uncoarsened for her age, and he had taken quite a shine to her. 'You must not mind James, Miss Hardwick. He has not been living here for three years and you are no doubt unused to the manner he has developed. Pray be comforted, ma'am, things can only get better.'

'I thank you, Mr Finlayson, you are most kind and attentive – such fine cambric as this handkerchief is, sir – London-made I suppose – we cannot get such things here. Forgive us if our reception of you was less polite than you could wish, Mr Finlayson, but we are still so upset . . .'

Great-Uncle Horace rose stiffly. 'I shall go home now, before it grows too dark,' he said, creaking out of the room with his wading-bird gait. Mary rose and accompanied him to the front door, where he stopped and said: 'I have been most impressed with James. I always thought he had sense, and I'm glad to see it has borne fruit. We shall have a proper master of Morholm at last.'

What James said was no idle boast. There was nothing of idleness in his character. From the day he took up residence at Morholm he worked ceaselessly. He got rid of Clarry and the maid and replaced them; he arranged for decorators, panellers and joiners from Peterborough to come in and restore the interior of the house; the library, which was mouldering and in disorder, he turned upside-down and made habitable single-handed; he went over the entire estate with Matthews, planning and re-arranging; he bought new farm-stock; he sold Kingsley's hunters and bought two stout horses for farm-work instead; he visited his tenants and talked earnestly with them of their affairs; with speed, energy and chilling efficiency he did everything George had not. As he had predicted, he soon became a figure much talked about and much admired. He was the man the family had been waiting for.

Yet he had scant regard for that family tradition he was upholding. He had left Morholm for London and the law as soon as he was old enough because he had only contempt for the life there. All through his younger years James

Hardwick had been surrounded by the aimless and complacent; he had set himself a purpose, something to strive after and finally master, unassisted by anyone else. The law was what he aimed at, and without doubt he would have become a successful lawyer had not these circumstances arisen. Now he faced a different challenge, and he did not flinch. He had broken free of what did not suit him to form a life of his own that did; now he decided he would change and shape what did not suit him into something that did, adapt the life he despised to his own forceful personality.

So within the space of a few weeks Morholm and everyone in it became submissive to the will and energy of James. Aunt Catherine pressed him to make calls around the area now that he had taken up residence, but he refused; he had no time for socializing. He rose early and retired late. Often Mary, sitting sleepless at her window in the early hours of the morning, would see him go striding across the fields, his boots glistening with dew and the tails of his dark sober coat flapping; or again, lying sleepless past midnight, she would get up and peer out across the landing and see the glow of light from the library where he was still working. He did not drink much: he took the occasional brandy-and-water, but it seemed to have no effect on him anyway. Once, when he was on the roof inspecting the slates and Mary was walking in the garden idly watching him, his foot slipped and he nearly fell. He saved himself by hanging on to the chimney-pot. She gasped and almost cried out when she saw him slip, and it struck her that that was the first unselfish burst of emotion she had felt since that terrible night. She was living entirely wrapped in her own sterile gloom; nothing outside it touched her. There was a kind of dreary immobile comfort in being so surrounded with one selfish feeling that nothing else mattered. She was lonely and she wanted no one; she was unoccupied and wanted nothing to do; she could see everything behind her in the past, and before her in the future she could see nothing. It was too much effort to look for hope, and she did not believe she would find any.

Yet through this black mood came gradually some rays of light, and they emanated from James. Without any feeling for him initially, she found she was developing a kind of passive admiration of James, his solidity and strength and his uncomplicated, impersonal manner. While everyone else crumbled James was steadfastly diligent, practical and untender, and that was perhaps the best thing for her at that time. She wanted no involvements of feeling; her heart, formerly so impressionable and so generous, was for the moment hard and empty – she could acknowledge nothing and she had nothing to give. She was not glad of James, for she could not be glad of anything, but he was the most preferable thing in her world.

May came with pink and orange skies, and grass that grew lusher and greener with a suggestion of fertility and richness coming to the surface, and Mary, contrasting in her mind this flowering and blossoming with her own spiritual barrenness, did not realize that by actually being able to frame such thoughts she was beginning to heal. Her long-neglected garden grew in a profusion of colours and scents. The leaves on the trees were shiny as if new-painted, yellow laburnums fluttered, ragged clumps of bluebells and primroses and almost stifling lilac broke out everywhere, and soon came honeysuckle and wild orchids, and in secluded places flaming poppies tossed their heads in scarlet scattered regiments. And in the cool green depths of the trees and hedgerows thrushes sang as if the world had just been made. A soul such as Mary's could not help but be affected, and as she began to take walks more and the moist grass rustled about her feet with a delicious freshness, little sorties of warm emotion were made on her heart, suddenly, like the splinter and crash of icicles in a thaw, even though, mistrustful of feeling, she tried to keep them away. A rabbit would bolt from a hedge and then stop and sit up, quivering with anxious whiskered life: children that she knew from the village would run up to her, pleasantly unaware of the dry monotonous grief deep within her and unaware even that such a thing could exist, and grab her hand and drag her off to see a puppy or their new baby sister: she would come across an old favourite spot that spring had made extra charming with clusters of buttercups and violets. Bees were swarming and she saw an old woman at the back of her cottage clanging a warming-pan to call them into her hive.

And stuck in the casements of cottage windows she saw branches of hawthorn blossom, put there by young men to signify their love of the girl who lived in the house. She thought the custom had been dying out but this year there were lots of them. All along the row of low thatched cottages that followed the stream south out of Aysthorpe ragged sprays of the pure white flowers hung from the windows, and stray petals were strewn over the path like drops of milk. She stopped to admire each one. But from the window of the last, most tumbledown cottage, with its feet almost in the stream and rents in the old thatch, hung a sprig of blackthorn. The blackthorn signified a quarrel or a rejection, something gone wrong. She tried to ignore it and turned away to look at the lovely hawthorn blossoms in their sweet, poetic perfection: but the sprig of blackthorn, intensely dark and knotted, seemed to imprint itself on her mind and burn deep.

In the end she turned and snatched it out of the casement and trod it underfoot as if it were the flowering of a guilt and remorse that could not be acknowledged.

When at last she walked back to Morholm, the country freshened and dripping from a sudden shower, she was surprised to find James in the garden, looking over it with his dogged, imperious thoroughness.

'Oh, it's you, Mary,' he said abstractedly. 'What a forest

this garden is! I think I shall have the whole thing cleared.'

'Oh, will you?' It was the first feeling of sadness outside her central grief. James caught her tone and turned round to focus his short-sighted, oddly penetrating gaze on her. 'You are fond of the garden, I take it?'

'Well . . .' She looked away. 'It is very overgrown.'

'If you like it, it shall stay. In fact you, Mary, shall supervise the weeding and improving of it. I shall get some workmen in, and you shall be in charge. And cousin, I do not want you to be afraid for your place at Morholm. I would not question your right to the protection and support of the master. Moreover I recognize that the place would scarcely have kept on its feet without you, no matter what happened recently. I am not an indulgent man, or a senti-mental or feeling or gay or easy man, as no doubt you are aware, but I am at least fair. And the garden will give you something to occupy your mind. I hardly expect you to be in high spirits, but you will destroy yourself by moping around forever.' He spoke firmly but not roughly.

'Thank you, James,' she said, feeling a growing gratitude and trust in him, and impulsively she touched his arm before he left her. She wished she had not. The mere feel of his firm young arm in its woollen sleeve brought back the twin phantoms of Jarrett and George, who haunted her and broke her rest at nights so that she woke calling out the names of first one and then the other.

Mr Finlayson and Aunt Catherine got on very well – that is to say he found her plump triviality comfortable and she found his placid Scots courtesy flattering. Moreover his company was something of a refuge for her from the increas-ingly harsh world of Morholm. She could no longer have her own way all the time; all her nagging, whining and browbeating were lost on James, who was inflexible in his role as master of the house. 'There are to be no more carriage-rides to the Townsends – you must go on horseback, or submit to the indignity of being fetched – and if the Townsends are such fatuous snobs as to judge a person by her means of transport then they are not worth calling on anyhow.' Restrictions such as these – and they were not few – on her long unbridled freedom left Aunt Catherine bemused and frustrated, as well as rather scared, and the look of martyrdom she had often affected became permanently fixed on her face.

One day towards dusk Finlayson went out to see where James had got to and found him in the fallow field close to the house mending a fence. 'My, but you're about it late, Hardwick,' he said, heaving his rag-bag body on to the gate. 'You've men to do that, have you not?'

'It's quicker to do it myself,' said James, not looking up from his work. 'I seem to have observed, Finlayson,' he went on after a pause, 'some friendly acquaintance blossoming between my aunt and yourself?'

'Ay, she's a talker, but I don't mind that – I'm nearly deaf in one ear anyway – and she's a damn pretty-figured woman, you know, Hardwick, though you told me she wasn't handsome. Still, you'll get to look at things differently when you come to my age.'

'Give me a hand with this beam,' said James in his peremptory fashion.

'H'm, I thought I wouldn't escape without doing any work,' grunted Finlayson, and for a while conversation ceased as, with much snorting and blowing, he assisted James in hoisting the beam into place.

'I would be glad to be rid of her,' said James, watching Finlayson mop his face with a handkerchief and loosen his stock to reveal a bull-frog neck that was, inevitably, snuff-brown. 'As you find her agreeable, you would be returning all the services I have done you if you were disposed to marry her –'

'Marry her?'

'– and take her to London to live with you. I hope you have not forgotten that it was I who virtually kept your practice alive a couple of years ago.'

'No, no, I have not forgotten, Hardwick. You did patch up those – professional errors of mine. But I have helped you too. The stewardship of this place for instance. It's a ticklish one. It seems likely your brother is dead, but it could be contested. Supposing he isn't? Supposing he turns up? There will be problems –'

'I will be responsible for that,' said James, his face stony. 'Besides, he will not come back.' He drew a deep breath. House martins swooped over the field to the stables. The sun was sinking below the woods to the west of Upton and taking all the day's warmth with it: it would be chill soon. 'Come then,' he said briskly, 'I hope you do not consider my request unreasonable. She has been sponging here too long – once you are married you can cut her down a bit, and anyway you are not poor. You say you like her – you will be without my company now that I am to live here – what do you say?'

'Well, I won't deny it had crossed my mind, Hardwick, but – will she have me? That's the question.'

'She must have you. She thinks I am using her poorly, and I can assure you that treatment will not improve, so she had better be under no illusions there. There shall be no more wasteful, indulgent life for her here. You had better impress that on her when you make your proposal.'

'Very well, very well, Hardwick, I know better than to argue with you. But come, she will bring something with her, I hope?'

'Yes, she has a little money settled on her.' He studied the beam: it was still not secure. 'Well, the light is fading. We had better go in.'

* * *

Mr Finlayson's opportunity came next day when James, saying he needed the servant who was to escort Aunt Catherine to Peterborough for her shopping, suggested that his friend should be her companion instead. So Mr Finlayson, on old Monmouth, and Aunt Catherine, mounted on the stoutest of the remaining three in the stable, and very fluttery and gratified, went jogging slowly out of Aysthorpe to the town where she, with a very strict allowance, was to buy linen. She did not sit at all easily, but, as she explained to her escort, 'I have been unused to such a means of perambulation, Mr Finlayson, of late, though in my young days I was known throughout the county as a horsewoman. And indeed I am very glad you are with me, Mr Finlayson, for I do not at all trust that new fellow James has employed – I am sure if we were to be set upon he would simply ride off and leave me to my fate. However, I am sure James knows what he is doing, and he is certainly on a course to bringing the family back into repute.'

'It is a pleasure to be your escort, ma'am,' said Mr Finlayson. 'I never dreamed when James invited me to come and stay at Morholm that I would find myself in such delightful company.' He took off his hat awkwardly and mopped his brow. 'But ma'am – may I take this opportunity – will you be offended if I ask a question that might be considered personal?'

'Why, Mr Finlayson, I am sure we are good enough friends for you to ask me anything, within the bounds of delicacy which I know you always observe, with perfect propriety.'

'You embolden me, ma'am. Then, can it be possible – you must correct my ignorance – can it be possible that you were never married, or engaged to be so?'

'Alas, 'tis true, sir. I have had my beaux – Lord knows, Mr Finlayson, I have had my beaux. I think I may say, at this remove, that I was once much sought after. Yet the right man never came my way, sir, and as my years grew on me – gracefully, I hope I may say –'

'Indeed you may!'

'– I resigned myself to unmarried status, and doing what I could to aid my brother Joseph at Morholm, and carrying his housekeeping keys – a role I continued with George – and hope to continue with James; and I have done my best to content myself, Mr Finlayson – but I have been a lonely woman, sir, though I have never complained of it – a lonely woman.'

'Pray do not say it, ma'am. You shame the whole male sex by such an admission.'

'Alas, Mr Finlayson, it is the way of the world. I wonder, sir – while we are talking in this confidential fashion – if I might ask something of you.'

'Anything, ma'am.'

'It is three years since James went to London to study with you, is it not? And in that time I daresay you have observed him – got to know his character?'

'As far as one may with James, yes, ma'am.'

'You see, when he was younger, living at home, he was very quiet, reserved – we thought him a little dull. Now that he has blossomed out, so to speak, I hardly know what to make of him. What I mean is, the severity of his measures in installing himself here – he is just the man we have been waiting for, of course – but am I to expect things . . . to go on . . . permanently . . .?' Her flow of words slowed and stopped.

'Ma'am, I have seen James develop into a man, and I feel bound to tell you it is a frugal, unbending and ruthless one, fair and never cruel, but austere and unsympathetic.'

Aunt Catherine looked a little pale and sick.

'But to return to my first point – you regret, then, Miss Hardwick, never having married? For I share your feeling there.'

'Then you have never had a wife, sir?'

'No, ma'am. I have always been a most devoted admirer of the sex, I assure you. As a young man, I believe, my entire time was spent in sighing and dreaming: but I was disappointed in my true love, ma'am, though I have never told this to anyone: I adored her and she turned out worthless, heartless.'

'How very sad! There was another, I suppose?'

Mr Finlayson nodded pensively. 'She married him – a tanner and leather dealer. Later she left him for a dragoon. A worthless creature she was – but captivating. When I say I have never told this before, I am wrong – I believe I once confided it to James – but he scoffs at such things. He is not a person of tender sensibilities, such as ourselves, ma'am. I dare say when he takes a wife, which he doubtless will soon, it will be some practical, hard-headed girl, who will be no trouble to him, and will carry his housekeeping keys.'

'You – think he will?'

'Oh, yes. I have felt the lack of a wife there, too, you know, ma'am – it takes a wife to make a home. I have a very comfortable house in Aldgate, quiet, but not unfashionable – and my income is comfortable too – and Mrs Granville who looks after me makes fine veal-pies, but still there is something missing, if you understand me, ma'am.'

Aunt Catherine and Mr Finlayson understood each other very well, and she had no hesitation in accepting him when, later that day, he proposed they get married to, as they agreed, 'unite their autumn years in comfortable and companionable fashion'.

2

At the end of May Mary was well enough to ride, and so she went to Stamford one morning, accompanied by the new groom, to call on her Great-Uncle Horace. The old man had had a cold and he seemed less incisive, more rambling and fussy. To her surprise she found herself thinking it a pity that staunch old Horace, for whom she had never felt much affection and indeed whom she had often found herself ranged inimically against, should show signs of age and decay; but it fitted in, she reflected, with the general air of change around. Gradually, as summer's scents and colours and sounds grew richer, the despairing shadow was lifting from her: she was beginning to open out, enjoy things with her old vigour for experience, face each morning with something like confidence. And what was even more hopeful, she could now face the thought of Jarrett and what he had done. He had left a scar on her spirit, but she was no longer afraid of looking at the scar. Only the thought of George, and the fear that grew each day there was no news of him, still troubled her dreams and pulsed like an abeyant pain at the back of her mind.

After an hour she left her great-uncle's and threaded her way down St Mary's Hill, which was busy and noisy. When she came to the yard of The George she looked around for the groom, but he was not there yet. She was about to go inside to see if a tankard had waylaid him when three young men spilled out of the door. She caught a glimpse of an angry landlord hurling their hats after them and then the door closed. The young men sprawled on the ground, braying with laughter and Mary, looking closer, recognized one as her brother William. She did not at all want an encounter with him in these circumstances, but even as she turned away he caught sight of her. 'Why it's Mary! Don't go away! Look, boys, here's my sister.' He staggered up to her and pumped her hand with drunken heartiness; his palm was sweaty and his breath was so tainted as it puffed in her face that it was like someone opening the door of a wine-cellar.

'Not *the* Mary Hardwick – the one they're all talking about!' sniggered one of his companions, and the other, breaking into coarse guffaws, cried: 'Do you know what they're saying about you, miss? Shall I tell you?' With growing distress she tried to move away but William had hold of her arm and though he was beckoning to his friends to be quiet he too was giggling.

'They say . . . they say, if anybody's low, they say to 'em – go to Mary Hardwick, she accommodates everybody –'

'And it'll be financially viable, as well!' The two youths collapsed together on the floor with yelps of hysterical laughter. Mary tore herself away from William with a wrench and hurried out of the yard, unwitting of where she was going, tears smarting in her eyes. 'Or if she's not around her cousin Julia will help out!' crowed the voices behind her.

She could feel the eyes of the people in the street all turned towards her and she bit her lip to keep her tears back. She heard running footsteps behind her and then William was at her side again. 'Look, sister, I am sorry. Ignore those idiots, they're drunk, and they are not really friends of mine, they just made me take a glass with them and, well, you know. Don't be offended.'

She was going to shrug his hand off her arm but thought better of it and said, trying to hold back a sniff, 'Oh – it's nothing, William.'

'I am glad I met you, in truth, sister, for I am in something of a predicament.'

'Oh?'

'James is living at Morholm now, is he not? You see, I'm without lodgings again – I've been staying with a friend but –'

'You were thrown out?'

'What a suspicious creature you are become, Mary!'

'You intend to ask James to lodge you?'

'Just for a while, yes. After all, there's plenty of room at Morholm, and –'

'William, I would not advise you to attempt this. I believe you will get but a poor reception from James.'

'What? Why, it's only for a little while – I am his cousin too, after all.'

William insisted on returning to Morholm with her, riding on the servant's horse and forcing him to walk. Formerly she would have stopped him doing this, but her old plucky spirit was not on its mettle. When they arrived at Morholm they found the stable doors open and James inside. He was crouching in shirt sleeves, examining the leg of a lame horse with firm untender hands, and at their approach he straightened and fixed his level gaze on them.

'What brings you here, cousin William?' he said. He wiped his hands and came out of the stable, squinting at the light.

'Winds of chance, cousin. A short stay, with the family dear to me. You are well, James?'

James made no reply but rubbed at a spot of blood on his sleeve. There was an odour of sweat about him and as he stood with his feet planted apart and his thick hair tousled he seemed very much like a young animal himself. He began to walk towards the house and they followed.

'You had better go back whence you came,' he said when they were almost at the door. 'There is no place for you here.'

'Come, James, there is room enough. I am not particular –'

'But I am particular about wasting my money looking after good-for-nothings like you. Morholm is very poor, it may interest you to know, cousin: your presence will not enrich it, in any sense.'

'Oh, come, cousin, surely I am not to suffer because of George's inadequacy –' William was attempting to push past him into the house but he found his arm seized and a pair of small intense eyes thrust before his face. 'You have no right to insult my brother's name, sir,' said James, 'contemptible as it may seem it can never be as contemptible as yourself.'

William looked half-defiant and half-pathetic. 'Why, what an insufferable prig you are, James,' he said, and the next moment was sprawling on the ground outside the door as James shoved him backwards. 'Leave him, Mary,' James snapped, and she followed him into the house.

In the hall he pulled on his coat from where he had left it on a chair. 'This has reminded me: I had forgot the date,' he said. 'Mary, who is that jawing with aunt in the parlour?'

'Mrs Townsend, I believe.'

'H'm, well, it cannot be helped,' he grunted, and strode in. She followed him again as if magnetized.

Mrs Townsend, seated with Aunt Catherine, Daniel and Kingsley, looked somewhat startled at James's informal appearance; but she was more startled when he snapped to Kingsley, who was lolling in an elbow-chair like a fat spaniel, 'Well, Kingsley, I hope that situation is procured. Your month is up.'

Kingsley, plump and complacent, smirked. 'You are not still harping on that, are you?' he said comfortably.

'Am I to take it you have not acted on my instruction?'

Kingsley merely snorted, and the next moment was hauled bodily from his seat, frog-marched out of the room and across the hall, and thrust outside beside the just rising William. 'Pack Mr Kingsley's things, he is leaving directly and for good,' said James to Mrs Reynolds in the hall, and returned to the parlour. 'I shall not afford you the same treatment, uncle, out of deference to your age,' he said to Daniel, who was gaping like a fat landed fish where he sat, 'unless you are so stubborn as to make it absolutely necessary. I am sure you will not be.'

Daniel was not; and the family that sat down to dinner later consisted only of James, Mary, Aunt Catherine and Mr Finlayson. Mrs Peach for the first time in her life was poorly and did not come down. The contrast with the old crowded, bustling Morholm struck Mary forcibly; and the silence was unearthly. Aunt Catherine's face, however, wore its most voluble expression of ill-usage, and every now and then she would break into some plaintive but feeble protest: 'Nephew – James – it really is too bad, I swear I shall never be able to look Mrs Townsend in the face again!'

'Well, as you are to be married next month and off to London, it will not matter; you will probably not see her again.'

'Ay, but – but where will Daniel and Kingsley go, nephew?'

'I am not concerned where they go: they may descend to the nether regions directly for all I care – they are sure to one day, anyhow. They are scoundrels, aunt, they do not merit your pity.'

Aunt Catherine produced a handkerchief. 'You have no concern for my tender heart, nephew. I am so easily upset. Now you have made me think of poor George again.'

'It might have been better, ma'am, if you had been so thoughtful of George when he was here,' said James. 'Your tears now can have no effect on him, and certainly none comparable to the effect your tongue had on him before. Now come, cease your whimpering and think of your coming

283

marriage; you can live in London then, and be vain and affected to your heart's content.'

Aunt Catherine opened her mouth to speak, but could say nothing, and in fact was silent for the rest of the meal.

'What the devil is all that knocking, Forrest?' said Horace Hardwick, standing in his dressing-gown at the top of his stairs and peering down into the gloomy hall across which the servant was shuffling to answer the thunderous knocks at the door. 'It is after midnight,' he muttered to himself as the footman fumbled with the bolts. 'Well, who is it?'

''Tis only us, Horace,' came the voice of Daniel, and followed by Kingsley he reeled over the threshold, pushing the astonished servant aside. They had been at The Black Bull since James had thrown them out of Morholm and were violently drunk; they had just suffered the indignity of being ejected from a house again, this time when the landlord had bustled them off his premises. Horace came a few steps further down and by the light of the candle the footman held his pinched face grew quite weasel-like as he scrutinized them. 'Why, what do you do here? Is there something amiss at Morholm?'

'Amiss?' said Daniel with a flourish of his arm. 'Ay, there's much amiss at Morholm. We are persecuted men, Horace, we have suffered at the hands of – of a mere puppy, in brief; you would not believe – I mean to say, Horace, I am a sick man, and to be treated thus –'

'You are both drunk, I see,' said Horace in sour starchy tones. He came creaking down to the foot of the stairs. 'Now what are you babbling about? Come, I am cold and tired.'

'We have been thrown out of Morholm by James,' said Kingsley, cutting off another rhetorical explosion by Daniel. He was leaning against a table and looked very ill.

'Indeed, indeed,' said Horace. 'Oh, bring us another

light, Forrest. And why is this? Was this a spontaneous act?'

'Well – well, he said something of it, you know . . . thought he was jesting. I . . . I am a sick man, you know!' Daniel finished in whining protest.

'H'm, well,' said Horace, scratching beneath his nightcap. 'I cannot say I am surprised. What reasons does James give?'

The footman returned with another candle which lit the two overfed faces a sickly yellow.

'He calls us scavengers –' said Daniel.

'Scoundrels –'

'Spongers –'

'Knaves –'

'Scavengers, us!' said Daniel. 'Now, Horace, I appeal to you –'

'Yes, yes, no more.' Horace came slowly into the hall, waving the swaying drunkards to silence. 'I must give this some thought tomorrow. I suppose you have no accommodation?'

''Swhy we've come to you,' said Daniel. 'You would not have us stop at an inn now, would you? 'Tis hardly becoming.'

'What's more, we were thrown out of there too,' said Kingsley. 'Our luggage is still there.'

'Well, you had better lie here the night – Forrest, have the two back rooms made up – but I wish you had come sooner. This is most inconvenient.'

'Thank you, Horace, thank you. One finds out who one's true friends are,' said Daniel. 'Send your man for our bags, will you? I believe I'll go up to bed now – I'm sadly weary, what with all –'

'Just a moment before you go.' Horace's voice seemed doubly dry and assertive in the crisp midnight silence. 'Let us establish one thing now. I am willing to accommodate you both overnight. But do not imagine that you may fasten yourselves here as you did at Morholm. Joseph and George may have been coined of the same metal, but I assure you, so are James and I.'

Daniel hovered around the stair and mumbled something incoherent.

'So long as that is clear,' said Horace. 'Never mind fetching the gentlemen's things, Forrest. They will not be staying long.'

Aunt Catherine and Mr Finlayson were married in Aysthorpe church towards the end of a delicious June when dawns seemed to come early as if the day could hardly wait to begin and dusk fell with the soft glimmering slowness of a dwindling candle, over a landscape rosy and sweet-smelling after tinkling rain-showers of poignant freshness. It was the first wedding Mary had been to and she loved it; to her relief she was not troubled by any unhappy sensations from the memory of this same ceremony she should have performed with Jarrett. The beauty of the season was like a balm to her bruised spirit. It even transformed this little church, normally as damp and mouldering as a hole in a river-bank: rays of sunlight pushed through the grimed windows and spread gold on the grey flags of the church floor, the scents of June stole in and dispersed the marshy vapours, and birdsong rose above the sawing of the viols in the choir. When the newly-wed couple left the church the villagers assembled round the door cheered and Aunt Catherine blushed and did not look as silly as Mary had thought, and Mr Finlayson beamed while looking rather anxious and perspiring. James had let them have a small reception for friends at Morholm, but refused to participate himself, although Mary pressed him. 'You work too ceaselessly,' she told him. 'It would do you good to mix and drink and be aimless for a while.'

'But cousin, I obtain my relaxation by going over accounts

or reading a book. Milling about with a set of foolish people will only irritate me and have the adverse effect.'

So he would not be persuaded: but she was not annoyed with him, for she found his character refreshingly uncomplicated and uncompromising; his very bluntness made him easy to get along with. His single-minded energy had roused her from her despair and carried her into his vigorous world where people could live without murky tangled involvements and still find fulfilment. It was because of his solid unsentimental presence, she realized, that she did not really fear the strangeness of Morholm without Aunt Catherine; he was so relentlessly practical that she began to reason, from his example, that nothing was worth so much regret, that she must go on.

But all the same, the morning after the wedding, when the time came for Aunt Catherine to leave for London with her new husband, she was moved, despite the fact that her aunt had often been irritating and unlovable. And in fact since James's coming Aunt Catherine had become softer and less strident; and before she went to the coach she embraced Mary and told her to be a good girl and not worry and said she would make someone a good wife yet. Then they were gone.

Now Morholm held only James, Mary, and Grandmother Peach – although Mr Matthews the steward was now much about the house – together with the servants. Grandmother Peach was a much subdued character too, incredible though it seemed. James refused her the long extravagant indulgence she was used to. Morholm was changed indeed. But it did not seem empty to Mary, for James's industry filled it with life: she was content to live in James's practical world – she was not happy, but she was content; she had not forgotten Jarrett, but she was successfully living on another plane, above the plane of emotion and involvement to which that memory belonged. Yet she was not cold and remote. She had enjoyed the wedding party immensely, touched by how kind everyone was to her, and she felt with pleasure the resurgence of the socializing instinct. But although his father and mother were there, she had noticed Henry Milton's absence. She was fond of him and would have liked to see him – yet he belonged to the world of Jarrett, love, feeling, the past, a part of her life she could not trust herself to revive: and the world of George especially. With the knowledge of Elizabeth Wainwright's marriage to Hugh Woodhouse she thought if Milton and herself met they might begin to exchange lamentations and that was the last thing she wanted, to stir up any old maudlin feelings now that she was growing strong again.

But she did meet him soon, after all.

As invitation arrived for the family at Morholm to stay at the country house of Mr and Mrs Hugh Woodhouse near Cotterstock. It was to be open house for a week to all the newly-wed couple's friends before they left to visit Mr Woodhouse's relations in Lincolnshire: there would be grand dinners, routs, hunting-parties, card-parties, and on Friday night a ball. James dismissed the invitation immediately. 'The last thing I have time for is a week tripping back and forth with the county society quizzing each other,' he said.

'But James, this is an open invitation,' said Mary. She had a great curiosity to see the woman who had turned down her friend with her rich new husband, and her old thirst for experience was fully awakened. 'We may go for as short or long a period as we like. Could we not attend just the ball? Even Lord Fitzwilliam will be there, I hear.'

'Is that so?' He looked at her keenly. 'Well . . .' He fingered the gold-lettered invitation. 'Just for the ball then. The one evening.'

She was content with that: and only the fact that she was

wearing the same gown that George had bought her for the ball at Stilton – the night that had begun it all – detracted from her excited pleasure as she rode in a hired carriage with James and Mrs Peach up the drive lined with lime-trees to the Woodhouse mansion. It was lit with coach-lamps all the way to the very large and very new Palladian house where crested carriages were already waiting and footmen in livery stood at the foot of a broad flight of steps. James's only remark at the ostentatious splendour was a dry, 'Woodhouse obviously means to impress.'

Inside, the fashionable society of Northamptonshire and Huntingdonshire paraded around the ballroom which, like the rest of the house, was capacious: the refreshment-room, Mary noticed with amusement, was larger than the biggest room at Morholm. French windows opened out at the end of the ballroom on to an illuminated part of the gardens where a fountain sparkled and there were seats beneath spreading trees. Mary saw many of the usual staid gentry of the area whom she knew well: the Townsends with their numerous daughters whom they could not get married off, the Villiers, Mr Van Druyten and his daughter Emma, who had ridden to the ball on her favourite hack and had worked up a good sweat that was now spangling the black hairs of her moustache. She knew also, from an occasional too-quick turn of the head, a warning cough as she passed by, that her appearance had set them talking again of the scandal of April – The Jilted Bride – and she felt an inward stiffening of pride. Let them talk. She felt stronger now than when William's friends had stung her with their cruel jibes, and was ready to meet anything.

There were also here several personages rather out of her sphere: Sir Robert Barnard from Thorpe Hall, Hugh Woodhouse's father Sir Geoffrey – an ancient, doddering and lecherous man who tended to paw at the ladies' skirts, and whom it would obviously be a relief to the family to be rid of – and, looking slightly bored, in a canary cutaway coat with striped revers in a fashion Mary had never seen before, the man with enormous influence over the Soke of Peterborough, Lord Fitzwilliam. She was startled when James, who was dressed as usual in sober black and was the only person in the room, it seemed, with no powder or pomade on his hair, left her side and made straight for him.

Left alone with Mrs Peach, she was content to take a glass of wine and watch the patched, beribboned figures around her: but suddenly she found herself being greeted by the Wainwrights. Mr Wainwright's shabby pinched demeanour was more incongruous than ever in this splendour, but his wife was in full regalia. Her hair was dressed extravagantly high in the shape of a heart with a jewelled arrow through it, her great moon of a face was thick with powder, and Mary could tell she was wearing plumpers in her cheeks to fill out the places where she had lost teeth. She had grown fatter than ever: there was the creak of corseting beneath her flowered apple-green gown, and there were rings on her puffy fingers that looked as if they would never come off again.

'Miss Hardwick, my dear, how are you?' she said. Mary could tell she was thinking of the scandal of the spring and searching for a way to mention it. 'How charming you look! We have not seen you in an age – but then that is understandable.'

Mary thought the best thing she could do was merely smile and thank her.

'We are glad to have you at my daughter's little assembly,' she went on. 'It is quite a pleasant house, is it not? Of course, it is still not all she could wish it – not entirely fitted up to the highest standards of elegance – my son-in-law Hugh lived at his father's place before the marriage and only used this house occasionally on hunting-parties, and you know what men are, and she has had such trouble with drapers and glaziers and what have you. I have told her, be firm with them, my dear – but she is such a mild creature. Tradesmen are such an exasperating, swindling crew, I have no patience with 'em.' Mary, thinking of Mrs Wainwright's origins, smiled inwardly at this. 'Hugh is in the process of clearing land for enclosure, is he not, Edward? – but he has had all kinds of difficulty with saucy locals kicking up a great fuss about common rights, and taking away some wretched footpath. He even received an anonymous threatening letter. If I found out who had sent it I would have him whipped at the cart's tail directly and no sparing. Ah, there is Hugh now – Hugh, have you met Miss Mary Hardwick? You must have heard so much about her of late.'

The big high-coloured man in a silver waistcoat gave Mary's hand a cursory shake. 'Charmed,' he said, not sounding it. 'From Morholm, ain't you? Any news of your cousin George yet?'

'No, I fear not.'

'Met him once, I believe. Didn't hunt.' Woodhouse sniffed. 'Seemed a poor sort of fellow.'

Mary stiffened. 'My cousin was nothing of the sort, sir, though I see that may be difficult for you to understand, basing as you do your estimate of a man's worth on his prowess in chasing down and killing small beasts.'

'Indeed?'

'Indeed. And anyone who speaks so of him I am bound to think a pretty poor fellow himself, large income and large belly notwithstanding.'

Mrs Wainwright's mouth was a little pursed O and she was swelling visibly, but Mary bowed calmly to her and moved away.

Mrs Peach related this story with cackling amusement a little later to James when he rejoined them. 'Well, it appears we have both made enemies tonight, Mary,' he said.

'How so?'

'I spoke to Lord Fitzwilliam of the forthcoming election at Peterborough, and my intention of standing for it.'

'To stand for Parliament!'

'Yes, why not? There are two seats and always the candidates are nominees of Fitzwilliam's and the election is scarcely contested. I suggested the time was right for an independent gentleman with land interest to stand. I fear he did not take kindly to the suggestion and we parted on unpleasant terms. Never mind, I shall press ahead. I feel sure many of the electors are of my mind and would welcome an opportunity to break the Fitzwilliam domination. And now, since we are both pariahs, cousin, will you dance with me?'

She was taken aback, and he laughed at her expression. The cotillion was just beginning. 'Just the one is all I ask – that will be quite enough for me, and you, I should think, for I dance like a bear. Come.'

So she danced with James. The orchestra was highly professional and James danced in sober and undemonstrative fashion. He seemed in such an unusually friendly mood that she was emboldened to ask him: 'And now, James, I can see you are enjoying it – why do you not indulge in social pleasures more?'

'Hm, then perhaps I could make an enemy of Lord Burghley too and have done with it,' he said. 'No thank you. Besides, it is my not doing so that has resulted in Morholm's becoming prosperous again.'

'That is true. But now that you have got things on a surer footing, can you not relax a little more? You work dreadfully hard.'

He smiled again, and the humanizing, softening influence it had on his hard face was remarkable: she was reminded of Julia's rare smiles. 'Well, perhaps I shall consider it,' he said. 'But you do not expect me to begin holding balls and parties?'

'No – but you might accept when invited to them.'

'Well, I shall consider it,' he said again. 'But I hope you would not have me become like my late brother?' he added.

She stopped. 'Why do you say "late"?'

'Come, Mary,' he said. 'Face the truth. George, I fear, must somehow have put an end to his life. You know what he was like, and he *was* last seen walking down by the river. And no word from him. It is the obvious solution.'

'Indeed it is not!' She had broken the dance by standing still and the couple next to them were frowning at her. 'Kindly move off the floor, madam –' began the man but she silenced him with a look. 'I refuse to believe that and I do not think well of you, James, for saying it!'

'I absolutely agree,' came a voice behind her, and she turned to see Henry Milton.

They were both moved to see each other and she squeezed his hand with impulsive affection. 'Dear Mr Milton,' she said as they moved out of the dance, 'I am heartily glad to see you.'

'Well,' said James dryly, 'as you two seem in such accord, I shall leave you to it.' Milton bowed to him without warmth and led Mary to a seat away from the crush. 'When I heard George's name mentioned I knew it must be you,' he said. 'We seem to be the only ones who have not given him up for dead.'

'I shall not do that,' said Mary, 'for if I were to do so, I fear I would . . .' Her throat tightened. 'Do you think of him often, Mr Milton?'

'Always,' he said, and they were silent, the spectre of Jarrett hovering between them, his name unspoken.

'And what of you?' he said. 'How are you now?'

She thought he looked gaunt and ill-favoured and abstracted. 'I am well, extremely well,' she said. 'Better than I ever expected. Perhaps it is merely the summer.'

'Are you not lonely at Morholm now? I have heard it is less full than it was.'

'No, indeed,' she said. 'James has been very good, you know, Mr Milton: we have our disagreements – as you have seen – but I fear I could not have got by without him.'

He smiled, and she noticed again what a hollow, abstracted smile it was, almost like a grimace of pain.

'I am sorry I have not called at Morholm since . . . since April,' he said, 'but . . .'

'I understand,' said Mary. 'And I expect you have been busy.'

'No, in fact I have not,' said Milton, uncomfortably. 'Well, in a way. I have been writing quite a good deal of late.'

'Oh, I am glad you have returned to it! Poetry?'

'Yes, some verse. Some essays, other pieces. That is partly why I am going away.'

'Oh? Not for long, I hope?'

'I do not know. I am going to London, you see.' He seemed very hot and tried to loosen his stock. 'I am hoping to get something published – and to earn my bread from my pen if possible. So, I am not planning on ever returning at the moment.'

'Oh.' She thought of the oafish Woodhouse, and his new wife, Elizabeth. 'You are not happy here, Mr Milton?' It was as much a statement as a question.

'I –' She watched his face struggle, contorted. It was not the face of George's old friend she knew. 'I do not know,' he said, turning to look at the dancers bowing to each other at the start of the minuet, a parade of colours, silks and satins, lace and ribbons and powder. 'No – no, I am not happy, I – no . . .'

'But do you think you will find happiness in the city?'

He shrugged, seemingly with irritation.

'I wish you were not going,' said Mary. 'I shall worry about you.'

'Oh – there is no need for that. I have written to Mr Matthew Bedford – a bookseller, an old friend of my father's. I met him a few years ago, and he has often asked me to come and stay with him. I can support myself as a hack-writer, if nothing else.'

'When do you go?'

He frowned. 'Tomorrow.'

'You will write to us at Morholm, will you not?'

'Yes – yes, indeed I will,' he said, seeming relieved at being able to make some show of warmth. 'Perhaps too I shall call on your aunt Miss Catherine – Mrs Finlayson rather – in London. And here – you will write me if there is any news of George?'

'Of course,' said Mary gravely.

'Well, it grows late, and I fear I am disinclined for the dancing.' He smiled, painfully. 'I had better say goodbye now.'

She took his hand. 'Goodbye, Mr Milton. Come back one day. We shall miss you.'

'Goodbye,' he said, and took a hasty, sweating leave. She watched his narrow figure wend its way through the mass of people to the doors. It had been a sad and uncomfortable meeting. His old shyness seemed to have hardened into an impenetrable reserve. And with her pity and sadness at his going there was a deeper emotion, for the sight of him had brought back with stirring, burning clarity the image of George. And now the little probing shoot growing in the back of her mind began to bud as at last she admitted to herself that not only must George be dead but that it was really she, blindly, unwittingly, but surely, who had killed him.

3

Henry Milton had been thinking of going to London for some time: but he had only made his decision the night before.

He had been at the Woodhouses' for three days. The invitation, when it arrived – he suspected it was Mrs Wainwright's doing, but whether it was intended as an act of kindness or reparation or spite he could not guess – could not even be considered: it was unthinkable: but in the end he had accepted, and he knew it was because he had to see Elizabeth again.

Since Elizabeth's marriage Milton had led a solitary, loveless life, of a monotony that gave a curious perverse comfort. He had talked to no one except when necessary, even his parents. He went about his father's few acres with dogged dislike; he rose early and alone, set himself odd unpleasant little tasks like the frequent taking of cold baths, or re-reading through 'Paradise Lost' in a night, taking a strange prickly pleasure in testing his stamina. He took to riding, or more often walking, far afield, roaming over the beautiful summer landscape, often unaware of exactly where he was. He went south into the rolling country of Northamptonshire and the edges of Rockingham Forest, north and east to the great Fens beyond Peterborough and Market Deeping where the country was like a vast black chess-board marked out with ditches that vanished with geometric straightness into the endless distance, where the horizon was dotted with windmills, and where he saw many ditchers, strange squat men with leather waistcoats, 'breedlings' from the fen. Along the Nene valley he would follow winding paths through woods and foxcoverts that suddenly opened to reveal a shining pasture or a cornfield of aching yellow stretched before him as if he had happened upon a seashore. He would follow streams and backwaters flanked by mossy overhanging trees where coots and moorhens slid on oozy banks and water-weed hung rank and densely green and there was a delicious dark moist coolness. He would trudge through lanes and backroads where woodcocks would fly up from the verges with a clatter and sometimes someone on horseback would clop past him with a friendly greeting. Twice he arrived, by accident, at the same tavern, half-hidden by a great chestnut tree, and a motherly landlady remembered him and was very kind and friendly. He crossed Helpston Heath to Langley Bush, a clearing round a great ancient tree where open courts were once held and where a gibbet still stood. Here he came across a gipsy encampment, and though they were swarthy and roughly dressed in mole-skins they invited him to a cup of ale with them. He saw to his surprise that they did indeed eat hedgehog as the gossips said. One man played a fiddle with amazing skill and when Milton finally left their open fire to tramp home they gave him good wishes and an ancient nut-brown gipsy woman took his face in her hands a moment and looked at him with black glittering eyes and said, 'There's a lady coming, ay, there's a lady.'

Yet he felt so cramped and mean inside that he avoided the tavern and the gipsies afterwards; he did not want to share any emotional exchange with anyone; he was afraid of it and contemptuous of it and at the same time he wished he could. He had not been to Morholm since his token visit when the London party had come home after Jarrett's flight. Then Mary had not been fit to see anyone; but somehow he had not wanted to see her. He felt strangely distanced from her, sealed in his own pain that prevented him pitying hers. With the love of his life gone the confidential but casual friend seemed to lose what significance she had had. And his capacity for trust had received a severe blow at the revelation of the true nature of Jarrett, a man who had been his friend and whom he had believed to be the most decent of men. Yet part of himself was angry at the rest for this attitude, and angry too because his parents were so calm and understanding and he was too festering and bitter to appreciate it.

But though he dismissed his invitation immediately, he found within himself a morbid desire to see Elizabeth in her new station. He still could not keep away from her, still he felt that irresistible attraction. His love for her was not dead, indeed it had swelled, become bloated, a monster that pursued him constantly, and it was this monster that had driven him, cursing himself, to accept the invitation.

He was prepared for an acute jealousy, bitterness, anger perhaps, on seeing Elizabeth; but nothing could have prepared him for the terrible, agonizing longing that broke over him in a wave when she greeted him from the grand portico of her new home. Milton thought himself grown hard since her marriage, hard and inaccessible – but this overwhelmed him. He could barely return her greeting as she stood with her arm through that of Hugh Woodhouse: he stammered and shook, he wanted to die and yet he wanted her, desperately. He was glad there were so many guests there so that he could sink back into silence and anonymity once the formalities were over.

There must have been well over two dozen people that night, he noticed, at the great dinner table in the stately dining-room with a gilded ceiling so high that every scrape of a knife produced a solemn echo. Elizabeth's father and mother were there and Mrs Wainwright, across the table, gave him a smile which he supposed was meant to be sweet but which he did not feel disposed to return. He was seated next to Wilhelmina Wainwright, who had a runny nose and whom he soon realized, to his horror, was trying to flirt with him. Eventually she left him to his silence and his gazing at her sister.

In the evening there was music and cards, and though Milton wanted to slip off to bed he was roped in to a card game with the Townsends from which he found it difficult to escape; and when he finally did Hugh Woodhouse himself engaged him in conversation, a conversation more dull and brutish than he could have imagined even of such a man as this. It was late when Milton finally reached a chilly and capacious bedroom where he lay in a kind of wakeful paralysis long into the night, his mind a noisy, bloody battlefield.

In the morning there was a hunting party, but he disliked the sport and declined to join it. Instead he walked about the parkland with a middle-aged gentleman guest who was interested in landscaping and did not cease to talk to him of it for an hour. When the gentleman returned to the house Milton continued to walk about the park, admiring in spite of himself the luscious turf and the spreading canopies of oak and cedar placed here and there with wooden seats in their shade. In one of these he sat for a long time, reflecting on the curiosity of feeling the same old emotions, being the same person, when the surroundings were so unfamiliar and extravagant. He was just considering getting up and wandering over to a summer-house he could see when he noticed, in the other direction towards the house, a tall fair figure in a white gown strolling alone, with her back to him. He felt the raw, sick sensation in his throat again and got to his feet. He wanted so desperately to speak to Elizabeth, to be near her, to be alone with her, that he had begun to run before he had even realized what he was doing. As he ran he wondered what he would say to her. A solitary meeting – if he could just explain his feelings – surely if you loved someone so much, and told them so, they must somehow return that love. He slowed down to a more dignified pace as he caught up with her, but he was directly level with her and she had looked round and smiled at him before he realized it was not Elizabeth but merely one of the Townsend girls.

He walked back to the house with her, feeling very stupid and with little to say.

That night Milton got drunk. Others of the guests were doing likewise so it did not matter, but they were not drinking for oblivion as he was. He was due to leave tomorrow evening after the ball and this was a way of erasing the time until then. It was midnight when he finally hauled himself away from the other men who were still drinking and bellowing, and staggered off to bed. Unfortunately he was so hazy and tired that he lost his bearings and found himself wandering in a quite different wing of the house from where his bedroom was. It was here that Elizabeth appeared, like a ghost, noiselessly turning a corner with a candle in her hand. She started when she saw him and they stood for a moment looking at each other in the flickering glow.

'Mr Milton,' she said finally. 'I . . .' He merely stood looking at her and she seemed somewhat at a loss. 'You . . . are unsure of your chamber, Mr Milton? I am not used to the house myself yet. Come, I shall lead you to it. Have you enjoyed your stay? Our domestic arrangements are not quite what we should wish them yet . . .'

Rattling on in this way she led him along the panelled corridors, a tall figure in a whispering silk gown, a halo of candlelight about her that lit up the exquisite white curve of her neck. He followed her, and in that peculiar sleepy intoxication and darkness and silence it seemed to Milton that he was following her, as the eternal lover, to the ends of the earth. She was the absolute dream, the paragon in some private mythology, impossible of realization, but whom it was happiness merely to follow in an endless, hopeless, sweet pursuit through this soundless glimmering world. Then she stopped and turned, holding up the candle to a door, and suddenly she was a beautiful but vain woman who had married someone else, and he was the jilted man, abject and morose, hanging around her and unable to tear himself away. The return to reality was crushing: he stood dumb and transfixed, painfully and inextricably knotted with longing, while she wished him good-night and turned away. She was descending the stairs.

'Elizabeth!' he said, in a voice torn from him like a cry of long-stifled pain. She made no reply, whether because she did not hear him or did not want to hear he never knew, and her foot-steps died away down the stairs. He went into his room and closed the door as if closing a door on a part of his life.

So his decision was made. But Mary was not quite the first person to learn of it. During the afternoon before the ball, whilst walking about the park, he met young Mr Francis Sedgmoor, Julia's unlucky fiancé, who was also staying there. Milton did not know the young man well but they found each other agreeable and soon Sedgmoor was inviting him to a supper-party at his father's home in Peterborough next week. That was when Milton told him he would be unable because he was going away to London.

The young man seemed to grow thoughtful at that. They had paused by an ornamental pool and Sedgmoor stirred the water with a stick before saying: 'Mr Milton, you are on good terms with the Hardwicks, you cannot be unaware of the details of what happened in April. Julia Hardwick and I were engaged to be married, as you know. It was merely a cover for the activities of her and Jarrett, but I – I suspected nothing of that. I – well, I am diffident with the female sex and she was the first lady I really knew and . . .' he smiled sadly. 'Well, that is over. In some ways I wish Jarrett had taken her with him as he promised her, as she loved him, but it seems he only wanted her for his pleasure. What I wanted to say is – well, Mr Milton, I am now to be engaged to Kate Wiley – you know her? She is a delightful girl, and

I am thankful of this second chance of happiness. But if – if in London you should happen to – it is a slight chance indeed, but if –'

'If I should see Miss Julia?'

'Yes, that is it,' said Sedgmoor gratefully. 'We assume she is still living in London – God knows how – since there has lately been no word from her. If you happen to see her, will you be so good as to give her a message from me?'

Sedgmoor hesitated. A swallow dipped over the pool where gnats hung in a humming cloud. Finally Milton said, 'Perhaps you could give me a letter –?'

'No,' said Sedgmoor, 'no, not a letter, I feel I could not say it in a letter. Just tell her I do not hold what has happened against her and I am willing to fulfil my promise to her if she wishes it. Ours was never a great romance, Mr Milton,' and the gentle frankness with which he said this made Milton like the young man very much, 'but I made her the promise. I know we could never love each other but I am prepared to honour it.'

Milton, moved, nodded. 'I will tell her, if it is possible.'

And so he retired to bed at last late that night back at Helpston with his mind troubled by images whose persistence he could not account for. Julia Hardwick and, most strangely, from his meeting with Mary, there lingered the antagonism and mistrust he felt for James.

July gave way to an even more splendid August and Mary watched her garden take shape into something far more beautiful than the old jungle. The men James had got in to work on it were droll, independent men from the fens and she realized how glorious it was to laugh again as she listened to their stories. She came to identify the clearing and improving of the garden with the gradual return to her old self that was steadily progressing through the influence of the lovely summer and the unobtrusive solidity of James.

Much of the wilderness of overgrown hedgerow that separated the garden from the farmland was torn up and replanted or replaced with fencing: but she intervened to save an ancient ragged hawthorn bush that James was going to have destroyed. The blossoms were long since over and soon there would be haws, but she was adamant, with an eagerness the gardeners did not understand and which she did not wholly understand herself, that it should stay. She wanted, obscurely but fervently, to see the day when it would flower again.

One day her cousin had to go into Peterborough on the election business that increasingly took up his time and would not be back till late, so Mary lingered long in the garden. She walked round with Mrs Peach until dusk, but after the old lady had gone inside she could not bring herself to leave the green scented world and stayed weeding and pruning until the light was almost gone. At last she turned to go in and noticed, from the corner of her eye, a figure moving behind the trees at the back of the garden. She went over to look more closely and the figure stepped out. For one leaping moment Mary thought that it was Julia come back. The last feeble glow on the horizon was directly behind the stranger so Mary saw her in a kind of rosy half-silhouette: she was a tallish woman, dressed plainly with a shawl thrown carelessly about her and an old-fashioned straw bonnet atop untidy black hair; she was heavily perfumed. She took a step nearer Mary and then stopped and they looked at each other. Mary searched in her mind to see if she knew the woman. Finally she said, 'Can I – are you looking for someone?'

The woman moved a little closer and Mary felt strangely afraid. 'This is Morholm?' the woman said at last. Mary nodded. 'And you must be Mary Hardwick.'

'Yes. Are you –'

'I am a friend of Mr James Hardwick,' said the woman, suddenly walking past Mary towards the house. Mary followed, rather relieved. 'Oh, I see,' she said. 'You knew him in London?'

The woman had stopped again and was gazing up at the house. 'What – what did you say?' she said abstractedly.

'I – wondered if you were acquainted in London?'

'Oh! Acquainted . . . yes. Is Mr Hardwick at home?'

'No, he is in Peterborough – he will not be home till much later.'

The woman turned again and looked at Mary, a quizzical, uncompromising look that Mary did not wholly like. 'Is no one else at home?'

'James's grandmother. Might I –'

'I thought there were more of them,' said the woman. 'A whole flock of relatives, James used to tell me. But perhaps he has cut off many of his dependants?'

'Yes, he has.'

'Yes! just like James. He has weeded out all the rank grass – and left the little blossoms, has he not?' She laughed a weary, unpleasant little laugh that was like a puff of black smoke in the sweet August air. 'You don't like me, do you?' she went on. 'You are suspicious and afraid. Why did I come sneaking through the garden? Isn't that what you want to ask me? Well, I wanted to look at the house. I was curious. James used occasionally to tell me about his father's home, though I could never get much from him – you know how close he is. I've been asking about it in the village. I am staying there, at that wretched little tavern; and very reluctant they were to take me, too. Therein lies another reason, you see: had I "called" in the proper manner, would your servants have let me in, do you suppose? Look at me.' As the woman moved closer Mary noticed that her face was heavily powdered and patched, and so were her neck and bare shoulders. She was over thirty. Her eyes were large, relentless, a little bloodshot; her mouth and nostrils were wide and made her look striking while missing beauty.

'Perhaps I should tell you who I am. My name is Sophia Goulding. I was James's mistress in London. There, are you shocked?'

'No,' said Mary, though she was.

'Good. It is really nothing so shattering, after all. And we were in love. You know what love is, don't you?' She turned her eyes, green and lamp-like, with a fierce intensity, on Mary.

'Yes.'

'But of course. James told me briefly what had happened just before he left London, the last time we saw each other. You were jilted, weren't you?' The woman leaned over and bent a rose towards her face and sniffed it. 'You see, James and I were not engaged in some sordid affair. Not to me was it so, anyway. I was his mistress, but . . . Well,' she straightened, 'that has all ended now. He was growing tired of me long before he left London. And now he's here, the local squire. Does he like living here?'

'I – think so.'

'Doesn't he say so? Does he confide in you? Does he? Does he confide in you?' The woman's voice grew hard and shrill.

'No, no, he doesn't,' said Mary, trembling in spite of herself.

'No?' The woman grew calm again. 'Good. Because it's the most wonderful thing in the world to be confidential, is it not, to be intimate in your own little world with someone.'

'Yes,' said Mary, feeling a tear in her eye.

'And then to be suddenly excluded – shut out! However, it is what invariably happens.' She paused and took off her bonnet and swung it idly by the ribbons. Then abruptly she said: 'Do you love James?'

Mary wanted to be offended, and turn away from this woman who had no right to corner her thus, but she found herself somehow compelled to speak. 'No; he is my cousin and I admire him. That is all.'

'Then you trust him?'

'Yes, I would trust James above all.'

The woman nodded. 'You seem a trusting creature . . . innocent.'

'I am not innocent,' said Mary.

'Well,' the woman said with a ghost of a smile, 'you no doubt think that. Everyone is always hot to deny that they are innocent. But let me advise you, my dear: do not trust anyone. Men least of all.' She put on her bonnet, made as if to move away, then stopped. 'The other one – James's brother – he disappeared without trace, did he not? I wonder why.'

The words were like a lash across Mary's back. 'Please go away . . .' she said, her voice breaking on a sob.

'Remember my advice then,' said the woman, and was gone. Mary let her tears flow for a while and then when her eyes were sufficiently cleared she looked out over the twilit field and dimly saw the tall figure of the woman, striding away towards the village.

Mary stayed up so that she might greet James when he came home. He finally arrived after ten, very tired and more grim and silent than ever. She sat with him a while as he ate the meal she had had kept warm for him. He did not speak to her until he had finished when, sinking back and pulling off his boots, he asked her what sort of day she had had. Then her resolutions of betraying nothing of what had happened melted and she burst into tears.

He did not console her, but merely waited until she had recovered herself before saying: 'What has upset you?'

Well, she had better tell it now. 'Today a woman named Sophia Goulding came here.' She hoped that would be enough.

'Indeed?' He rose and walked up and down thoughtfully. 'What did she want?'

'I – I do not truly know – she came and spoke to me in the garden, told me about you and her.'

James stood, square and dogged, above her sitting figure. 'And do you feel you can no longer respect me, be friends with me, because this woman was my mistress?'

'No, no, James, it does not concern me –'

'Because she was,' he went on. 'I cannot pretend otherwise. Stupid, selfish folly in me it was ever to get so involved: exactly the kind of youthful folly I have despised and prided myself on being free of. However, it is all long since over. And I was never bad to her, Mary. I hope you can believe that of me.'

'Yes, James, I can,' said Mary. 'But I believe she is still in love with you.'

'Is that what she talked to you about?'

She turned her head as she felt tears prickle again. 'Yes, partly.'

'She distressed you?' said James. 'It would be typical of her. I see she has.'

'It is nothing, James,' said Mary trying to smile, 'but I wish she would not come here again.'

'She will not. I shall see to it,' said James. 'Well! now I am going to retire, and do you likewise. My grandmother is well?'

'Yes.' Mary dried her eyes, already ashamed of the weakness the strange woman seemed to have tapped in her. 'Thank you, cousin.'

Mary came down next morning to find talking to James in the parlour the blond, thick-set person of John Newman, the son of the old farmer who had been her friend. They were delighted to see each other and he took her hand in his great golden-haired one and said it was a treat to look at her again. 'If only the old man could see you, mistress: but he's living over near Lynn with an old friend of his, a farmer, who took him in.'

'How is he, John? It's so long since I saw him.'

'He's well and fine, mistress. Changed though. He's turned Methody. He went wi' his friend to Lynn to see one o' they preachers at a meeting in market square, and they both of 'em found salvation that day and joined the connection. The Lord ha' seen fit to take them up out o' the fiery pit and set their feet upon a rock of everlasting mercy.'

She was surprised at this language from the young man and he smiled in an embarrassed way. 'Well, I joined the brethren myself for a while, mistress, though I've strayed since. 'Twas too much of the next world and not enough of this for me, and I don't reckon to be leaving this'n yet. I been doing well, mistress, though I say it, and that's what I been speaking to Squire about. I been hoping to take up the old farm again. I got a bit of money, and I was hoping master and me could come to some arrangement. I know how to work that land, you see, as you'd expect, so I was hoping –'

'Oh, it would be fine to have you living there again! You do agree, don't you, James?'

'H'm, I don't know; what assurance can I have of this young man's character?' said James.

'Why, mine! Truly, James, you could not wish for a better man to work the farm.'

'Well, as you lived on the farm since boyhood . . .'

'Yis, sir, twenty year.'

'It seems a practical idea – the place has been standing empty for too long – provided you are prepared to work.'

John Newman was more than prepared to work: and so was Mary, who was indefatigable in helping him to settle in. They found the house in a sorry state. Just to get to the front door Newman had to struggle through a thorny wall of weeds that had sprung up with tropical speed. There were holes in the thatch and colonies of rats and mice and damp had rotted the beams. But Newman set to work with a will and Mary came to the cottage almost every day, taking an interest in it almost as strong as his own and helping him, despite his protests, to scrub the floor and walls, polish and arrange the few bits of furniture he had, and supplementing it with various pieces she herself produced; curtains, a vase with flowers, a quilt. She took a delight in helping to make a home, somewhere for someone to live. Occasionally James would come over to see how work was progressing, and he said it was a good thing for her to have another interest to keep her busy.

With John Newman she got on better than ever, but she was surprised to find what a thoughtful man he had become. He often startled her, while in the middle of some laborious manual task, by raising a question or opinion of a profundity that her mind had not dared to touch since the catastrophe of the spring. It was not difficult to draw John Newman out; and gradually they began to exchange thoughts with a freedom that many would have thought improper between two people of such disparate status.

One thing they never mentioned, however, was that very catastrophe of April until one day, when Newman was up a ladder mending the roof and she was below weeding the patch of garden, it somehow slid into the conversation. He was telling her she reminded him of the blackbird that he heard in the mornings, lovely and cheerful and heartening, and she laughed and said she would be pecking for worms next, and he said: 'But are you really cheerful as you seem, Miss Mary? Truly?'

'Yes, John,' said Mary, 'I believe I am now.'

John sighed. 'Because I think you're marvellous strong and brave, if you don't mind my saying so, after what happened.'

Standing there in the magnificent August sun with the miles of cornfield shimmering about her, Mary did not mind: she felt strong and brave, as he had said; she could think back to the terrible night without fear. 'I *was* in despair, for a time, John,' she said. 'I wasn't plucky. I gave in. I am still surprised I ever lifted myself out of it. Well, in truth I did not: my cousin James helped me out of it. He is still not very approachable or easy to be fond of, it's true; but he has behaved justly to me and done me a power of good. And you have helped me too, John.'

'I'm glad to hear that, Miss Mary. Y'see – I been thinking. There's a powerful lot of suffering, ain't there?' He stopped and wiped his broad tanned brow. 'Well, I been looking at it and, well, there's so much unnecessary, I can't understand it. Like I say, I turned Methody but I were soon back in the toils o' sin and the pride of life, as preacher'd call it. I couldn't be doing wi' it. Thass a rare comfort to the old 'un, but to me it axed more questions than it answered. Take Mr George, now – wherever he is – I mean I don't blame him though he threw us out of here – he never meant no harm, I reckon – he were a dreadful unhappy man, even I could tell. How can we blame him? Which brings us to that bastard Jarrett – pardon me – can we lay it all to him? It seems like we always have to find someone to blame else we go mad. What d'ye think, mistress?'

She did not know what to think, and knew that in some respects she did not want to. Forgiveness and goodwill came so naturally to her she never thought about them: but one thing she knew for certain was what she would do if ever she saw Thomas Jarrett again.

James told Mary that he had warned Sophia Goulding to leave her alone, and though she often saw the woman still hanging about the village she did not speak to Mary again. All the same she always felt oddly nervous whenever she saw the slatternly, lamp-eyed figure slouching across the common like some trollopy, unromantic witch. But her life was a secure one with two such solid men as her cousin and the young farmer, and her old life seemed a hundred years distant until one day a visit to Peterborough brought it back with disquieting clarity.

She always loved to go into the town on market days: and today she left the groom who was escorting her at the Talbot Inn to thread her way through the crowds alone. The Long Causeway was almost entirely blocked by the cattle market, and only sedan chairs could fight their way through the jostling, noisy mass of people and livestock. In the narrow Cumbergate was the skin market and the smell here under the hot August sun could turn a stomach not used to it. Beneath the arches of the Guildhall broad, squat Fen-women bellowed their wares in the butter market and from The Talbot across the square there was a great rattling and thundering of hooves as the Norwich Self-Defence lurched out of the inn yard pursued by screaming little ragged children. Mary watched the coach move off towards the Wisbech road with a grating rumble of iron-shod wheels and was just turning to walk down to the cathedral precincts when a hand touched her arm.

Daniel was looking considerably less well-fed and seemed unable to meet her eyes. His old snuff-brown suit was stained and worn and when he spoke his voice had none of the arrogant volume that demanded to be heard. He was living in a lodging-house in Priestgate, he said. Yes, he was well enough. He sometimes did errands and little jobs for Squire's Bank, who often had need of a man of genteel bearing. How much of that was true she did not know but she felt more sorry for him than she ever could have imagined. When she asked after Kingsley he said nothing, but took her hand and led her past the Butcher's Row and into Cumbergate.

'You don't mean he's in *here*?' she cried.

They had stopped before the House of Correction, a narrow gaunt building with high latticed windows that admitted no light. Daniel nodded.

An old pensioner in a skull-cap who worked as the gaoler admitted them, grumbling, and showed them to a long work-room where it was almost as dark as night. Here the petty offenders of the town were set to work beating hemp and amongst the drunks and vagrants and prentice-boys caught gaming they found Kingsley. There was an atrocious stench in the crowded room.

Unshaven, a dirty cap in place of his wig, Kingsley was barely recognizable. Mary had not the tender nostrils that ladies were expected to have but she had to hold her handkerchief to her nose at the foul smell and could only gasp his name. He looked up at her from his bench with a flicker of recognition and then looked away.

''Twas a squabble in The Angel . . . gambling at a cock-fight. Kingsley was accused of cheating and there were blows,' said Daniel in a low voice.

'Cousin Kingsley, I am indeed sorry to see you like this,' said Mary. She scarcely knew what else to say.

'Do not distress yourself, Mary,' said Kingsley. He did not look up at her. 'At least you know you will never descend to this condition. You were lucky enough to be born of the right sex to use in gaining favour.'

'What do you mean by that?' Mary said, ignoring Daniel who was motioning him to be quiet.

'Just what I say,' said Kingsley. 'I hope you are nice and cosy with James. Dear, dear, *you* will always be well placed with the master of Morholm – whoever he may be.'

Mary drew a shuddering breath of the fetid air. 'I came here in pity for you, Kingsley. And still I feel it. I do not say James was right to turn you out. But you do me an injustice!'

'He doesn't mean what he says, you know,' said Daniel anxiously. 'This place – affects a man.'

'Is this what you truly think of me, Kingsley?' said Mary. Kingsley said nothing, but lowered his head and returned to his work. Anger overcame her. 'I think we had better go,' she said. 'Come, uncle.'

So this was it. She had gone through the summer, recovering, feeling stronger, oblivious of any wagging tongues: but all the time they had been there. She came to the door and gulped at the fresh air – which even with the smell of the market seemed marvellously sweet – and blinked at the light. Daniel joined her and laid a hand on her arm. 'I am sorry for that, Mary,' he said. 'But I thought you should see him.'

She was silent, struggling with herself. With anger were mixed other emotions. There was no strong physical resemblance among the younger Hardwicks: only between James and Julia were there echoes in the lines of the face: but strangely, in the sight of Kingsley, despite his degradation, she had seen something intimately recognizable that had not been discernible in his old plump sleepy self. It was as much a visible manifestation of a mutinous, uncompromising streak as a particular facial feature, a streak that was in George, in Julia, in James, in herself. At the same moment she saw that James's measures had been wrong. When he had thrown them out she had felt little but surprise: she had no illusions about Daniel and Kingsley: they were freeloaders and rogues.

But the spirit of Joseph – and of George – was stronger in her.

She turned and went back into the building.

The old gaoler was not pleased about letting her in again. 'An't you seen enough?' he grunted, breathing stale gin over her.

'What do these people get to eat?' she demanded.

He looked her up and down warily and then spat before replying. 'Sixpence a day victuals,' he said.

She fumbled in her purse. 'And what of water – washing?'

He sniffed. 'What d'ye think? There an't no water supply here, mistress. May be as you've mistook it for the Bishop's Palace –'

'Hold your tongue.' She counted out two pounds. 'Here.

Send across to the Cross Keys for some soup and pies and a jug of ale.' The inmates of the long vault-like room were all looking at her, dumbly, even Kingsley now. 'And also ewers of fresh water so that they can wash.'

The old man looked at the money and sucked his gums and then spat again. 'Nay. Thass more'n I could do, mistress. Sixpence a day victualling they're allowed, wi' a straw mat to sleep on. Thass all settled by the wardens. I couldn't go handing 'em out extra –'

'Several of the churchwardens are personal friends of mine, and so is Earl Fitzwilliam,' she said with the haughtiest manner she could muster. She did not know any of them but she must brazen it out. 'I am sure they would be interested if I were to tell them of the foul condition of this place and that their pensioner was neglecting his duties. And probably pocketing the prisoners' sixpences if truth were told.'

He was sweating and frightened now. That last bit had come to her on the spur of the moment, but she seemed to have hit on something. 'Nay, mistress, I'll do as ye say,' he said, cringingly. ''Twas only as I mistook your meaning as ye might say. No call to git mardy. I'll send across . . .'

Hastily she went over to Kingsley and pressed her last shillings into his blistered hand. Daniel, who had followed her, was staring at her as they left the House.

'What's the matter, uncle?' she said, feeling a little shaky now.

He shook his head, still looking at her. 'Nothing, nothing, Mary. Just for a minute there you made me think of old Joseph.'

That pleased her more than anything.

4

It was harvest-time and James was out in the fields for most of the long burnished day. Only late in the evening would he return to the house, tanned and weary, and quickly eat supper and glance at a book and tell Mary how the work was going – it looked to be one of the best harvests in years, which would be a relief to the country-side after such a cruel winter – before retiring to bed. In the morning he would be up fresh and early to ride into Peterborough on his election canvassing before Mary had breakfasted. John Newman, having no crops of his own in the derelict fields at the farm, also worked on the Morholm harvest, so for much of the day she was alone, but she did not mind; she would watch the men working in the fields from a distance, seeing their bodies becoming a wavering blur in the shimmering summer heat and the blades of their scythes glinting rhythmically as if in some strange signalling code. She watched the gleaners following them, women with little children scarcely weaned or no higher than the sheaves. While Newman was at work she put finishing touches to his cottage, and she would leave sprays of foxglove and larkspur and clusters of glowing marigold and roses of unendurable sweetness in jugs about the rooms for when he came home. She did not wait for his return because a young girl from the village came in now to prepare his meals for him and if she found Mary there when it was time for John to come home she was hostile underneath a frigid deference. Her name was Jenny Lake, and she was a long slender girl with masses of corn-coloured hair and full lips that tended to give her a sullen expression. She moved with casual deftness and the sleeves of her coarse linsey-woolsey frock were rolled up above arms that were creamy and freckled and stabbed by ears of barley from her work in the fields. Mary could see that the girl doted on Newman and though she could never get her to be friendly she thought what a good wife she would make the young farmer.

Mary was returning home late one afternoon after watching some Scottish drovers with their herds of little stumpy cattle crossing Lolham Bridges. The wandering herdsmen often came this far south to fatten their cattle on the rich fenland pasture and they were a strange spectacle with their colourful kilted dresses and uncouth highland voices. She met Newman returning through the village from harvest. His shirt was flung loosely about him, stained with sweat, and his hands were raw and chapped, but they were on such good terms that they walked along together like a brother and sister at an assembly. She decided to sound him out about Jenny Lake and so she said experimentally: 'Now that you have a proper home, John, do you not feel the lack of a wife to share it? After all, there are Newmans in the place again now and it would be a pity not to continue the line: you are young and comely and I am sure there are a dozen girls who would look on you with favour.'

Newman smiled and shook his head and said well, he didn't know, he didn't want to go and marry a girl he didn't love. 'Who do you think of then, Miss Mary?'

'Well – well, Jenny Lake seems a lovely girl, and she is quite set on you, you know, John.'

John smiled and shook his head again and said Jenny, well, he didn't know, perhaps Miss Mary was mistaken . . .

'Oh, no, you are not to escape that easily: it is as sure as you were born. Jenny is very pretty, is she not?'

'Ay, I won't deny that – and, well, it's very fine in a way, though in another way a bit worrying, to know that someone's thinking of you that way, but –' He hesitated and ran his hand through his thick blond hair that grew like a profusion of untended grass. 'You see, I look at some of the courtings and weddings around me, and – well, can you start to love someone, just to order like? Is love so – well, so easy, so open a thing?' Before she could answer – and in fact she was stuck for an answer – he went on: 'And is it right, do you think, to have a try at loving someone because they love you? Have we got a – sort of duty – to love someone back if they really love us?' He had been gesturing excitedly and he suddenly stopped and looked rather abashed. 'I'm sorry to go on – you probably think I'm a right muddlehead – but I just get to thinking. Y'see –' he was off again – 'the way I see it, love is something that creeps up on you. Thass what I couldn't swallow about the Methody conversion – the way the spirit's supposed to enter you in one go and change you for ever. Nothing works like that. I reckon love can come out o' simple friendship or respect or maybe dislike – something you can't fathom – and it gets into you and takes root before you really know it. D'you follow me?'

She had only been in love once, and that had not been at all like what he talked about. But still she could not help feeling there was something in what he said; and it gave her hope that perhaps this process might bring him to love Jenny Lake. So she said 'Yes . . . Yes, I understand, John. But do not go and worry about this now. You have enough on your hands.'

They parted at the lane leading to his farm. Going up the drive to Morholm she stopped to look at the old house. Under James's rule it was much changed. The building had been newly roofed, the walls were stripped and cleaned of ivy, many of the old draughty casements had been replaced, the gates were painted. But a cloud seemed to come across the glorious August day and she felt cold inside. It was not the Morholm she knew. George was not there.

*   *   *

On the road to London Henry Milton watched through the coach window a countryside deliciously healthy and fertile with harvest. Larks sang in skies of pale rarefied blue and the tall elms that lined the route were green and shapely and the scents wafting in from the tawny fields were beautifully rich. He came into a London rank and suffocating with heat, where tempers were short and the refuse stank in the gutters and the horses had staring flanks and gasping breath and the strong sunlight bounced glaringly off the high rooftops. Milton felt again the mixture of attraction and repulsion the city had produced in him last time he had been here.

Mr Matthew Bedford lived in a cloistered, respectable street off Holborn near Gray's Inn. He had been a close friend of Henry's father when Dr Milton was studying to be a physician, and he and Henry had got on well when Mr Bedford had visited Helpston a few years ago. Now he had asked Milton to stay with him until such time as he had his own lodgings and means. He was retired from publishing now and living comfortably on the profits he had struggled for during the last thirty years. Being a bookseller and publisher was a hazardous, competitive and often sleazy business, but Matthew Bedford had come through it: he had mainly been involved in the most genteel areas of his trade, and did not share the wholesale unscrupulousness of many of his colleagues, though he was certainly shrewd and businesslike, and it was rumoured that as a young man he had been an associate of the Unspeakable Curll, the most infamous and piratical man ever in the profession.

However, Milton thought such a thing unlikely of the man who greeted him in the hall of his roomy respectable town-house. Mr Bedford was a smallish man of unprepossessing appearance, dressed carefully in a frogged coat with a beautifully curled bag-wig – personal vanity was his weakness. His face had a pleasantly aquiline nose and a row of white teeth, and though nearly sixty he was sprightly and alert, as was his wife, a woman with a dolly face who shared a touch of vanity with her husband which manifested itself in a fondness for large and lacy caps.

'How are you, my young friend,' Mr Bedford said, shaking his hand heartily, and 'You are most welcome, Mr Milton,' said Mrs Bedford, and after they had loaded him with pleasantries and enquiries he was led up to his room to prepare himself and dress for dinner.

They had given him a charming room, and as he washed and put on his best bottle-green coat with the velvet collar he reflected that he had not thought about Elizabeth – till now – for several hours. The change must be doing him good. He combed his hair, for the first time in what seemed an age, and put a new ribbon in the back. He realized that from his country life he was rather brown, and would probably be thought very rustic in town; but that did not worry him. His only real trouble was that the Bedfords still had their youngest daughter, Hannah, who had not long finished schooling, living with them. Now he did not relish the prospect of meeting her; he had developed since Elizabeth's marriage to Hugh Woodhouse a sour animosity towards women in general which was very different to his old romanticism. He hated the thought of having to maintain the courteous smiling chatter expected between young gentlemen and ladies and knew he would start being defensive and unpleasant. He had done it several times with visitors at home, so much had his disappointed love embittered him. And he despised himself for this.

They dined, he, Mr and Mrs Bedford and Hannah, in a deliciously warm and cosy dining-room amongst furniture of polished oak which shone burnished red by the light of a fire which was kept roaring despite the warmth of the evening outside. He was placed next to Hannah, but if he was afraid she might remind him of Elizabeth he was very far from the truth. Hannah Bedford, a few years his junior, was a short girl with a trim figure, silky honey-coloured hair kept simply and unpowdered, and a round, open face, clear-skinned with large eyes and generous mouth. She was cheerful, friendly and very talkative, and with such characteristics seemed designed to provoke Milton's prejudices that sprang from his own reticence, let alone his new bitterness towards her sex in general. Thus his replies to her were short and undemonstrative, but it did not matter as her rapid conversation was rarely directed exclusively at him but fired off at the company in general. She was an unsubtle, ingenuous girl, incapable of dissembling; she was unaffectedly emotional and Milton thought he detected an element of hysteria beneath her rattling cheeriness.

'And how are things down in the country your way, Mr Milton?' asked Mr Bedford when his daughter was silent for a moment.

Milton said a few commonplaces, not choosing to mention the events in the Morholm household.

'And did I not hear, Mr Milton, some time ago in one of your good father's letters, of your being about to get engaged to be married?' asked Mrs Bedford.

'Oh! no,' said Milton, 'no, no, I fear not, that is quite a wrong idea. I anticipate remaining a bachelor for the foreseeable future.'

'Ah, that is something they all say,' said Mrs Bedford. 'I remember all our three – John, Walter, and Frank too, all vowing the same thing. We must have you attend balls and routs while you are here, Mr Milton.'

'And what work have you brought with you, Milton?' said Mr Bedford. 'I am out of the business now – and well out of it, I say,' he added with a laugh, 'but I shall still be interested in looking it over, if you've a mind.'

'Thank you, sir,' said Milton. 'I have some verse, some

essays, and a draft of a short romance, about the length of Dr Johnson's *Rasselas*.'

'Indeed, indeed? Perhaps we shall make another Johnson of you, my young friend. You may see the original in town, if you are lucky.'

'Have you ever met him, sir?'

'I have never spoken a word with him,' said Mr Bedford, 'though I have seen him often enough about the coffee houses. He has a very loud and emphatic voice which drowns out all other conversation – no doubt the reason for his being called a wit – his are the only words to be heard. But I would like to see this work, when you have a moment. The bookseller I shall put you in touch with is Mr Isaac Carey – a shrewd fellow, I have known him a long time. You will perhaps find him a little daunting: he is full of odd humours and peculiarities. But he tells me he is in need of temporary verse writers – the kind of stuff, light, decent, that sells well amongst the ladies – and possibly he needs work for serious pamphleteering. You are willing to work as a hack, I hope?'

'I wish to earn a living writing, so I must be.'

'How long do you intend to stay in town, Mr Milton?' asked Hannah, turning her round bland face to him.

'I have no plans to leave it, Miss Bedford. There is nothing at home to attract me.'

'I hope you will find a satisfying social life. I always think a social life completes a person, don't you? Do you dance, Mr Milton?'

'Only under far greater prompting than I hope to find in London, Miss Bedford. I fear I am disinclined for such things.'

'The poetic temperament, you see, my dear,' smiled Mr Bedford. 'I could never get his father to go anywhere with me till a time when he came out of his shell, suddenly, when he was nearly thirty.'

'How interesting!' said Miss Bedford. 'I am so very differ-ent! I love to dance and talk and meet people. Perhaps I am too fond of such things,' with a smile at her parents, 'I am sure Papa disapproves a lot of the time. And what of society where you live, Mr Milton, is it frightfully rural?'

'Society is there, to be had by those who want it,' said Milton. 'Speaking for myself my greatest pleasure is in the countryside – its beauty and solitude.'

'I cannot speak of that,' said Miss Bedford, 'for I have hardly visited the country proper. I love the town; though it is true I have only known its more pleasant side. What is your novel about, Mr Milton?'

'Oh . . . it is no very adventurous undertaking. I have tried to make it an insight into the human heart as Mr Richardson did.'

'Really? I have read each of Mr Richardson's books a hundred times over, and Mr Mackenzie's, and Mr Fielding's too, though Mama does not like me to say that. Is it a story of love, Mr Milton?'

Milton hesitated. 'Love comes into it, Miss Bedford.'

'Oh, I do hope you have success with it! I would love to read it. I am a voracious reader – though I suppose that is to be expected.'

In the drawing-room Hannah played the harpsichord and sang in a high flutey voice for them. Afterwards she talked to Milton indefatigably. 'I have such a shrill voice, I fear,' she said, sitting down with him on a long sofa. 'Miss Castle always used to say so. Now my friend Jane Waters – she is a charming girl, perhaps you will meet her – she has such a thrillingly low voice – I am dreadfully envious of her. Do you sing, Mr Milton?'

'Only when I wish to clear the room, Miss Bedford.'

'How you do speak your mind! But I think it much preferable to the kind of duplicity we get here in town. I saw your father once, long ago when I was small – he came

322

to visit Papa – he seemed a specially agreeable man. Is he still so?'

'Yes, indeed – I have an immense love and admiration for my parents.'

'How charming! So have I, but it is not always the case, is it – I know many of my friends live in frightful discord with their father and mother. How lucky we are to have such excellent parents!'

'Yes,' said Milton, and it struck him for the first time. 'Yes, you are right.'

'You said there was nothing to keep you at home, Mr Milton,' she went on, 'but will you not miss your friends in the country? Have you many friends there?'

Milton did not wish to unbosom, least of all to this chatty pleasant girl: since losing Elizabeth he had cut himself off with a contemptuous mistrust from any kind of intimacy or confidence: but he could not see any way out of telling her, and in spite of himself he was enjoying talking, so he told her, briefly, about Elizabeth.

'Oh, Mr Milton,' she said when he had finished, putting a hand impulsively on his arm. 'I am sorry to have reminded you of such a thing, though I suppose it is not an easy thing for you to forget. Do you know, Mr Milton,' she lowered her voice a little and leaned closer to him, direct and ingenuous, 'when I first saw you I wondered why you were so grave-faced. I am sorry now I ever thought such a thing.'

'Never fear, Miss Bedford,' said Milton. 'People have thought me glum and solemn even in my happiest moments. My face was made that way.'

'It is exactly the opposite with me. They say I am forever grinning. How opposite we are! And yet you understand me so well. I suppose that is your author's understanding. I am sure your work must be very penetrating, now that I have met you. I am sure you will get it published at last. Papa is such a pessimist, though he calls it being businesslike. I do detest pessimism, don't you? It is such a cowardly attitude all in all, so easy to retreat into. But I am running on again – and you are too polite to stop me – you are such a good listener.'

'Listening to intelligent conversation is no difficult thing – it is making it that presents the difficulty.'

'How well you put it! You must write that down: but in truth it is difficult to listen to idle chatter without becoming impatient. But see! Mama is beckoning me to retire, so you must put up with me no longer. It has been a great pleasure meeting you, Mr Milton – good-night, sir – good-night, Papa –' and she was gone.

Milton retired about half-an-hour later. After he had undressed he warmed his hands over his candle for a while and reflected. Against his will he had enjoyed talking to Hannah Bedford: he mistrusted this impulse but could not deny it. He had begun meaning to be defensive and distant, but her kind-hearted effusiveness had somehow drawn him out. As he warmed his hands it occurred to him – and his reaction to it was something of mistrust and something of gladness – that his heart too felt as if it might be beginning to warm up and thaw. Eventually he snuffed the candle and turned to sleep.

What he did not as yet guess was that Hannah Bedford had fallen very much in love with him.

Mr Bedford took Milton to see Mr Isaac Carey next morning. 'I shall just introduce you,' he said as they went up the steps to a grimy and unimposing house in Cheapside, 'and then I must leave you. I hope we shall be lucky enough to find him in a good temper.'

They were let in by a maid with a face that looked to Milton to have come straight from an Italian caricatura.

'How is your master, Polly?' said Mr Bedford, but the old

woman merely grimaced and shook her head and jerked a thumb towards a door at the end of the hall.

As she shuffled away the door opened and a little man in spectacles was forcibly ejected out into the hall to land on his hands and knees on the floor. His wig had fallen off but it was hurled after him by the figure who appeared in the doorway, bellowing '. . . and never come back, sir, if you value your hide!' The little man, barely pausing to put on his wig, was gone in a moment. His assailant turned to them truculently as if prepared for further conflict.

'Well, and what do you –' he began. 'Oh, 'tis you, Bedford.'

'Carey, this is the young gentleman I was telling you of. Milton, Mr Isaac Carey.'

Mr Carey was a man of middle height and thin build but formidable appearance. He was dressed in a very old coat with flared skirts: in place of his wig a filthy cap covered his head and he wore no waistcoat. He was beetle-browed and had a long fiddle-shaped face, and his jowls bristled with stubble. His eyes were of a pale, watery, transparent blue, but keen and darting. 'What do you bring me, then, sir?' he said, extending a hand. Milton delivered to him his precious bundle of manuscripts. 'Well, I must leave you,' said Mr Bedford. He patted Milton's shoulder. 'I shall see you at dinner, Milton.'

'Come into my office, Mr Milton,' said Mr Carey, leading him into a room that looked like a library in which a troupe of monkeys had been let loose. Books, pamphlets, broadsheets and yellow manuscripts covered every available space. 'That insolent fellow I just got rid of – claimed I had credited a work to him that was not his – "capitalizing on his name", if you please! As if his name were anything but dirt.'

Mr Carey had a way of grinding his jaws as if he were chewing on some invisible piece of gristle, and he did this as he pawed through Milton's manuscripts. Milton tried not to feel offended at the bony grubby hands rifling with such carelessness through the work on which he had spent so much labour.

'Milton, h'm, an apt name for a poet,' grunted Mr Carey at last. 'Though it is a pity some of this does the name no credit. Not that anyone reads Milton these days anyway. At least you write a fair hand: some of these young princocks expect me to read the most childish scrawl. H'm, these essays will not do; no one reads essays, unless some famous oaf has scribbled them. Sermons perhaps. Ah, lover's poems – yes, these are pretty, I may have something for you there. What is this? A romance?'

'Yes, sir. That is the work on which I lay my chief hopes, the work into which I poured most feeling.'

'Hm, feeling, sir, what is feeling, can it be bought, can it be sold, is it marketable, sir, can it be advertised on the title-page? No, you will be useful to me for your tinkling verses, sir, but if you want this romance publishing you must find a patron. Find me a wealthy man to back you and I will venture it, but not before. However' – he rose and returned Milton's bundle to him – 'come with me now, sir, and I shall find you some work.' Mr Carey removed his cap, took his wig from where it rested on a Roman bust, and put it on; it was such an old-fashioned one, almost a full-bottomed peruke, that Milton gaped a little. Then Mr Carey took a stick from the corner and, grasping it like a cudgel, led Milton out into the street. He walked at a very brisk pace and Milton had a job to keep up with him.

'You shall see Grub Street at its least wholesome, Mr Milton – I shall show you one of my hacks at home. I provide them with lodging in exchange for their scribbling. Bah, get out of my way, sirrah!' he exclaimed as a beggar stepped out before him with outstretched hand. 'D'you think I have money to throw around, when 'tis as much as I can do to keep myself from descending to your condition?' He turned abruptly down a side-street and Milton had to trot to keep up with him. Down here the ordure of the gutters was piled high like snowdrifts and little rickety children rooted amongst it like insects: Milton had to hold his handkerchief to his nose. 'Ah, you are not used to the stench of the city yet, h'm, Mr Milton?' said Mr Carey, turning his pallid roving eyes to him. 'Not like the sweet scents of the country, eh, eh, the lilac and the lime and the babbling brook? You should have stayed there, Mr Milton, far healthier for mind and body than this stinking ants-nest. Ah, when you have been here a few years your nose will be as insensitive as mine, and your soul too: that is the inevitable effect of the place. In the meantime you had better soak your handkerchief in vinegar.'

They came to a crossing: a little half-starved crossing-sweeper had cleared it and Mr Carey threw him a handful of pennies. 'Ha, you are surprised, Mr Milton? I am not such an ogre as you supposed, eh? In fact, Mr Milton, I *am* an ogre: I perform such acts of charity to salve my conscience. I never step inside a church, you see, sir, for I am a vicious unbeliever, an atheist, they say with horror. Are you shocked?'

Milton said he was not a religious man himself.

'Ah? Good! I cannot abide a man who is preachy. You see, if I do things like that every now and then, I can assure myself I am doing some good in the world, should it turn out that one's behaviour really does affect one's future life, as these spouting Wesleyans never tire of telling us. Personally I entertain little hope of that. H'm, and what a fool I was to give away so much. That was no lying miser's whine back there, you know; I have been in the sponging-house and the debtor's prison many a time. Not like old Bedford. The old fellow has always been lucky, and can afford to dress himself up like a peacock. You do not think

I dress in this way from choice, do you? Here we are.' They mounted the steps of a smoky and ramshackle terrace and Carey led him in without knocking and up a flight of perilous stairs. He stopped at a door on the top floor and hammered at it with his stick. There was shuffling and whispering within and then a woman's voice cried: 'Mr Foulkes is not at home.'

'Eh, what is this, not at home to Isaac Carey, this will never do!' growled Mr Carey. Immediately the door opened and a harassed-looking woman with a baby against her shoulder smiled anxiously at them. 'So sorry, Mr Carey – we thought it was the tailor.' An equally harassed-looking man in his thirties, clad in an old dressing-gown and slippers, appeared from behind the door where he had been hiding. 'I am a little in arrears with my tailor for my breeches, you see, sir,' he said with a nervous smile.

'H'm, I hope you are not in arrears with your work, Foulkes?' said Mr Carey, leading Milton into the room. It was a dirty, dark and humid place, steamy from a bubbling pot and a string of baby clothes hung over the fire. Apart from the bed the only piece of furniture was a desk, littered with papers, beneath the tiny window.

'Oh, no, Mr Carey, it's all up to date,' said Mr Foulkes, scrabbling among the papers. 'Here it is, sir.'

Mr Carey glanced through the greasy sheets. He made no explanation of Milton's presence, and none seemed to be expected. 'H'm, good, good. See here, Milton, we have a series of verses written by a consumptive poet to his fair one . . . the sort of thing the ladies like. The sheets are selling well so we are continuing the series. You know the sort of thing, modern, pretty, elegant – they weep over it one day and it is used for curling-papers the next. And we have here some "True and Original Correspondence from a Lady of Fashion to her Lover in the –th Regiment". Foulkes has been doing it so far, but I do not think he has an elegant enough style. I want a dozen more letters between the lovers, plus a few from her outraged mother and his colonel, leading to their elopement and his being killed in a duel with her brother.' He thrust a bundle of papers into Milton's hands. 'Now, Foulkes,' he produced more papers from the pockets of his coat, 'here is an outline of "The Amours within the Convent", from the French. I want you to fill it out suitably. Can you have it ready by Friday?'

'Oh, yes, sir,' said Mr Foulkes, though Milton thought from his expression he would be hard pressed to do so.

'Good. Now, Milton, let us be going,' said Mr Carey, and his hand was on the door-knob when Mr Foulkes cried: 'Oh, Mr Carey – if I might – if I might ask –'

'Well, what is it?' said Mr Carey, glowering at him from under his beetle brows and champing as if at an invisible bit.

'I am a little pressed by creditors, and it is two weeks since last you gave me –'

'You wish for money, sir, when in those two weeks you have hardly done a stroke, no indeed sir, when you have finished that commission and not a penny before, sir!'

Milton followed Mr Carey out and down the stairs. 'Now, Milton, get that done for next week, and then I may have some more work for you,' said Mr Carey over his shoulder. 'By-the-by, I am having the Bedfords to dinner on Thursday, I shall expect you too. I'll leave you now.'

He left Milton to make his own way home: and this took him some uncertain wandering about Holborn before he got his bearings. The ceaseless tide of strange faces that confronted him wherever he went in the city was something he had yet to get used to: and it was this that made him wonder if the face he had glimpsed crossing Snow Hill was really that of Thomas Jarrett.

5

September came in, but the summer showed no signs of being on the wane at Morholm, and the only hints of autumn were the clouds of tiny black smuts that drifted across the country from the stubble-burning in the fields. Mary saw less and less of James. Now that the harvest was nearly in he spent much of his time in Peterborough and the villages around, drumming up support for the forthcoming election. One warm and fragrant evening, a week before the hustings, he came home so tired that he declined supper and went straight to bed. Mary, who still found sleep difficult, remained in the garden and went to look as she often did at the old hawthorn bush. The haws were budding and the foliage was beginning to tinge with brilliant flaming colour. The sky was streaked with rose and purple clouds that looked like stained cobwebs, and she was falling into a dreamy contemplation when she saw three figures coming up the drive to the house. She went round the stables to meet them and they gave her a short greeting.

'Good even to you, ma'am,' said one, a short, round and sweaty man who licked his lips nervously. 'Is Mr James Hardwick at home?'

'He is, but he has retired early. Can I help?'

'We shall wake him from his dreams, then,' said the second, a stocky, bull-like man in an old velvet coat, and he grabbed at the door-handle.

'Just a moment,' said Mary, pushing in front of him. 'I have told you he is gone to bed. Now, if you have business with him –'

'Yes, business we do have,' said the third, a clerkly man

330

in spectacles. 'And very urgent. It concerns the election in Peterborough.'

''Tis urgent, ma'am,' said the short man. 'We wouldn't intrude otherwise.' He glanced at the others anxiously. 'Perhaps so be as you'd listen to what we've to say, if you wouldn't mind.'

'Very well.' Mary opened the door. 'Come in.'

'I still say we should wake him and have it out right now,' said the bull-like man. Mary turned to him. 'You may take your choice. Say what you have to say to me, or go.'

'No need for that,' said the short man, frowning at his companion. 'I reckon we can sort this out civilized, without your mardies, Jack Wistow.'

She took them into the front parlour where they would be quiet, and the clerkly man spoke up.

'The matter is this, ma'am. My name is Hackthorn and I'm a chandler in Peterborough. This here is Mr Fenstanton, miller,' indicating the short man, 'and this is Mr Wistow, farmer. We've all a vote in the election next month.'

'Ay, and 'tis my first,' growled Wistow.

'Quite. And what we want to say to Mr Hardwick is, well, we want him to stand down and not contest the election.'

'Indeed?' said Mary. 'And so you have come here to threaten him.'

'Now, now, no one –' began Fenstanton, but Wistow cut him off. 'If need be,' he said. 'If that's the only way he'll see sense, I'll –'

'Wait, Jack.' The clerkly man silenced him. 'Mr Hardwick is standing outside the Fitzwilliam interest, as no doubt you know, ma'am. Now, we've got nothing against that – indeed, 'tis about time it happened. I would willingly vote for him, if . . . You see, there is a question of influence. If I were to vote for him I might be ruined.'

'You mean Lord Fitzwilliam would apply pressure?' said Mary.

'Mebbe not him as such,' said Fenstanton, blinking and sweating. 'But two of the candidates are nominees of his – the ones that are expected to win – and one buys most of my grain. If he knew I'd withdrawn my support . . .' He shrugged.

'An election upset might mean trouble for all of us,' said Hackthorn. 'Mr Hardwick is interfering in a system that's always worked. We've got our way of doing things, and he's upset it.'

Mary sighed. 'I understand your position. But you do not know James as I do. He is a very determined man, and I doubt the opposition of the whole town would move him –'

'That's all we need to know,' said Wistow grimly, and strode to the door. 'I know another means of persuasion –'

'Wait!' Mary pulled him back forcibly. 'That does not mean he will give way to violence either! Now I will tell him what you said and put your case for you, but if you are intending to settle this business with fists you must use them on me first!' She faced the bullish man – it seemed fearlessly, though inside she was afraid.

'Ay, come, Jack,' said Fenstanton, eyeing her with a new respect. 'The lady has spoken fairly. We'd better go.'

'Mebbe.' Wistow shrugged and he followed the others out to the front door. Then on the threshold he stopped and turned. 'But standing an election is an expensive business, if you're not in some lord's pocket. What I want to know, mistress, is where the money's coming from. Good-night.'

Mary had no answer to that: for she was wondering the same herself.

Henry Milton was often frightened and disgusted in London and often he longed for the Helpston countryside, but he found himself, almost against his will, liking the city and feeling its grip of fascination tightening the more he saw of it. All the same his new life was a very different one and he might have felt lonely had it not been for the continual kindness of the Bedfords. Mr Bedford, despite his vanity and some very occasional fits of ill-temper, was unremittingly hospitable and good-natured; Mrs Bedford was like a mother to him; and Hannah, in spite of all his affected coldness, was so friendly to him that he could not be sullen and defensive with her for long. He found some lodgings, modest but not thankfully of the squalid kind he had seen when accompanying Mr Carey, but every evening and frequently at other times he went to the Bedfords' at their request. The work Mr Carey gave him was in no way difficult but it was rather tedious and stultifying, and though Milton realized he was lucky to be earning money in so genteel a fashion in comparison with many of his colleagues, and acknowledged the debt he owed to Mr Bedford's influence here, he still felt that his novel demanded the attention of the world.

But in the evenings, when he was with the Bedfords, he felt a kind of contentment stealing upon him that he had almost forgotten. After their excellent dinners the Bedfords would retire to a drawing-room of delightful cosiness. Mr and Mrs Bedford would converse with him unobtrusively and intelligently, and Hannah would ask about his work and his life and his views with unaffected interest. And gradually, where he had begun by holding aloof from her, he found her directness refreshing and engaging. After months of sourness and self-inflicted loneliness, to be hauled by the scruff of the neck back to warmth and communication was undeniably pleasant. One evening she even persuaded him to sing with her, something of which he had always had a positive terror back home, and when they had finished and Mr and Mrs Bedford were clapping and they sat down again on the long sofa she said to him: 'There, you see, you have a charming voice and you never use it. It just shows it is better to do as I tell you,' and they laughed together under a glimmer of yellow candlelight. She looked rather attractive today in a clean healthy way and her large eyes sparkled. 'And I have got you to smile,' she went on. Her parents were talking between themselves so they were unattended. 'I despaired of ever doing so when you first came. You look so much more agreeable when you smile. You are to dine with us at Mr Carey's tomorrow, I hope?'

'Yes, he has invited me.'

'Oh, good! Of course,' she lowered her voice and touched his arm, a gesture she often made, 'you have seen Mr Carey's eccentricities – you must not be surprised when they manifest themselves at his dinners. I cannot count the number of times we have had the soup and the fish and the tarts in a very peculiar order, or have had Mr Carey's spaniels sitting on the table as we ate.' They laughed again and Milton asked, remembering something he had wondered about: 'Tell me, is there a Mrs Carey?'

Hannah shook her head. 'I understand there was, a very lovely creature, but she died quite young. Mr Carey never mentions it and indeed, shows no signs of ever having been tender and loving with anyone in his life.'

Milton grew thoughtful at this and remembered Elizabeth. Something of this must have shown in his face for Hannah said gently: 'Oh, Mr Milton, have I made you think of – that lady at home – talking like this? I am so sorry. I had hoped to help you forget that – or at least not to forget – but to soften the memory.'

He smiled. 'No, no. Well, I suppose my grief is a common enough one among men and women everywhere – the oldest story in the world – the one you love marrying another. I have made a great fool of myself over it. It was the chief reason for my leaving home – being unable to bear to be in the same place with her. But – perhaps there is something wrong with me – somehow I have been unable to forget. I am afraid mine is a very resentful, brooding spirit, Miss

334

Bedford: but I must say since I came to London I have been much happier.'

Hannah was silent for a moment, and then she said something that surprised him. 'Do not blame the lady, Mr Milton. I dare say she never meant to hurt you. But if you find you do not really love someone there is no pretending. It is best if you sever it altogether. There was a young gentleman last year who paid court to me, and indeed I liked him initially, but when I saw how serious he was I realized I could never match that seriousness in regard to him. I simply did not love him, and I find when you cannot return someone's ardent love, even your liking or affection for them cools and becomes a matter of discomfort. You cannot help it.'

'I do not blame the lady,' said Milton, though deep down he knew he did. 'But the man she married . . . a rich oaf –'

'There, you see, you are blaming her,' she said. 'And are you sure, in that case, that the lady was really suited to you?'

A twinge of annoyance went through Milton. He had not faced such questions, he had not wanted to face them. 'I don't know . . . yes . . . no, perhaps not, but that makes it no easier. You are attributing to love a logicality that it does not possess.'

She smiled suddenly and understandingly.

'I know. It is very easy for me to lecture like this. But I think you are a very kind and understanding person, Mr Milton, and I should hate to see that swallowed up by your bitterness. And most of all I should hate to think that what you are in love with is really the idea of being in love itself. To be in love with love is very easy and pretty: but it always leads to heartbreak, unless you learn what real love means.'

Besides Milton and the Bedfords there were only a very old couple who were both stone deaf at Mr Carey's the next

335

night, but still the dinner was very frugal. There was some palatable mutton, some uneatable beef, a partridge, and some fillet of veal which Mr Carey took all for himself. Afterwards they had a few tarts which were cold. There was no shortage of wine, however, and Mr Carey, who engaged Milton in conversation, drank plentifully of it. 'And how goes your work, Milton?' he asked. 'Tired of it yet? I dare say you think it very beneath you: you think your talents are being wasted, and that your real work is being ignored by the world, h'm? It is always the case with you young men. What about that romance of yours, eh – still holding on to it? You really hope for success in that quarter?'

'Richardson, Fielding, Smollett have all done so.'

'Ah! and a thousand others have not. And Richardson, sir, was a mere humbug. And so was Fielding, come to that, though a shade livelier. But I am glad you make mention of Mr Smollett . . . now there was a great man, the greatest author we have had since Swift. And now he is gone too.'

'Do you not find Smollett's misanthropy a little unhealthy, sir?' said Milton.

'What? Unhealthy, d'you call it? Life is unhealthy, Milton, and Smollett's response to it was the truest. But you would have no success in writing like him anyway, tastes are becoming too delicate. You had better fill volumes with nonsense like *Tristram Shandy* . . .' Mr Carey appeared to be growing rather heated and Milton was about to turn from him to talk to Hannah when he spoke again. 'But if you are truly serious, Milton, there is a gentleman I know who you might approach as a patron. His name is Whitwell, he is foully rich, and takes an interest in letters. I shall give you his address. If you were to petition him to help you you might have some success. Write him a crawling dedication to the book and try and get him to accept it. He is a generous man. Persuade him to back you and I shall consider it.'

It was at this dinner that Milton realized that Hannah

Bedford was in love with him. When, after taking port, they joined the ladies in the drawing-room which, like the rest of Mr Carey's house, was cluttered and old-fashioned Hannah got him to repeat their duet together while she played on the antiquated spinet that stood in the corner on rickety legs like some ancient, faithful dog. As they sang she looked at him earnestly with her big moist expressive eyes and when they had finished he took her hand as they acknowledged the applause and the warm pressure of her fingers could not be mistaken.

Of course it was gratifying to know, especially after so short an acquaintance; he could not help feeling flattered at being the object of 'love at first sight'. But it was also disquieting. Milton was enjoying the pleasure and warmth she was bringing back into his life but he could no more love her, he felt, than he could stop loving Elizabeth. And at the same time he hoped that his loneliness and frustration would not lead him to accept her love and involve himself in something in which he was not sincere – and which would ultimately hurt her.

He thought about this all evening, even as he talked to Hannah and found his fears confirmed by her every word. At last, when he was handing her into Mr Bedford's carriage and her parents were a little way off, saying good-night to Mr Carey, he decided to say something to her, something to clear the air, anything. 'Miss Bedford –' he began, but he had no idea how to go on. But she laid a hand on his arm and said: 'Please, Mr Milton, I wish you would call me Hannah when mama and papa are not by.' And after that he decided it was no use saying anything, so he merely murmured, 'Oh, nothing . . .' and waited to hand Mrs Bedford into the carriage.

Milton went, with the manuscript of his novel and a servile dedication he had tacked on, to the very grand house of Mr Josiah Whitwell in Portman Square. He had a letter

337

from Mr Carey urging Mr Whitwell, 'who is known as a munificent and discerning friend to the literary world, to launch this young author, this germinal star into the firmament of letters'.

He was let in by an insolent young footman who looked him up and down with barely concealed mockery and finally led him to an ante-room. 'Mr Whitwell should be back within the hour,' he said. 'He may see you then. I don't know.'

As it happened he was kept waiting only twenty minutes before an amanuensis appeared and ushered him into the presence of Mr Whitwell.

Milton, on entering the luxurious library scented with the perfume of many fine books, was surprised to find that Mr Whitwell was not the thin scholarly man he had pictured but large, portly, gouty and high-coloured and dressed in a silver coat with so much lace at his cuffs that for a moment Milton had the impression that he had no hands. He seemed pleasant but Milton was still horribly nervous as he falteringly explained his petition, couched in the flattering phrases Mr Bedford had suggested to him, while Mr Whitwell sat up in a carved oak desk-chair like a big good-humoured boar and clasped and unclasped his pink hands on the chair-arms as if trying to squeeze them out of shape. And while Mr Whitwell, with unreadable hums and grunts, glanced through his manuscript, Milton stood and fumbled with his hat and the cane he had taken to carrying with the scented herbs in the top and stared at the great writing-desk and thought how like an altar it was. At last Mr Whitwell blew through big blue lips and said: 'I am fond of novels, Mr –'

'Milton.'

'Quite so. Yes, I dare say this is not without promise: but I really cannot say anything on it now. I must go out of town for a couple of weeks – I am an exceedingly busy man

338

– and I would like to take this with me, look at it further. I may be able to do something for you . . .' And Milton was soon being shown out, rather regretful at leaving his precious book in the hands of a stranger, but conscious that the visit had really been a remarkable success.

In the ante-room as he went out he saw a handsome man in his thirties, striding up and down and bending a pair of fearsome brows to the floor. Milton recognized him as Mr Alden, George Hardwick's old tutor. He had been well acquainted with Alden – he was after all a more scholarly character than George and he and Alden had often discussed books together when he had visited Morholm as a youth.

'Sir – my name is Henry Milton – do you recollect –?' said Milton, holding out his hand.

Mr Alden glanced up a little impatiently and then his face softened with recognition. 'Mr Milton, I remember well,' he said, shaking his hand heartily. 'What a lucky meeting! It must be four years. How are you sir, how are you?'

They sat down together on the only two chairs in the room with great cordiality and Milton felt old forgotten memories of his youth come alive again. 'You are waiting to see Whitwell too?' said Mr Alden.

'I have just seen him,' said Milton. 'Yes, I am seeking favour.'

'Precisely my errand! Is this your first time of coming?'

'Yes.'

'Indeed! You were lucky to be let in. I was turned away many times before they would even admit me. And I have been lingering about Whitwell's ante-rooms for a week now and have still not seen him. Not that he is so bad a patron: I have known some monsters. He is a good-natured man, but thoughtless. I am still working as a teacher, you see, but I hope for success with my pen too. You are living in London, Mr Milton?'

'Yes, I came here a few weeks since.'

'And what of dear old Morholm? The last thing I heard was the death of old Mr Joseph, a year ago.'

Milton told him the story of Mary, Jarrett and Julia.

'Good God, what an evil history to come from sleepy old Morholm!' said Mr Alden at last. 'For this Mary – she came to Morholm the day I left for Europe with George, as I recall – it must have been a very shattering business.'

'Yes, but she has come out of it very well. Of course she was in a sad distress at first, but James, who is there now, has looked after her and brought her out of it. She relies very much on him now.'

Mr Alden glanced up and there was a deep cleft between his black brows. 'You seem troubled,' said Milton.

'Well . . .' Mr Alden's frown deepened. 'Perhaps it is merely my own prejudices about James, but I would be uneasy about leaving a trusting young girl there with him.'

'Why?'

'Well, as I say, I did not like James. He was a diligent scholar – more so than George – and I could never really find a fault with him; but when it comes to trust – real trust, not trustworthiness – I would prefer his brother. James never does anything without a motive. He is, I think, a completely calculating, untender person, his head always ruling his heart. Certainly when I knew him I felt his reason had usurped his conscience.'

'I never thought of anything like this. When I left Mary I remember thinking she would be most secure under James's guardianship.'

'Perhaps I am being a little sensational. All I am saying is, when James wants something, he will do all in his power to get it; he considers his wanting it perfectly reasonable, whatever it may be, so long as he works for it. I would feel easier about Morholm if George went back straight away.'

Milton looked at him, startled. 'Oh – you don't understand – George disappeared in April, and since then there has been no news – he was in a very depressed state of mind and it was assumed he took his life.'

'There certainly must be a misunderstanding,' said Mr Alden. 'George is here in London. I spoke to him but three days ago.'

The last load of corn was brought in from the harvest, and at Morholm James held the Harvest Home supper for the labourers. Trestle tables were placed in the big hall and it was a noisy and convivial gathering; James had not the popularity of old Joseph but he treated everyone fairly. As was the custom the oldest labourer on the estate stood up to propose a toast to the master: he was a man of nearly seventy, six feet tall, from Ufford, and after the toast they sang the old song, 'Drink up your liquor and turn the bowl over'. Mary was touched when, after the song and much cheering and stamping, the old man also proposed a toast to her, and John Newman at the end of the table gave a loud huzzah.

Nat Royle, the blacksmith, got insensibly drunk at the supper, and that may have had something to do with what happened next morning, when the housekeeper hurried in to tell Mary and Mrs Peach at breakfast that the blacksmith's shop was on fire and other cottages were like to go up any minute from the flames it was throwing out. Mary flung her shawl about her and ran out of the house. As she ran across the common she thought it was unlucky James had ridden into Peterborough early: if he were here he would doubtless take charge of the situation. As she came panting up to the crowd gathered around the forge she saw that it was now only a black shell, but it was still blazing redly within and thick purple smoke came clawing from the wreckage as if trying to escape. Timbers crashed and the clucking villagers drew back from the showers of sparks. Mary plucked at the elbow of an old man standing near her.

'Is everyone out of the building?' she shouted in his ear.

'Eh?'

'Is there –' she began, but broke off, spotting in the crowd Nat the blacksmith standing with his hands on his hips gazing dumbly into the fire. 'Where is his wife?' she said aloud, and a woman nearby answered: 'John Newman's in there trying to get her,' and shook her head.

Mary felt sweat break out over her skin like a wave. She pushed forward through the crowd and into the blazing wreckage as far as the heat and smoke would allow her, but even as she stopped and chokingly called 'John!' a roof-beam fell with a roar a few inches from her and she was driven back. 'John!' she cried again, with desperation, and then she saw a figure emerge from the smoke and materialize as John Newman, coughing and staggering but gallantly supporting in his arms the swooning form of the blacksmith's wife. He delivered her to Nat and a sympathetic knot of women and then sank on to the charred grass. Mary ran to his side. 'John! Oh, how foolish you are, and how brave! Are you all right?'

John coughed and smiled weakly and coughed again. 'I'm all right, mistress, once I get my breath back.' He swept blackened gritty sweat from his brow. 'They were going to just leave her there, you know.' He looked wearily round at the crackling wreckage. 'Poor Nat, he's hardly had the shop but a few months. I reckon he's not used to keeping the forge fire proper – that's what must have started it.'

When he had recovered he got to his feet again and waved away the praises of the villagers. 'I reckon I'll go home and get a wash,' he said with his amiable smile and his pale blue eyes rather bleared.

'You are sure you are recovered?' Mary asked him, but he nodded and loped away, unheroically.

As the evening drew on and the purple sky darkened and

the last ribbons of smoke trailed away across the fields Mary stayed in the village, helping to sort through the remains and do what she could to aid the heartbroken Royles. She was making ready to return home when she noticed, in a group with Jenny Lake and a couple of other village girls, the strange woman Sophia Goulding. They were standing by the rear fence of what had been the smithy and looking most pointedly at her, and when she turned Sophia Goulding said: 'Good even to you, Mary Hardwick. These girls have been telling me all about you.'

There was a kind of challenge in her words which Mary was going to ignore, but she found herself going up to them and looking the woman in the face. 'Indeed, Miss Goulding?' she said, trying not to flinch beneath the green ardent gaze.

'Indeed,' said the woman, and there was a neural twitch about her mouth that did not quite become a smile. 'It seems you are talked of in the village . . . quite a prodigy . . .'

'What do you mean?' said Mary, facing each of them in turn. The two other girls lowered their eyes, embarrassed, and made as if to move away, but Jenny Lake presented her a face of bold hostility. 'Come, Miss Hardwick, you know well what is meant,' she said. The girls giggled and went red but Jenny was unrelenting.

'Tell me,' said Mary.

'Well, what with young Mr Jarrett and all, and then Mr George, going off like that – mysterious-like – and now Mr James looking after you so nicely and all – people have talked.' Sophia Goulding sniggered but Jenny turned her hostility to her for a moment and cried: 'Not that I ever held wi' any of that daft talk. Folk have said about how lucky Mary Hardwick always lands on her feet, but I reckon you've had a damned bad time of it. But what I want to say is –' Suddenly she seemed to lose her confidence. Mary, her cheeks burning, told her to go on. 'Well – what do you mean with John Newman?' blurted Jenny finally, and tossed her thick strawy hair back and looked at Mary in her sullen pretty challenging way.

Mary's heart pounded. So here it was again. The talk, the stupid vicious gossip. She could have wrung Sophia Goulding's powdered neck. 'I mean to be his friend and to help him all I can because in the past he and his father and mother were very kind to me! Good God, what minds people have – if there is no dirt they must create some. Cannot I be on good terms with a young farmer who is an old friend without you folk imagining some wicked liaison between us?'

Jenny Lake, looking half-contrite and half-aggressive, muttered, 'Well, you can't blame us, the way you are for ever along of him, and at his cottage . . .'

'That does not mean I am anything but his friend who wants to help him get started in life. Please, Jenny,' Mary's voice grew softer and she tried to touch the girl's hand but could not find it in the gloom, 'I know you are in love with him – no, why deny it? – I do not blame you, he is a comely man and a good man. I have suggested to him myself what a good idea it would be for you to marry.' Here Sophia Goulding snorted but Mary ignored her. 'But to suggest that between me and John . . . I know this woman must have been poisoning your mind. Will you still continue your hostility to me, Jenny?'

Jenny said nothing but moved away, drooping and frowning and confused, and her girl friends went with her. But Sophia Goulding remained behind, her face frozen in a sneer as she stared with feline intensity at Mary. 'Well,' she said finally, 'what a taking way you have! Is that how you get round James, eh?'

Mary raised a bitter laugh. 'Shouldn't you know what pleases him, Miss Goulding?' she said, and turned away, contemptuously, to hide her fear.

6

Milton sat in the most respectable of the two rooms making up his lodgings, papers idly strewn before him, gazing out of the window into the cool September evening. The light was fading, gently and slowly, but greyly, without the soft pink flush of summer, and gave a hint of the approaching autumn. Milton's window looked out on to the black backs of rows of houses, smoky and serried and uncommunicative. The dusk was silent and he was deep in thought, still clutching his pen as if paralysed.

He had been more than a month in London now. In that time he had got used to the fairly regular work Mr Carey gave him, had become like one of the family in the Bedfords' household, and had also worked off much of his gloom. The change had succeeded; though his love of the country forced him to take a boat out of the city occasionally to smell the green fields again, he liked London and had learned to conquer his fear and disgust at its darker side. And there was no doubt that Hannah Bedford had played a great part in bringing him back to life.

And he wished he could be more grateful, instead of finding himself so confused and frustrated about his relationship with her. She was an engaging, refreshing personality, and the time he had spent with her recently had been enjoyable. Mr and Mrs Bedford, perceiving the partiality of their daughter for their young friend, had not stood in the way; most evenings they were left to talk together, last week he had escorted her to a small party where there was dancing and he had partnered her several times, and last night they had gone to Vauxhall Gardens together. He thought the gardens rather vulgar with their lamps and decorations and coy little arbours, and he hated the great press of people around them and the young bucks who congregated in the narrow walks calling out remarks to the ladies, but she seemed to love walking round it with him, and when an Italian opera-singer sang from a balcony she stood and listened as if in a trance. People were milling around them and trying to get past and Milton felt uncomfortable, but she never seemed to share his embarrassment at such things. 'I love to hear a truly good voice, don't you?' she said to him when it was over. 'Papa hates the opera, he says there is no understanding a word of it. Do you like it, Mr Milton?'

He said he had had little opportunity to find out.

'No, I suppose that is true in the country. But then books are your forte, aren't they? I am fond of reading too, but it is music that I love most. I love to hear it: I wish I were more talented at it.'

'That is always the case – I wish I were more talented at my writing.'

'Oh, but you are! By the by, when is Mr Whitwell to return?'

'He did not say precisely when, but it should be soon. I must just keep calling until I find him there.'

In this amiable, talkative way they had passed the evening; and when, at the Bedfords', he finally took his leave, her eyes were still shining tirelessly at him as she said: 'And have you thought of the lady today?' It was noticeable that they had never mentioned Elizabeth's name, only referred to her as 'the lady' who had married someone else.

'No,' he had said, 'she is as far from my mind as she is from my person.' And she seemed delighted and pressed his hand with a secret, tender gesture and he was wretchedly confused because he could not share her single-minded geniality.

It was true that during his time in London he had thought of Elizabeth less and less. The edges had been filed off his bitterness; he no longer ached for love of her, only felt a lingering pain at her memory, a bitter-sweet regret for the past joy of those days that now seemed impossibly far off. He wondered if he could love her now, supposing by some miraculous chance she should turn to him again: it seemed as if in rejecting him she had cut away something, cut away the capacity to love. Yet there was still a space in his soul, and an emptiness, a need for a love that could not be found. He felt certain that he was no longer in love with Elizabeth; she was Mrs Woodhouse now, a woman who, if she had ever loved him, certainly did not now. If there was anything he was still in love with, it was the Elizabeth Wainwright who no longer existed in name or in person. But though he was certain of all this, he was also certain that though Hannah Bedford loved him he did not love Hannah Bedford.

He had tried, but he knew he could not. He found her agreeable and pretty, but he never thought about her except in the context of this problem, he never longed for her, he felt no regret at parting from her. She felt so much more for him: and he hated having to disappoint her by not matching her delight when they were together. Perhaps, he asked himself, he ought to be content with Hannah: perhaps he ought to make her happy by forcing himself to love her? But no, that was impossible. It seemed like a kind of ingratitude to reject so much love, but there was still a void within him that Hannah could not fill.

And now, there was the stunning shock of what Mr Alden had told him. 'George is in London . . .' He thought the tutor must have been mistaken, for though refusing to admit it to himself he had finally given George up for dead. But no: Alden had met and talked to him three days before. ''Twas in the Turks Head coffee-house, in the Strand,' Mr Alden had said. 'He looked well, preoccupied perhaps, but

347

well. He told me he had been some months on the Continent again – France, I believe. We could not talk long, for he was in something of a hurry, but it was a pleasant meeting.' Milton's reaction, after the first surprise, was an overwhelming joy: but on top of that he was deeply disturbed by Alden's remarks about James. If only he himself could get in touch with George. But in the great city he hardly knew how he could do so.

He sighed and tried to turn his attention to the work on the desk before him: but there was another side to the problem of Hannah. As Mr Bedford had warned him, Mr Carey had commissioned him to write something of a somewhat indecent nature. He had been given a series of lewd engravings and told to string a narrative around them. Whether it was an effect of this, whether it was the influence of London with its many prostitutes and courtesans, or whether it was merely a consequence of his coming back to life after a summer of sterile solitude, he did not know, but the fact was that he had begun to feel physically frustrated, unusually carnal. He was not a lascivious man by nature; his love for Elizabeth had included sexual attraction, but it had been integral, healthy, not all-embracing. Now he found himself, against his will, irritatingly libidinous. And here was another danger in his relationship with Hannah: that he should be tempted by his frustration into exploiting her. That would be an atrocious thing to do and a danger he must at all costs keep out of.

He glanced at his watch. It was time he got ready; Mr Carey had invited him to a dinner at his house, this time an all-male affair. From what he had heard these were just excuses for heavy drinking bouts and a spot of gambling, but he could not refuse Mr Carey, and anyway he meant to come away before the drinking became in earnest. He dressed and arrived at Mr Carey's punctually.

Mr Carey's other guests, assembled in a chilly room where

a spare fire had just, it seemed, been grudgingly lit, were a mixed crew of cynical, shrew-featured old men of Mr Carey's own type, fat middle-aged epicures, and various hopeful young scribblers like Milton himself. As Mr Carey was talking to his colleagues, Milton engaged in a rather gloomy dead-end conversation with two doom-eyed young poets, and he was glad when they all went into dinner, and he found himself able to talk to Mr Carey.

Milton never knew what to make of Mr Carey; he often felt that he would find much to like in the old bookseller, but he was too unapproachable; it was as if a kind of hard scab had formed over Carey's spirit, through cynicism or suffering or experience, and made it impossible to touch. He chaffed Milton about the work he was doing. 'I hope you are setting your wits to work on that, eh, Milton?' he said, poking food methodically into his cadaverous mouth as if he were posting letters. 'Plenty of scope for the mind, eh? Not that those engravings leave much to the imagination. In actual fact, you know, Milton, they were drawn by a man who's seventy if a day, and used to be a parish priest. He was defrocked,' he added with a cackle. One of his old and smelly spaniels jumped into his lap and he began feeding it titbits from the table. 'And what of Whitwell? Is he returned yet?'

'No, he was not when I called today.'

'Ah, the indolent old windbag, he is probably going to remain at his country place till next season now, cannot be bothered to return, and your book will probably end up as wrapping-paper in the kitchens of his mansion.'

Milton was used to the consistently sour note of Mr Carey's remarks by now and paid little heed to this. In fact for most of the dinner he was occupied with the reflections that had troubled him earlier. When dinner was over and he was trying to conceal his distaste as the men began to use the chamber-pot in the corner – chamber-potting in company was something he had yet to get used to, never having observed it at home – he resolved to take the first opportunity to leave. But somehow, probably because of the fiery nature of Mr Carey's liquor and because the others were drinking with such liberality, he found himself rapidly getting very drunk and suddenly not at all disposed to leave. As he went further and further into intoxication the evening became hazy, an amorphous mass of loud, bawdy talk and pipe-smoke and abandoned card-games. The room seemed to grow very hot and everything about him took on a fierce magnitude. Then it was suggested by one of the fat men that they go along to a place he knew – but a few streets away – and soon he was stumbling down the steps with the rest of them into a night that struck horribly chill on his heated body. He followed them, too stupefied to ask where they were going. They went along in a noisy, staggering cluster and the few people in the streets avoided them. Finally they arrived at a dark plain-looking house in a narrow sequestered street off the Haymarket: but when they got inside Milton wished he had never come. This was quite obviously a brothel, and not one of the highest class. He stood reeling in a dimly lit hall decorated with crude un-framed prints; the air was cheaply perfumed to mask – unsuccessfully – various unpleasant odours that Milton de-tected. He leant back against the wall, feeling faint and revolted as one of the old men fumbled with a painted whore, who in turn fumbled in his pockets. The others were pairing off with women in a rapid and business-like manner, it seemed; he felt only cruelly embarrassed and disgusted – there were girls here, he noticed, who seemed no older than ten or eleven; all the carnal urges he had felt stirring in him disappeared. And then a woman, powerfully scented and in a bodice that exposed her breasts completely, approached him and began to caress him, tapping his pockets expertly to see that there was money in them and continuing to caress him when she found there was. Her breath was on his face, surprisingly sweet breath, sweet and warm and blowing away all traces of the squalid and making her into a creature of charm and loveliness . . . Then abruptly as if all the liquor had drained out of him and left him deadly sober he was overcome with disgust at the squalor and degradation and he broke free of her with a wrench of loathing, loathing of himself for the overpowering attraction he had felt. He heard people laughing at him as he struggled in the gloom to find the door. At last he found it and hauled it open and stepped out eager for the slap of the healthy outside air. But he had lost his bearings, and this was not the front door; he had merely stumbled into another room, a sort of filthy scullery where a woman was bending down to get some bottles of gin from a case on the floor. Lank hair hung down round her face but when he burst in she pushed it back and looked round at him. It was Julia Hardwick.

He stared at her and she stared back. A woman shut the door on them, saying with a laugh, 'He's found something to suit him,' and then they were alone in the grimy little room. 'Miss Hardwick,' he said, and at any other time might have been struck by the absurdity of this formality in such circumstances.

'If you want my services, Mr Milton, let us go upstairs,' she said in a flat voice.

That sickened him most of all. 'Oh, my God, Miss Hardwick,' he said, passing a hand across his face.

'You are surprised to see me here, Mr Milton?' said Julia, putting the bottles on a shelf, her voice still flat and indifferent. 'I am surprised to see you here.'

He looked at her with shocked distress. Her skin, never of the whitest complexion, was now a sickly grey, and powder did little to disguise it. Her dress was of the low-cut alluring kind to show her large breasts, but it was dirty and worn; and she looked underfed. She gazed back at him, as he stood transfixed and appalled, from the baleful eyes that now looked fathomlessly, soullessly vacant.

'Good God, Miss Hardwick . . .' he stammered, hardly knowing what to say, 'how – how long have you been here?'

'How long? Well, after that day in April I stayed at inns for as long as I could, a couple of weeks. You see I had only a little money. Tom Jarrett took all the rest you know. So then they took me in here. I was very lucky,' she added, and Milton felt sick with distress.

'But why . . . why would you not go back to your family?' he said.

'I could not!' said Julia vehemently, and there was a sudden brightness in her dull eyes. 'I could not face them, Aunt, George – and Mary – could I? After what I had done!'

'Your family were worried about you . . . Mary especially.'

Suddenly she sank down on to a stool and gazed at the floor with inexpressible thoughtfulness. Then she muttered, 'Poor Mary . . . poor George . . . poor all of us –' and with that all her drab indifference seemed to break down and she began to weep in dry, stuttering sobs that seemed to be wrenched from somewhere deep inside her where they had been long confined. Milton did not know what to do but he felt strangely a little easier, a little more confident, now that she had cried. Finally he said, trying to sound brisk and forceful, 'We must get you out of here – right away.'

She seemed to ignore this completely but stopped crying. 'How strange,' she said hoarsely, 'that it should be you, Mr Milton, who finds me.'

'Miss Hardwick, we must get you out of this place! You must not stay here a moment longer.'

She looked up at him with tear-stained scorn. 'I shall never leave this place,' she said. 'You don't understand, do you? I have not been out of it for weeks and weeks. I have been shutting myself away.'

'Why?' said Milton, and the word came dry and futile from his throat. She gazed before her, calm now with some of the glazed dullness returning. 'I cannot face anything, cannot go out, have no need to go out. I just stay here, do my work,' and the atonal indifference with which she said this was sickening, 'and do most of the kitchen work. Not so very different from Morholm. Get me out of here, Mr Milton? What is to be done with me? Will you support me and lodge me? Apologize to your landlady for bringing home a stray whore?'

'If necessary, yes,' said Milton stoutly. 'And then I can return you to your family, Miss Hardwick. Truly, they would dearly love to see you back at Morholm – Mary for a certainty loves you and would –'

'You are citing "love" to me, Mr Milton? That is no way to persuade me – I am no friend to love. Thomas Jarrett "loved" me. Can you offer me no better security than that?'

'Please, Miss Hardwick, you must leave here – you cannot go on living like this –'

'Selling my body?' She looked at him with a trace of the old stubborn, sardonic defiance. 'Why, what does that mean to me? Thomas Jarrett took it all long ago, took all the passion and love out of me. Whatever of pleasure the fools who come here find in me they are welcome to. I am only a shell.'

'Miss Hardwick, at Morholm you will find only James, Mary and your grandmother. George went away and I believe is somewhere in London. Your aunt is married and no longer lives there. Daniel and Kingsley are gone too. I feel sure you need fear no persecution there – you will be received with total kindness – it must be better than staying here.'

She was silent and he thought he saw some wistfulness for her old life in her face. Then her eyes hardened and she turned away.

'It is no use, Mr Milton. I cannot go back. Even supposing I should wish to, I cannot leave here.'

There was a thunderous hammering at the door at the back of the kitchen. Julia got up to unbolt it and was almost thrown back against the wall as the man burst in. 'Strike me, woman, why d'ye bolt the door?' he said, kicking it shut behind him. 'I got to come and go, don't I?' He was a big man well in his forties, like a decayed prizefighter, with close-cropped hair and a large coloured neckerchief. He gave Milton a brief glance and then looked at Julia. 'What's this?' he said. 'There's bedrooms aloft, an't there?'

'This isn't what you think, Gully,' said Julia, with the old proud note of contempt in her voice.

'Isn't it, though? What a jemmy miss it is, giving herself airs!' He put his huge hand on the back of her neck. 'I thought as how we'd cured her of those.'

'Miss Hardwick is an old friend of mine,' said Milton. 'Who the devil are you?'

'Please Mr Milton, don't interfere.'

'Damn right,' snapped the man. There was a smell of cheap spirits from him and his eyes were red-rimmed and mutinous. 'Unless you got real business here, choker – get out.' He turned to Julia again with a laugh. 'What's amiss with him? Couldn't he fill the pipe? Not that I'm surprised – look at you, woman,' he struck Julia across the face, 'paint yourself, can't you? Who do you think'll pay push for a judy looking like you?'

'Oh *God*, Gully, you are *filth*!' screamed Julia, trying to shove him away. He hit her again across the face and then gave a bellow of pain as Milton came at him from behind and flung his arms round his neck. 'I'm taking her out of here,' he said, trying to tighten his grip on the thug's bristly throat: but Gully thrust back with his giant fist, doubling Milton up and sending him crashing back against the door.

Milton had a glimpse of Julia's tear-stained face crying, 'I told you it's no good, Mr Milton! Now do you understand?' before Gully lifted him and threw him bodily out of the back door on to a cobbled yard. 'The tarts here do as I tell them,' he growled before closing and bolting the door.

Somehow Milton got back to his lodgings – he never remembered how – and laid his bruised body on his bed. But he slept little, and only to fall into dreams shot through with horror at the state in which he had seen Julia Hardwick. And when finally he lay awake and watched the square of grey light in the window grow brighter and heard the sounds of the costers and street musicians below bringing the city to life he continued to think of Julia. He forgot Hannah, Mr Carey, George. He forgot Elizabeth: she seemed to have as much connection with reality as a fairy-tale princess. The image of Julia was etched on his mind's eye as with acid. He lay and gathered his strength.

At last he got up. His landlady, making her daily sortie from her kitchen where she sat and brewed tea and read sentimental novels, brought up his basin of water and he washed his face and shaved himself and changed his clothes. Then he looked about his two rooms for something to take with him. There was little in the way of furnishings: a desk, some frowsy upholstered chairs, a glass-fronted bookcase, an old Dutch clock: but in the hearth was a rusty iron poker. That would have to do. He put it inside his coat and set out.

He found the brothel again with little difficulty: in the daylight the house looked grimy and less innocent. One of the painted little girls opened the door to him. The sight of her pocked face had the effect of increasing both his revulsion and his determination. 'I want Miss Julia Hardwick,' he said, pushing his way in.

'Who's that coming at this time o' day?' came a familiar

voice, and the man Gully, in shirt sleeves, appeared from the kitchen. 'Oh – 'tis you.'

'I've come to take Julia Hardwick out of here,' said Milton.

The big man seemed in a different stage of drink from last night: now he was slurring, greasily avuncular.

'Listen, my friend,' he said, hitching up his breeches. 'You want her for the proper purposes, you take her upstairs and be my guest. But she don't stir from here. She does what I tell her. I'm the cash-carrier here, see? Keep things in order. Now if –'

'You filthy bastard,' said Milton.

The man sighed. 'Go on out o' the way, Letty,' he said to the little girl.

Milton caught sight of Julia, appearing at the top of the stairs, before he pulled the poker from his coat and rushed at Gully. The first blow glanced across the man's head with a sickening sound of iron on bone; but to Milton's astonishment, after the man had staggered back against the staircase, he rose up again and charged like a bull. The poker was twisted laceratingly in Milton's hand and then wrenched from him and thrown to the floor with a metallic clatter: and then there was foul breath on his face and Gully's great hands clasped his throat. Milton gagged and a shimmering red light filled his vision: then with a last impulse of strength and anger that seemed to come from impossible depths within him he wrenched one of the hands free and punched the man across the cheekbone. He staggered backwards again and Julia, who came headlong down the staircase, was behind the thug and had pinioned his arms. 'Hit him!' she screamed at Milton. 'For God's sake, strike him dead!'

With smarting knuckles Milton hit the man again as hard as he could and he reeled over on the floor, groaning. Julia stood over him, her eyes glazed in a kind of ferocious trance, until Milton seized her hand. 'Come,' he said, urgently. 'Before he recovers. Come, hurry.' He half-dragged her across the hall and out of the house and the painted child, still standing there blankly calm, watched them go without a trace of expression.

Once outside Julia tensed like a frightened animal. 'Oh, God – I cannot. They will stare at me – the world will stare at me – accuse me –'

'No one will stare. Come, it is not far.'

'Where will we go?' She clung to his arm, no longer towering and fierce, but small and afraid.

'To my lodgings. My landlady has a spare room you can take.' Though whether she would approve was a different matter. 'Please. I am under no financial pressure, I can pay for your keep. Let us go.'

All the time as they walked she clung to his arm with a tense frightened grip and kept her flushed face averted and looked at the ground. In an effort to relieve the tension and to cover his own agitation he talked to her, in a nervous inarticulate stream, of his own concerns, when he had come to London, what he was doing, what an odd man Mr Carey the bookseller was. He did not know how much of this she heeded, but it seemed to have a calming effect on her. Eventually he was able to lead her through the noise and press of the busiest streets, though she still hung her head and gripped his arm as if she were walking through a beast-infested forest: but their journey would have gone perfectly well, had they not turned the corner of Charterhouse Street to meet Hannah Bedford.

She was walking, with bonnet and parasol, with a lady of her own age, and a servant was loping along behind them. Her eyes at first flashed with delight at seeing Milton, but then she saw his companion. She looked as if the ground had opened before her. Milton felt miserably embarrassed and sorry for her, but in a way he could feel glad at this mischance: perhaps this would throw Hannah off him, and ultimately be to the good. He took off his hat and tried to appear natural and unconcerned. 'Miss Bedford,' he said, and gave a bow to her companion, 'an unexpected pleasure. This is Miss Julia Hardwick, the sister of my friend George, whom you have heard me mention. By lucky chance we have met in town.' And in this way he chatted with an appearance of trivial, cheery unconcern for a few minutes, Julia never saying a word or lifting her head, Hannah saying very little and gazing at them in perplexed fashion. At last they parted and went their ways and Milton breathed out a long sigh of relief. Julia, however, was now stiff and trembling so he hurried her on to his lodgings.

There he sat her in one of his two chairs and gave her a little brandy that he had in a cupboard. She grew gradually calmer and soon was able to talk to him. He told her the story of George's disappearance, and his discovery that he was alive and in London.

'Mr Milton – you said my aunt was married – when was this?'

He was glad she wanted Morholm news. ''Twas in June, I think: a Mr Finlayson, a friend of your brother James. They are living in London, though not near here. You need not fear seeing them.'

'So James is master of Morholm now. What became of Daniel and Kingsley?'

'The last I saw of them they were living in Peterborough. Apparently James threw them out with very little ceremony.'

There was the ghost of a smile on her colourless lips as he said this; but it was quickly gone and she asked, with a quaver in her voice, 'And . . . Mary?'

Julia bit her lip and the knuckles of the hand that held the cup of brandy went white. 'But how can I face her – how can I, Mr Milton?'

'Do you know so little of your cousin to think that she –

Mary of all people – would blame you, blame you for being charmed by Tom Jarrett? I, too, I admired him more than any man I knew, was his friend for ten years or more. All you must do is go back and show you are willing to begin life again as she has done.' He was called away at that moment by a knock at the door. It was the paper-seller come to collect a debt. When Milton had argued with him and finally fobbed him off with half of what he owed – it was all he could afford that day – he came back to Julia to find her looking at his work which lay on the desk. Thankfully it was not the smut he had to write for Mr Carey but some rather sentimental love verses.

'Did you write these?' she asked.

'Yes,' said Milton, a little abashed because he thought them pretty feeble. But Julia seemed interested and read them all carefully. When she had finished she did not look up.

'Miss Hardwick . . . Julia, I should tell you – before I left home I spoke with Francis Sedgmoor –'

She gave a groan and sobs began to shake her body. 'Oh, no, don't.'

'Julia, listen to me. He does not blame you in that Jarrett business. He told me to say to you that he will still honour his promise to you if you should wish it. He does not think badly of you: no one blames you, no one – rather you are the object of pity and concern. Jarrett took everybody in, myself included.' Her sobs grew louder and more wretched and instinctively he put his arms about her. All her cool impassivity was gone: she clung to him and he remembered long afterwards the strange joy of that moment, with Julia sobbing against his chest, and dryly stuttering, her voice muffled by his coat, 'Oh, God, I never meant any harm to Mary, to Mr Sedgmoor. I didn't think – I just didn't think. It all seemed so convenient and easy. I never meant to hurt anyone, believe me, Mr Milton. Oh, God, I have been so wretched – thank heaven you came. How I wish I had never seen Tom Jarrett – he just – he just seemed to put me under a spell – I never meant any harm.'

It was a long time before she was quiet and could sit down to wipe her eyes with little exhausted gasps. 'You are taking on a very difficult burden, Mr Milton,' she said. She indicated the tawdry dress and old shawl she wore. 'These are all the clothes I have.'

'My landlady will lend you some,' said Milton, realizing he was counting rather heavily on the good nature of his landlady. 'I shall go down and speak to her now. No, you need not come.'

He was rather more afraid of the old lady than he had been of the pimp Gully: but in the end he appealed to her motherly instincts and to the vein of romanticism cultivated by her reading of the sentimental novels, by elaborating a story around the presence of Julia. She became an old family friend who had been held against her will by a wicked dandy in the city and he had liberated her from his fiendish clutches. Well, it was not too far from the truth. That evening found Julia established in the spare room across the hall from Milton's, dressed in an old-fashioned tight-waisted frock of his landlady's, her body bathed and her hair washed and her eyes at last, he saw with a strange moved delight, losing their dead vacancy and beginning to sparkle.

But in the night he woke to hear such desolate weeping from her room that he had to get up and steal across the hall to knock at her door. 'Julia,' he said softly, 'Julia, please, what is it?' He heard the sound of her sobs and then she opened the door. She was in her shift and her loosened hair hung in dark strands over the white contours of her shoulders. 'Oh, Mr Milton, I'm sorry. I am a fool. I am so happy and yet – still afraid. Oh, I am so afraid, Mr Milton.'

He put his arms around her and she clung to him again, tightly. Then they went to his bed and she curled up in his arms, her sobs gradually dying away as he stroked her hair, until at last she drifted off to sleep: and like that they stayed till morning.

The week before the Peterborough election Great-Uncle Horace came to stay at Morholm for a day. It was unusual for him to go visiting and Mary suspected that he had come to inspect the new Morholm – for such it seemed – for himself. The old man was little changed, merely becoming daily more pinched, acerbic and fastidious; he had lately taken to flapping everywhere with a scented handkerchief. He seemed highly impressed with the effect James's diligence had had and repeatedly praised him for restoring the good name of the Hardwicks and re-establishing their respected tradition.

'Not that the old families mean so much nowadays,' he muttered over dinner. 'What about that Hugh Woodhouse fellow – *Sir* Hugh now, for his father met his long-overdue decease last week – making a great noise with his new bride and house and tasteless extravagance. Vulgar.' He grumbled with testy regret for a time that was irretrievably gone, the time of his youth and the beginning of the century. 'Not that solid fellows like yourself will not have the edge over his kind in the long run, you know, James, setting yourself up in the proper manner – Woodhouse will be burnt out in a couple of years and they'll have to go begging to his wife's parents. And now this fighting in America. Danger from France because of it. I knew the whole thing would end in chaos. World's going mad.'

Mary and James accompanied Horace on his ride back to Stamford next day, they both having shopping to do; and as they rode back through a late afternoon that was a little chilly and gusty with approaching autumn, the enormous sky speckled with the shapes of the last departing swallows, Mary felt a too-rare sensation of peace. But this was shattered when she entered the house ahead of James to find Sophia Goulding seated with Mrs Peach in the parlour, her bonnet swinging by its strings from one hand, her hair straggling Medusa-like about her intense disquieting face.

'Ah, Mary,' said Mrs Peach, 'this lady says she knows you and James. She came in from the garden and we have been having the most pleasant talk.'

Sophia Goulding's eyes were fixed on Mary's, a ghostly tireless green, and they flashed with wry malice before lifting and fixing on something behind Mary. It was James who had appeared in the doorway. Mary stood mesmerized by the electric glare that the two exchanged.

'Who let you in?' said James in a level voice.

'Oh, grandson, I thought 'twould do no harm. She has been so agreeable – she came in through the back,' said Mrs Peach, indicating the open french windows. 'She said she knew you.'

The woman stood up and walked over to James and Mary, swinging her bonnet idly. 'So here you are, both of you, together,' she said.

'I told you to stay away from here,' said James. 'Go back to London where you belong. You've no business here.'

'Leave you alone?' she said. 'Leave you alone with your tempting, obliging cousin – spinning her webs and trapping you like all the rest?'

James stepped in front of Mary and faced the woman. They were of exactly the same height and their eyes seemed to be locked together. Mary sensed here a fierce and passionate battle of souls that she could not trespass upon even if she wanted to.

'What do you want, for God's sake?' said James. 'Money? I have given you enough of that.'

'I do not want your money, James.'

'Then get away from Morholm!' James's vehemence made

362

Mary start. 'You, and that poisonous tongue of yours! You may hook your claws in me, Sophia, because I can fight back, but I will not see you prey on those with whom you have no business! You will leave this house now and if you are found in this parish again I shall apply to the magistrates to have you thrown out or sent down for vagrancy! Is that clear?'

Mary thought the woman was going to cry, but she did not cry. Her eyes bulged in a curious manner: then she spat at James and turned and left the way she had come in, slowly and sullenly.

James was silent and preoccupied for the rest of that evening, and the next morning he was up and about his work before Mary rose. Haunted by the thought of Sophia Goulding and yesterday's encounter, which filled her with unease, she made her way across the moist stripped fields to see John Newman. She found him, blond and robust and untiring, at the top of a rickety ladder, mending a hole in the thatch of the cottage that was by now neat and homely and nestled, like a solitary egg in a ragged nest, amongst a tangle of roses and blackberries and hollyhocks. He was going to come down but she said she did not want to disturb him and stood at the bottom of the ladder, squinting up at him in the gold September sun and chatting just as they were. She had told him nothing of her exchange with Jenny Lake the day of the fire and still she bore no malice against the girl. John, however, seemed quiet of late and did not seem able to look her in the face with his old frankness. His intelligent blue eyes seemed to have lost some of their pellucid vitality and become shadowed and languid. But she knew he would not mind her mentioning it and so she said: 'John, are you quite well of late? Are you very tired, or unhappy? Somehow, I don't feel . . . If I'm being inquisitive tell me to mind my own business.'

'Oh, I'm well and fine, mistress,' he replied, pausing in his work but not looking down at her. 'I –'

'Tell me, John. Are you lonely?'

'Well, not as you'd say lonely . . .'

He half-turned towards her on the ladder, and she saw his strong blond head framed a glowing golden against the brightness of the sky. ''Tisn't exactly that, mistress – perhaps in a way –' He seemed to be struggling for words.

'Does Jenny still cook your meals for you?'

'Ay, and very well. She makes fine pies . . . and she's a fine girl. I like her very much.'

'Then what is making you unhappy?' said Mary gently. 'Can you not repay Jenny's affection? Are you in love with someone else?'

'In – in a way,' said John, and she could see beads of sweat shining like tiny pearls on his brow. 'Well, Miss Mary, I'm fond of Jenny, but what stops me giving her my love, well, if you've fallen in love with someone who's – who's not for you, and there's another love sort of, in the making, like, should you sweep that love away?'

The truth began to dawn on Mary.

'If that love is hopeless?' she said, looking up at him.

'Ay – hopeless.'

She felt so sad and sick that she wanted to die, would willingly have died at that moment if she could save him pain. The world suddenly seemed such a place of infinite tragedy that she doubted her ability ever to do or say the right thing again in her life.

'John,' she said, 'I have only ever had one love – though I suppose that was no love at all in truth – but I shall never have another. I feel no bitterness or sorrow at that, but a certainty. Tom took my heart, you see, and no matter what the truth about him was, I can never give my heart again. I know too well that love is a thing not easily submitted to reason, but John – when I say this I speak as your friend who has a great fondness for you – to remain faithful to a hopeless love is to destroy yourself. I would not say this if I truly did not mean it. I understand now, John,' she said, looking steadily up at him, 'and believe me when I say it would be better for you to forget. Please, John, can you not forget, knowing you will always have, till my dying day, my affection and gratitude?'

'But no more,' he said huskily.

'But no more.' She felt so immensely sad and sorry for him at that moment she was afraid she would burst into tears: but she would not cry. She owed it to him not to cry. There was a long silence and then he finally spoke. 'Thank you, mistress. I'm glad we've spoken this way.'

'Do you hate me, John?'

'No.' He looked at her, startled. 'No, never. Never.'

When Mary had gone John sighed and shook his head and returned to his work. He did not get on very well at first because his eyes kept blurring oddly and he had to wipe them, but eventually he had a grip on himself and even managed to whistle.

He had decided to stop loving someone, who could not love him, in case he hurt her: he had been far braver this hour, though he did not know it, than when he had plunged into the burning forge.

He did not hate her: but she hated herself.

Mary was normally a woman given to viewing her own acts critically, and never made excuses for herself; and it was in anguish that she returned to Morholm and shut herself in her room. She had lied to John, she knew. She could not love him but there was one man she could love and did. She could not give her heart again because she knew now – though stupidly, blindly, she had not known before – she knew now with a bitter desperation that it had belonged to him all the time.

In a bizarre way she now saw the Mary of the last year as an entirely separate person, one she knew well but who in no way partook of her identity. In a detached light she looked over her actions in the past as if she were reading a book about herself. She saw her consuming passion for Thomas Jarrett, the blindness to everything else that he had engendered in her, with a kind of horror. It was a horror that till this moment she had never really let sink in, still in some corner of her heart willing herself to believe that she could not have been so wrong. She saw all the mistakes, the misunderstandings, the wilful demon that had brought her life to this pass. And she saw the man who in his own way had offered her his love and found it refused, indeed scarcely even noticed or comprehended for what it was.

But this was the worst part of the story: that character had disappeared. That man whose love, she realized with a lacerating regret, she had failed to see and now needed most of all, was gone and she feared he would not return.

7

The Bedfords, together with their young friend Mr Milton, were invited to a ball on the eleventh of October. It was held by a *nouveau riche* friend of Mr Bedford's, but there would be many distinguished people there and it was a conspicuous, if solitary fault in Mr Bedford's character that he was anxious to impress on Milton when he called how remarkable it was for a former bookseller like himself to have reached such an eminence.

'It may not seem much to you, Milton,' he said, caressing the lace on his chest, 'but I tell you thirty years ago I would never have believed that I would one day attend an assembly at which there are titles – many titles. I think my pride on this point is pardonable. However, you need not worry about feeling out of place, you have a genteel bearing and manner. Hannah will do most of the talking.'

Milton was not, in fact, much worried about feeling out of place; for he did not think he would go to the ball. But he was afraid that whatever happened he was going to hurt Hannah. What made the situation worse was the fact that he had told her, the day after she had seen him with Julia, something about the girl, explaining that she was an old acquaintance whom he had found living in some distress and was trying to help. Somehow he could not keep her deliberately under an illusion: but after that she had renewed her courting of him.

And yet his explanation about Julia was really no longer true, he realized, and was glad of it and was fired with a secret, explosive tenderness even as he smiled and chatted with Mr Bedford.

Julia had been living at his landlady's house for a week now. She rarely ventured out, for the turbulent London streets still made her flinch somewhat: but while he was there with her they talked and in talking she seemed to blossom like some vivid and neglected wild flower, making him laugh and cry and sometimes both. She told him of the long months in the brothel, the enslavement of the wretched girls beneath the brutal Gully, the livid, unconscionable shame that had overcome her after Jarrett had left, such that retreating to the life of a whore was almost a relief. 'I really felt that after what I had done, it was the only place for me, that it was where I belonged. I felt that if I were to once go out into the world I would instantly be branded, accused, recognized for what I was. And then you appeared in that place, looking so decent and – and *real*, part of a life I'd lost . . .' While he was out she made fair copies of some of his work in a large round hand and later would talk to him of it. She had a highly original mind and after the initial shock of hurt pride at her criticisms he found them a revelation.

At nights, in the dark and silence, she still grew lost and afraid and the business continued, faintly farcical, of creeping across the hall to lie in his arms in order to calm down and sleep. But last night there had been no element of farce as when they lay there and her breathing grew deep and untroubled his lips had sought hers and found there a responsive tenderness and passion.

And so he found as he pulled the heavy sensual warmth of her body to his that the love he had thought about and suffered over and tried to write out of himself in verse and prose was no love at all but really just another of his fictions: and that the heart had dark and tender places never touched by the pretty gestures of sentiment.

'You know you will not be the first, Henry,' she had whispered. 'But I believe for me it will be just as if you were.

I believe for the first time it will be as it always should be
. . . with love.'

'Milton – I say, Milton.'

Milton came out of his reverie. 'Oh, I am sorry, Mr
Bedford. You were saying –?'

'I was saying that Whitwell returns to town today. I heard
it from a friend of his last night. So now you may find out
the fate of that novel of yours. Of course you must not be
downhearted if he won't have anything to do with it. You
were very fortunate to get so far – I thought you would
merely be given a small sum and shown the door. There are
others to approach, you know, and all the time in the world.'

But it was not as simple as that, Milton reflected; and he
took his leave and set off for Mr Carey's deep in thought.

The streets were noisy, rank and oppressive at this time,
with everyone jostling to avoid the stinking dirt of the
gutters, which were swelled and overflowing from recent
rain: but today he walked heedless of the filth and heat
around him. The spectre of Hannah haunted him: but with
her, the image of Julia, bright with the rays of the strange
exhilarating love that had burst upon him. So, he had come
to London to escape Elizabeth: but now, though it had
created new problems, London had eradicated the original
one. Julia could now go back to Morholm. And he must go
with her.

For a while now he had felt the pull of the old country,
the place of his birth, the flat geometric fields and dykes and
the tall elms and the green, slow-moving rivers. That was
an extra reason. And he must get away from Hannah.

Of course it would hurt her when he left so abruptly; but
it would hurt her much more if he stayed and continued to
play out this wretched game until finally there would be the
inevitable shattering of her illusions. And so he decided that,
as soon as he possibly could, he would leave the city and go
back with Julia to Northamptonshire.

And when he had decided, when the resolution was taken, he felt an immense relief; relief that he was going to be free of the noisome city and back in his beloved fenland, free of the monotonous hack-work he was doing, free of the complications of his life here. He went with elation up the steps to Mr Carey's house, wondering how to tell him.

Mr Carey was squatting on the floor of his untidy study with an incongruous look of delight on his lean face. One of his spaniels had had puppies, just where it wanted to, of course, and he was rapturously examining them. 'Milton! Look at this! Sheba's first time, and what a litter!' he exclaimed.

Milton looked on with amused eyes; he never ceased to be surprised at the odd mixture of Mr Carey's personality. When finally Milton had the old bookseller's attention, however, he came straight to the point.

'So, we are to lose you so soon, eh, Milton?' said Mr Carey, throwing him a piercing glance. 'It is seldom that young fellows like you buckle under the strain so quickly.'

'Indeed it is not the work,' said Milton. 'There are –'

'Personal reasons, I suppose? Oh, yes, you see, Milton, I do know such things exist, I am capable of understanding the passions too. Love problems, I suppose?'

Mr Carey's manner was so blunt – likeably so – that Milton could not help but be quite as direct in return. 'Yes,' he said.

Mr Carey sat down at his desk and gazed with sour pensiveness at the floor. 'Ah! Love! What a thing that is! How it quickens the blood, how it makes life worth living! How it lifts man into the heavens! How it distorts, how it twists, how it complicates!' He laughed softly. 'Ah, you are thinking, what can this old embittered cynic know? He is not young, he is old and stale, he has forgotten that pulsating rapture! No, I have not, Milton, but when you have reached my age you will see that love, far from being the simple business they make out, wears many faces, and very, very rarely the ones you expect.'

Milton did not entirely know what to make of this; but he delivered his last work to Mr Carey, received his last fee, and took his last farewell with a mixture of regret and relief. Now it remained to wait on Mr Whitwell again. It would be difficult now if Whitwell had decided to subscribe for his book, since that would mean his staying in London; but he need not have worried, since when he called at the grand house in Portman Square he was received only by the amanuensis who curtly handed him his manuscript. Mr Whitwell's only comment, the man told him with obvious relish, was 'sickly sentimental nonsense': and Milton had to smile as, standing on the steps of the white mansion, he leafed through the tattered pages and found he agreed entirely. It was really about Elizabeth: and Elizabeth, he now knew, had largely been the creation of his own mind in the first place.

Now all that remained was to tell the Bedfords of his decision to leave directly. This would be the most difficult thing of all.

He arrived at the Bedfords' house in the early afternoon after lunching at a coffee-house. The servant who admitted him told him that the master and mistress were out. He hesitated for a moment and was about to say he would call back later when Hannah's voice called from the top of the stairs, 'It's all right, Campbell. Please walk up, Mr Milton.'

He went up to the little sitting-room on the first floor but found it empty. He stepped out into the passage again, nonplussed, and then he heard Hannah's voice from a room further down. 'I am in here, Mr Milton. Please come in.'

It was her bedroom, a fresh and pleasant room that suited her, with whitewashed walls and an old porcelain clock and books in an alcove. Hannah was sitting in a wicker chair by the bed dressed only in a morning-coat, her neck and shoulders and the curve of her small breasts gleaming creamy white in the afternoon sun that filtered through half-drawn green damask curtains, her light glossy hair brushed. She looked very young as she sat and gazed at him from eyes that were limpid and unreadable in the soft oval of her face.

He stood still, unable to speak.

'You have come to tell us you are leaving,' she said. 'Am I right?'

With a dry feeling in his throat he nodded, and looked away.

'I knew, somehow. I could see it coming. You are taking that unfortunate girl back to her family?'

Again he nodded.

'And you too are going home and not coming back.' She sighed and turned her head to gaze in the direction of the window and the light pencilled the rounded line of her jaw. 'Mama and Papa will be sorry to have missed you,' she went on, and he saw that there were tears in her eyes. 'When do you go?'

'Very soon. Miss Bedford, I –'

'I wish you were not going,' she said in a breaking voice and before he knew what he was doing he had sat down on the bed near her and had taken her hand, still not knowing what to say. Her tears had not brimmed over and they remained like a film over her eyes as she turned to look at him.

'Miss Bedford – Hannah – I shall not forget you, for knowing you has helped me, saved me from –' He did not say any more for she was kissing him with a deep disturbing tenderness.

But as his mind struggled to find some way out of this she sensed his turmoil. She drew back her head and looked at him. 'I beg of you, Hannah,' he said breathlessly, 'do not let me forget myself.'

She touched his face lightly and kept her hand there. 'It is all right, Mr Milton,' she said. 'It is my fault: for how can I love a man who is not there? For though I have seen you and talked to you and touched you – and loved you – all the time you were not here at all, were you, but still back in your dear Fen country in your heart.'

He knew she was right. 'I am so deeply sorry, Hannah.'

'I am not sorry. I have been so happy. I shall not forget you either, Mr Milton. Tell me, is it that lady who married that draws you back?'

He shook his head. 'I – can scarcely say.'

'I had hoped to cure you of her.'

'And indeed you did.' He gripped her hand and she returned the pressure. 'You brought me back from the dead, Hannah.'

'But now you must return to your home.'

'Now I must return.'

She stirred and looking down at the floor said: 'It is such a pity you will miss the grand assemblies in the new year. They are so gay. Mama and Papa say I make them giddy at that time for I never rest a moment – and I shall be gay this year too . . . be my old self and have lots of beaux. But not for a little while yet . . . not for a little while.' And as her tears finally brimmed over she said, 'Will you hold me – just hold me for a moment,' and he held her, unable to trust himself to say a word.

Her voice muffled against his shoulder, she said, 'Do you know that poem, "My love is of a birth as rare . . . It was begotten by despair, Upon impossibility" – Love is so unfathomable, its roots going down so deep and far and long ago that you can never trace them – unless a poet can. That is what you must try, Mr Milton.' She gently pulled away and stood up and looked at him. 'You had better go now.'

Her eyes were not crying now: they were wide and luminous but endlessly deep, as if lost in wistful reflection. He took her hand and said goodbye. 'I hope you have a safe journey home,' she said with a gentle smile, and then, as he went to the door, 'And I hope you will both be very happy.'

Milton was very weary when at last he arrived back at his lodgings at dusk and registered only a mild flicker of surprise when he saw the tall male figure in his window on the first floor. Only as he was going up the stairs did he suddenly think of the face that he had seen in Snow Hill and could have sworn to be Jarrett's. Fear and rage tightened at his breast and he sprinted up the stairs four at a time, calling Julia's name.

She was in his room, sitting in an armchair, smiling, and the tall figure at the window turned as he came in.

'Hello, Milton,' said George.

The first greetings and exclamations were over, and Milton was so shaken with emotion that Julia had laughingly pressed him into a chair and fanned his face with a page of his manuscript. But almost the first thing George had said to him was: 'How is Mary?'

'She – she's well, or was when I left home. Has Julia told you then, about Jarrett, about what happened?'

'I knew,' said George, 'or at least, I found out about a fortnight after Jarrett's escape. I was in France by that time, and –'

'France! So Alden was right. I met him in town and he said he'd seen you, but I still hardly believed – But why France?'

George smiled. His hair, brushed back and tied in a ribbon, was unpowdered and showed its natural dark coppery colour. His face was tanned, and the sickly lines that Milton remembered in it were gone, though the faintly rakish look was still discernible. There was a spark in George that Milton had not seen in a long time. 'Same old Milton,' he said. 'Must always be a reason.' There was tea on a tray on the table and George poured a cup and handed it to his friend. 'Here, drink this and stop shaking. Well, when I had my Tour in '71 after finishing my education I knew a couple of friends in France – friends of father's originally – and I liked the country and, well, I had to get away. You know the state I was in – half-mad, drinking. God knows how I survived. On impulse I thought going abroad might keep me from the brink – it was worth trying. The last thing I wanted was a lot of fuss about farewells. A trifle melodramatic as an exit, I'll acknowledge, but then I was not in a way to think rationally. So I left with nothing and was on the Boston coach before I could change my mind.'

'I thought you had –'

'Done away with myself?' George smiled, but there was pain behind the smile. 'Fool and damned fool I have been in my time, but luckily I was not such a fool as that. Not that I did not consider it.' He looked at them soberly. 'France was really a last desperate attempt to – save myself, I suppose. When I was on the voyage across and had the decks beneath my feet I felt somewhat better – one of the few things I can say to my credit is that I am a good sailor, and it was cheering to tuck into salt beef whilst the other passengers were turning shades of green. But it was not the trip in itself that saved me. It was when at last I heard what Jarrett had done, and that he had escaped across the Channel, and I knew that he was probably in the very same country as I, another Englishman, liable to be marked.' His voice hardened. 'That gave me a new purpose. Then I wanted to live.'

'You mean you tracked him down?' said Milton. He saw that Julia was quivering and he laid his hand on hers.

'With much labour,' said George, noticing the gesture

with approval. 'It was a long business of trying all the Channel ports, asking and asking. Englishmen a-plenty come and go to smuggle but few actually stay. I thought he might be recollected by someone. At last, in a foul little smuggling tavern in a fishing village near Dieppe – Jarrett and his accomplice had some very seedy contacts – I heard news of them, from the very smugglers who had facilitated their escape. But then that was the last I heard of them for weeks: for I was told they had gone to Paris, and to find them there – an impossible task. Then they lent me a hand themselves.' He paused and drew breath, and Milton could read the quiet satisfaction within him: there had been more than an element of crusade in this. 'One of father's friends, M. Marqueste, whom I had met on my travels, wrote me from Rouen. Englishmen are less popular than ever in France at the moment, with this American War – the French are very much on the side of the rebels – and M. Marqueste told me that two Englishmen like the ones I was seeking had raised a great outcry at a coaching inn in the town by getting very drunk and loudly condemning – in bad French – the Americans as a parcel of rogues who deserved to be put down. They barely escaped from the local *paysans* with their lives. It appears then they thought they might be safer back in England, and I traced them here to London.' He sighed and half-turned to the window, so that his lean sensitive profile showed its unquiet against the dwindling dusk light. 'Even here they have not let the grass grow under their feet, and have kept me on the hop. Last week I arrived at an inn on Primrose Hill but an hour after they had left it.'

'I *did* see Jarrett then,' said Milton. 'Here in the city, some time ago.'

George nodded gravely. 'He is here all right. But I have lost track of him completely. However, now I am not the only one who seeks him. He is wanted for murder.'

'Great God!' breathed Milton: but Julia nodded. 'I can believe it,' she said in a low voice.

'I should not have spoken of his accomplice, Macmillan, in the present tense,' went on George. 'Three days ago Jarrett stabbed him to death, in a quarrel over the division of their rapidly diminishing spoils, in a lodging-house in Lambeth. Constables are seeking him all over town. When he is caught he is sure to be hanged. The law, having let him through its fingers once, does not intend for that to happen again.'

Julia got up and joined her brother at the window and looked out. 'I hope they catch him soon,' she said, her voice muffled. 'For if I were to see him I would not be able to restrain myself.'

George looked at her soberly. 'Amen to that, sister.' He turned to Milton. 'Julia has told me all about her life these past months – the longest talk I think we've ever had. And your part in ending that life.' He gripped Milton's hand. 'So it's doubly good to see your solemn old face again. I have a great deal to thank you for.' Then he laughed, shyly. 'At least tracking *you* down has been less difficult!' He pulled a paper from his coat pocket. 'I was browsing in a bookseller's in Cheapside and came across the name of an author I knew well at the bottom of these rather sentimental verses. I inquired of the bookseller – a ferocious old person name of Carey – and was directed here.' He glanced at Julia and smiled. 'To find a double pleasure.' His sister, with something of her old drooping defiance and something of the gentleness Milton knew, turned and kissed him. Their separate experiences had broken down old barriers. George looked at Milton again and laughed. 'Henry, I beg you to stop looking at me as if I were a ghost. I'm sorry you didn't hear from me, but I felt, rather uncharitably, that I wanted to sever my every tie with my old life completely. But you must have heard from James what I was doing.'

'James?' Milton was startled. 'James has never said a word of it. He said he firmly believed you were dead.'

George's face froze. Outside in the empty street a brewer's dray rumbled past with a hollow clop of hoofs and then left the twilit silence to settle again.

'What the devil – But it was from James that I learnt about the Jarrett affair! When I arrived in France I wrote to him at Gray's Inn, turning over to him the running of Morholm until I returned, and asking him to explain to the rest of the family. He wrote back saying he would be glad to, and told me of Jarrett's flight, and so I stayed in France to seek him out. I sent a note to Wiley's Bank authorizing James to make drafts on the estate account.'

'George – we knew nothing of this,' stammered Milton. 'James gave out that there was no news of you . . . established himself as master of Morholm.' He got up and fumbled among the papers on his desk. 'I have a letter here from Mary, from a couple of weeks since. She tells me James is standing for the parliamentary election at Peterborough.'

George took the letter and Milton noticed the trembling gentleness with which he held it. 'James? What in God's name is he up to? What of the rest of my family?'

Milton shrugged, trying to cover the mounting unease within him. 'Your grandmother Mrs Peach is still there, I believe, but the rest James turfed out of Morholm one way or another. Apart from that, there is . . .'

'Only Mary,' said George, and the trembling of the hand with which he held Mary's letter grew more violent.

8

The Peterborough election and the Bridge Fair were held on the same day in October, throwing the city into a ferment such as it had not seen in many years.

Even among the gentry in their staid solid houses in Cowgate and Priestgate the occasion was of some excitement: the name of Hardwick was suddenly spoken of with an interest missing for fifty years or more. And Lord Fitzwilliam was to be at the hustings too, having come into town for the purpose, and the night before had attended the recently opened Theatre in Queen Street to see 'She Stoops to Conquer' with a large circle of noble friends whose elegance had created quite a stir.

James had gone in the day before – by hired carriage, for the right effect – to stay with old Mr Sedgmoor, the lawyer and his close confidant in the election canvass, at his house in Westgate, and to attend the election dinner at The Talbot. Mary rode to Peterborough on the election morning, with the groom as escort, and the Longthorpe road into the city was already busy, with carts full of cheering labourers from the Fitzwilliam estate lurching past her. From the east and north roads came sturdy breedlings from the Fens, on wagons or on foot, for their red-letter day of the year. The inns and taverns and gin-shops would be open all day and it was going to be a rollicking occasion.

They left their horses at The Talbot, and though the groom said James had instructed him to stay by her, she told him to go and enjoy himself: she was quite capable of looking after herself. She liked to look around the fair without having to drag someone after her making sure she didn't step in a puddle.

The Bridge Fair covered the low-lying meadows around the Nene bridge out towards Fletton, spilling over up Bridge Street and into the Marketstede where the wooden hustings had already been erected, ready for the election in the afternoon. The weather had been rainy and the bridge fields, always prone to flooding, had been covered with straw to counteract the mud. She arrived in time to see the procession of magistrates and the Feoffees, who virtually ran the town, led by the High Bailiff and the town crier who read the proclamation opening the fair. Thousands of sheep, cattle, horses, geese and fowls were herded into enclosures by the bridge for marketing and the noise of the animals and of auctioning and haggling was cacophonous. Mary passed quickly through the first field, where the serious marketing went on. The sight of the lone striking girl in the riding-habit and small green tricorne hat elicited a few remarks and whistles from the farmers and she tried to ignore them and tried not to show she was flattered. She would prefer their rough admiration to the simpering compliments of rich fops any day. In the next field there was more to interest her, with tradesmen and pedlars selling everything from second-hand wigs to a lucky touch, good for curing the scrofula, from a lamed man who had been the only one of the crew to survive a shipwreck in Biscay. There were quacks selling, with an endless repetitive patter, nostrums and elixirs that would cure fits and rheumatism and dropsy, men with hurdy-gurdies and fiddlers and ballad-singers, and hawkers selling cheap broadsheets purporting to be the confessions of a murderer who was to be hanged at Norwich that day.

She bought some gingerbread and went into a booth to see a live Chinaman and an Eskimo on display, and was fascinated by their bizarre Mongol features. She stood in a crowded tent and laughed at a troupe of mummers performing St George and the Dragon with much noisy slapstick humour. She saw a contortionist with a wide grin put his foot in his mouth, and paid a penny with a tipsy crowd to see an execrable side-show supposed to represent the beheading of Charles I. It was here among the hooting laughter and thrown orange-peel that Sophia Goulding suddenly appeared beside her.

'What rustic delights you country folk enjoy!' she said with superficial brightness. She was wearing a purple cloak and long silver earrings dangled amongst the dark coils of her hair. 'I declare I am quite fazed with the gaiety of it all!'

Mary looked at her with distaste. 'People here get precious little amusement in their lives,' she said. 'If it disgusts you, Miss Goulding, I suggest you leave it.'

'Oh, but they are pure animals!' said the woman, as a young man tipsy on cheap beer from a booth jostled by her. 'They stink like their cattle and grow to resemble them as soon as they are past twenty.'

'So would you if you had to live as they,' said Mary, her old feelings of strange mistrust of the woman resolving into simple hatred.

'But my dear, that is the point! I choose not to. Why, there is scarce a good-looking man amongst them. Though I tell a lie. I could make an exception for the blond clown who is your beau – honest young John.'

'He is not my beau,' said Mary levelly, 'but he is worth ten of you.'

'Oh, I believe you!' said Miss Goulding, and looked her up and down with her wide green eyes. 'I am worth very little, I assure you. But then perhaps James has not grown tired of you yet.'

'I wish to God you would cease your wretched innuendoes and say what you mean,' said Mary. 'If you are implying –'

'Why, my dear,' smiled Miss Goulding, and put her hand on Mary's arm. She shook it off. 'I really believe you *don't* know. Never mind. You'll find out.'

'Miss Mary!' came a familiar voice.

She had never been more glad to see John Newman, and with him Jenny Lake, who came pushing through the crowd towards her. Sophia Goulding looked at them with one of her over-bright smiles. 'Well! 'Tis the maid and her swain. Though it's a case of maiden no more, I'll wager –'

Jenny calmly lashed out and slapped the woman across the face. 'You get out of here,' she said, 'filthy lying trollop.'

There was a red mark on Miss Goulding's face and she put her fingers to it for a moment. 'Very well,' she said. She spat on the ground and left them.

Jenny turned to Mary and smiled shyly. 'I reckon we want no more of that woman,' she said. 'Well, John, are you not going to speak up?'

John, who was standing stiff with muscular blue-eyed embarrassment, stammered, 'Well, we – we wanted you to be the first to know, Miss Mary. Jenny and me, we're going to be . . .'

Mary finished it for him. 'Oh, I'm so glad,' she said and kissed Jenny and then impulsively, to the murmurs of the people around them in the tent, reached up and kissed John. 'Let me steal one, Jenny,' she laughed, 'for he will have plenty more for you.'

She was more glad than she could say, and the beaming pride on both their faces suggested that it was a sincere attachment. 'When is it to be?'

'We been to see Parson Medhurst yest'day, and the banns'll be called next week,' said John. 'We hope as how you'll come to see us wed.'

'I shall be honoured,' said Mary. 'And you will live in the cottage?'

'For the time being,' said John, a little uneasily.

''Twould be best to get a little place of our own,' said Jenny. 'My father's said as he'd help.'

'The thing is, Miss Mary,' said John, 'there's some bad feeling on Morholm estate about Mr James, and I'd better prefer to be out of it before it gets worse.'

'James?' said Mary. 'But – I thought he was always very fair.'

'So he was,' said John. 'And still is to me. But Luke Whittle, him as has a holding over to Barnack, 'd say he's selling off land without a by-your-leave –'

'Selling land?' said Mary.

'Ay, mistress – I thought you'd know of it.'

'No,' said Mary thoughtfully, 'no, I didn't.'

'Well, as I say, there's beginning to be bad feeling, so we'd rather get out before long. 'Tis a rare pity, for I've a fondness for the old place.'

Mary stayed with them for the rest of the morning – though she was now somewhat preoccupied – and at noon they went into a refreshment booth to eat hot pies and drink a cup of spiced ale. Soon the ground, even with the straw, was resolving into a liquid mash and ragged people, including tiny children, were fighting and reeling from the gin-booths, so they left the fair and walked up Bridge Street with a tide of people to the market square to see the election.

The hustings platform had been erected in front of the Guildhall and already the square was filled with people, the rival factions bellowing slogans at each other. In the upper windows of the houses and shops round the square ladies had gathered to watch the proceedings in safety. In the highest window of The Talbot Mary saw the figures of three very grand ladies. One was Countess Fitzwilliam: the other two were Mrs Wainwright and her daughter Elizabeth, now Lady Woodhouse. Clearly the ambitions of the Wainwrights did not stop at owning most of the commercial interests of Stamford. Mrs Wainwright was using her daughter's new title to haul herself up further. Mary preferred to be in the midst of the excitement and with John and Jenny she pressed forward as far as she could to see the figures who were already on the platform. Many notables of the city were there with the candidates: Matthew Wyldbore, long a member and a well-known figure: a young man called Richard Benyon: a fairly unknown man called Phipps: and James, in his severe dark coat, his hands behind his back, with old Mr Sedgmoor. Lord Fitzwilliam was also there, looking very relaxed: he was used to this. Mary knew it was an uphill battle for James. The Fitzwilliams' Whig nominees had held the city virtually un-contested for years: they and their patron had most of the city's property. James had the prestige of his name and the ground-swell of opposition to the Fitzwilliams on his side, but little else. When she had told him about the three angry electors who had come to Morholm the other week she had not known how to take his reply: 'Well, I shall just have to buy their votes, that's all.'

The poll was being declared open: the City Bailiff, as returning officer, was making the proclamation, but she could scarcely hear because a fight had broken out between rival supporters in the crowd near her, and she had to use her elbows to keep standing in the swaying crush. There were calls for order from the platform and finally there was a degree of quiet and the polling began.

Many of the electors who stepped forward on the platform to record their vote she did not know: but she instantly recognized Hugh Woodhouse – now Sir Hugh – who had inherited his father's property in the city with his title. She looked at his pot belly and swaggering walk with contempt. 'Mr Wyldbore and Mr Benyon.' Well, that was no surprise. A vote for Phipps and Hardwick would constitute the strong-est rejection of the Fitzwilliam interest, but there were few of them coming. 'Mr Wyldbore and Mr Benyon.' 'Mr Wyldbore and Mr Benyon.' But some electors kept a foot in both camps. Dr Villiers, tall and lean and hard-faced, stepped up. 'Mr Wyldbore and Mr Hardwick.' That was typical of the canny surgeon. Old Mr Sedgmoor in his long bag-wig stepped up for his own turn. 'Mr Hardwick and Mr Phipps.' Loudly and emphatically, as if to make a point.

There were cheers from parts of the crowd and Mary's mixed feelings began to give way to pure excitement. Then she saw Wistow, the bullish man who had come to Morholm with his threats, step up. He looked nervous and cleared his throat and the recorder had to ask him to repeat his vote because of the noise of the crowd. 'Mr Wyldbore and Mr Benyon.' She saw James throw him a cold glance. But the other two men who had come that day were next: Fenstanton, the squat one. 'Mr Hardwick and Mr Phipps.' And Hackthorn, the clerkly one. 'Mr Hardwick and Mr Phipps.' James's face was expressionless. So he had brought them round, thought Mary – somehow.

The crowd was swelling and swaying back and forth in a roaring, unruly tide, making the platform shake, hoping for a rout now that the pattern seemed to have changed. Mary had long lost count, but James's seemed to be the most frequent name. 'Mr Hardwick and Mr Phipps.' 'Mr Hardwick and Mr Phipps.' Lord Fitzwilliam was dabbing his nose with a handkerchief. A sudden sideways surge almost lifted Mary off her feet and she found herself separated from John and Jenny. There was a commotion in the packed bodies directly in front of her and then they parted and the figure of her brother William burst from them and fell in the mud at her feet. 'Mary! Sister, save me, they'll tear me apart!' he cried, staggering to his feet and clinging to her. His bony face was white with fear. Two men who had been pursuing him burst through the crowd and then, seeing Mary, stopped. 'Leave him go, mistress,' said one. 'We want him.'

'I will not,' she said, and placed her trembling brother behind her. 'If you want him so badly you must come and get him.'

The two men looked at the slender girl with the fearless eyes and then sidled away. 'Damn coward – hiding behind a woman,' one said.

'All right, they are gone,' said Mary. 'Now what is this

all –' She caught sight of some papers in his pocket and grabbed at one. He made a move to snatch it back but stopped and grinned, shamefacedly.

It was a cheaply printed and scurrilous broadsheet, purporting to be 'Some Facts about the Hardwicks of Morholm which a Disinterested Observer feels should be brought to the Attention of the Electors of Peterborough. Price One Penny.' Amongst the crude character assassination of James that followed another passage caught her eye: 'Mr *Joseph* Hardwick, the candidate's father, was known throughout the County as a Half-Wit or all but: and the Infamy of his Brother *George*, a notorious Rake-Hell and Lecher who fathered many illegitimate Brats before his strange Disappearance, when he probably ended his Existence in Deserved Remorse, need hardly be Recounted . . .'

She threw the paper down and ground it into the mud with her toe. 'Now, sister –' he began.

'And *you* have been distributing these – these foul slanders, lies! William, you are shameful! And your own cousins –'

'I was paid, Mary, I was paid, I needed the money, I was desperate . . . folk in the opposing camp stood to gain, they paid me,' he gabbled. 'Those men there – supporters of James's side – did not take it kindly.'

'I almost wish I had left you to them,' she said, and seizing the rest of the sheets from William threw them into the mud. 'Well, you shall spread no more of this –'

An almighty roar arose from the crowd and there was another surge forward towards the hustings. The result of the poll was being announced. Mary strained to hear above the din.

'Benyon . . . Mr Wyldbore, one hundred and fifteen . . . Mr Hardwick, one hundred and eight . . . declare . . . Mr Benyon and Mr Wyldbore elected as members –'

It was all over. James had lost by seven votes. The crowd bellowed, an animal sound, part delight, part rage, and one of the wooden beams supporting the hustings was almost knocked away, so that the whole structure wobbled alarmingly. On the platform there was confusion. James and Mr Phipps, after a brief consultation with old Sedgmoor, were contesting the result. Mary caught the sound of James's voice, struggling to be heard: 'Somewhere an illegal rate has been charged to create more voters . . . it is illegal . . . I contest . . . not valid . . .' Phipps was shaking his fist at Lord Fitzwilliam. Then, mainly it seemed from fear at the rapidly disintegrating platform, the poll was hurriedly declared closed and the candidates began to clatter down the steps at the back.

Immediately the crowd began to tear down the hustings plank by plank. Already well-oiled and vociferous from the fair and the excitement, the controversy of the result had incited them further: moreover so much firewood for the coming winter could not be left standing there. Mary saw James hurrying across the square to The Talbot and she ran after him. 'James!' she called. 'Wait!'

His face was darker than she had ever seen it as he turned to her. 'Come on,' he said. 'We had better leave at once. We can send for your horse later. Things may turn ugly. The whole thing is nothing but bribery and intimidation.'

In the yard of The Talbot he ordered his hired carriage to be hitched up and while they waited they heard the roaring of the crowd in the square and the splintering of timbers as the hustings was demolished. 'They might well screech,' muttered James. 'Fitzwilliam has them all in his pocket.'

He was silent again as they climbed into the carriage and they were just about to start off when William came half-running, half-staggering into the inn yard. His face was bloody and terrified as he hammered on the carriage window. 'James! Please let me in! Save me!' he cried.

'Dear God, it's those men – they'll kill him,' breathed Mary.

James looked at her and then, abruptly, flung open the door. 'Get in,' he snapped, and as Mary helped the sobbing William into the carriage James tapped on the roof to the coachman. William's pursuers came up just as the carriage began to move and one pulled open the door. James lunged forward and hit him on the chin and then heaved the door shut just as with a great sickening lurch they swung out of the inn yard.

As soon as they reached the turnpike road at the edge of the town James stopped the coach again. 'You should be safe now,' he said to William. 'So out with you.'

'A thousand thanks, cousin,' said William, who was beginning to look his old swaggering self again now that he was out of danger.

'Your thanks be damned,' said James as the young man climbed out. 'You needn't think I am unaware of the ill services you have done me with your infernal broadsheets. Drive on.'

James sat grimly silent for a while as they rattled on. At last Mary asked him, 'Was the election truly not fair, James?'

'Of course not,' he said. 'The Overseers had met in private and trumped up a rate so that a few more submissive voters could be found. The thing was settled before I ever made my foolish decision to stand. It seems that ambition is little valued in this forsaken place.'

She looked at him soberly. 'Ambition, when it is for worthy aims, is good, but ambition simply for its own sake . . .'

He looked at her, an odd, disconcerting look that he seemed to be using more and more with her: it was very different from the old impersonal gaze. He sighed. 'I read an old fable about a group of frogs in a pond, who wished for their own private god to worship. Zeus sent them a reed, but it bent and swayed and they soon despised it. So he sent them a heron, which promptly ate them all up. Rather like the Hardwicks, is it not? George the reed, and I fancied myself the heron. But now I have faltered, failed.'

'And what if you *have* failed?' said Mary. 'That does not mean the end of the world.'

'Failure is not in my scheme of things,' said James.

Evening was coming down with autumnal swiftness and when they got back to Morholm Mrs Peach was hobbling across the hall to the stairs. 'Well, grandson, and what's the result? Are we to have another Hardwick at Westminster after all these years?' she said.

'Are you not going to bed, grandmother?' snapped James.

'Very well, very well,' she said. She knew better than to cross this grandson, but there was a cold, shrewd speculation in the glance she threw at him before tottering up to bed.

James drank several glasses of brandy in the evening, which was unusual for him, and though Mary tried to concentrate on her sewing she felt very uneasy. He stood silent before the fire and each time she looked up at him he was looking at her with an odd mixture of interrogation and anticipation. Presently he went over and snuffed one of the candles, leaving the room in a soft, red half-light. It was then she put her work down and spoke the thought that had been troubling her. 'James, why did you help my brother like that? Last time you met you were hostile —'

'You think I did it for that sot's own sake? I should have left him to his fate.' He put down his glass and stepped closer to her. The remaining candles were behind him so she could see little of his face but a faint, hard glint from his eyes. 'What have I done everything of late for, do you suppose? Can you really not see?'

His voice alarmed her. She lowered her face in confusion. 'If . . . for my sake you have done this, you need not. I don't want that.'

'Then for God's sake what do you want?' His voice grew harsher.

'I don't understand,' said Mary, baffled and frightened by this change in James.

'Of course you do,' he said in a tone of contempt. 'You have been playing out of my reach for just long enough.'

'James, I – I don't understand what – I thought – you have been very kind to me but I never –'

'Kind? Ay, damn kind I have been,' he said, and paced across the room. She could see his face now, square and aggressive. 'As if I have not had enough to do, I have spent a great deal of time and effort on you recently.' He stopped and looked at her with eyes that were almost animal in their glassy intensity. 'Do you really think –' He broke off, clenching his fists. 'I haven't been so extravagant through the goodness of my heart, you know! Have you ever known me do anything through the goodness of my heart? Without motive? And then I go and risk my neck helping that wretch of a brother for you –'

'But I don't want that,' said Mary, a sob rising with searing, choking tightness in her throat.

'Then what do you want?' he said again.

'I don't want anything. I don't understand. I just want us to carry on as we were . . . companions.'

'You think I let you stay here merely so that we may carry on as cosy companions, like some doddering old brother and sister round their hearth?'

She tried to move away, unable to bear this any longer. 'I'm going to bed,' she stammered, but she found herself seized by James's iron hands and prevented. 'Oh, no,' he hissed, 'you will not sidle away like that – hold me off once again. I suppose this is the kind of provoking behaviour that drove my brother off –' Mary, bewildered, uncomprehending, and now furious, screamed at him: '*Damn* you, James! You have no right to say that!' His grip on her wrists was painful. 'George would never behave like this!' she cried, her voice choking with sobs.

'No, he was not man enough,' said James, thrusting his face close to hers. 'But I shall leave you in no doubt as to my superiority in that respect.' His teeth were clenched and the veins on his brow bulged. 'You owe me something, Mary, whether you acknowledge it or not: in my system of doing things you owe me something and cannot refuse me after I have paid my part of the bargain.'

He was too strong for her. Before she could even cry out he had pushed her down on to the sofa and she felt his hands on her breasts and the dead weight of him pressing and pinning her down and his breath on her face. But she was a fighter. She struggled and kicked at his shins. With strength she did not know she had she pulled her wrist free from his grip and put her nails up to his cheek. She actually heard the tearing sound of flesh as she clawed at him, and the pain made him recoil a moment, a moment long enough for her to stretch back, feeling as if her spine would break, and seize a heavy candlestick from the table behind her. She swung it with all the force she could muster against his head and face, again and again. Stunned, he rolled off her, clutching his hand to his head, and she sprang up and ran from the room, pulling up her torn clothes.

He had not succeeded in his intent but the assault could not have been of greater horror. Blindly she ran across the echoing hall, pulled back the heavy bolts of the front door. Two at the top. One at the bottom. Rusted and stuck. Would not budge. Almost taking the skin off her fingers it flew back at last with a screech. Gasping with panic she tugged at the door. She could hear James in the parlour rising to his feet. Tears streamed down her cheeks and jaw as she rattled, hopelessly, at the unmoving door.

'It's locked, cousin,' said James, appearing behind her, blocking her way to the kitchen passage. 'I have the key.'

She screamed until her lungs felt seared, as if she had inhaled fire, and ran for the stairs, calling for Grandmother Peach, for Mrs Reynolds, anybody. She had reached the top stair when he caught her, tugging at the hem of her gown. She kicked out at him but fell. Her own cries drowned out the noise of a thunderous rattling in the hall, and she felt a waft of cool air. For a moment James's hands were on her again: then he was lifted bodily away and hurled to the bottom of the stairs.

Other hands were touching her now, gently; and for a moment the nightmare seemed to have turned into a dream of sweetness as she looked up and saw George's face above her. She clung to him as he lifted her and carried her down to the hall and when he set her on her feet she clung to him still. He squeezed her hand and then turned to face James, who was standing unsteadily, holding his hand to his ribs in pain. Blood was running from the cuts on his cheek.

'What in the name of heaven have you done to my house, James?' he said.

James took a deep shuddering breath. '*Your* house, George?' he said, his voice flutey with pain and anger. 'Oh, no. No, no. You abandoned it. You left it. Turned it over to me. You weren't fit to run it. Look around you. Improvements. Great improvements. Mine. I am master of Morholm. My achievements say so.' His voice rose hysterically. '*I* am the master now, do you hear? Get off my property!'

The two brothers faced each other across the empty hall. George made a sudden move forward but Mary tugged him back. 'Please, George,' she sobbed, 'let us just *go*.'

He looked at her, a tender concern softening the anger on his face. 'All right,' he said. He turned back to James. 'I shall go, brother. To take Mary away – where *you* cannot reach her. But believe me, I shall come back, James. I promise you that.'

Outside, in the twilit drive, they found Sophia Goulding, a shawl about her shoulders, waiting. She looked at them both with interest. 'Good,' she said, 'it's come at last, then,' and with a small bare smile she passed them and walked into the house.

9

The ceiling of the room in The George Inn at Stamford was divided by two stout beams of stained oak, one slightly larger than the other and tapering a little at one end. The smaller had two knotholes, a few inches apart, that faintly made the shape of a face, and a long silver filament of cobweb was strung diagonally across its width. Mary knew all this because she had been lying on the bed dully staring at it for over an hour, until the light from the diamond-paned window grew too dim to see.

Even then she did not move. The events of the day circled her mind in a garish meaningless train and she felt that she just wanted to lie here absolutely motionless for ever.

They had come to the inn from Morholm – George and herself – in the hired post-chaise in which Milton, Julia and George had ridden from London. George had insisted that Milton and Julia should wait at the inn. He had wished to go alone to Morholm. George had obtained rooms for himself and Julia and Mary and here they had left her to rest – how long ago? Time seemed to have stretched and dilated to absurd, incomprehensible dimensions today. She could not believe that this morning she had been eating gingerbread at Peterborough Bridge Fair.

It was an effort even to turn her head when there was a tap at the door and Julia came softly in. Mary, looking at her cousin, thought her grown thinner, her features less heavy and more openly vital than before.

'Are you feeling better?' said Julia.

'Yes.' Mary sat up and strength seemed to flow slowly

back into her. She took Julia's hand. 'Yes, everything's all right now.'

Julia gripped her hand feverishly: then abruptly dropped it. 'How can you bear to touch me?' she burst out. 'Don't you remember the last time you saw me, in the street, in the rain . . . that terrible night in London?'

'Yes, I remember.'

'I struck you then. I wish now you would strike me, for before God I deserve it! What I did! D'you know how I lived in London all those months? I was a whore. I had to be – because that's what I already was. Jarrett left me unclean, dirty. It was the only place for me after what I'd done. Strike me, Mary! I was having an affair with Jarrett. I could have told you about him but I let him deceive you, so how can you bear to touch me so –' She burst into stormy tears and flung herself on the bed beside Mary.

'You didn't because you felt for him as I did,' said Mary, cradling Julia in her arms. 'And we were both deceived. All that is something we have in common, not something to come between us.' She felt a tear running down her own cheek. 'Let us be friends, Julia.'

Julia slowly sat up and pushed back her masses of tangled black hair. 'But there is more than this,' she said. 'I – have a new love – a *real* love, Mary. I don't deserve it for one moment but I *will* take it. But only . . . only if you will give me your blessing.'

'You mean – Mr Milton? Oh, Julia, he is a dear good man and of course you have my blessing. A thousand, a thousand, both of you.'

They looked at each other and laughed, with relief, at their tear-streaked faces and tumbled hair. Keeping hold of her hand, Julia stood up. 'George and Henry are downstairs, in a supper-room. Will you come down?'

'Well,' Mary smiled, 'I believe I do have an appetite.'

George and Milton, in the little panelled candle-lit

supper-room, were talking in low voices when the two women came in. They both got up, anxiously, and stared dumbly at Mary until she had to laugh. 'I'm all right,' she said. 'And I'm that glad to see you. And I'm *hungry*.'

So over supper George told Mary his story: of his going to the continent, tracking down Jarrett and pursuing him to London: and that now he was wanted for murder, and could not be found. And all the time George looked at her, with an anxious tenderness, especially when she blanched and her lips tightened at the thought of Jarrett, the man she was to marry, the murderer. Then Julia and Milton told their story, and how they had met up with George: and finally how they had all, seized with fear for her that they could not wholly explain, come back from London in a post-chaise, and arrived at Morholm in fortunate time.

'I knew something was very wrong when Milton told me James had hidden the fact that I was alive and kicking,' said George.

'He tried to convince me you were dead,' said Mary.

'You are not to be rid of me so easily, I'm afraid,' said George. 'I walked up to see Thornton Wiley whilst you were resting, and learned that James has been laying out huge sums of the income from the estate.'

'The election,' said Mary. 'I see now. The Peterborough election today – James stood for it.' She remembered again the three electors who had come to Morholm. 'The money, I suspect – and he has been selling land too – was spent on buying votes, but he did not buy enough.'

George sighed and shook his head. 'What an infernal family we are! And that villain of a brother of mine has almost scattered us to the four winds. Are you quite sure you wish to marry into this dreadful clan, Milton?'

Milton looked startled, and both he and Julia coloured.

'Well, I am not blind,' laughed George, 'and there is no sense in havering about and being mealy-mouthed about these things. That's one lesson at least I – learnt myself,' he added softly. 'So come, tell me! Are you prepared to take the risk of joining this strange brood?'

Milton looked at Julia. 'If it will have me, then very much so.'

They laughed. Mary caught George's eye and looked away and tried to hide the blurred and liquid emotion resolving within her.

Later, after supper, Milton set off for Helpston to see his parents, leaving his luggage at the inn, and the others retired. Mary's room was at the back of the rambling old inn and the window looked out across the road to the grassy bank of the Welland. She stood and watched the October mist stealing down the river with its phantom whiteness until there was a tap at the door.

George came in, his suntanned face, still mobile and sensitive, tense with anxiety. 'Are you truly recovered from your shock?' he said, softly.

'Yes. I'm well and fine. It's all right.' She turned to the window again, looked out without seeing. 'As long as – as long as you will not leave me, George.'

'Never,' he said, his voice very quiet with a complete conviction. 'I must go back to Morholm tomorrow: I have not forgotten James. But otherwise . . . I have come back to haunt you, Mary, for good – if you will let me.'

He came up and touched her shoulders and was startled when she shrank away. 'I'm sorry. I should have realized – after what happened today –'

She shook her head and swallowed. 'No, no, it's not *that*. I am no lent lily to snap off at the first touch,' she said, with a painful smile. 'It's just – oh, George, I don't *deserve* to have your love after – after everything I did – all that time I was obsessed with Jarrett, and you – you were unhappy. I don't *deserve* it, George. I think you had much better be horrible to me for a while, until I hate myself a little less.' She stared out of the window, afraid she might cry, a draught from the casement stirring the brown unruly hair across her cheek.

He let her go on, looking at her calmly and tenderly. 'Well, now let me tell you something,' he said. 'I have been afraid of this moment, meeting you again. Oh, I have looked forward to it. It has kept me alive, it was with me all the time I was in France, but I was afraid in just the same shamefaced way as you. I was not kind to you in the past, Mary – I did many cruel things – though you have chosen to forget those in your dear, typical, Mary-way.'

'Oh, but you had *reason* to,' she gulped, 'you –'

'I thought I had, no doubt,' he said. 'Reasons in my jealousy, my resentment, my damn-fool immaturity. I could simply never tell you how I loved you – couldn't speak out. How you tolerated me as you did I don't know.'

'Oh, George, you'll break my heart.'

'No, I won't. It's too dear to me. Mary,' he touched her arm and she did not move away, 'all that dead weight of the past – past and pain – I want to throw off. But I can only do that with you.'

She turned, abruptly, and buried her face in his chest, tugging him to her with all her strength. She wanted to press his body into hers until they were joined and merged and could not be separated. Her voice came muffled. 'George, I *am* yours, *always*. I realized that, in my wretched blind stupidity, when it was too late, when I *thought* it was too late. But it's not too late. You're here.'

'I'm here,' he said, 'and intend staying, I assure you.'

She touched his face with her light fingertips, looked at his grey serious eyes, his lean face and wry humorous mouth. He was so inexpressibly dear – so real in her arms – that she was afraid she would cry again. 'And you really forgive me?' she said.

'I would forgive you anything,' he said, 'though that doesn't apply as there's nothing to forgive.'

'And – you can find it in your heart to love the most foolish girl who ever lived –'

'Yes and no: for you are not a foolish girl, you are my most dear, my most lovely Mary, but yes, I think I can find it in my heart, for I have loved you ever since I came home and we met in the garden at Morholm.'

He lifted her chin gently and kissed her and she knew as with a single bright flame of feeling that shot up through their pressed bodies that at last she had found the place where she belonged – where she had always belonged – and which she would never forsake.

'I have so much to make up to you,' she whispered, 'so much time I wasted.'

'That's not much,' he said, 'out of a lifetime.'

And so the dead weight of past and pain was thrown off. And soon the place where she had thought there was only everlasting barren desolation blossomed as it never had before.

Milton spent the night at Helpston and returned to The George early in the morning to find the landlord, rather mystified but delighted at the presence of his three distinguished guests, serving them breakfast in the dining-room. George invited him to join them.

'You have eaten little yourself, George,' said Mary.

'I cannot pretend I have a stomach for it,' said George. 'I must go back to Morholm, and somehow gain entrance to my own house. I do not intend that we should stay at inns for ever.'

'Let me come with you,' said Milton.

'Yes, and me, George,' said Mary. 'You saw James last night . . . half-mad. He would stop at nothing.'

George held up his hand. 'I shall go alone,' he said. 'This is a matter between James and myself.'

'Take care, brother,' said Julia, and with a sudden clumsy affection reached over and kissed him. 'We have only just got you back; and for me it is as if I have only just come to know you. We don't want to lose you just yet.'

'No fear of that,' said George, lightly, but clearly moved. 'I have a very tender regard for my own safety. Well,' he got up from the table, 'if I can hire a horse from this well-named inn, I shall be off.'

'Take mine, George,' said Milton. He looked at Julia. 'I shall remain in Stamford today, I think.'

Mary went with George out to the inn yard. 'What Julia said just now,' she said. 'You know that goes for me too.'

He bent and kissed her. 'Never fear, my lover,' he said. 'I shall be back soon, inheritance firmly wrestled from usurper, like Richard the Lionheart – and then we shall return to Morholm.' He put on his hat and buttoned his riding coat.

'I'll be waiting for you,' she said.

Milton and Julia were going to take a walk about the town, but when they asked Mary if she would go with them she said no. 'You go,' she said with a smile. 'I shall stay here and wait for George.' And so she sat at the window of her room, watching the boats go up the river to the wharf, the carts and sedan-chairs passing up St Mary's Hill with the stream of bonnets and three-cornered hats, and listening to the bells chiming the hours from the many churches of the town, and waited.

Milton and Julia strolled about the town, seeing again the familiar landmarks, the Assembly Rooms, the great tower of All Saints, the new theatre. But they only really saw each other: there was still a kind of rarefied wonder in the simple fact of each other's company, and only a sudden shower of

399

rain roused them. They took shelter under the pillared portico that led to the market. When Milton saw young Mr Francis Sedgmoor coming towards them he felt Julia's grip tighten on his arm but she whispered: 'It's all right, my love.'

The young man with his decent nervous face extended his hand. 'Mr Milton! I'm indeed delighted to see you again!' He shook Milton's hand. 'And – and you, Miss Hardwick,' and held out his hand to her.

'Mr Sedgmoor, Henry has told me of what you said and I can scarcely believe that anyone can be so kind but if you really do forgive me then I shall be honoured to shake your hand,' said Julia in a breathless rush: and then shook his hand in a numbing grip.

Sedgmoor flushed and then said, embarrassment aggravating his stammer, 'And w-what of your literary venture in London, Mr Milton? W-was it a success?'

'It was an experience I am glad not to have missed,' said Milton, 'but the life was not for me.'

'So you are back for good? Then you are the very man I wish to s-see. I have been about some business in the town that may be of interest to you. I am setting up in the profession of printer and bookseller – much to father's chagrin, he says it is barely respectable. He would rather I carried on his business, but the law repels me. I have been purchasing a printing-press, stock and premises from old Sam Holland, who is retiring. It is but a short walk and I want you both to see it. Will you come?'

So, chattering enthusiastically, he led them to an old peeling house in Scotgate that slumped over the street like a drunkard. At the back was a printing-press and two closet-like offices: the rest of the house was packed with mildewed books, pamphlets, broadsheets, prints and galley-proofs.

'I must begin in a small way,' said Sedgmoor, showing them round the cramped shop. 'The Vicar of Peterborough is a friend of father's and has promised me some sermons which I shall publish as pamphlets.'

Milton found an edition of Mackenzie's *Man of Feeling* and was glancing through the pages that had affected him so much when it first appeared, and finding them to his amusement rather sickly, when Sedgmoor said: 'Good heavens, some of this stuff! See this, Miss Hardwick. "True and Original Correspondence from a Lady of Fashion to her Lover in the –th Regiment".'

'Good God,' said Milton. 'May I see?'

'Do you know it?' said Julia, passing him some tattered sheets. Milton glanced down the ill-printed columns and remembered his dingy rooms overlooking a smoke-blackened London.

'I wrote it,' he said.

'Truly?' said Sedgmoor, delighted. 'Your own work?'

'Well, I was given the subject. The Lover was killed in a duel with the Lady's brother,' he added with a smile. 'Imagine its reaching Stamford!'

'Well, I shall demand only the highest price for it,' said Sedgmoor. 'And now, what do you think of the place?'

'It looks fascinating. I wish you the very best of luck,' said Milton.

'Oh – but you don't seem to understand,' said the young man. 'I am asking you to be my partner.'

Milton was startled. 'Mr Sedgmoor! You are very good, but I fear you cannot be aware how very little capital I have.' A portion from his father and a few guineas from a set of poems that Mr Carey in London had specially liked were all the money he had in the world.

'Oh, if it were a question of capital I would be going to some woodenhead like Mr Townsend,' said Sedgmoor. 'No, it is your pen and your brains which I wish to pick, Mr

Milton, and I reason they will be worth far more. What do you say?'

Milton looked at Julia. 'In that case,' he said, 'I shall be happy – on one condition.'

'What is it?'

'That you let me keep this,' said Milton, indicating the 'True and Original Correspondence'. He felt Julia slip her hand in his. 'I have nothing of the work I had published in London – I fear little of it was worth keeping – but I would wish to have this, as a souvenir.'

At Morholm Grandmother Peach sat in the wicker rocking-chair by the window in her bedroom looking out over the stables, where she had been all night.

You didn't need so much sleep when you got to her age and after all that business yesterday evening there was no chance of it anyway. She had heard Mary's screams and hobbled out on to the landing and peered over the banisters to see George turn up out of the blue and knock James clean down the stairs. That had been exciting, and so had the sight of James angrily ordering them out. They needed a bit of excitement around here. She had felt some respect for James when he had first come to take over Morholm: he was made of stern stuff like herself. And now she was the only one who had survived here. She had greatly enjoyed seeing those loafers Daniel and Kingsley thrown out on their ears. She had always despised the Hardwicks, and would never have had anything to do with them if her daughter Anne had not married the great loblolly Joseph, and brought her to live here when Mr Peach had died. She had never thought much of the marriage or the family – an idle, foolish set, she thought, decaying in their comfortable self-importance in this flat wasteland. She had made sure to live well off them at any rate. And her grandson James, she thought, had something more about him. But what he had tried to do last night . . . that was too much. And now George had taken Mary off and James was in the parlour with that mistress of his . . . nothing but a nasty painted trollop with her roving eyes and sneering ways.

They had been there all night, that she knew: she had gone down about ten last night and seen them there, and since then they had not come out. Mrs Peach had lived a fashionable life in London in her youth and considered herself broad-minded enough, but really it was not decent. She had seen James – sober, unbending James – sprawled on a sofa, drunk, in shirt and open breeches, and that Goulding woman was perched beside him. Her tawdry frock was half-way down her arms, exposing her breasts, her skirts were drawn up above her spread knees, and her hair hung down in black strands as she poured brandy from a glass into James's mouth. A guttering candle, almost gone, lit the room fitfully. There were several empty wine-bottles on the floor. James had merely snapped at his grandmother and ordered her to go back to her room, and she had needed no pressing.

But now, now it was morning, they had changed their tune. They were having a thunderous row – she could hear their voices below – and occasionally there was a smash of something being thrown. Once she had heard Mrs Reynolds go to the parlour and be brusquely ordered to go back to the kitchen by James. She herself knew better than to stick her nose in: but there was a worm of fear inside her that she could not account for and she was glad when she saw, from the window, the figure of George coming up to the house from the back way.

'George!' she called, in a kind of shouted whisper, throwing open the window.

George looked up. He had tethered his horse at the back of the garden and skirted the stables and the brew-house to reach the kitchen door.

'Where's James?' he called.

'Back parlour. With *her*. Going to turn him out, are ye?'

'If I have to,' said George. 'Close your window and stay in your room.'

The old lady did so and George opened the kitchen door. Mrs Reynolds, with a maid he did not know, gave a start when he came in.

'Oh, Mr George! 'Tis really you! I'm so afeared. Your brother and that woman – having a fearful row –'

'It's all right, Reynolds. Stay here.'

He went softly into the hall, past the broad staircase and the old brown portraits. Strange that this place, which had once become so repugnant to him that he could bear to be in it no longer, now filled him with a new, possessive warmth. He had laid those old ghosts, those phantoms of memory and despair. He had laid his hand on the handle of the parlour door when it was flung open and James appeared. He was in shirt sleeves and George was shocked at the grim haggard lines of his face.

'You,' said James. He closed the door behind him.

'It would be better if we did not come to blows, James,' said George, 'but by God I could kill you for –'

'I know it,' snapped James, his black eyes fixed intently on his brother. 'Don't you think I expect it?' Then he seemed to relax and sighed, leaning on the door-frame. 'You have changed, brother. I thought you at least might comprehend. A constant, searching sense of responsibility for all our actions . . . that would be wonderfully convenient. I must confess that I have often tried to convince myself that I have it. But it is impossible. The phantoms and demons, the passions, are always there to destroy it – you of all people should know that, George. You, and Julia. We are three of a kind, despite it all. D'you not believe in fate, George, or something like it? If only we could go back over the ground of our actions, but we have already been shaped by them. Have you looked around at Morholm?' He waved an arm. 'Great improvements. Great house again.' He laughed, a hollow sound. 'A mere shell – with rottenness at its heart. And now you have come to take it back.'

'I never lost it,' said George, half to himself. 'Why did you hide the news that I was alive, James? Did you want to be master of Morholm so badly?'

'I felt it really belonged to me, that only I could make a success of it. I doubted that you would come back, at least for a long time. Ambition, George. Pure and simple – or not so simple, and certainly not pure. It's all gone now. Broken. Never have ambitions, brother, for when they are destroyed . . .'

'You speak as if your life were over,' said George. 'There are a thousand things you still could do –'

'Great-Uncle Horace very much approves of me,' said James, cutting him off. 'I have been the true head of the family they have been waiting for at last.' He laughed bitterly again. 'At least I have exposed what a wretched sham all that is. You could thank me for that, brother, before I go. But before I leave Morholm to you, allow me to sermonize a moment, in case you and Mary think me a monster. Let me tell you there are no monsters. There are no monstrous villains as I know there are no angels and bogles and will-o'-the-wisps that scare the clowns on the Fen after a night at the alehouse. There is something too heroic about ogres and villains. The truth about us is always smaller, sourer.'

'The truth about us is never final, James,' said George, looking at his brother. It was a long time since they had talked alone like this – almost the first time. 'Believe me in that. Yes, I have changed, I suppose. "Experience" is the usual canting explanation for it, but that's not true. You can go through fire and ice and still be the same person after all. You've always coveted this place, haven't you? Yet you never came out and said so.'

'Oh, I would never admit it, of course. Even to myself I would not admit I was jealous,' said James.

'Another family trait,' said George. 'And one we would all have been better without. Odd that we are all so alike and yet have been always at each other's throats in one way or another. Where will you go? Back to London?'

'I suppose so. Where else –' began James, when the door behind him opened and Sophia Goulding appeared from the parlour. Her face was raw and flushed, her eyes bloodshot with drink. She was in her shift and her arms glowed whitely in the shadowy hall. 'Well, and so you are having a cosy talk with your dear brother, James! What in shite's name are you doing? Never tell me you're going to leave –'

George saw James's face wince with a kind of pained fury. 'Get out, woman!' James cried. 'Faugh, how you stink!'

'Stink yourself, and cess on you!' screamed the woman, hideous with rage, and began beating her fists on James's square figure. 'You are no man, you are a boy, you are a wretch, a pitiable piss-pot weakling –'

'When will I be rid of you, woman!' he hissed, struggling with her. 'I believe you have been sent to torment me!'

'How you change your tune – how you blow hot and cold! What would you have? Perhaps you would better prefer to tumble your pretty little cousin or some such simpering baggage!'

James struck her a stinging slap across the face at that and George heard the slap echo across the hall. 'You she-devil,' he said, his voice quivering. The woman turned and bolted back into the parlour. 'If I must leave, you shall go first, Sophia!' roared James. 'It's *over*. I never want you in my sight again, woman!' He went and pulled open the front door so that a waft of cool autumn air came in. 'Come!' he shouted. 'Get your things and be gone!'

Sophia reappeared from the parlour. In one hand she held her frock and in the other the little duelling pistol that hung on the wall, pointing straight at James.

'Great God,' murmured George. 'James, don't –'

'Give that to me, Sophia,' said James, moving towards her.

'Don't come one step closer, James!' the woman screamed. 'I warn you! Not one *step*!'

George saw the look on his brother's face: it was like a sudden clearing – like relief. Deliberately James took a step forward and in the same moment George grabbed his arm and tried to pull him aside as the shot rang out.

The explosion seemed to rake the furthest corners of the hall, dragging out all the clangorous echoes that had ever resounded there down the years. James was flung backwards with his hands to his face and Sophia ran like a cat out of the open front door.

George knelt beside his brother, aware now of cold sweat clinging to his whole body. James's hands were still pressed to his face and George saw with horror the blood seeping between his fingers. 'Let her go, brother,' gasped James. 'She is mad.'

George pressed his brother's arm. Behind him Mrs Reynolds screamed as she came running into the hall. 'Reynolds, find the groom and send him for Dr Villiers. Hurry,' said George. 'It's all right, James. The doctor will soon be here.' And he thought of how James had taken that step forward with the look on his face as if he were inviting the shot that came.

Mary, in the window-seat of her room at The George, had fallen into a half-waking reverie, lulled by the soft rays of autumn sunlight and the flowing of the river below, when the tap at her door came. 'George, you're back, thank –' she cried, and then stopped.

She did not at first recognize the figure who had entered. He was in a long green riding-coat and only when he removed the muffler that covered his pale unshaven face did she murmur his name.

'Jarrett.'

'Mary,' he said, closing the door behind him. 'I regret this intrusion, my dear, but you are my last hope. As you were my first . . .'

Her first thought was that she must be asleep, that he must be part of the nightmare of the past that she thought was gone. Then he took a step towards her and she rose from her seat. 'Don't you *dare* come near me!'

'I understand your feelings entirely, my dear, indeed I do.' He was smiling, the old handsome smile. But his eyes were dark-ringed, with a hard glitter, and the smile came out as a grimace. 'I know what I did – I can never make it up to you. But you look so lovely still, I wish you'd let me try.'

She felt she could spit in his face. 'You filth,' she said.

'All right.' He nodded, submissively. 'It was too much to hope, and more than I deserve. All I ask is your help, Mary – help for old times' sake. No one will help me. I – you must know I am on the run. I fled here a few days ago from London thinking to find old friends. Old friends. But I have been refused, betrayed. I went to an old friend in the town yesterday, asking him to help me. But he refused, turned me away! And now he has alerted the constables. Look at me, my dear. I have slept rough these three nights. Surely you don't wish to see me like this – see anyone like this? It's not *fair*. No friends left, no one to trust. And then I saw you last night, from the street, coming here with George, Milton and Julia. All old friends, but especially you, Mary. Don't tell me those old times mean nothing to you?'

'Ah yes – those old times,' she said. 'How sweet that sounds – a suggestion of golden days, and love. Those old times when you smiled and kissed me and planned to rob me and desert me.' She looked at him and felt nauseous with contempt. 'George will kill you as you killed Macmillan.'

'But George isn't here,' he said, with the same skull-like smile. 'I watched him go earlier. And I *had* to kill Macmillan! He wasn't being fair. The money was nearly all gone. He tried to cheat me – *cheat* me of my last share!'

'Did he, indeed! Oh, how outrageous! And you with your fine feelings, Thomas, your fine moral susceptibilities – I can see why you are hurt. God, you are despicable,' she said, shaking her head. 'I don't know whether to be sick or to laugh at you.'

'Don't antagonize me, my dear, I warn you –'

'Why, what will you do?' she said. 'Your threats are as empty and hollow as everything about you.'

'Look – very well,' he spread his hands and took a step nearer, 'I am all you say. I admit it! But I've no money left at all now, not a penny of it, it's all gone. *That*'s my punishment, surely, the cruel irony. The constables are seeking me in the town, Mary. I'll swing if I'm caught, you know that. I was going to ask you to hide me here, just till dark, but I know now you won't do that. Just give me some money – a little – enough for me to ride out of here – Scotland, the north, the coast, anywhere. You're my last hope, Mary. I've no one else to turn to. Give me a little money, I beg you, enough to get a saddle-horse or the mail-coach – and then raise the alert, eh? A sporting chance, like the fox-hunt.'

'I won't do anything for you,' said Mary coolly.

Jarrett stared at her and then pulled from the pocket of his coat a small gleaming knife. 'You *will*, my dear,' he said, 'and that is an *order*.'

Mary laughed. 'Why, you are too much of a coward. Your hand shakes. You won't do it. Put it down, you poor man, you are absurd.'

Beads of sweat were running down Jarrett's brow and the hand that held the knife trembled as if he had a palsy. 'You bitch,' he breathed. There was a knock on the door behind him.

'Mary, it's me, George.'

Jarrett wheeled round with feline agility and got behind Mary and held the knife to her throat. With his other hand he yanked her wrists behind her back. 'Come in, George,' he said.

The cold point of the knife pressed harder against her throat as the door opened and George stood there. For a second she thought he would fly at Jarrett. But he stood quite still. He had gone white.

'You've interrupted our little chat, George,' said Jarrett, his words sibilant in her ear. 'But I must be going anyway.' He pressed the knife a little harder until she thought it must break her skin. 'And here is my safe passage. So, George, make yourself useful and go down and hire one of the inn's excellent post-chaises, for a gentleman and lady who are leaving directly.' He moved so that his arm encircled her waist and the knife point was pressed against her stomach. 'We shall descend the stairs thus, my dear – a cloak over the lady perhaps – a sweet couple in an attitude of charming familiarity, unable to bring themselves to break their loving embrace even as they set out on their journey.' He moved the knife back to her throat with a laugh, a rattling metallic sound. 'How delightful.'

She bit his hand. She bit so hard through the fleshy part of his thumb she was sure her teeth met. With a bellow of pain he dropped the knife and she pulled away from him. He stooped to retrieve it but found his hand pressed to the floor by the toe of George's boot.

'By God, I've waited for this,' said George.

Jarrett wrenched his hand free and staggered back to the open window. 'You shall not even have that satisfaction,

George,' he said, and in a moment was over the window-ledge.

Mary ran to the window and craned out, expecting to see Jarrett's body on the ground below: but the rambling old building provided many footholds for an agile man. Just below her Jarrett was clinging to the thickly knotted ivy that covered the rough stone wall and feeling carefully down with his foot.

'He's climbing down,' said Mary. 'Quickly.'

Together they ran headlong down the dark haphazard stairs, one flight, two flights, the old banisters creaking in protest at their rough handling. In the vestibule they had to shoulder through a group of travellers from the Boston coach and George shouted over their heads to the innkeeper 'Raise the constables, man, there's a murderer . . .' When they reached the outside Jarrett was running across the west road to the paddock behind Lord Burghley's hospital next to the river. He began to bank left but George, running full pelt after him, had anticipated him. Jarrett swerved and nearly fell in the damp grass and then swung round the long projecting hospital building, parallel with the river. But as he ran on down the side of the hospital the strip of grassy bank between it and the river grew narrower until it petered out and the hospital walls dropped straight into the water for several yards before joining the first buttress of the town bridge. George was coming up behind him, fast. His long travels in France had hardened George and he would run all day if he had to to catch him. There was a low arched culvert cut under the building that came out beneath the other side of the bridge. Nothing else for it. Jarrett bent double and waded into the culvert. Rank scummy weed clung to his legs as he pushed his way into the dark tunnel. Mary, breathlessly coming round the corner of the hospital, called out to George. 'The bridge, George! We'll get up on to the bridge!'

By now the hue-and-cry was raised and when they re-crossed the paddock and ran up on to the bridge there were several people there from The George and a constable was running up from St Martin's. Jarrett's name was already notorious in the town. When they reached the bridge they craned over the far side wall and saw Jarrett emerge from beneath the arch, into the deeper water, swimming strongly. 'There he is!' cried George. Jarrett reached out and clung to a rotten spar of wood projecting from the steep walls of the bank. There was no place to climb up here. The coach-guard from the inn had come across to see the excitement and the constable commandeered his musket. 'Give yourself up, man!' he shouted down at Jarrett. 'Stay there and we'll throw you down a rope. Attempt to go further and I fire!' Jarrett turned his head a moment and then released the spar and plunged on again, moving diagonally towards the opposite bank where there were a few handholds.

The constable raised his musket and fired. A little white fountain of water spouted up a few feet from Jarrett's figure.

Jarrett managed to glance over his shoulder again. The bastards were shooting at him! His breath was coming shorter now. But he was a good swimmer, he knew he could carry on. This damned riding-coat didn't help. But if he could reach the opposite bank . . . that was where the back of Water Street was. The brothel he had used to visit. They would help him. He should have gone there in the first place, instead of relying on so-called friends, betrayers. They would help him there now, if he could haul himself up to the back of the house. He was popular there. Most of the women were poxy drabs, but a few were really delicious creatures – they would do anything.

A second shot rang out and ploughed the water inches from him. On the bridge George had wrested the musket from the constable and his aim was better. Next time he would be hit. But he was nearly there. An old rotten wooden jetty came in reach and he grabbed at it. Flakes of crumbly wood came away in his hand and he grabbed again, desperately, with both hands, scrabbling, feeling the current pulling his body. Rotted timbers fell forward into the water with a kind of slurping creak and one struck his head. He floundered back, swallowing water, his breath going, his ears singing, the current sucking at him greedily. Oh God – if only he could get up there – to those girls who would help him – those girls with their soft silken bodies . . . Their images swelled and filled his mind till the currents that tugged at his limbs seemed to be their caressing fingers and he ceased to fight and gave himself up to their cold and dank embrace.

'Fire again! Fire again, George!' Julia had come running down the hill to the bridge with Milton panting behind her and was screaming at George to fire again, hysterically, over and over, until Milton had to take her in his arms and hold her still. George raised the musket to his shoulder but Mary clutched his arm. 'No, George,' she said, 'I think there is no need now . . .'

10

The woods to the north were one fiery mass of deep-burnt orange against a vast white fen sky brushed with the first tints of dusk. From Fitzwilliam land to the south came a faint, pleasantly acrid smell of smoke from burning leaves, and to the east Mary could just make out the thin purple line that marked the edge of the furze and brake of Helpston Heath. And to the east were the chimneys of Morholm. And by her side, his arm gently about her waist, was George.

Henry Milton was at Morholm, with Julia, and Mrs Peach: so they had slipped out to walk about the fields and smell the autumn evening air and taste the berries that were drooping in glossy clusters from the bramble hedges. It was cool and fresh and dew was glistening on George's boots as they rustled through the thick grass.

It was their first day back to normal at Morholm. Three days ago the body of Thomas Jarrett had been washed up on the north bank of the Welland where the river ran out of the town into the flood plain that bordered the fen. And then there had been James to tend. As soon as he had been fit enough to be moved he had insisted he leave Morholm. He was adamant that he could not stay in the house. They had both protested that he should remain: but Great-Uncle Horace had come over and in a burst of strange long-stifled tenderness offered to take care of the young man at his house in Stamford. And James had seemed to want to go there. Mary thought of his face as he had lain in bed propped up with pillows. Ironically the scarring was really not much. The shot had glanced off the very tip of the bridge of the nose and altered his features little: but the splintering had been enough to blind him. Dr Villiers had said ah, would he ever regain his sight, well, h'm, it might be possible, and made it clear he didn't know.

'Will James be all right with Great-Uncle Horace, do you think?' said Mary, breaking their long silence of content.

'I wondered myself,' said George. 'They are two of a kind, at any rate. The old fellow's offer startled me, as did James's acceptance. I would willingly have looked after him here – but he said he did not belong at Morholm.'

They were silent again and stopped at a fence to watch a flock of wild ducks descend into the gloom of the sallows by the stream that ran twisting out of Aysthorpe. The wind coming unimpeded off the fen traced shifting patterns in the grass.

'Soon I must see about that land James sold off,' said George. 'The transaction was not legal, of course, but that means even more difficulties, and I fear we will not get our money back.'

'And the income from the harvest? He used that too?'

'Mostly. We shall stay just solvent this year, but it will be a pinch.'

'I don't mind that. Do you?'

'I have you, remember.' He smiled and squeezed her hand. 'You'll fetch a fair price in the market if the worst comes to the worst.'

She laughed. 'Very flattering. You had better not spoil the goods. But seriously, George, we've *got* what's really important, have we not? Oh, we are lucky too – we have health, home, food to eat, clothes to wear – but if two people love each other, then no matter what happens, what circumstances, what – external things, if they've got that, then nothing else matters, does it? And without that, all those other things don't have any meaning.'

He kissed her. 'I can't add to that.'

They walked on, back towards Morholm, and the day

began to wane with bars of smoky salmon-pink cloud arching above them. A late thrush was singing somewhere among the trees as they came into the garden and at the sound of their tread it flew up with a shrill clatter. Mary stopped before the rambling old hawthorn bush, which was brightly studded with shiny red berries. 'It will flower again,' she said softly. 'I began to doubt it once.'

He looked at her quizzically.

'Oh – it's just a fancy of mine, George,' she said. 'When spring comes I shall tell you about it.'

In the distance a wisp of smoke curled from the chimney of the Newman farm.

'I had forgot to tell you,' she said. 'John Newman is back there now.'

'I shall go and see him tomorrow,' said George. 'If I remember rightly I owe him an apology.'

She squeezed his hand. 'It's all right, George. John is very happy now. He is soon to marry.'

'Is he? Well . . .' He paused, and his dark eyes twinkled as he looked out towards the farm. 'It seems to be quite the fashion just now.'

'Of course. And really, in our position, it would not do for us to be unfashionable, my lover.'

They passed on down the avenue of trees to the house through the wickerwork of shadows and emerged into the tender pink light of the lovely dusk, and somewhere in the depths of the wood the thrush began his song again.